Robin Wallace-Crab .... .our earlier
Essington Holt novels. He has a particular interest
in the visual arts, writes about them from time to
time, and revels in the twin acts of painting and
drawing. He lives in Canberra and on a farm an
hour and a half away.

The book's cover shows *Etude d'une femme*, 1947,
42 x 59.5cm, *fusain et estompe sur papier Montval*.
Essington Holt forgery of an Henri Matisse drawing. Private collection. Provenance: acquired by the
present owner from the Stan Kriticos collection.

The Forger

The Forger

Robin Wallace-Crabbe

[signature: Rob Wallace-Crabbe]

D
S

Duffy & Snellgrove
Sydney

Published by Duffy & Snellgrove in 2003
PO Box 177 Potts Point NSW 1335 Australia
info@duffyandsnellgrove.com.au

Distributed by Pan Macmillan

Cover design by Alex Snellgrove
Typeset by Cooper Graphics
Printed by Griffin Press

ISBN 1 876631 82 1

visit our website: www.duffyandsnellgrove.com.au

For Virginia

*When an artist reasons, it's because he
no longer understands anything.*

André Derain.

Chapter 1

Before I could think of selling the apartment, I had to evict the motivational speaker who'd conned his way into a lease on it. At the same time I needed to disengage the managing estate agent.

I just couldn't believe it when, in the most recent email I'd received from this clown, he told me there were things to do with the apartment's plumbing requiring attention. He reckoned the curtains were stained and torn, plus several of the chichi electric light fittings needed replacement. I replied with 'How can this be true?' because we purchased the apartment only two years earlier, off the plan. I had promotional photographs to demonstrate that I had bought something between a place to live and the set for a Hollywood film about bed-jumping glitterati.

Once, by chance I caught Damien, the agent, on the blower. 'You're telling me the fabric of the joint is damaged! So why didn't you let me know this before?'

'I did.'

Don't you hate being lied to? 'And this deterioration, it was instantaneous?'

'Of course not, wear and tear.'

'Wait a minute, the apartment's condition is your job. You recall the word "inspections" in our contract? There's a bond each time you let it. When people trash the joint we throw them out and keep the bond, if that doesn't cover it then you take them to court – they are liable to pay for the damage.'

'Mr Holt, I …'

'I'm not a charity.'

'Now you wait a minute, Mr Holt …'

'Damien, you listen to me. How could the condition be otherwise than like new? Think about it, I bought it through you and Gerald Sparrow. He was my good friend, do you remember that? And, for reasons I can't begin to comprehend, you seemed to be his. Do you mind me asking, Damien, what exactly was your business relationship with Sparrow?'

'I find that offensive, the truth is …' Damien hanging in there, putting up a bit of fight.

Out of the past one of my father's many sour truths has stuck with me: Never trust a man who starts a sentence with 'to tell the truth'. And I never do. I certainly don't trust my own motives when I sense the words 'the truth is' starting to form at the back of my brain.

Once I'd hung up on Damien it took a great deal of self-control not to whip around to his office and finish the apartment business once and for all time – with the assistance of something along the lines of an aluminum baseball bat.

There is much of my father living on in me. A few wise sayings, a two-shilling piece with King George V on one side that I keep in my wallet, and a tendency to lose it.

Me, I am an artist, as in painting. A bit of a scam artist as well to tell the truth. When I paint paintings I do fakes. Deceiving people gives me a buzz, but I do get a big kick out of the great works of art. And like any other lost dog on the street, I respond to random acts of kindness.

While in Sydney, doing the apartment thing, my personal business plan involved becoming known to be a respectable citizen with pots of money and the milk of human kindness flowing through his veins. I was hoping for the occasional mention in the social pages, to make a few significant contacts – being one more nice guy around the town. Contemptuous of the way human society works, my father used to say that if I wanted to get ahead I should dress nicely and turn up to charity balls and opening nights. That's precisely what he reckoned his sister had set out to do. God, how my father despised her for marrying well. He despised her for her early widowhood too, not to mention the fortune her husband left.

Fifteen years ago she left me a mansion on Saint-Jean-Cap-Ferrat in the south of France, together with enough money invested in international stocks and in property to secure the life-style to which I instantly became accustomed. It was five years, at least, before it hit me that setting me up in such comfort had been her way of getting back at her brother. How spiritual was that?

Brooding on Damien, I waited for my wife Karen to pop out of bed on the far side of the world, in France, so we could talk over the apartment problem. Killing time I sat in my hotel suite watching a movie about this world-famous oboe player who returns to his birthplace, a small town in Brazil, and makes everybody feel good by playing his oboe. And then he dies. It seemed to me to be art about art, which can be very nice; it can also be a total pain in the neck.

As an accompaniment for the movie I had asked room service to rustle up the one thing that didn't look too bad on the menu, kidneys with artichoke hearts and thyme. Plus, I had set my sights on a middle-aged bottle of merlot. The meal had just arrived when the phone rang.

'Essington?'

'Who is this speaking, please?'

'Stan ... I missed our appointment, sorry about that.

But you know how it is.'

Being so far from home, first off I was asking myself, Stan who? Then I was thinking, why would Stan ring me in Australia? 'Where are you ringing from?'

'To tell the truth, I am standing at my window watching the ferry coming in from Corsica. It looks nice, the scene: calm sea, reflection of palm trees in the water, the sun up in the sky. Very aesthetic. But I'm not at all happy, Essington.'

He had said 'To tell the truth'!

'You rang to say you are not happy? Get yourself a psychiatrist.'

'No, it's because we were going to meet, remember? But I got tied up and missed our appointment.'

'How did you get this number?'

'I rang your wife.'

'And she gave it to you, just like that?'

'Actually, it was the other one, what's her name, Dawn something?'

'So?' I asked.

'Just keeping in touch, that's all. That and, it's to do with the art deals we've done.'

'What about them?'

'The paintings, you told me you'd guarantee their quality, remember?'

'Stan, that's a fine art collection you've put together for yourself.'

'You said it.'

'What you have there are works by some of the greatest names, so of course they are quality. I don't need to have guaranteed anything, you've got the quality suspended there on your walls.'

'Essington, don't try back-peddling on me, okay?'

'I'm not trying anything on you, Stan. I'm explaining to you how it works when I buy a painting for a client.'

4

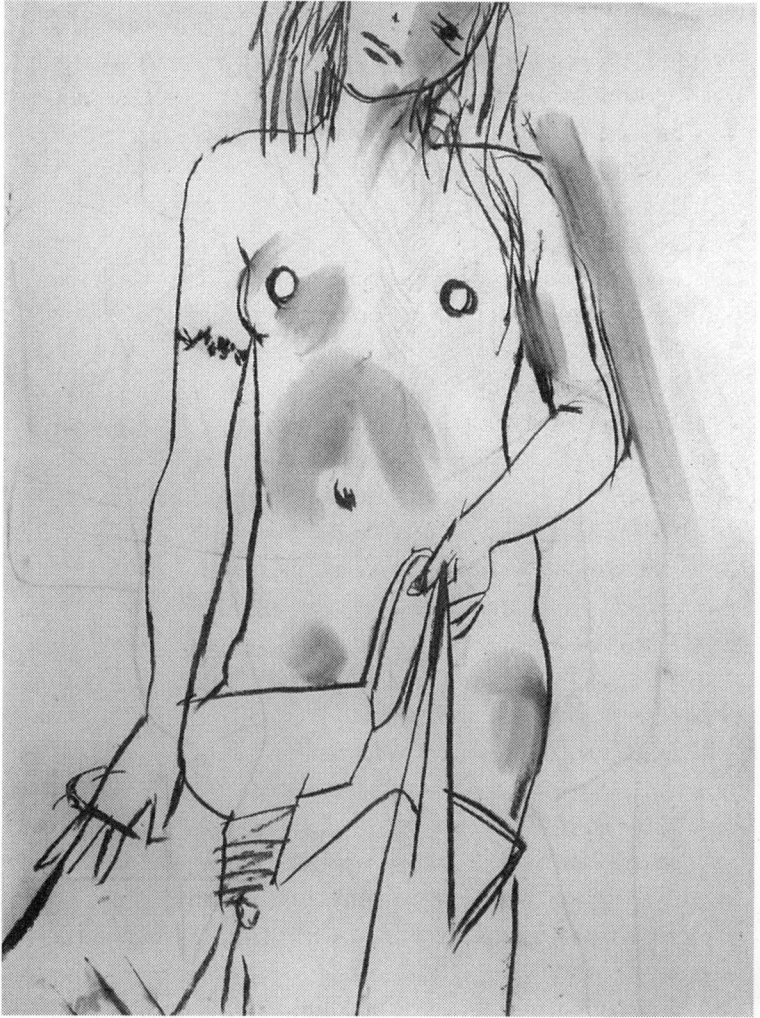

'You guaranteed the quality, and now you're going to honour the guarantee by buying the collection back. Of course there'll be a margin in it for you. I deal straight with people, you hear what I'm saying? I will make it worth your while to buy them back. You get to keep the quality you guaranteed, I have the money now, when I could do with it, to tell you the truth, and you keep fifteen percent of the total value.'

'See you round,' I said.

'I don't think you are listening to what I'm telling you, Essington.'

'I've heard enough, it's bullshit. I am not going to do it, end of discussion.'

'I believe you will do what I want, my friend.'

'Oh yes, and why's that?'

'Because if you don't you will be sorry. I've made you a reasonable offer because I am a reasonable man. Are you listening to me, Essington? You knock it back then you are dead.' Raising his voice at this point to repeat the threat. 'You heard me, you're going to finish up more dead than dead if you don't.'

I nursed the phone back into its cradle.

The double 'dead' talk was echoing inside my head. I guess I thought to myself, well that's Stan for you. And then attempted a little bit more of a think. But I failed.

So I poured a glass of merlot, took a gulp to savour those complex chocolate flavours the wine list assured me I'd find drowned in there somewhere. Question: Why would Stan Kriticos imagine I'd buy back his art collection?

Answer: He'd blown a fuse somewhere inside his head.

Question: Why would he threaten to kill me?

Same answer plus a fresh question: Was he joking or was he for real?

Answer: He had to be up to something because he could take what he had hanging there on his walls anywhere, to a dealer, an auction room, you name it, sell the lot without trouble. Or I could do it for him, charge him fifteen percent of the money as it came in. What I certainly wasn't going to do was buy them back. Because, unlike Stan, I knew they were fakes. Unless …

And more disturbing: Did he know that too? And if so, how could that be?

Next question: What did he believe I'd do now? Was I supposed to piss my pants, or what?

On the TV screen the movie was still playing: some people were wheeling a coffin around and there were pigeons circling in the Brazilian sky. But I'd lost the thread of the story. More wine. I forked a mouthful of kidney followed by an artichoke heart. It tasted really life-affirming. More wine.

Just as I was wondering what he'd do next, the phone jangled and, like a dog trained by Pavlov, I picked up to hear Stan warn me never to hang up on him again. 'I repeat, never, don't even think about it, you hear what I'm telling you?' So, being essentially nice I asked why he didn't sell the paintings on the open market like any normal person would, and learn to live with the profit he'd make. To which he responded that he didn't have the time to frig around with art type people. He elaborated, 'Essington, I'm offering you a real opportunity here, to get the paintings back for what I paid in the first place, less fifteen percent, plus you get to take the rise in value as more commission. The way I see it is that I'm handing you what, a thirty or forty percent gain if you play it right? It has to be that much, maybe more. And you are the expert in this market, correct?'

'It's just not the way I do business. What's more it's not the way I want to start doing business. Oh, and the other thing, I don't have the fucking money.'

'Borrow it, that's what we have banks for.'

'It's a very generous offer, Stan, and I appreciate you making it.'

'You're telling me it's generous. Look, Essington, you and me … I am sorry for losing it when I called the first time. I have

7

a short fuse, you know that, I'm supposed to be famous for it.'

'At least you're famous for something. According to Andy Warhol sometime in the future we will all get to be famous for fifteen minutes.'

'According to who?'

'All the same, Stan, I don't see why you don't sell them yourself, and take the profit.'

'Because I don't want to, you arsehole.'

'Neither do I.' I hung up again and rang reception to tell them not to put any further calls through to my room, thank you very much. Then back to the film, which was all but over. So I switched the set off and stared at its dead screen's reflection of me and the soulless room.

Andy Warhol had also said that the more you look at something the more the meaning of it goes away and the better and emptier you feel.

Half an hour later I wasn't feeling any better or any emptier at all.

I'd eaten more than half the meal. The kidneys had that faint urine taste to them that Karen always reckoned is a man's eating thing. She was strictly a no offal person, even before her recent drift into Buddhism. Along with the meditation, abstinence from sex and the constant questioning of my materialistic values, this religious thing had turned her into a vegetarian. There were retreats as well. She'd been to one in Paris for a week, another in Riberac up in the Perigord, at a village called Senzelles that I wasn't able to find in the Michelin Guide. Still, no skin off my nose, or so I thought at the time, knowing too well that salvation through religion wasn't my style.

I refilled my glass and punched a long line of digits into the telephone. Our friend Dawn picked up. Dawn is sort of part of the family, though how things finished up that way I've never been quite sure. Two women, one child, a beautiful dog and a man who has never been all that reliable, that's the Holt household over there in France. Me, Essington Holt, that same household's head, if in name only.

Dawn is neat with short-cropped hair bleached blond at the tips. Amazing honey-coloured skin. Answering the phone she'd be dressed in Issey Miyake or something with a lot of crushed pleats. And the fact is that anywhere, the beach, in the mountains, she'd be fixing her attention on a nice looking girl in the middle distance with a neat butt, small breasts, the kind of girl who seemed to be a fraction light on gender specifics.

Dawn said, 'It's you. I suppose you want Karen.'

'Be nice.'

'You telling me to be nice, I don't believe you, Essington.'

'It would be nice to talk with Karen, that's what I meant.'

'Meaning I'm a pain in the arse?'

'Dawn, no games, all right, just get her, please.'

'Now you are being nice, saying please.'

That sort of talk can go on between Dawn and me pretty much forever.

I asked, 'By the way, did Stan Kriticos ring and ask for my number?'

'Stan who?'

'Dawn, you must remember Kriticos. Did anybody ask you for this number, where I am staying?'

'Not from me, they didn't.'

'You absolutely sure about that?'

'A hundred percent. Except your friend Sparrow, of course. The only calls for you we're having are from Gerald Sparrow. He's ringing four or five times a day. Sounds particularly desperate. Maybe you should do something there.'

'He knows I'm not going to talk to him.'

'Claims it's a matter of life and death.'

'With any luck, death, his death.'

'He was your friend.'

9

She got the tense right. Sparrow had been my friend for a long time. Since childhood. A relationship which had lasted longer than the good faith that underpinned it. He'd given me legal advice over the years as well.

'Thanks for the reminder, Dawn,' I said. Then Karen came on the line.

Straight up Karen wanted to know how many times had she told me to stay away from Gerald Sparrow and his destructive ideas? 'Now he's ringing here I can't remember how many times. See, Essington, it's best you're out there in Australia, out of contact. It has occurred to me that, while you are at it, you might take the trouble to check if there was anything on top of the normal legal costs in it for your Mister Sparrow. Finding that out might make you face up to the fact that he has taken us down.'

Adopting a hard tone when talking to me was a recent thing with Karen. Talking to other people she was all sensitivity and concern – even for the ants, in case we trod on them. We'd been over this ground too often already. I hadn't wanted to cross the world to sell the pissy piece of real estate I hadn't needed to buy in the first place. I am the stay-at-home type. I possess a cave man's strongly developed domestic instincts. Away from home I can lose my grip on reality and I have been known to get into trouble.

'I might have gone about it the wrong way, I've admitted that already, but Karen, investing in the apartment was your idea, remember?'

I believe it was being in business with Dawn that had made Karen hard. Now she was off: 'Not paying rent, and it's our fault according to the agent! I don't believe I'm hearing this! Move in on them, Essington.' She didn't raise her voice. The fact that she didn't do that with me, not ever, was unnerving. 'That's it, move in, try playing some of what you like to call real music. That ought to flush the bastard out. While you're at it pig out on take-aways, develop dysentery, occupy the bathroom.'

'There are two bathrooms and three toilets.'

'The big selling point, how could I forget? So, occupy the lot.'

'Could be beyond me.'

'I don't believe I heard you say that. Get him out of there, one way or another. Make it up as you go along, like you normally do.'

'Thanks a lot, Karen. Oh, and by the way, how's the Buddhism?'

'Don't ask me, because you are not interested.'

'I love you.'

'Me too.' She hung up.

I sat on the hotel room's big bed considering what she might mean by saying 'me too'. Me just sitting there, semi-collapsed, mind pondering big questions like that. Karen had got my head so scrambled, so full of guilt and inadequacy, that I couldn't think straight.

I felt she was drifting away from me, and that the Buddhism was some kind of ERT – Essington Replacement Therapy.

I decided that Stan Kriticos had simply been letting off steam. He was the highly-strung type, Stan, product of one of those claustrophobic Greek families that force-feed moussaka, baklava and Greek-bred wives to their boys. So he had to present himself to himself and the world as the kind of person who wins and who sustains the upper hand in relationships, whatever. I concluded that something must have gone wrong inside his universe and he'd taken it out on whoever he could find at the other end of the phone line. Still, I was pissed off at not knowing how he'd got my number. The hotel room phone number too; not my mobile, which was a brand new contract and number anyway. Being connected to the world by mobile was a totally new thing for me and I didn't like the idea of it all

11

that much. Being a stay-at-home man who had been known to wander, I wasn't sure I wanted to be always within my world's reach.

Stan had treated me with a lack of respect before. There had been the occasion when I'd turned up at his supposed-to-be smart, Kriticos-built apartment overlooking the anchorage at Villefranche-sur-Mer. I'd been delivering a painting by Wassily Kandinsky, had it tucked under my arm in fact, wrapped in plain brown paper. A really nice piece of art, the Kandinsky. The title was *Schloß and Church*. The size, from memory, 30 x 40 cm. There had been a whole lot of pencil writing on the back of the canvas stretcher, some in Russian Cyrillic and the rest in French. It was dated May 1909; a painting produced at the beginning of that summer in southern Germany. There was a blue-green lake foreshore with the white front wall of the schloß and mountains behind forming a zigzag against the sky. All broadly sketched in with a strident use of obliques in the upper two-thirds of the composition. And the colour: undiluted cobalt blue, cadmium orange, pure red, a rich purple madder that read as a kind of brown. The composition was a textbook example of pre-WWI, Die Brücke group, expressionism. For a brief and brilliant moment Kandinsky had flirted with that set of artists and their style. Me, I was genuinely proud to have brought such a masterpiece into this world.

You had to know something to understand it was a major work I was offering Stan that day. The price was more than reasonable at US$500,000. If you knew nothing and didn't have it in you to respond to innovation and freshness in art you might think it the work of a rank amateur with mild psychological problems.

Stan, not a big man, but wiry, hirsute and sun-bronzed, had stood there in the doorway of his apartment, his arms aggressively folded, blocking my way in. His greasy black hair was cut short on top and at the back it curled down over his neck. Grabbing at my parcel, he ripped the wrapping off and held the painting out at arms' length, a contemptuous know-nothing expression spread across his face. 'You have to be kidding.' Then – at the time I couldn't believe it – he tossed US$500,000 of rare art so it hit the floor, bounced and ended up askew with one corner of the frame resting against the wall.

'Fuck you, Stan, that's only a Kandinsky. You don't handle great paintings like that. When there used to be what was called civilization you'd get thrown off a cliff for doing something dumb as that.'

'Only kidding.' Stan did a spaniel thing with his deep brown eyes. That was it, he could put on this I've-been-a-naughty-boy expression. Then lose it again just as quickly. Mercurial.

'That's the problem with quick money people like you, Stan, pig ignorant. Get rich then come to believe that you know things you aren't capable of ever knowing. Bloody philistine.'

A frowning silence followed, then he said, 'I know what I like, okay?'

'Never, you hear what I'm saying, Stan, never do that to a work of art. It's close to a hundred years old, a milestone in art history.'

'Essington, you treat me like a cash cow. All right, so tell me what's so good about this one. I mean, it's obvious the man can't draw. But at least try and do some work for your percentage. I am only asking you to convince me.'

'You are so …'

'I'm waiting.'

'Stan, if you don't get the painting, what's the use of learning what to say about it? Art is all about silence. I told you that once before. You look at a painting, and it communicates with you or it doesn't. Like this brilliant Kandinsky. It doesn't matter that it was done when a group of young artists were in revolt against the art culture of Munich; or that Munich was the world capital of sentimental, green-brown landscapes and domestic interiors for the new burgher class to hang on their walls; hang it on their walls with the same dumb attitude you're showing me right now. In fact, Stan, if you weren't so Greek they would have loved you in Munich back then.'

'Watch it, there's a line and you are so close to crossing it.'

'You've already crossed the line from where I'm looking at the world.'

By then I was clutching the Kandinsky to my chest, protectively. Well, I'd put a lot of work into it, hadn't I? And he was standing, still blocking his doorway, a guard, arms crossed again, looking aggressive. 'You're a fucking control freak, but you're not going to control me.'

'Be more fun training a slug to race.'

But he had got back in contact that same day, just before sunset. I was standing out on the front lawn of Villa du Phare, watching a US warship negotiating the tip of Saint-Jean-Cap-Ferrat. The dog, Desdemona, was sitting a little way off, imitating the Sphinx as always, watching Yassir the gardener do absolutely nothing in the garden. I was sipping wine and admiring the colour gradations above the warship, up there in the western sky, when Karen announced I was wanted on the phone.

Unrepentant in manner, sure, but suddenly Stan had a great need to own the painting. I explained that it would cost him ten percent more now because the seller was so offended when I had explained what happened that he sacked me as the agent. Worse, he had wanted the painting checked over by a conservator to make sure none of the paint had come away from the canvas as a result of the jarring it received from being chucked on the floor. I put it to Stan that to go forward I was going to have to crawl back into my side of the deal. That and the conservator was going to cost money. All together I reckoned it was going to cost another US$50,000 easily.'

'Just do it, Essington, okay?' Stan loved to instruct lesser beings in that perfunctory fashion. I sometimes wondered how he came to adopt the attitude with me when I had a lot more cash at hand than he would ever see. Property developers, they are usually 10 percent of what they've signed their name to away from bankruptcy.

He hung up. Yassir was still loitering amongst the gardening implements, Desdemona still watching him. An intuitive type, Yassir, who kept to himself mostly. He approached me. Then stopped a couple of metres away. His mouth slightly open, something close to a smile hanging there. All his upper front teeth missing. 'Some kind of trouble?' he wanted to know.

'On the contrary.'

If there was trouble, Yassir was there. He'd proved that over the years. His ears had been cut off in some torture compound where he'd been pushed around with stock prodders, had his balls cut out. No family any more.

Most of the real garden work at Villa du Phare he left for his friends to do on a daily basis. Yassir principally liked to ponder the meaning of life.

Chapter 2

It was attempting to be night outside my Sydney hotel. Standing on a balcony just wide enough to fit a dining chair sideways, I was breathing in the city's rising fumes and swallowing night cap number– I must have given up counting. The Harbour Bridge was lit so brightly that above it seabirds circled like the damned – souls doomed to fly forever, believing that there can be no night.

At the time we bought the apartment, Karen and Dawn had calculated that Australian real estate was about to take off after a slow and restrained recovery from lows established during a property crash in the previous decade. Dawn enjoys all that stuff. She gets off on investment cycles, the relationship between bonds, equities and property, she adores words like leverage, warrant, put-and-call option, concepts like buying off the plan. She lets her juices flow over graphs predicting a company's stock price on the basis of past performance. And mostly Karen likes what Dawn likes. As usual they had turned out to be right. Dawn flew out to Australia to check what real estate was for sale and to say hi to her family while she was at it. Once she'd reported back, my job had been to get in touch with my friend Gerald Sparrow the lawyer and set the wheels in motion. That was when I hit on the notion of leaving buying the place up to Sparrow and the agent he was so warmly recommending.

See, from the start I wasn't interested. I didn't need any more money. From the way I saw it, all we were doing was investing a lousy A$500,000. That's a lot of money, sure, but you know, in the greater scheme of things – well you couldn't buy a small Kandinsky for that, could you? Life is much too short to squander on roofs and walls, on property deals.

Encouraged by Dawn, Karen confidently expected us to pocket a hundred percent profit inside three years.

'Half a million dollars, Essington, not to be sneezed at.'

'I'm not sneezing at anything, it's just that a deal like this, it's so uncreative.'

'Doubling money is uncreative?'

'Frankly, yes. Karen, you're the one who's supposed to be on a spiritual journey. While he was sitting by the river making oom sounds, was the Buddha planning real estate deals in Calcutta, do you think so?'

'The world was different then.'

'That the world becomes different, surely that's an illusion. I would have thought you had to realise that to become a Buddhist.'

16

'Essington, you're forever turning the art you purport to love into money, isn't that the ultimate in materialism?'

'Art gives us something, it transports meaning from one century to the next. Anyway, I'm not supposed to be spiritual. But an apartment is just a series of interconnected spaces, and these days the stuff on the floors, the tiles on the bathroom walls, bench surfaces, it's all so tacky. Look underneath anything and you see chip board and gang nails. If we were investing in an apartment designed by, say, Walter Gropius, if we were buying a meaningful work of art to live in, then my attitude would be altogether different. Anyway, how many times must I point out we don't need to make half a million dollars. What are we going to do with half a million dollars? Invest it in something else, invest it in what, for Christ's sake?'

We'd been doing that argument for years. Each of us had our lines down pat. Progress was never made – how Buddhist was that?

Of course I lost, so we bought the place and rented it out, furnished just as it had appeared in the glossy promotional brochure. Short-term leases, high rent. How could we lose? Ho, ho, ho.

Shabby idea, lousy outcome.

Three days before leaving for Australia, I had been informed by Damien that a once-was rock-and-roll star from the US of A, now motivational speaker, happened to be leasing the joint. 'No problems with this one, Mr Holt.'

Consider myself assured.

I guess that was Damien's first unconscious admission that there had been problems with previous tenants. It seemed that our talk-freak worked under the name of Mister D and was now doing his motivational thing at business conferences and other classy gigs like that. I nearly threw up when I heard about it. Worse, the angle he was taking was that he had been reborn through Jesus Christ Our Lord as a motivational speaker. He was delivering a series of performances titled 'JESUS CAN MAKE YOU RICH'. I got a picture in my head of fellers with hard-ons for Christ being baptized by Mister D in a paddle pool brim-full of pink bubbly. My best guess was that Damien had to be tied in to the whole sick, motivational joke somehow. Or just star-struck.

And what was Sparrow's role?

A quick search of the net via my laptop had revealed that in Mister D's case the term 'has-been' was kind. How had the mighty fallen? In the early 1980s he'd moved from the United States to the Bahamas in the wake of a damaging carnal knowledge charge. I wouldn't have much problem with that, myself. But in the mid 1990s he'd been arrested by police in Wales for downloading buckets of kiddy porn. Not so nice, really. He got off the charge on a technicality. In the tabloid journalistic detail there had been the unsurprising suggestion of substance abuse. Indulging myself, I right-clicked on the image of Mister D and then clicked 'save as'. I had him stored in my mugs gallery of friends and acquaintances – reduced to a JPEG file.

Although not Buddhist, I like to kid myself that I am on the side of the little guy who can't pay his rent; that I stand shoulder to shoulder with the man who jumps the turn-stiles to ride for free on the Metro in Paris, who lifts a half-pint of scotch from a bottle shop in Soho and then runs for his life. But at the same time, I don't like to be jerked around by arseholes like Damien Berry, Mister D or, indeed, Gerald Sparrow.

So, off I went to the apartment, not so much to extract what I was owed by the tenant as to get right up the nose of Damien, our property manager from hell. On arrival I stood on the pavement, looking up at the building's front face. Not particularly nice. At street level there was dense garden planting up to the edge of some uninviting, concrete-lined, two-metre-wide void.

I was thinking what to do next when this street bum came up, a crazy-looking character. Matted blond hair. Looked a hundred, probably thirty. Even in the gloom I caught an ice-blue glow from his eyes.

'You wouldn't have a dollar?'

The truth was I didn't. I had a hundred dollar note, a bunch of them in my wallet, but that was all. He was watching me, I suspect working on a line of abuse.

I gave him a hundred. That pinned his ears back.

He was swallowed by the garden planting, where I guess he lived.

The owner's key to the street door, sent to me at the time of settlement, didn't seem to work, if it ever had. I managed to get through the apartment block's street level security entrance by schmoozing an aged tenant who was bearing a gigantic bunch of red roses. Surprisingly though, tackling the door of the apartment I discovered that, despite slipping behind with the rent, Mister D had not considered changing the lock.

I let myself in and set to checking the place out. I'd imagined we owned up-to-the-minute if slightly tacky-looking Italian designer chairs and couches ready to shoot off into space, glass-top coffee tables, a lot of beech veneer, black leather and chrome, huge mirrors with beveled edges hanging from the walls where civilized people used to hang paintings. It had all been there, pristine, in the promotional brochure, and was listed piece by piece in the inventory.

Well, forget about the furniture, Essington. Most of that had disappeared and been replaced by cardboard boxes and plastic milk crates. The slim-line Venetian blinds controlling light off the harbour were buckled and belted about. Their strings were missing, tangled or hanging out of line and loose. Beer cans were scattered here and there, some no doubt to catch the occasional cigarette butt, though it looked as though most of those had ended their smouldering lives on the black and white bold-design scatter rugs or the polished Tasmanian oak parquetry flooring. CDs and tape cassettes together with or apart from their brittle plastic boxes were here, there and everywhere. Adding a touch of motivational class was a half-empty case of sparkling burgundy parked in the middle of the open-plan living area, no doubt in readiness for the next drug and booze soaked Jesus-mega-cum event.

The main bedroom featured one elephant-size bed in serious disarray. Looking a lot like a piece of Young British Art, its surface was littered with damp towels, old socks, underpants, you name it. Above this mess was a watch-me-humping mirror, taken, I suspected, off the living area wall and inexpertly attached, somewhat askew, to the ceiling by means of cup hooks and lengths of picture wire. Blue-tacked to one wall was a soft-focus, life-size, full-colour photo of a frizzy-haired nubile girl wearing nothing but leg warmers, her legs thoughtfully spread for the camera while she fiddled with the protruding pale pink nipples of partly developed breasts.

Feeling pretty pissed off with the state of our property, indeed agitated and in need of calm I guess, my sugar levels all shot (Dawn was always going on about sugar levels) I popped a can of beer, the closest thing to food that I could spot in the refrigerator. Then, grabbing the remote, I snapped on the tenant-owned mega-size, flat-screen TV with the lot. Both video player and DVD player were buried beneath a stack of tapes and disks, some in and most out of boxes featuring lurid graphics. Surfing the channels showed me pretty quickly that there was nothing on so I hit play for the video and dived smack into the middle of a reasonably unimaginative sex scene, mostly two girls, one naked, the other older and clothed. They were trying to beat the shit out of each other as the naked one made frantic attempts to get the jeans off her opponent. It looked fairly nasty by yesterday's standards. It got worse when a heavy-set guy wearing only a tee shirt stepped in from out of shot and thumped the naked girl with a length of plastic hose. The volume control permitted me to sample the performers' discordant screaming and the man's voice saying 'You fucking bitch, I'm going to make you pay' while jacking himself off.

I hit the off button before he got further along with the enterprise. I swigged my beer. I wondered what to do with myself next.

I sort of started going through the videotapes' boxes, scanning come-on titles like *Ukrainian Fairy Tale 3, Little Angelina and the Gypsy, Snow White and the Seven Dykes, Whacked Out Baby*. Predictable, maybe, but there was a lot of this kind of product there, demonstrating that notwithstanding his earlier tangle with the law, Mister D's predilection for porn, underage and violent and whatever, was still alive and extremely well.

I pulled a digital camera from my jacket pocket and wandered from room to room, the flash flashing, shooting twenty or so images to record damage to the place. Most were wide angle, some close-ups of specific damage. To do so seemed sensible at the time.

For me, the waiting landlord, time was passing very slowly. Back with the television I found a pay channel playing a program on volcanoes and became interested in an island that had appeared out of the sea not so long ago and had already become the breeding ground for a species of North Atlantic sea bird. I concentrated on birds hatching, lava flowing down hillsides and diagrams of the earth's centre. I might have been arriving at the conclusion that the earth is a fertilized egg when I dozed off.

And awoke to gaze, fuzzy-brained, at a creature whose polished head reflected the gleam of a reading light over the far side of the room. The television had been switched to off.

'Hey! Somebody's been eating my porridge and we scored ourselves a little wee bear in here, Bobby.'

From outside my line of sight: 'This qualifies as a break in.

You better believe it. A high security apartment block, you told me! It's high enough, but security – oh mate, you've got to be joking. I should be getting danger money.'

I noticed that what I assumed to be Mister D was squeezed into a corset beneath the cover of his four-button black satin suit. I noticed as well that he appeared to be talking to one of our own. The two of them there, confident, sounding as if discovering me, a total stranger, on the premises didn't threaten them one little bit. More like I was some kind of joke.

'You're employed as the bodyguard, Bobby, which is to guard my body. There can't be danger money on top of what I'm already paying you to do.'

'It's my second day on the job.' Long silence. 'Only kidding.'

Now that I could actually see Bobby, the first thing I picked up was his deadeye stare, the look you can get from a night-club bouncer – or Stan Kriticos in one of his moods. Possibly it connected more with someone who has done a bit of time in prison? His clothes were neat, too neat really, kind of awkward and at a tangent to fashion trends – dark brown jacket with a high collar, immaculate pale blue jeans with emphatic ironed creases front and back, pseudo alligator-skin cowboy boots. Your classic out-of-date male with attitude.

I must have stood up about then, trying to get on top of the situation while, no doubt, to those two appearing totally confused.

Mister D was asking Bobby if, maybe, I could be the police.

'Oh mate, doesn't have to matter, the law or not, he's blown it. In this country you can't break and enter unless you show a warrant or something. I'm going to throw the prick out.'

Suddenly I was working extra hard to concentrate my attention.

'Your play, Bobby.'

And, right on cue, Bobby stepped up wearing the same empty expression as before, and out of nowhere punched me in the stomach. I suppose at some level of consciousness

I knew he would do that.

But not nice.

Next he spun me round, twisted an arm up behind my back, much too high, and too hard. I might even have thought 'unnecessary force' if the pain hadn't cancelled out thinking.

'Time for Goldilocks to go to bed so, fatso, out you go.'

Gasping for breath from the whack I'd taken in the stomach, I was putting up no resistance at all while he steered me out the bedroom door, making certain that in passing my head connected with the woodwork.

Only when replaying the scene for my own entertainment later did it strike me as comic that Bobby, whose hair was cut short and bottle-bleached yellow, should refer to Mister D, with his head bald as a billiard ball, as Goldilocks. But right then, in the moment, droll word games were zooming straight over my head.

When your head is smashed against a doorjamb is when you really come to resent the presence of scum on this planet. The funny side of motivational speakers and their pals trashing your place while paying no rent evaporates altogether. Nothing in this life is going to get a giggle out of you until the scales of justice are set to horizontal again. Add physical pain to that loss of a sense of humour, not to mention the humiliation, plus the frustration of finding no way to fight back; tot all that up and multiply your total by being called 'fatso', and first thing you find is that head injuries and an ever-present guilt concerning just about everything in this life, plus the beer, and the fact of you're generally feeling down … well. Arguments for reasonable outcomes vanish like tiny accidental white clouds into a blue sky on a clear, warm day.

Suddenly you are concentrating on the moment only.

Confident he is on a winner, Bobby steers you to the apartment's entrance foyer, opens the door, and for good measure bangs your head on that jamb as well, then he hurls you into space so hard that you collapse against one of the two stainless steel elevator doors opposite. Doors everywhere!

Bobby pushes the elevator's 'down' button and your guess would be that a light comes on behind an arrow indicating that one or other of the machines has registered the message.

Slam.

That is your own apartment's door saying goodbye. You are locked out of your own property! Out of your own goddamn high-in-the-sky strata title!

You are roaring. Karen says I never grew up, emotionally, that's why I roar. Whatever.

It is a minute, could be less, before you have the key back in the lock and are turning it. Your head's hurting too much to care about knocking first. Inside, there's Mister D, standing, flat-footed, all surprise! Which is nice. Maybe he has been standing up against the door looking through the peephole at you outside, in distress, or maybe it has just occurred to him – as it turns out a fraction late – to snap the security chain into place. He appears amazed to see you again so soon. So he wasn't looking through the peephole then. But hardly does the fact of your physical presence register on his born again motivational brain before your shoulder has caught him in the solar plexus and cannoned him hard against the scuff-marked, off-white plaster render. Whereupon Mister D lets loose the kind of noiseless gasp fish make when flipped out of water. That is followed by a howl and 'Bobby (inaudible gasp) … I'm …!' He fails to articulate even the most fundamental of his thoughts because you hit him in the mouth. Yes, so sweet, connecting precisely where he orates from, so hard that it has to leave tooth marks across your knuckles. And he falls full length, half on and half off a stained, pink-with-black-blobs, modernist scatter rug. The rest of him, mostly the legs, are splayed across the pale oak parquetry.

In the nick of time, too. Because here comes the salaried muscle running at you while swinging a full, sparkling bur-

gundy wine bottle like a club. It comes at your head, misses, and that turns out to be his big mistake of the night. Because on semi-automatic you kick him in the groin as he follows through.

The kick causes him to drop the bottle.

It bounces.

He doubles over.

You kick him in the face.

At about that moment your brain catches fire and you lose it altogether.

Directly following a fight I tend to be set adrift on a calm blue sea somewhere inside my head. My sails go slack and I just sort of float on a plane of contentment. I suppose it's my system's way of seeking and finding equilibrium. It's always been like that with me, right back to my early teens when we were kids fighting for no reason other than to feel alive.

While Bobby was bleeding from cuts around the head, and wandering in and out of consciousness, I tied his wrists to his ankles with strips torn from the bed sheets, to keep him from having another go. I stuffed a sock in his mouth for good measure and secured that with a gag tied behind his head. Then I dragged him to a capacious broom cupboard in the laundry, whacked him over the head a few times with volume one, A–K, of the Sydney telephone book, and shut the door.

Goodnight sweet prince.

The befuddled gaze of the tarnished motivational star held me from where he lay on his back on the floor. He was groaning a lot, and I'd have to say, fairly damaged.

I was just starting to come down off cloud nine as I dialled the agent. No answering machine. I let it ring till I heard a tone change as it switched to some secondary telephonic device. Eventually it rang out. So I dialled again. And again.

'Mr Holt …!' Indignant. 'You do realise that it's after midnight?'

'Damien, I want you to forget about the time of day, even if it happens to be closer to two-thirty.'

'I'm going to hang up this phone now.'

I had a totally weird guy in this Damien. I just don't get his type. You'd think he'd attempt to placate me at any time, day or night, after screwing us around the way he had. Wouldn't he worry about his reputation as an estate agent, fret over his capacity to remain in business once I set my mind to nailing him and his real estate agent's license? Mightn't he even cling to the faint hope that one day I could engage him to organise the apartment's sale?

'Hold on a minute, Damien, and listen. I'm calling from the apartment.'

'You're in the apartment?'

'Even as we speak.'

'You don't have the right, unless you arrange it through me. By law the tenant must be protected.'

'Oh, he's protected, don't you worry.'

'It's a security building, how'd you …?'

'Just get your arse over here.'

Inside a minute the phone rang. I picked up and put it down again.

Out of my post-violence calm, the problem was what to do next. It was dawning on me that I had a complex legal situation. For instance, I could be charged with assault. It would be my word against theirs. I liked to imagine that my word would win out, but Mister D had Jesus on his side. Of course he also had a lot of compromising videos to explain. But still, I was starting to understand that I needed someone to back me up.

Karen and Dawn's old school friend Giovanna Cecchini had replaced Gerald Sparrow as our legal representative in Sydney after an unrelated incident – on his advice I had nearly purchased his interest in a small company heading for insolvency. This had been the end of a long and not always beautiful friendship.

I dialled the home number for Cecchini that Karen had thoughtfully loaded into my new mobile phone. Abrupt, but apparently unsurprised to be dragged out of bed, she agreed to come around straight away.

Suddenly I was pacing from room to room, picking objects up, putting them down again. My hands started to tremble as the next stage after violence set in. I couldn't stay still. A couple of times I approached the laundry cupboard to check on muffled sounds coming from the gagged and bound Bobby. I suppressed the urge to shut him up for good. A few minutes later I asked if he wanted a drink but couldn't understand the answer, because of the gag.

There is nothing in this world worse than waiting.

Then, like some runaway child coming down from the high of escape, next thing all I wanted was to go home, to lie down on my own bed amongst my own things, wrap my arms around Karen, clutch our son Henry, too; and of course Desdemona the Second – that's the dog. Jeez, I love that dog.

I was even missing Paula Bartels, Henry's middle-aged nanny.

Yet I had to confront the reality that I was trapped up there in our investment with harbour views, flashy veneers and generally degraded decor. I had to face the fact that I was just one more sleepless papa on a business trip to hell. And of no significance.

Over the intercom the terse announcement of Giovanna Cecchini's arrival at the street entrance had me pressing the button to buzz her inside the building. A couple of minutes later she was hitting another buzzer at the apartment's door. What I captured of her appearance at first glance didn't have much effect. She looked tidy, okay, and concentrated too. Unfortunately I would have to add that she appeared extremely annoyed. Gazing through the doorway, peering through the foyer with its damaged motivator still recovering on the floor, and beyond into the vast, open-plan, junk-strewn lounge-dining area, she took the lot in, turned back to me and said, with considerable emphasis: 'I find it difficult to believe you'd do something like this.'

Yet she didn't appear shocked.

Hearing this fresh voice come amongst us, Mister D rolled onto his side, took a quick look, closed his eyes again and bunched into one more unconvincing version of the foetal position.

Then she added: 'Or do I?'

'Me? I did what? These bastards have wrecked the place, Karen's and my place, check it out for yourself.'

'Men!' Her practiced, judgmental response contrasted with what I had started to focus on, the unblemished olive complexion of a virgin on the streets of Naples. Other than lipstick, Ms Cecchini didn't need make up. She wore those large gold-rimmed glasses loaded with focal lengths that warp straight lines. Her clothes were elegant but understated and mostly dark blue, with a crisp white cotton blouse for contrast. In the no-go hours of that particular morning she was groomed the way you'd expect a professional to be when turning up at the office at 8.30. In her hand a slim satchel of soft, dark brown leather.

'Karen said to move in.'

'Must you be so literal?' Dropping her gaze to scrutinise for a second time the fresh bloodstains on the floor, a metre or so inside the front door. Next she was shaking her head, theatrically, feigning incomprehension while letting air escape between high coloured, gloss-gleaming, pursed lips, creating a small whistling sound, as though making absolutely certain I understood that she couldn't believe it.

I was beginning to think that despite or because of her having been snatched from slumber, there was more to this lawyer than I had gathered at first glance – more of just about everything. She had entered my small world looking fresh, okay, but the attraction was building on the fact of a slight puffiness under the eyes, and hair still a touch wet – from stepping under the shower?

Before she and I could venture further down the road of mutual misunderstanding the door buzzer buzzed. As they will even in the wee small hours.

I opened up.

This had to be Damien Berry, Mr Real Estate. He was the only visitor who wouldn't need to ring through to the apartment from street level. He was eating a Mars Bar. Behind a translucent mask of nonchalance and mastery over this poor world, Damien could have been letting some uncertainty show – by eating that Mars Bar, for instance. As well there was the way his eyes wandered about the place, checking everything, anxious to be seen to be doing so. Possibly casting about for signs of something more important to him than simply being found out for having stuffed up as managing agent.

Yet, signs of what exactly? Was it just the DVDs and videos? Possibly. And that he was a particular pal of this Mister D – most probably that as well.

A neat man of light build. Designer label all over. You'd lay money on Calvin Klein underpants. As well the blue-violet of his eyes had to come from tinted contacts. Despite having complained at being disturbed at such an ungodly hour, he seemed to have found time to blow wave an enviable head of mid brown, boy-cut hair. Mobile phone clipped to his belt. One of those watches that cost the equivalent of a week with call girls at a five star hotel. One diminutive golden sleeper in the lobe of his right ear. Smelling like the perfume department of a big city store.

I cut away from Damien to the watchful Ms Cecchini – one wee golden sleeper in each of her ears. I looked back to Damien to find that the Mars Bar had been devoured and he was rolling the wrapper into a ball between the palms of his hands.

I wasn't trembling any more, I'd gone all calm again, and felt light enough to float to the ceiling. I wanted to hurt Damien, of course. But not in front of Giovanna, because I seemed to be developing plans for her of an altogether more tender variety.

Regarding Damien, part of me was like: should I care about this arsehole's business? I was after economic justice where the apartment was concerned, and nothing else. Wasn't I? I had to repeat that like a mantra to stay focused. Whatever these people were into that I might not like, it wasn't as if the law and I were ever going to be playing on the same team. If Mister D was into kiddy smut, into illegal substances, snuff movies, whatever, and Damien Berry happened to be part of that same scene, it was no business of mine. Anyway, when in the past I'd speculated about what others were up to, invariably I got it wrong, particularly where sex was concerned.

Mister D had recovered sufficiently to crawl across the floor and rest the upper part of his body on a couple of stained pillows that just happened to be lying there. He'd folded his arms around his head as if to keep the world out of that anatomical arena. Damien gasped at Mister D's appearance, but like a Christian on holidays stopped short of offering comfort.

When I instructed Mister D to get up, he obeyed, scrambling to his feet, appearing surprised to have accomplished the manoeuvre. He didn't look at the other two, only at me, having wisely locked in place a kind of 'What next, boss' expression. Meanwhile, sticking to legal mode, in her hand a fat file spirited from the soft leather satchel, a stern, controlled Giovanna was explaining to the increasingly uneasy Damien that he had been the recipient of four letters from her office, all relating to his mismanagement of the property. What was more, she went on, copies of the last two of those letters had been sent to the real estate agent's registration body. She couldn't believe that entity hadn't been in touch with him already over the matter?

And so on. Our lawyer doing what we paid her to do. Her small breasts pushing indignantly against the snow-white fabric of her pure cotton blouse. When she was through and I'd extracted the hired help from the cupboard and they'd handed over the keys, I rode the lift down with Damien, Bobby and Mister D, herding them into the street where the homeless character I'd given a hundred dollars to was standing stiffly in the block's garden and declaring a whole lot of stuff to an unhearing world.

Giovanna drove me to a down-market eating spot in Surry Hills, where cab drivers and other live-wires of the pre-dawn were drinking coffee, swapping rumours and devouring greasy food. Suited me to a tee. I got into a reviving hamburger with the lot while she alternated an espresso and a glass of European-label, still mineral water.

We hadn't said anything while driving through the all but empty streets. Ordering at the counter we still hadn't done much more than be polite with each other. Now, as I wrestled the hamburger to my mouth, Giovanna was looking at me with what I hoped was fresh interest, peering through the big glasses, her eyes narrowed. Or was she merely calculating what to say next without causing too much offence?

Eventually: 'Your head, you might need to take yourself off to a doctor.'

'It heals.'

'So, you do this kind of thing often, Essington?'

'I live on Saint-Jean-Cap-Ferrat. Have you any idea what that's like socially? Of course I don't beat people up on the Riviera.'

'I should hope not, for Karen's sake.'

'What are you trying to say?'

'The proverbial bull in a china shop.'

'Wait a minute, let me tell you exactly what went on.' I dabbed the lump on my forehead with a handkerchief; the stain indicated the lesion was still oozing blood and serum. Giovanna averted her gaze. I asked 'Do you think I was born with this? I didn't do a thing till that Bobby what's-his-name used my head as a battering ram.'

'Unprovoked?'

'Totally. I do not tell a lie.'

'I am a witness to how you repaid him for that. I must say I find it hard to accept. Would you describe what you did as involving a rational use of force?'

'There were two of them. And one of me, one Essington Holt.'

Of course what she was saying made sense. Once we'd hauled him out of the cupboard even I'd felt bad seeing the damage I'd done to Bobby. He was just the hired help and, hadn't he said that it was only his second day in the job? How about that for a piece of bad luck? Yet I hadn't been able to suppress a smile, either. From the way he was nursing it I suspected I had fractured some bone in his left arm. Only part of the damage.

'A fight between grown men is a fight, Giovanna. A person can get killed.'

'So I see.'

'Bobby isn't the type to say sorry. He wasn't even feeling sorry for himself, did you notice?'

My impression was that his eyes had been telling me we weren't finished yet.

I chewed, she sipped.

Then, as if inspired, I pulled out my digital camera, held it aloft, popped a shot of her across the table. Flash went the flash.

'You can't do that to people,' she snapped. 'They were right, you really are a little crazy, aren't you?'

'Sorry, I should have asked. Anyhow, the reason I brought

the camera out is to let you see I've used it to put together a record of the damage the tenants have done to the place.'

'At least that's useful.'

I passed her the camera. She examined it carefully, first the front, then the back. Next she pressed the shutter button, another flash, taking a shot of nothing in particular.

She passed the camera back.

'Three point three mega pixels, what does that mean?'

'I wouldn't have a clue,' I replied, 'I bought it because Dawn told me it was the best of that size, to put in your pocket.'

Chapter 3

'Do you mind leaning forward a bit more, Alison, and move your head around so I get a profile.' She did as she was told. 'Nice,' I said. 'Now fix your gaze on that crappy piece of hotel art up there on the wall, if you can stand it, of course.'

'Sensitive little thing like me.' Playing a part, she gave that 'thing' something approximating a Southern twang.

'That's better.' Reclining on top of the walnut veneer desk in my hotel room, Alison looked like one of those Modigliani nudes they used to hang prints of on coffee lounge walls, in the days when Paris was king and the avant-garde wore berets: long thin torso, narrow waist swelling to hips and thighs, a bush of red pubic hair.

'You're right though, there's not much art about it.'

'About what, Alison?'

'Whatever it is you told me to look at.'

'It's an etching, as in "Come up and see my …" ' Safe subject, tasteful print, a line drawing of a lotus leaf on a pond, a frog on the lotus leaf, printed in turquoise with a lot of plate tone. Whoever rented the room, Catholic priest, Mullah, Baptist weirdo, nobody was going to find fault with that print. I guess it was a middle-class Buddhist's wet-dream.

'Come up and see your what, Essington?'

'Oh, when gentlemen used to put in work seducing girls, one line they'd take was asking them home to see their etchings. Images of sexually suggestive subjects, ripe figs, people dancing the tango, you know.'

'Sweet.' Alison got a dreamy look in her eyes. Maybe she reckoned a bit of oblique conversation before getting down to the screwing part of a night out might be nice, could even be romantic. That or she found the subject boring.

Christ knows what the do-no-evil, see-no-evil management thought when Alison asked for me at the reception desk at ten o'clock in the morning. Dressed in scuffed workman's boots, baggy grey cotton twill trousers with a tear below the left buttock, grubby tee shirt bearing a 'Save Nature' message for all the world to read, Community Aid Abroad shoulder bag. At the price charged for my suite you'd have hoped they'd show her the door.

Happily, appearances can deceive. Stark naked, Alison was amazing. Well, naked except for a length of turquoise silk wrapped turban-style around her head. She had brought the silk with her. 'Just an idea.'

'An idea of what?'

That her hair was no more than an inch long might have had something to do with the idea.

'The agency said you wanted to do arty drawings with dress-ups. I thought you might be thinking along Matisse lines, you know, the exoticism of North Africa, that sort of thing.'

Snap.

'You an art student?'

She said 'No' by shaking her head. Whatever, by naming Henri Matisse, Alison had hit one of my many sensitive spots. Matisse happened to be very much on my mind just then. So much so that the master's name out loud caused me to break the stick of charcoal I'd been holding between my fingers.

Interesting.

'You'd know a Matisse if you saw one?'

'All right then, I did go to art school for a year and a half.'

'And?'

'Total wank. I knew more when I started than when I gave up.'

'And now?'

'Mostly I do this kind of thing … occasionally I get to hang pictures for an auction house. My father's brother …'

'Your uncle?'

'I never think of him as an uncle.'

'Help hang, dressed as you were at my door?'

'No way, they are very concerned with appearances.'

'And I'm not? I'm paying you to model!'

'You want my clothes off, that's all, so what difference does it make what I'm wearing to start with?'

'Every difference, Alison.' Why was I talking bullshit?

She was charming, I liked her a lot, she smelled of soap.

I wasn't sure, though, about the auction house connection. And naming Matisse had disturbed me. Still, I filed what she had told me in my head, under A for Alison. And for Auction.

With Alison, turban or no turban, I wasn't trying for Matisse-style drawings, because I wasn't capable of getting that result when working from the model. The drawings I do for myself are much more prosaic than those Matisse produced. I can't let a line flow as if it had a mind of its own the way the master could, even when he was sick and dependent on his wheelchair to get around the studio. The only way I can replicate a Matisse line is by copying one or by tracing and retracing over a light table until I get it right. And even then I'll rework it maybe twenty times until making the mark becomes the reflex of a muscular memory.

For my chosen profession I was used to analysing the work of modernist masters right down to the last brushstroke. A practice which rendered me acutely aware of my limitations as an artist. So, the purpose of drawing Alison was to learn more about drawing, and about my own, unique responses to the motif. I was, you might say, getting into a spot of self-improvement. Mid-life crisis?

Dangerous.

While in the air, heading for Sydney, I had decided to put into practice what I had been thinking about doing back home, which was devoting part of my time each day to drawing. Matisse did a lot of drawing like that. He'd just sit in the studio and draw some half-naked woman reclining on a sofa, producing the most casual pen and ink studies, maybe just a handful of lines on the sheet of paper, no more. Most of the models believed he possessed no talent at all. And maybe he didn't. I read somewhere that he used to get some of his models through Auguste Renoir, who lived a bit further west along the Mediterranean coast and who reckoned Matisse was a nice enough character but light on artistic ability.

Drawing Alison and other models connected with an undertaking to keep my activities inside the law. Karen had made me promise that. She argued that now I was a father it was time to consider the effects criminality might have on our children's lives. Soon as Henry was born she had taken to putting questions like, Did I want to have the children visit me in gaol?

'If they smuggled angel wire so I could saw through the bars, why not?'

'I'm serious, Essington.'

But even with the best intentions in the world, I couldn't give up on forging great masterpieces. I was addicted to my craft. At home, if I sat in the sun on a top floor balcony, gazing out over the Mediterranean, chilled bottle of rosé by my side for comfort, it was only a matter of time before I would be planning the complex sequence of activities leading to floating one more forgery onto the choppy waters of the international art market. I have been told that gamblers are like that, they can't stop getting the hots for the odds, despite the often terrible consequences of their passion.

But travel can lead a person to make reckless decisions. So my promise to Karen went out the window the instant I was instructed to head off to Australia and fix up the apartment mess. Somehow, planning to break the law in the southern hemisphere didn't seem so bad – promises had to be hemisphere-specific, yes?

I was having trouble with one of Alison's arms, the elbow of which was pointing directly at me. What I had managed on the paper looked more like a tree stump than a piece of human anatomy. While I muttered recriminations to myself for screwing up, and rubbed the bad drawing back to grey with a piece of paper towel, Alison returned to the subject of Matisse.

She wanted to know if he made passes at his models.

'What sort of a question is that? What's Matisse got to do with anything? Looking at you, I was thinking more like Modigliani.'

'Who?'

'Never mind.' Strange that she rattled on about Matisse but had never heard of Modigliani. 'How about when I finish this – or rip it up – we try something a little bit Balthus.' Balthus is nubile-sexy, 'transgressive' might be a better word. He's like the photographer David Hamilton but pretending a higher purpose.

'Never heard of him either.'

I couldn't get the arm right on the second try so I tore the sheet of paper in half. I guess I just couldn't adapt my heavy-handed style to foreshortening. Occasionally I fluked it, but mostly I failed. It wasn't just that I couldn't learn the trick involved in making something in a drawing seem to be coming towards you, rather, for me to draw an arm I wanted it to say 'arm', to be representative of all arms. But drawing naked women, avoiding things coming straight at you wasn't always possible.

Why had she mentioned Matisse again? Criminal intentions can turn a man into a total paranoiac.

'You don't like the scarf around my head?'

'Not a problem, it looks great. But you'd look good without it, too.'

'Should I take it off, then?'

'Why not.'

As she unwound the length of silk I thought that what I really wanted to capture in my drawing was something of the lithe animal being she presented. Question: did I want to draw her at all, or would I prefer to be crawling around the floor with her, buck naked? The pair of us being lithe animals together. A breeding pair, maybe. Answer: I think I wanted to keep on drawing.

New pose, still with foreshortening, one forearm behind her head and the other bent at the elbow, bringing her knuckles up against her neck. She was partially on her back with the far hip pushing up so the tangle of red hair of her pubic triangle was at the center of the volume below her waist. I'd cut my drawing off half-way along her thighs so her hips balanced her shoulders, arms and head at the other end. Now she was looking directly at me; strong, straight nose, thin lips and the fragile dome of her head beneath the short-cropped, hot-red hair. The magical beauty of another human was spread out before me, just about perfect – even with a butterfly tattooed directly above her pubic hair.

'You get much work as a model?' I asked, not expecting the truth.

'I live in hope.'

I'd thought of taking a few photos as well, so I could feed them into my laptop to use as references for more drawings. I hadn't tried that, but it was an idea. When I asked if that would be acceptable Alison said she didn't mind at all, seemed pleased in fact, so I took one, then took another zooming in on her face. So beautiful, just eyes, nose, lips filling the viewer's rectangle. Next thing the phone rang.

It was Giovanna Cecchini who wanted to know, was I busy?

I said, yes I was, I was drawing a model.

'A model of what?'

'Naked, beautiful, if you're interested you'll have to arrange it with the Pretty Girls agency.'

'Why on earth would I do that?'

'To please me, of course.'

No comment. She said she'd received a call from a friend of mine, Gerald Sparrow.

'And?'

'He is anxious that I let you know he'd called.'

'How could he know to contact me through you?'

Alison broke the pose and mouthed the word 'bathroom' at me. Pity really, the drawing had shown promise. Still, I had the photos.

'Through Damien, of course. Think about it, Essington. You told me that they worked together on buying that property.'

'Did you give him this number?'

'No.'

'Did he ask for it?'

'Yes.'

'So?'

'He said he'd be in touch anyway. Oh, and he mentioned someone called Stan Kriticos.'

'In relation to?'

'He didn't say.'

The reason I like drawing in charcoal is it's so forgiving. You can smear areas to produce grey background tones and draw back over the top, defining body shapes with strokes of velvety black. Or you can rub back to white with an eraser. It was a lot of fun recording aspects of Alison, my hired friend of almost two hours. Already I liked her a lot.

'Would you like a drink, Alison?'

'It's not lunchtime yet.'

'So?'

'Okay, yes.'

'Vodka? Your choice.'

'A vodka would go down fine.'

'It's not too strong for you before lunch?'

'For me, no, right now it's still before breakfast, so meal-wise I guess it's still last night. They have anything to eat in this hotel, Essington?'

'Yes, they have food.'

Drawing can be frustrating, particularly if you've looked too closely at too much art for too long and for the wrong reasons. As I have. Again and again I get this feeling of failing the subject as much as I fail myself. I had been failing the beautiful Alison, with her oh-so-white skin and red hair. She downed her share of a platter of oysters and accepted two vodkas from the chilled bottle, and was relaxed. She was on the bed, lying on her back with one leg up and the other down. Trying another drawing I figured the trick was to start at the middle and work out in all directions. So I rubbed a smudge to mark the spot in the lower center of my page, and was plotting dots out from there, thinking about interlocking triangles. Then I set to delineating her vulva and the way her buttocks swelled beneath.

Working in silence now.

After not too long she appeared in danger of going to sleep, so I asked, 'What else do you do, to earn a living?'

'Mostly just modelling like this.'

'In art schools?'

'Hell no, they don't pay enough, and it's boring. They make

you sit in the same spot for hours on end.'

'I'm paying above the art school rate?'

'Well, yes, double, because with the agency it's mostly one on one.'

I went quiet after that, requiring all the concentration I could muster to check the proportions I had sketched in, noting straight off that the knees were out of place in relation to the position of the head. I'd kind of squashed the image up too much. And again the foreshortening posed a problem, with her head farthest away from me and feet closest, somehow they were wrong in relationship to the smudge and lines I'd drawn indicating genitalia. The real difficulty for me was to keep her head back there, while at the same time elevating my point of view so that the work would be somewhere between a perspective view, like a photograph, and a plan drawing.

Eventually I asked, 'One on one, does that mean ...'

'Look, Essington, I'm twenty-four years old, what I do to make a buck is my own business.'

'I was only making small talk. I couldn't give a toss what you do.'

'Sorry.'

'Tell me about the last person you posed for.'

'It was not so much modelling as ...'

But again I'd lost interest in the conversation. I was having too much trouble making the legs join on to the torso in an anatomically reasonable fashion. I knew Cézanne developed the idea that all of nature could be understood in terms of simple geometric solids and I was attempting to apply that to the problem. For Cézanne, the leg would have to be analysed in terms of two pieces of pipe joining at the knee. I tried to resolve how the pipe would be when pointing directly at me the way one upper leg was doing.

'I'll tell you about a job I had a couple of months ago, if you pour another vodka.'

'You driving?'

'I am just so far from being able to afford running a car.'

I was working tone into the leg, having repositioned the knee. There was the idea of the pipe, I'd got that pretty right. Next I was softening the profiles while attempting to get a sense of the structure of her buttock on that side, the way it tucked up behind her vulva. But in becoming analytical I'd lost the sensuality. There was no rhythmic flow through the body.

'I do a bit of exotic dancing.'

'Which means?'

'Mostly you don't want to know. Sometimes I do this lesbian act, you know, at bucks' parties, business conventions, that sort of thing. The fellers get their thrills. Then, of course, afterwards it's back to the wife and kids, boring the family shitless with lies about sales graphs and motivational sessions.'

There was that Mister D word, motivational. 'And?'

'This time with my friend we were booked to do a show at a bikies' weekend down the South Coast, outside Batemans Bay. We were driving down in Pixie's car ... what a bomb.'

'Bikies wouldn't talk about sales graphs.'

'Unless it's amphetamines ... no wife and kids either, would have pissed off years ago – just restraining orders and the Harley.'

'Who's Pixie?'

'She'd be forty something, a primary school teacher. Like we do this schoolgirl and teacher act. They go for it, love the exercise books, the rulers, spanking, stuff we do with the pencils and erasers – avant-garde, we are.'

'Pencils! Hope you don't chew the ends.'

'Chew the ends? You are weird, Essington, anybody ever tell you that?'

'Never.'

'There's a first time for everything. For instance, take a look at yourself. You've got sticking plaster wrapped around the knuckles of– would that be the hand you'd punch the walls out with? And you're asking me these pervy questions! Why don't I ask you some of my own?'

'Go ahead.'

'Well, what are you trying to do here? These drawings, I could just about do them. At the same time you haven't made a pass at me or anything. So, what are we here for? Weird. With the bikies what you see is pretty much what you get. With you I just wouldn't know.'

Apparently it had taken Alison and Pixie longer than they'd calculated to get down to Batemans Bay and it was dark by the time the car spluttered to a halt ten minutes outside town. Alison had sat there smoking a joint, feeling pissed off with the whole adventure, trying to shift blame onto Pixie who was playing at being practical by opening the bonnet and poking her head under it, but seeing nothing because it was so dark. Eventually a farm truck pulled up in front of them and a hayseed came walking back to lend a hand. His arrival caused Alison to remember there was a light set into the end of one of several vibrators they'd brought along to keep the fellers entertained. The Good Samaritan accepted it without comment, switched it on and used it to find and fix the problem.

What really stuck in her mind about the guy was the way, having finished, he shook each of them by the hand. 'He asked us where we were off to and when we kind of explained he just said, "Safe home, girls". Can you imagine it? I mean he didn't seem to have a clue, did he? Neither did I by that stage – too stoned.'

'You reckoned I was weird! But really I'm just like that farmer helping you out.'

'While paying for this hotel suite? I don't believe it. Anyway, those bikies were stuffed full of booze and speed. But Pixie was amazing, so confident. It's the teacher in her. She reckoned she could keep them under control, well enough for us to get out of there in one piece. She told me it's what they show them at teachers' college. If it works on a room full of kids it will work on a bunch of drunks, even if they have sawn-off shotguns in their pannier bags.'

'And?'

'It didn't.'

'You're telling me …?'

'I'm not telling you anything too exciting, Essington. Just that Pixie wasn't able to control those animals. A bunch of them got completely out of hand, grabbing at me, you know, trying to have a go and everything. It wasn't nice.'

'And you let them?'

'Didn't look like we had much choice, did it? Until along came our knight in shining armour.'

'Who was?'

'By that stage Pixie was up against it, being the lesbian school teacher. They were going to show her who's boss. I mean, at first I couldn't believe it, what chance for us two girls against that lot. But all of a sudden there's this group of men bust in through the door. Not too many of them. But they weren't off their faces, were they? Weren't motorbike club types either.' My drawing came to a halt. 'It was the farmer who'd stopped and got our car going. He'd come in with his mates, to save us. Like, Essington, they gave it to the bikies who were fighting amongst themselves anyway by that stage. Possibly some of them weren't so keen on gang-raping us girls.'

'You lived happily ever after.'

'I lived. Seems our farmer had this notion that something could go wrong for us. Intuition. Said he believed things stuff up in threes, that's what he said.'

'But there were only two things, the car and then the audience turning on you.'

'The third thing was, Pixie shacked up with the farmer. She's still down there, loves it, the country life.'

'Two bad things, one good.'

'Good! Those lesbian acts with Pixie paid so well.'

That drawing turned out better than I could have hoped. It had the right kind of tension between being an abstract arrangement of lines and a description of Alison in repose. Some sensuality in there as well. Maybe the story she told kept my mind from pushing too hard at the problems of proportion and space. I'd also forgotten her mention of Matisse.

Plus I'd consumed a bit of vodka.

Oh, and I'd swallowed a lot of oysters along with the story.

Thinking of Sparrow trying to get in touch, I found myself brooding over Stan Kriticos. So it hadn't been Sparrow who gave Stan my telephone number at the hotel, not if Giovanna was to be believed. The big question for me was, why would he insist on me buying back the art I'd so assiduously acquired for him? It didn't make sense. I'd roll this over again and again in my head, trying to work out what he was hoping to achieve.

Of course it occurred to me that he'd twigged to the idea that the paintings were all forgeries. If that was the case it would make sense he'd want his money back. Yet it seemed very un-Stan not to come straight to the point and accuse me of dudding him.

If he could prove they were forgeries, he could hold it over me that he would call in the police. But again, to do that would be very un-Stan. Both of us would know that once police and the idea of fakes were involved none of the paintings would ever be worth anything. I'd be in the slammer and he'd be down a lot of cash.

Anyway, what he had were exceptional examples of the forger's art, even if I say so myself. No way would Stan or any-body who saw them on his walls have picked the difference, they would need to have resorted to DNA testing, and the rest. And why the hell would he bother with esoteric stuff like that?

Still, it was a worry. But then, Stan was always a worry. And his motives hard to fathom.

I don't do my art transactions for the money. Money I have, I'm over my head in it and I know too well how it takes the zap out of this, your one life. With too much in the bank, you wonder why you bother to get up in the morning, there isn't the necessity of foraging for food, battling for shelter, holding onto your tribal land. A set of golf clubs and memberships around the world are not a substitute for reality. I need risk on a daily basis. We all do, the possibility that we might not eat.

Most highly valued works of art, forged or otherwise, don't just sit around waiting to be discovered, their reputations are tied up with the social prestige of those who handle them along the way. Big for me, psychologically, is the prospect of entrapping culture snobs, because it really pisses me off when important paintings finish up the property of people incapable of understanding what they are looking at. I am addicted to that adrenalin buzz you get from flogging fakes to the high and the mighty.

The quickest way to establish art credentials is to present yourself as a loud, bidding presence at a prestigious art auction house. Either that or get your fat butt over to the local public gallery and donate something big. Or, just donate them a bucket full of cash. You do any of those things and you are respected, as an art lover – and a source of paintings going up for auction. I'd already checked out the art auction houses in Sydney and it seemed I had a few weeks before I could get my glad rags on and throw any money around. Stand out in the crowd. Now that I'd met Alison, I also had the possibility of using her uncle connection. I wasn't sure about that one because Alison didn't seem the type for art world contacts, knowledge of Matisse notwithstanding. There was a chance that the self-proclaimed star turn in a lesbian act for bikies could be up to telling the occasional little white lie.

The next morning, after Alison had gone, there was a message at reception from Giovanna telling me to ring Gerald Sparrow, she had supplied his number. After thinking about it for a while I crushed the piece of paper with the number into a tight ball and goaled it into a wastepaper basket.

Gerald bloody Sparrow, dear oh dear. I'd known him since secondary school. Early on he developed a particular way of talking to people, as if he had been in receipt of information from a higher source. He became a firm believer in British values, the Westminster system, the Crown, the entire disaster. I could remember him saying stuff like 'The French could never have produced a Shakespeare. Molière doesn't stand up, too superficial, not the depth.' Shit like that while still in his teens.

I knew he'd read about as much Shakespeare and Molière as I had.

Yes, that's what he had been, an embarrassment who clung to me because I was everything he wasn't. I was doomed to become an uneducated non-professional who could draw the testicles out of a sheep with my teeth. How was I to know he'd turn out to be one of those people you wish you'd never met?

A dedicated, ambitious student, he had studied law at Sydney University, following that up with working the regulation time in some big law firm, identified as partner material, talented at schmoozing political wheelers and dealers, the rich and powerful. Natty dresser too. Most importantly, at least from his point of view, he set himself up as a man about town, with an interest in property developments, the arts, government, the lot. He became president of the thrombosis something or other – raised money for medical research.

Before I inherited I had seemed to be getting poorer at about the same pace Sparrow was amassing a small fortune, and becoming increasingly uppity with it. I had even sold him a couple of paintings I had picked up at auction. Nothing too flash, two 19th century Australian landscapes that were better as art than the punters had believed.

To clear my head of Sparrow and the past I connected digital camera to laptop and downloaded its images. Then I cleared the camera's memory stick, clicked open my image-editing program, and checked out thirty-four JPEGs. The first twenty were prosaic enough, reminding me again just how trashed our apartment was. Then came Giovanna facing me across the table at the hamburger joint in Surry Hills. Being a close-up her nose looked too big and her eyes were red from the flash. The shutter had caught her between expressions, she appeared neither angry nor legalistic, more like somebody's daughter. Thick black hair was kicking out either side of her face. To me she looked beautiful. Next shot was of the café's wall, in the frame's bottom corner the top of a customer's head.

I looked at that shot of Giovanna for a long time before printing it out on my little A4 printer. Then I tucked the image under the bottom edge of one of the framed, hotel-art prints adorning my suite.

The rest of the images were of Alison variously undressed. I checked them, one by one, but they failed to supply any fresh art ideas.

And there were the still-fresh memories of a night with Alison, in the middle of which she had popped what I supposed to be a dance party drug. Whatever, it did the trick and concentrated all her attention on abandoning responsibility on behalf of us both. She had appeared to enjoy the game of whispering into my ear, 'You are the oldest man I've ever fucked.' She had repeated it over and over like some circuit had gone wrong inside her head.

And I replied, 'And you're my first woman,' over and over and over.

A wonderful laugh, Alison.

There was a point when I'd been lost in a world of my own between her legs, my tongue exploring the detail, her legs holding me in place, trapping me more like it, the tips of her fingers massaging my bald patch.

Next thing she'd been sitting on top of me, her hands spread on my belly to control the action as she raised and lowered herself, determining the pace and the pleasure till, tilting forward like a jockey entering the straight, she pretty much took the whip to my flanks as I kept on going after she had let loose with a howl that dropped down to a groan and finished as a mere sigh.

Rolled off me.

'Hail Mary, mother of God.' Then silence. Lying on her back, gazing at the ceiling, till out of the blue she asked, 'Who is Giovanna?'

'Giovanna who?'

'That's what I want to find out. Not that I care, of course, but you called me Giovanna a couple of times and I just wondered if she was a wife or something.'

'Called you Giovanna! I don't believe it. She isn't even a something, she's my solicitor.'

'You fuck her?'

'You sure I called you that, Alison? It could have just been me slurring my words.'

'And I'm Mickey Mouse.'

'Minnie, you'd be,' I kissed her on the stomach, the start of my mouth's next journey south.

'You realize you haven't kissed me on the lips yet. Would it be any different if I was a solicitor?'

Too late, I was down there and she was spreading her legs.

Chapter 4

I like to conduct at least part of my business on the wrong side of the law, but that doesn't mean the two detectives had a right to work me over verbally the way they did. I told them straight out that I had been in the apartment, okay, having let myself in the front door. But then I owned the place, didn't I?

For a second or a third time my answer was that this fool had jumped me, bashed my head against the building's structure when showing me the door. 'Throwing me out my own god-damned door, officer!' They had done damage to the Essington Holt forehead, a little to the face as well. So, give me a break. In fact, I don't think I have any more to say, officer.

'I'll be the judge of how much more you might or might not have to say, Mr Holt.'

We were in my hotel suite, the three of us. We did all this a few more times, backwards and forwards without getting anywhere. They couldn't believe I'd turned up at the apartment without any plan in my head.

The cops obviously didn't like me. I wasn't their type. For instance, they wanted to know where I got my anti-police attitude, labouring the point that if I wasn't going to be in some trouble with the law then why not cooperate, just tell them how it was and get over it.

Giovanna Cecchini breezed in, digested information regarding my status as the perpetrator of an alleged assault and checked out what the police had in mind for me. Eventually she asked if there was evidence of some crime having been committed other than her client being attacked on his own property by two men who had, prior to the attack, ceased to qualify as tenants in good standing – or something along those lines.

Her amazing skin! I checked the expression on her face – was she concerned for me?

No. Not the beautiful Giovanna. Heartless.

Her eyes so clear, so bright behind those enormous spectacles.

Another question from the police was coming at me as I played with the fantasy of Giovanna wearing nothing but those spectacles, reaching her hand up to remove them, and me saying, 'No, leave them, please.'

A little out of control where my feelings were concerned. Was that a by-product of my erotic exploration of Alison the day before? Was I indeed papa on a business trip eager to lose it altogether in Sydney, Australia? A guy who couldn't be in the presence of a woman without imagining some kind of sexual adventure?

'Let me remind you that Mr Holt didn't break in because he didn't need to ... the property belongs to him. To be precise, it is owned by a company of which he and his wife are the sole directors.'

At the word 'wife' she shot me a look.

I added, 'I had a key, that's not breaking in.'

But whenever I had a go at saying something, Giovanna bit down on her lower lip and scowled.

The accusation of assault came from Mister D, not from Bobby. His witness, Damien Berry. Wouldn't you just know it?

Well, stuff them.

Giovanna won the day. And the officers were just leaving when, before the door of my suite had the time to close behind them, we were fronted by an expressionless character holding out his identification. Another cop! At least this one was wearing a pinstripe that buttoned up without looking about to burst at the seams. He had the pallid skin of someone suffering a liver complaint. In his gaze was the recollection of some terrible event. He explained that he too would like to talk with me about what had happened at the apartment.

Standing very straight, Giovanna objected. Nice like that,

I thought. Her long neck, the little bejeweled cross on a fine golden chain. Her breasts, the cloth over them still pulling slightly.

The first pair of detectives followed the newcomer back inside. One, sitting down uninvited, drumming his fingers on an occasional table, said, 'Would you believe this is not a movie, Missus Cecchini. Chief Inspector Schwartz here, each one of us, all we want to do is work out what's been going on, sign off on the complaint and go home to our wives and families, just the same as everybody else in the world, no doubt even yourself.'

Giovanna. 'I'm not married, but like you I am here to do a job, nothing more.'

'Then let's do it,' said Schwartz.

I couldn't help but notice that the other two treated him with some deference. And that the three of them weren't used to working together.

Schwartz was not their pal.

'My problem, in the job you understand,' facetious, 'is I have reason to be interested in Mr Holt's business plans here in Australia.'

I thought, Jesus Christ!

Schwartz, shaking his head now as if hunting up some detail lost from memory.

I began to say something but Giovanna placed her hand on my arm.

Such a nice gesture. Her touch, such a nice touch. But there was no follow through.

When he announced that he'd received information connecting me with unscrupulous art dealing, I asked, 'What kind of information?'

Out loud Giovanna instructed me not to say anything.

Schwartz went on to explain that he'd known I was associated with the private company which owned the apartment and by pure chance had come across the fact that there was an assault complaint against the apartment's owner.

I started to ask if that meant he'd been watching the apartment, but Giovanna cut me off.

Just managing to contain my indignation, I sat there for the rest of the session watching as Giovanna swung her head to look my way and emphasise a point, or shut me up, or fix her attention on one or other of the men. The whole thing was a bit of a mystery as we went over it again, with a few vague references to art from Schwartz. Disturbing, but apparently pointless. I found my attention wandering. It was wonderful the way Giovanna's straight, jet-black hair flared. Her lips shone, as though wet, and behind the glasses those eyes continued to flash fresh and clear. She made me feel older and even more beaten up than I was.

She was dressed in dark blue trousers and a matching jacket, plus a white linen blouse with little flowers embroidered into the cloth and the first two buttons undone. Her satchel was stuffed with documents so, when it was all over, gallant to a fault, I carried it to where her black, two-door Lexus was parked. Before she opened the driver's side door she said, more as an inquiry than a statement of fact, 'Schwartz is in the fraud squad.'

'Why would the fraud squad be interested in what went on in the apartment?'

'Precisely what I was asking myself.'

'Neutral-looking bugger in that suit. Seemed to me as if he was kind of unconnected, dispassionate, you know what I'm trying to say?'

'Why do you think the fraud squad would be interested in you, Mr Holt?'

'Call me Essington, please.' I said I had no idea.

She asked, 'Are you up to something?'

'Me?'

'These things happen all day every day, and dealing with

them is of no assistance to a police officer's career. Particularly if you are a fraud investigator. So, why this interest? You understand I can't represent you adequately if you are keeping the truth regarding your business dealings from me.'

'You are a very beautiful woman.'

'You didn't answer my question.'

'Absolutely nothing.'

From where I was placed, time appeared to equal nothingness in Sydney. Maybe I should have got away from the harbour and walked the ocean beaches, a mere twenty minutes taxi ride east. There at least I might have sensed the existence of another world, on the far side of the Pacific. Instead, I was biding my time in the CBD, wondering if I should sell the apartment, squinting at bright light bouncing off high-gloss painted steel, off asphalt and concrete, walls of glass, watching fully employed sleepwalkers in their colourless clothing.

On top of all the edgy stuff headlined in the daily papers, there didn't seem to be a great deal happening in the world capable of surprising me, so I took to doing the word puzzle. In my time the Holt head had taken a lot of blows, the Holt psychology likewise, and I'd been a dud at school. Yet there I was getting twenty-one words from the nine letters set out in the square grid, plus the long word, AWESTRUCK. According to the score sheet that rated 'excellent'. Which didn't say much for the intellectual capabilities of the citizenry.

Maybe I should have reserved intellectual energy expended on the word puzzle for a reassessment of the plans for forgery I'd carried with me to Australia. But I wasn't up to that yet. Instead, I tried to work out what somebody like Chief Inspector Schwartz could have found out about me, and from which source that information had come. I believed I had a clean sheet up to that point. Well, maybe a few stains on it, but I'd never been convicted of an offence related to marketing artworks or the attribution of paintings appearing on the market. In my profession if you come under suspicion once then that's it. No serious art player will deal with you again. But I'd never been suspected, let alone charged. Yet now, first Kriticos, now Schwartz.

The following day, 10.30 am. Another model turned up courtesy of Phyllis at the agency. Paloma, she was, and wearing a dinner suit a couple of sizes too big, a formal shirt with front pleats, wide red suspenders holding up the trousers. When I whistled a few bars of La Paloma she said: 'Old men do that to me, but I've never heard the song anywhere else.'

'We old men are an endangered species.' She rolled her eyes. 'They are destroying our habitats, we will die out like the Tasmanian tiger.'

'I don't think so.'

'Have you done modelling before?'

Shyly she answered 'No.'

But yes, she would like a vodka. 'Sure you're of legal age to accept hard liquor from old men?'

'That's my problem.'

I was on the second drawing when she told me she'd once worked at a table dancing club.

'Jesus Christ! I thought you were going to tell me a table tennis club.'

Breaking the pose, she refilled her glass. 'It wasn't me, not really, these guys stuffing ten dollar notes into my G string, and going for a bit of a feel with it.'

'Paloma, you were up there on the table swinging your thing at them!'

She blushed. Blond, blue eyes, she watched me finish the drawing. 'What do I do now?' she asked.

'On the table, of course, I play music, you dance.' Only there wasn't a table.

Next Paloma was sitting on the floor, one leg up one leg down, the dinner suit trousers hanging off the corner of a painting 'The man running that place, he was the worst, all he wanted to do was shag my brains out.'

A bit later on, both of us a little under the weather but the drawings coming along. 'My Polish grandmother gave me the name, Paloma. Said I was her little white dove.'

'Italian word, but she was Polish?'

'Actually no, Ukrainian, she met my grandfather at this migrant camp in Victoria, he was Polish.'

'How old are you?'

She asked: 'Have you ever done this before?'

'You think I'm pretending to be an artist?'

'What you've done so far, none of them look a bit like me.'

'How old are you?'

'Eighteen, why?'

'I was thinking about the table dancing club.'

'What?'

'You must have known what to expect.'

'I suppose I did, it's just that I imagined it would be a bit more, you know, classy.'

'I don't believe you.'

Her mood changed. 'What do you want me to say?'

'I don't know, but there's always going to be consequences if you start gyrating in a G string with a lot of pissed guys standing round.'

'How was I to know?'

'You could have asked your grandfather about the Russian army in Poland.'

'I can't do that. He's dead.'

I held up the drawing, 'That looks more like you?'

'You really think so?'

2.00 am. On the telephone to Karen. She didn't even ask how

I was. Instead, playing Ms Efficiency rather than the Buddhist convert with begging bowl, she went straight to the subject of the apartment. Of course, hearing her voice I didn't feel all that chipper. For one thing I could still taste Alison on my fingers, like Pilate, or whoever, 'Will these hands ne'er be clean?' No time for self-recrimination, though, Karen and I were into deci-sion-making. She wanted to know if I was intending to offload the apartment as is into what might prove be the late stages of a buoyant housing market, or risk taking time to return it to its former, glory. She reckoned I should take my time and do it up first, which worried me because it meant that I'd have to stay away longer. Was a spouse supposed to be unconcerned at having a husband in exile?

I didn't think so.

Dear oh dear, I was missing home and Karen and Henry, not of course to forget the dog. In fact, when not otherwise engaged, one of my favourite pastimes had become working out the order in which I missed that lot – sometimes it was Henry then the dog then Karen. Depended on how I felt.

Still talking empty junk to Karen on the far side of the world, checking myself in the mirror to see if any of the guilt showed, I was surprised to discover, gazing straight back at me, this fairly decrepit-looking character with a fading bruise on his forehead and what looked very much like a couple of bloodshot eyes lurking there beneath. The folds of flesh either side above the belt line, my body going kind of soft all over, that shoul-der-length hair held back in a pony-tail turning grey, and those bloodshot eyes brim-full with pity for what they were regarding. The mirror told me that my time had come and gone, in the winking of some third, cosmic eye.

Night outside. Vodka in the freezer, Lou Reed on the player. American football on television.

Karen terminated the conversation and some time later I hung up and donned a pair of mirror sunglasses with fat yellow plastic frames. I looked better in them, for sure, but then again I could also have been thought to look a great deal worse.

On an average morning I might take an hour or so to decide if I should shave off two, three or four days growth. Or should I trim back my nose hair. Do some push-ups? Too much on my own, I seemed to be developing this thing about myself as an object that wasn't being looked after properly.

There remained the problem of unfulfilled desire for the family's Australian solicitor. My photographic image of her had been taken off the wall by a cleaner and thoughtfully placed face down on my bedside table.

I had her on the case, chasing after the rent bond and quite a lot of money beyond that to cover the lost furniture and so on. But much more I wanted her in my bed, spinning yarns and magic, even if only just a little bit and for a little while. With Alison I had demonstrated to myself what was possible in Sydney, Australia.

Damn.

There in my hotel, eating an early breakfast of porridge with honey and raisins followed by bacon and eggs with the lot, having already consumed a small bottle of gin and one of brandy out of the mini bar, gazing blankly at a French language news channel on television, permitting my thoughts to wander all over the place, suddenly in my mind's eye there was a small golden ring snug in the lobe of Giovanna's ear.

Then I was removing a shoe from Giovanna's foot. I was kissing her cute little toes. This little piggy …

Burying my face in her hair.

Telephone rang. Reception. A parcel for me.

It's a risk sending valuables through the post. At the same time, they don't advertise themselves as being valuables if they come in a cardboard tube. On the customs certificate the contents of

60

my parcel were marked down as drawing paper, and the value 500 francs. What kind of petty official was going to get excited about that? As it happened, someone had. The tube had been opened and then resealed without whoever did it taking a lot of care over the job.

I pulled off some sticky tape, removed the cover from one end of the tube, and tapped out the contents. Good quality drawing paper, yes, and sandwiched in the middle of the sheets was a well-aged modernist nude painted in browns and greys on very fine Belgium linen canvas. No signature on the painting, yet. So no laws broken. Because the sheets of paper were a lot bigger than the canvas, somebody checking the parcel's contents would have difficulty picking that it was there.

Posted to myself in Sydney before I left France, I was hoping to drift it into the local art world as a genuine Andre Derain. And have a bit of fun along the way. Not a great deal of money involved. So, what I planned to do hardly represented a breach of my promise to Karen to give the forgery game away.

But now I had to take the Inspector Schwartz factor into account. What had caused him to become interested in me? And if he was so interested, wouldn't he have had the contents of my parcel checked? Did that explain why it had been opened?

Should I be worried?

My choice of the artist, Andre Derain, wasn't an accident. He was just the right kind of painter to launch into the relatively small Australian art auction scene. In all the books, he had been part of the first thrust of modernism, one of the Fauves or wild beasts as they were called, up there for an instant with Matisse and Picasso. But the work he produced after about 1918 became increasingly conservative and recently had failed to reach the big prices it once commanded. So, putting a non-Fauves Derain up for sale in Australia wouldn't seem all that crazy. In fact, if the cards played the way I anticipated, the Australian collectors' relatively conservative taste was going to provide the right market for my minor masterpiece, and provide me with a modicum of the pleasure which accompanies sending another fake work of art out into the world.

I put the drawing paper on the table to flatten, weighted down with telephone books. The painting went into the top of the cupboard under the spare pillows. I rolled up the drawings I had done so far and stored them in the tube.

Alison turned up only half an hour late, at 10.30. This time she'd come up with the idea of wearing angel's wings, and from God knows where had picked up a paper bag of white feathers to scatter around the suite, setting the scene.

'What's wrong with angels?'

'It's just all these feathers …'

'You're not allergic? Or is it … to tell the truth, you don't look so good.'

'I'm fine, it's just, you know …'

'What should I know? Only that you stink of booze, you're not drunk already?'

'There's an idea. Giovanna, would you like a drink?'

'The name is Alison.'

'Only joking.'

Regarding the feathers, she explained she'd been looking at girls on a soft porn site on the internet, wanting to come up with something really nice for me to draw.

'Thank you, very thoughtful.'

'Oh don't thank me, I'm the one supposed to be getting the kicks out of this.'

I poured her a glass of traminer riesling from a chilled bottle I'd shoved in the mini bar a day or two earlier, took a swig out of the bottle myself, and we got down to it.

First up, magic, I produced a really good drawing of her lying on her back, legs spread as if to give birth, or get checked

over by the gynaecologist, holding the wings at arms' length above her, as if she'd just ripped them off a passing albatross. I went for a generalized smudging of the genitalia at the drawing's center, and kind of let the body and feathered wings she was holding grow out from there.

Next I took a few photos of her moving around the room, keeping the shutter slow so she'd read as a blur.

I said, tentatively, 'Alison, I hope you don't feel …'

'Playing at being Giovanna, whoever she might be, it's not a problem, Essington. I'm just someone you hire, okay? One night I'm your lay, this morning one of the heavenly host.'

'Gabriella.'

'Stuff you talk to me about, weird, but it turns me on a bit.'

'Isn't that just the booze, Alison?'

'Speaking of which?'

'The stuff I talk about, how about you? You describe a lesbian act for bikies as if it's as tricky as setting the table, Jesus Christ, what can I have told you to match that?'

Unfortunately the break in my concentration had screwed the drawing.

'Funny thing is, you've really told me nothing about anything.' Alison bringing her knees together, sitting up, looking straight at me, her big eyes, even the lashes were red.

'Why aren't you a vegetarian, Alison?'

'What sort of question is that?'

'Nothing, it's just that you look like one. Ever been a Buddhist?'

'People aren't Buddhists the way they might be, say, a surfie. It's a life thing.'

'Like vegetarianism?'

'I wouldn't say so, I was a vegetarian between about ten and fifteen. But then I just got to be so anaemic.'

When room service arrived, she answered the door, white skin, red pubic hair, angel's wings held in place on her back by white satin ribbons. I guess the room service man must have reckoned he'd died in the lift and my suite was paradise.

Nice as it seemed, it turned out there was no way I could sit up in my hotel suite drawing models twenty-four hours a day. Two hours a day was about all I could take. There was a lot of hard looking involved, not to mention anxiety over making a wrong mark, so after another night of fucking, and another guilty and extended phone conversation with Karen, it didn't take long for me to be swearing at myself, erasing what I had done, and on the next attempt getting the drawing even more wrong.

Suddenly it seemed to me like a good idea to go off and meet Alison's uncle.

'You can't just breeze in, Essington.'

'Well?'

'Ring him, why don't you, find out the way a proper person would.'

I looked up Johnstone & Lang in the book, did as she commanded, and indeed, Julian Anderson would like to meet me. Over the phone he was telling me of a corporate collection they were preparing to auction. Enthusiasm showing without him having a clue if I was a tyre-kicker or in for the big art purchase.

Very British over the phone.

The collection, he explained unnecessarily, had belonged to an insurance company, one of several that had imploded and now had liquidators realising assets found amongst the rubble.

I told him, thank you very much, if it was Australian art it was probably not my cup of tea but I'd be there in about an hour if that was all right, to take a look.

He suggested lunch.

I forgot to mention that I'd be bringing his niece. Still, it seemed a good way of sucking up to the man and Alison was over the moon at the suggestion.

The auction house had its office in a terrace shop front that looked to have been a general store years ago before Paddington went up-market. This latest function was celebrated by gold sign writing and a fresh and shiny coat of deep-green paint all over the façade.

A tight-lipped young man with golden locks tumbling to his shoulders sat at a computer. We stood mute while he continued typing.

After quite some time Alison gave a little cough.

'With you in a minute, Al.'

I thought, fuck this, I'm out of here and was making for the door when, 'Can I do something for you?'

'Doesn't look like it.'

'Oh, then …'

Alison, 'He's meeting Julian.'

'I'll check if he's in, who shall I say?'

Before I could reply, a smiling gentleman came bumbling through the rear door, 'Well, well, well … and you must be …?' Red over-shaved skin. The bluest blue eyes. Military-looking tie.

He was in his shirt sleeves, gold cufflinks. Rimless spectacles worn half way down the bridge of his nose. I don't know why but straight off I reckoned I liked him. Well, maybe I did know why. On this visit to Australia he was the first man I had come face to face with who didn't appear to pose some sort of threat – one or two hotel staff, taxi drivers and waiters excepted, possibly.

It wasn't just the tie but everything. I thought military. British army. Could have been one of those chaps they breed out in their forests, trained to kill you with a single blow, but dress like fairies. Tuck linen handkerchiefs up their coat sleeves. Alison was concentrating on the little shit who'd greeted us in such an offhand manner. Julian Anderson was checking his watch the way people do when they already know the time. Time for lunch.

Walking along the street, he was telling me how hard it was to get established. Big ticket items, he said, were oxygen to an auction house. 'Not so many of them around. Small market. Enthusiastic but small.' I indicated sympathy. 'Lots of buyers under a hundred thousand, most five, ten, fifteen. Decorators. Gold frames. Water gilding, just adore water gilding. Blue skies, too, golden grass sort of thing.'

We arrived at the door of a neat little restaurant off Oxford Street. The welcome told me this was Johnstone & Lang's other office: Julian nodding and smiling at waiters and customers alike. Seated, Alison dedicated herself to ordering and the possibility of eating up big while I discussed commissions and he went over what they had in their next sale. But mostly he told me how it was, starting out. The two international auction houses operating in Australia, Sotheby's and Christie's, had direct links to offices in London and New York. With Johnstone & Lang only operating within Australia, it would seem an unwise choice for the sale of a really good European painting, indeed anything that was worth a great deal of money.

'Internet, Essington. That's where we can catch up with the majors. Give me a Michelangelo, I'll sell it from Tierra del Fuego over the internet. Global medium.'

'Rub themselves all over with whale oil in Tierra del Fuego,' said Alison. Grinning at me.

'Get thee to a nunnery.' Julian signalling a waiter. He was an alert man, a lot of charm. No sign of knowing a thing about art. Didn't matter. Almost nobody does.

'Makes the skin shine, uncle.'

These two, I was asking myself, was he a real uncle or what? Alison ordered salmon on a bed of something smart. I asked for the same. Julian said to make that three. A bottle of white wine. Water. Yes, bread. Yes, steamed vegetables. I was checking to see if pepper and salt were chargeable extras.

Sticking with the art market, 'You're telling me you could handle a painting with serious international credentials. How would that work, internet or no internet? Buyers have to know to look for you first. Forget about Tierra del Fuego, is someone in New York going to find Johnstone & Lang on the internet? And here, inside Australia, surely there isn't the pressure of money. Not enough people, marginal currency.'

'Individual paintings, they are about contacts, person to person.'

'You know who's in the market, looking?'

'Precisely.'

He went on to explain at length that there wasn't a Johnstone or a Lang attached to the company any more. They had been a general auction house. Julian and a unnamed associate of substantial means had bought the business five years earlier and transformed it into a specialist art auction business.

I received this information politely. If I was to go ahead with the plan, then maybe Johnstone & Lang would do. They'd been placed in my path by fortune, and Julian Anderson and I were getting along. You don't want an auction house just to sell a painting, you want them to look after your interests rather than returning a favour for whoever happened to be on the other end of the deal.

My mind came back into focus when out of the blue Julian started talking about the highlight of his sale year to date, a small Andre Derain still life from fairly soon after the First World War, A$65,000, five above the estimate.

'Particularly good work, that.'

I suggested another bottle of wine.

'Not been a great deal of French art from that period floating around Australia, Essington. Not out of the Australian collector's price range directly after the Great War. 1920, per capita this country was rich by comparison with Europe. But still taking its cultural lead from old England.'

'You lot.'

'Brought up there, lived there most of my life, but Australian born.'

Alison intruded, 'I don't get it, all those paintings by dead people, what's the point? Isn't art about being alive?'

'Derain, run over by a truck, whichever year it was.'

'That rings a bell,' I said.

'There'd been problems, since the start of World War Two. He was one of the more compliant French artists. Retreated from modernism, came to be celebrated by the Nazis as an upholder of the true French artistic tradition.'

Okay, he was showing off a little, but this art auctioning uncle of Alison's knew a bit. The prospect of running my Derain past a Derain specialist got the adrenalin flowing. I emptied my glass. The waiter poured.

I asked Julian how he came to know so much.

'It's my period, I did … well half of a masters degree on the Fauves and somehow Derain stuck with me. Before I joined the army. Derain attracted me because he developed an ambivalent attitude to painting. A father of French modernism, the way his mind was structured, the way it worked, disbarred him from committing to the enterprise without qualification.'

Alison was wiping her plate clean with a crust of bread. 'Time passes and it becomes history. There's so much going on right now, at any given moment, all over the world, isn't that enough?'

'You will see things in a different light when you are older.' The perfect uncle.

'You mean wiser, don't you? I don't believe it, Julian.'

He looked to me for support just as Alison was running a foot up my leg. I sipped wine, smiled at each of them in turn.

She laughed.

'Is she pulling my leg, Essington?'

'Not just yours, Julian.'

'Tearaway.' His suggestion of dessert was eagerly taken up by Alison. I was happy with coffee, and a cognac on the side. 'By the 1920s all the modernists had retreated from experimentation and innovation, Picasso and Matisse turning for inspiration to the late works of Renoir. Quite extraordinary when you think about it. Of course nobody does think about it today, do they? Derain was considered the height of fashion at a time when his confidence began to falter. He said, "Concentrating on a painting, being too close to it, I believe I can see the shapes I want to portray and it is these shapes that are killing me. When I try to disengage myself from a choice between two known shapes, everything falls apart."'

'He said that?' Wasn't I suffering from pretty much the same confusion?

Alison, right on cue, 'You don't seem to have that problem, Essington.'

'Problem?' Julian wanted to know. Bemused by his niece seeming comfortable with an old geezer like me.

'Oh, I do a bit of drawing. A hobby, nothing more.'

'At least you do it now, in real time.' Alison supportive.

Julian: 'Precisely what is the connection between you and Mr Holt, Alison?'

She laughed. 'You don't want to know, let's say I help him with his drawings.'

'Good lord, you're an artist's model! That's a first for the family.'

'Artist is an overstatement.'

One of those pauses in conversation that go on and on.

I broke it. 'I seem to remember Derain also claimed he'd never seen a painting as beautiful as a motorcar.'

'I can relate to that,' Alison said, observing the one serve of dessert for our table land directly in front of her. 'What are they

after all, these paintings people rave about? Just a form of decoration. Dance music is more connecting, it has a real impact on
people in real time, and doesn't gather dust.'

Chapter 5

Giovanna said that if we were going to seek compensation I
couldn't make any moves doing up the apartment till the
damage was assessed. At the same time she advised me against
seeking compensation. She reckoned, in her own chillingly
practical fashion, Mister D would turn out to be a bankrupt.
And so, in her opinion legal action against him was liable to cost
more than it would end up being worth.

I accepted that. At the same time I reckoned that Damien
Berry had to be good for the money. I had found that when
replaying the whole apartment thing in my imagination it was
Berry, the one I didn't get to lay a hand on, who I really wanted
to punish. Because he was such a cocky little bastard. And
because he was liable to report back to Gerald Sparrow, let him
know exactly how I felt.

'You have had your pound of flesh already,' Giovanna said.

'Regard that as the entrée. Just thinking about the apartment makes me so angry.'

'Mightn't that be because it was you who made the wrong
initial decisions?'

'Have I ever told you how much I'd like to …?'

'You should leave the business deals up to Karen.'

That was how things stood, Giovanna perfecting her freeze-out-
Essington technique – had probably been practicing it before
the mirror. And, me, I kept on inventing reasons for staying in
touch with her.

I'd ring and ask her to meet somewhere around town – $250 or was it $300 an hour those meetings cost me! She'd arrive late and look at me pretty much the way you'd expect a smart young female lawyer on the way up to look at a pile of dirty washing.

How many times did I ask if she would join me for dinner?

Always she'd respond that it was delightful of me to offer but no, thank you very much.

I would gaze at her.

She would return the gaze till I turned away.

Did I ever mention how full and glisteningly moist her lips are? How silk-like her skin?

When I explained to Karen that Giovanna was playing games with me, Karen wanted to know, 'What kind of games, Essington?' She'd go on to point out that Giovanna happened to be a nice person and an extremely loyal friend. So, would I do my best not to put her offside. 'I mean, Ess, we've tried your pick of the Sydney lawyers, haven't we? Gerald Sparrow!'

Dawn, Karen and Giovanna had been friends at high school in one of Sydney's southern suburbs. Dawn turned out the type of girl who places a great deal of importance on building close friendships with other women. They developed different sexual preferences, the three of them, but at the same time got to know too much about each other. Dawn is the definitive woman for her time, horny as a sailor on leave, a mind working at the speed of light, not too much empathy bouncing around in there. Give Dawn a product and she can sell it, can't stop herself. The success of Karen's fabric design and printing business being a case in point. Give her a tricky emotional situation and she's out of there at the speed of light.

I knew that if I tried to hit on Giovanna the other two would snap to it instantly, even from the other side of the globe. Call it morphic resonance, whatever. And yet, you know how it is, the fact of Giovanna being totally off limits increased the temptation to transgress.

Skin, bouncing jet-black hair, her obvious disdain, those lips. Oh dear.

Always a fool for beauty, some part of me had gone for art early on, maybe because of those big Australian landscapes suggesting something precious, if unobtainable beyond the mountains. So art equalled possibility. As well, it promised fulfillment. And, I guess, quietude of a kind. I certainly needed something to calm me down; from my mid teens I'd been losing it too easily in football games, going crazy in the scrums, gouging, head-butting, generally acting super agro in most of life's arenas.

Later, there had been moments when, lying on my back on a stained palliasse in some fibro shack out in the bush, my mind would be calculating where the studs were in walls so I wouldn't break my hands if I took to punching out the lining. When there was lining.

Pursuing art as an escape, I began heading into the landscape wherever I was working at the time, to paint those blue hills off in the distance, maybe put the fat silver-grey trunk of a gum tree in the foreground, whatever; I was copying and composing what nature had rolled out before my eyes. Very traditional paintings they were, and after a while not too bad. If there happened to be some problem I couldn't solve, I'd go into the library of the nearest town, hunt up solutions from one of the few art books they'd have on the shelves. I wasn't thinking about what some dickheads might term 'high' art back then, just getting some sort of control over my reactions to the knock-out visual stuff nature throws in your face. By degrees my paintings developed from relatively naïve attempts to capture an impression of bush landscapes to where I got to play around with the elements of those landscapes. And with how paint was applied. I experimented with glazing tints over opaque underpainting, with scumbling translucent whites and ochres on top of strong reds and browns. I'd try doing bright red hills, or rendering the paddocks purple, that sort of thing as well, just to see what would happen. From the start I knew I wasn't a genius.

I hadn't got much chance to practice drawing the human figure the way I knew they had taught it in the old academies. So, drawing was what I was turning to in middle life. Possibly for the same reason I'd taken up painting so long ago.

To keep from punching out the walls.

Drawing, hanging about, plotting an art fraud, I kind of lost count of the days. Eventually I put a tape measure in my pocket and took a taxi to a commercial art gallery down at Brighton le Sands, south of the CBD. I'd been ringing round and this gallery, called The Blue Boy, seemed just what I was looking for. It turned out to be hung floor to ceiling with sentimental landscapes, most pre-WWII, a lot European – the kind of stuff displaced, aspiring middle class migrants brought with them after that war. Checking the walls, and the store room out the back, finally I lighted on what I was after, an image of the Pont Royale in Paris, France, fairly broadly painted in dirty greys and yellow-greens and with a whited out cobalt blue sky featuring puffy clumps of flake-white representing summer clouds. There was a signature in the bottom right-hand corner, just the initials, HV.

The owner of the gallery kept on showing me more stuff but I was insisting I had just one tight space on my cluttered wall and the painting had to fit it. Pretending shock at my lack of appreciation of the art content of any of the dross I'd been sifting through, he watched me check dimensions with the tape measure. Raised eyebrows, little swallowing sounds. The Pont Royale was the perfect painting. Exactly the right size, which was important, in fact it was a standard-size French canvas of its time, the sort of canvas an artist would have bought from any mainstream art supply store. The stretcher, with its original corner wedges still in place and a silverfish-eaten label on the back, featured a few sale-room chalk marks as well. I loved them. There were neat rows of rusted tacks holding the tension of the canvas. All original.

We haggled over the price for a while till finally I offered five one-hundred dollar bills, saving him tax while preserving my anonymity. He counted them out loud, 'One, two, three, four, five.'

'Can you do that all the way to ten?'

'Have to, occasionally.'

'Somebody asks what's going on?'

'You have it on approval. No deal done yet. Why, you expect someone to ask?'

'Can't imagine who would bother.'

We shook hands. Not a bad character. You can come across much worse in the art world. I was doing well, first Julian Anderson, now … I'd forgotten to ask him his name.

Jane was carrying a big bag of clothes in one hand while swinging her car keys in the other. A small white cuddly toy with glass eyes was attached to the car keys. Jane didn't look happy.

I asked would she like a glass of water, a cup of coffee, anything?

No, she wouldn't. 'Where are we doing this?'

'Right here. That's why there's a drawing board, paper and stuff.'

'Oh.'

I was thinking I could have a problem here. I was saying: 'You comfortable, doing this?'

She looked at me, I looked at her. Obviously not.

She stripped. Just like that. She was standing there, pink, not a hint of body hair. Standing, feet set apart like someone holding balance on a boat's deck in a storm.

'Try putting something back on and, please, sit down, you are making me nervous.'

She seemed just so angry.

'What are you doing this for?'

'The money.'

'Well, there's no way I can draw if you're going to be like this.'

'How am I being?'

'Why don't I just pay you and you go home?'

'No.'

I stuffed up a drawing.

'What else have you got in the bag, Jane?'

What didn't she have? Crushed up there was the sort of hat society wives wear to the Melbourne Cup, a feather boa, and thigh-length, deep purple patent leather boots, lots of scraps of lingerie. She even had a bright yellow plastic mackintosh.

She put on a flimsy little dress, the hat too, the boa, and sat in front of the mirror. She was still looking very pissed off with this life. Yet while I did the drawing she was checking in a mirror to see how she looked.

I asked her what she did. She replied that she didn't do much at all since she found out she was pregnant.

'You don't look pregnant.'

'I only just found out.'

'You feel like throwing up?'

'Some of the time I do, even before I got pregnant.'

I went back to the drawing, producing a lot of strokes for the feathers. No sound in the room, just the charcoal on the paper, till I said, 'I didn't think people got pregnant any more. Well, not till they owned everything they wanted, the BMW, the timeshare in north Queensland.'

'You reckon I wanted this to happen?'

'And the father to be …?'

'Do we have to talk about it?'

It was late afternoon and the sun was bouncing off the harbour. The golden light of early autumn. The bridge looking like nothing so much as a model of itself set on a hand-coloured papier-mâché harbour-scape, with cleverly crafted ferries and yachts scudding about a choppy sea. In the distance an aeroplane was circling, waiting for traffic control to permit a landing. Nice view I had at six hundred bucks a day, a panorama of modern life the way we are meant to experience it, nothing exploding, everything working and rational and neat. A brisk sea breeze blew the smog inland.

I was drinking my way through a bottle of riesling, starting at the top, working down. It was nice.

Reception called to announce a visitor, who turned out to be an intense-looking girl named Thea. When I told her that she wasn't due till the following morning, she said something about always getting things wrong, or being given the wrong message. Finally arriving at the conclusion that it had to be because of her star sign, she became visibly upset.

I didn't bother to ask which star sign that was.

'I'm a Sagittarius,' she said.

'Oh!'

'And my life is turning to shit.'

So I said, okay, let's go to it.

She asked, 'You're not drunk?'

'And if I am do I get to spend the rest of the day in peace?'

A puzzled look.

Thea's parents must have originated somewhere along the east Asian seaboard. Her eyes might have been painted onto the translucent, sallow porcelain of her face a long, long time ago by a master calligrapher. Her naturally jet black hair was streaked with auburn and stacked up on top in a cute fashion with a number of fine plaited strands hanging down either side of her face.

Could I have been correct to suspect Thea was at least a little out of it?

Or was she just edgy?

I guess I made whatever was upsetting her worse by covertly checking for signs of drug abuse, because no way in the world did I want to get involved with a walking casualty of the free market economy. But Thea seemed clean. When she took off her clothes I noticed two small, circular tattoos, one on her stomach just above the line of her 'European' trimmed pubic hair, the other in a corresponding rear position, high on her left buttock – as if representing the entry and exit points of a spiritual spear, driven straight through an ovary, perchance.

Chatting idly while opening another bottle of riesling, and then while making a few tentative marks on the paper with my stick of charcoal, it hit me that she was totally uninterested in what I was telling her about the martyrdom of Saint Ursula.

I was saying how there had been a thousand virgins in the boat she'd taken to France.

'Who took to France?'

'I was telling you about Saint Ursula.'

'When was this you're talking about?'

'In the middle ages, or earlier. They let themselves get killed rather than raped by a bunch of Huns.'

Thea narrowed her eyes, 'That'd be, like suicide?'

First set to Thea.

I told her about how when you are drawing you have to think about the piece of paper being a flat surface. It was just for something to say, really.

All she could do was roll her eyes and say, 'How flat is a piece of paper?' Then, 'Maybe I will have a glass of wine.'

'I never offered you one.'

Still I poured, and then gave up on the talking altogether.

I wanted to lift my game. I wanted to capture what a particular pose meant, screw the formal qualities. I guess I was attempting to make a shape or group of shapes that summed up my looking at the model – the way I felt, how she seemed to feel as well, I was after the electricity of the two of us trapped by an outdated artistic convention in this weird situation – me observing, recording, her being looked at. Certainly I wasn't trying for anything structural, anything about what critics used to call significant form. I felt that had to be a given, like breathing. How could one form in a composition, in the world, be more significant than any other, and who was to judge?

I guess I was attempting a seeing-mind thing. Or something.

The next pose, standing on one leg, the other foot up on the arm of a chair, she was painting her toenails the colour of dried blood. I started at where her fingers gripping the little brush were connecting with the raised foot. Next thing I was drawing that exquisite, almond-shaped eye, setting it into the side of her face as if I were working away in ancient Egypt, and she was a temple dancer.

Thea looked really nice like that, and even if the proportions of the drawing were out to buggery, the image had a naturalness about it; maybe because she was acting out one of a day's small routines.

Her wine glass empty beside the leg of a chair.

The phone rang.

I put the stick of charcoal down, crossed the room, picked up.

Thea broke the pose as I gazed back at her.

Picking up the glass, she was watching me with a certain intensity.

The phone said that there was a gentleman in the foyer wanting to deliver a package. I replied that I was busy at that moment and couldn't he just leave it with them, at reception? There followed what I assumed to be some discussion at that end. Then, no, it was necessary for me to sign for the package.

'Get him to come on up to the room, then.'

More discussion. 'He would prefer for you to come down to collect it.' The hotel employee I was dealing with sounded Indian, or Pakistani.

Next thing, Christ knows why, I was heading down to the hotel foyer. Where there wasn't any man delivering anything to anyone.

Not at the desk.

Nowhere in sight.

Worse, nobody on the desk appeared to be from the Indian sub-continent.

I inquired.

No, I was told, there had been no attempt at a delivery for me. However, checking the pigeon holes – it was nice the way in our electronic age my hotel still had pigeon holes – there was a message.

I read it on the way back up in the elevator. It was from the management, the cleaning staff wondered if I might use a floor sheet for whatever I was doing that was trampling black powder into the carpet. Would I please request one at the reception desk. Plus a terse, legalistic reminder that I was liable for any damage to the suite.

Which was fine, sure. But suddenly I didn't like the idea of the non-delivered package.

Or the idea of Thea up there unsupervised.

As I came in the door as quietly as I could, I found Thea, still naked but standing at my desk. She was holding my digital camera, the lens cap off.

'Hold it right there, Mr Holt,' she framed me in the view-finder, clicked off a shot, the flash flashed.

Neat idea, I thought, naked girl with camera photographing a clothed man. Kind of an art piece in itself.

But I was pissed off with the bogus delivery call.

To get over it I brought out the vodka.

My hand assisted by more vodka, the drawings seemed to be working well; I had produced six more while the sky beyond my windows turned the purple of bruises. Nearly all the yachts had scurried off the harbour to the safety of marinas. Lights were gleaming just about everywhere. And the souls of the damned were already circling over the bridge.

Thea was lying on her stomach supported by a pile of pillows, her butt sticking up in the air, her head down so her left cheek was pressing against the room's only marginally despoiled carpet. She appeared to have gone to sleep while I was working out how much anatomical detail to go for across and down her back; asking myself if I should just rely on the outlines to suggest form or model up the sensual subtleties of backbone and muscle. Difficult decision really. Yet on the paper the space which was supposed to be her back seemed short on real information. Or was that because the outlines I had drawn lacked the kind of energy that could express the volumes?

I was rubbing out a failed attempt at suggesting the row of knobs that was her spine when there was a tentative knocking at the door. Straight off, of course, I thought of the aborted package delivery. But when I opened up I found myself looking directly into the clear and piercingly blue eyes of a young woman with long blonde hair. There was a lot of flesh showing between her top and the hip-hugging belt line of her jeans.

'Thea here?'

I asked, 'Should she be?'

'She told me this is where to come.'

'Sorry,' I said and shut the door before, from behind me Thea asked, 'Mandy, is that you?' And breaking the pose, Thea was moving towards the door. I grabbed her by the arm. 'You wait a minute.'

'Please, Mr Holt, we thought you might like to try two models.'

'You thought! And Phyllis at the agency?'

'Just Mandy and me, we thought it would be fun.' She was blushing while laughing nervously.

Suddenly I saw myself as one more man not keeping up with life.

When another knock sounded at the door I said, 'Okay, you get it.' But not without misgivings. I was losing control of the situation.

As Mandy stepped inside I said, 'Can't be too careful.'

Mandy, 'Too careful of what, Mr Holt?' She passed me with the expectant spring in her step of a girl eager to party.

Which was, as it turned out, sort of what we did.

The rest of that session, tell me about it.

I have this idea that I kept on calling up booze and quantities of food from room service. As well I seem to remember designer drugs, out of Mandy's survival kit. Or am I mixing the drugs up with the night I'd spent with Alison? Whatever, the two girls were having a great time doing girl on girl poses for – by that stage I was offering double the money? And producing masterpieces? Had to be. On the art front it seemed I had discovered a whole new way to go.

I was using big sweeps of pure colour delivered with sticks of soft pastel and then working black pastel and charcoal back in over the top. Untold damage done to the carpet. More booze, another tablet, Thea bouncing on Mandy's lap. Me with the camera aiming and clicking away. Mandy picking up a stick of charcoal, adding a moustache to the last head I'd drawn.

Was I still drawing? or was I taking photos? or was I dreaming when Thea slipped a hand between her thighs, those long fingers working their way inside, Mandy kissing her on the mouth?

Next I was in the bathroom, naked, in the bath itself with Mandy and a mountain of soap suds; Thea aiming the camera and its flash shooting off time after time. Me trying to get on with it, Mandy telling me I was a very naughty boy.

Did I recall Thea saying, 'This is going to cost you a lot more than double the agency rate, Essington.'

Then I was clambering out of the bath, the two of them drying me with towels, leading me off to the big bad bed.

Outside, I guess there must have been stars. Oh yes, there would have been stars.

And those damned birds still circling.

Me coming awake to find silence. Solitude. A pile of drawings.

It was a relief to discover the digital camera still there.

The next day, out of the blue, and interrupting the flow of guilt over a night of sexual indulgence, I got a phone call from Inspector Schwartz. He was wondering if he might drop around, check over a few details.

'Like what, for instance?'

'I am keen to learn more about the workings of the art market.'

'What's that got to do with anything real, Inspector?'

'Actually, I was hoping that you could offer me some advice.'

Slippery bastard. I said I'd meet him on level three in the Bounty Bar at twelve-thirty.

'Okey-dokey,' he replied.

Hard to believe the 'okey-dokey' bit. But I had to admit I was interested in talking with him. If he was trying to find out about me, then, without incriminating myself, I wanted to know what kind of information had triggered his curiosity.

I assumed correctly that there would be no model arriving at my door that morning, which left me with an hour and a half to puzzle over Inspector Schwartz's intentions. Something I didn't want to do too much of, partly because I wasn't up to it with my head enclosing a woofer thumping out big decibels.

An hour and a half was sufficient time to walk across Circular Quay into the Rocks area and pay a visit to the art supply shop up on Argyle Street. It used to be a great shop, years ago, and I had found it still listed in the Yellow Pages, still in the same spot in this forever changing world.

Nice bright sunshiny day bursting through the lifting veil of a light fog. Circular Quay was crowded with the usual suspects from all over the globe, taking photographs of each other standing in front of silver-painted buskers pretending to be sculptures, and/or beside Aboriginal guys with ochre body paint growling down didgeridoos. There was an old Vietnamese man plucking at the strings of a guitar-like instrument, the sound of which couldn't be heard above the traffic, the ferries and the constant chattering of our blessed species.

It wasn't till I was making my way up a narrow passage between two buildings, and suddenly very much on my own that I got this feeling of being followed. Looking behind me there wasn't anybody there, just the narrow walkway with two sets of steps ascending in the direction from which I'd come.

Leading away from the harbour there are several stepped pathways between the tight-packed 19th century buildings that have been given over to selling clothing and tourist souvenirs, carbohydrates, coffee, and opals. The area is a tarted-up rabbit warren. In case the feeling of being followed connected to reality, I ducked and wove through retail outlets, in the back out the front and vice-versa, making it an extremely indirect route to the art supply shop. And yet still I suffered from this being-followed feeling. Of course I knew who it would be, if it was anybody. It had to be Schwartz or one of his side-kicks. It figured that he'd want to know where I had gone between receiving his phone call and meeting him for lunch.

The idea that Schwartz was trying to pin some illicit art deal on me wasn't too much of a worry. Well, it didn't worry me as much as the thought that somebody could have fed him information against me. In which case I needed to know who might have done that. And why. People don't feed the law information about art forgery unless there is going to be something in it them. As a crime, art forgery doesn't have a public moral indignation side to it, because it's the rich or well-funded public institutions staffed with arrogant public servants that are the losers. Mine is a very Robin Hood profession, leaving out the give-to-the-poor bit.

But on the information available he had to have got me all wrong. Innocent of just about everything criminal known to man, I was out buying art supplies in Sydney. John Citizen, weekend painter, eat your heart out.

Brownscombe Art Supplies is divided into two sections. On one side of the entrance there's a picture-framing business that also puts together canvas stretchers, on the other side a crowd of island displays offers an amazing range of art materials manufactured all around the world, French printing inks, Dutch oil paints, papers from Japan, Nepal, Italy, Germany, the USA. Me, inside there I was a kid in a lolly shop. All that stuff so sweet to gaze upon.

Between the shop's two sections there was a glass counter with an antique cash register. In attendance this big guy in white tee shirt saying Vincent van Hog, and regulation black jeans. He looked at me. I looked back at him while explaining that I was just browsing.

'Enjoy,' he commanded.

After I'd been picking up bottles and tubes, reading labels, checking colour charts for five minutes, I didn't spot anybody who could have been following me coming in the door. So I relaxed and began ordering a lot of stuff.

It was when I was on my hands and knees comparing three brands of canvas pliers that, sensing something, I glanced to the side and saw a pair of New Balance trainers pull up beside me. Turning awkwardly and attempting to rise I took a kick to the solar plexus that threw me back onto the artist's quality gouache display stand. It went with me, collecting a stand of pencils and pastels on the way down.

I came up breathless but in a mind to swing at nothing and anything. As it turned out, at nothing. Because the sales assistant had my assailant, who had one arm in a sling already, in a head lock, while an older man in an apron was closing in with a heavy stick of gilded framing timber held in both hands, high, ready to strike.

'Bobby, what the …?'

He growled, 'You fucking loser.' Mostly into the glass counter. His eyeballs close to popping.

The man in the apron: 'If you know each other, take your fight outside.'

Still gasping for breath, it took a little while to get the words out. But I got them out. 'Not really, no. He followed me here.'

'Who pays for the damage?' The big guy in his Vincent van Hog tee shirt.

By degrees breathing more regularly, 'Ring the police, let them sort it out.' I couldn't see much point avoiding the law since I was having lunch with Schwartz within the hour.

Bobby, his face pressed into the glass counter. But watching me.

I asked him, 'You got a better suggestion?' No response. 'Because, if that's how you tackle life's little problems, someone ought to put you out of the way till you learn.'

Suddenly I changed my mind. Bobby was concerned about something. If I hadn't known better I might have thought his hard exterior masked some complex inner life.

'You want to talk, before I call the police?'

The reams of paper, pastels, boxes of charcoal and pressure packs of fixative would be delivered by courier the next day. I took a pair of canvas pliers and a tack hammer along with me as Bobby and I walked off for a quiet chat at a George Street bar.

Settled in, I found myself liking the guy. Don't ask me why – I guess I was desperate. We had a long talk about nothing much. And over my third glass of chilled wine and his second lemon lime and bitters, we came to what I hoped might turn out to be a mutually beneficial arrangement. I was going to pay him a retainer and set him up with a mobile phone account. He was going to stay out of sight, cause me no grief, stop shadowing me, and even perform the occasional job of work.

'Like what?' He wanted to know.

'I wouldn't have a clue. But, say, talking to someone on the telephone. Is that too passive for you?'

It had to be an offer impossible for him to refuse.

'Who knows, Bobby, we could turn out friends.'

'Mate, I don't think so.'

Great start that was.

I asked why he was into soft drinks.

He responded, 'None of your business.' Then, 'Think about it, fellers like you, the harm the booze does them.'

'It shows?'

'Oh, mate.'

Bobby and me, if we had got much closer we might have ended up married. Probably would have anyway, if he'd been able to iron shirts.

Back at the hotel, I climbed into a lightweight mid-grey flannel suit, white shirt, Italian silk tie featuring this dinky pattern of little horses and even littler foxes, and made it to the Bounty Bar. There was the beginning of a lunch crowd gathering, and Schwartz sitting at a table all on his lonesome, doing here's the church, here's the steeple open the doors and here's all the people, with his policeman's firm fingers. There was a beer and a bowl of nuts positioned directly in front of him. He was wearing a different pinstripe suit to last time, the background grey a darker tone. A handkerchief matching his tie stuck casually in his top pocket.

I turned away, pulled out my camera, took a quick snap with him dead center, wide angle, slipped the camera back into my pocket.

Sensing something, I guess, he looked in my direction.

'I've just been talking with one of the guys I was supposed to have assaulted in my apartment, Inspector. The two of us getting along like a house on fire.'

'Rogues together. From what I hear you've been doing a lot of things.'

'It's called living. What other things have I been doing that could be of interest to you?'

'Visiting auction houses, art galleries that don't really deal in your kind of art.'

'Which is?'

'Excuse me, but I wouldn't have thought that gallery was dealing in art up to your standard.'

'Other people's taste is a perpetual mystery, you must know that already, Inspector. I'd reckon someone really important must have said that once upon a time.'

'You just did.'

'Ah, but I'm not important.'

'A proposition I'm aiming to disprove.'

I took a nut out of the bowl. Only when he asked if I wanted a drink did I realize how much I didn't need one. With Bobby I'd already had more drinks than the doctors recommend. What was required here was a clear head. I said, 'mineral water, Indian tonic … no we'd better keep it flat.'

Schwartz signaled a waiter, ordered, said to me, 'Funny, from the first I recognised that boozy look about you, but you want me to believe you don't drink. Problems with alcohol in the past?'

'With respect, Schwartz, that isn't any of your business.' Quoting Bobby already.

'Give me some room, please. Can't I demonstrate an interest in the health, the inner well-being of my fellow man? Did it ever occur to you we may desire the same outcomes in life, you and me?'

'What might those be?'

The mineral water arrived with two menus. Schwartz suggested something to eat, a sandwich? And set to studying the snacks and light meals list. Neither of us said anything for quite a while. He took a sip of his beer, ate a handful of nuts, went for another sip.

I told him I liked the idea of the law, but sometimes its execution was, 'how should I say, rushed?'

'I felt that about you from the start, antagonism.'

'We all know that what goes around comes around.'

'Rubbish.'

'It's true, Inspector. A person has one bad experience with the police, that's it for life. He's never going to cooperate again. I'm accumulating so many bad experiences, here, there and everywhere. For instance, the fact that you know I've been to an auction house, to a gallery as well, I wouldn't have thought that this is the way things are done in a democracy. I'm being watched for no good reason. Think Prague, 1970, sure, but in sunny Australia?'

He held up his hand, the stop sign. 'In my experience, when a citizen experiences problems with the law it's because he or she has transgressed in some way. Hardly ever have I constructed a case against a villain than he's claimed victimisation. Either at that particular moment, or a memory of it from somewhere back in time. It's as though nobody is responsible for their own actions. "I fiddled the books because something nasty happened to me when I was three." I am meant to swallow that?'

A waiter showed up and I ordered the shepherd's pie that

had found its way onto the menu. Schwartz went for bruschetta with smoked ham, tomato and haloumi on top.

I asked, 'What's haloumi?'

Having his mouth full of the last of the nuts, all he could do was shrug his shoulders in answer. Once his mouth was empty he said, 'Let's suppose for a minute I share your enthusiasm for the visual arts.'

'It wouldn't prove I'm not being spied upon.'

'Possibly not, no,' pointing to my empty glass, 'you want another one of those?'

'I reckon a double vodka and ice.'

'One minute on the wagon, next diving into the pond.'

'That's offensive.'

While I climbed indignantly to my feet he pulled a waiter, ordered another beer and my vodka.

'Please don't go, I have a proposition to put to you.'

'Do I need to hear this?'

'Your lawyer's a very attractive woman, if you don't mind my saying so.' Long meaningful pause. 'She gave me the impression that you were a gentleman of leisure with a certain obsessive interest in the visual arts.'

'And?'

'Nothing more.'

'If you asked about my habits at this hotel, as I am sure you have, they would have said there is a problem concerning the state of the carpet in my suite. From which you would conclude?'

'Why would they tell me that?'

'At reception, they would have been particularly interested to check your identification, to learn you are with the fraud squad. Make their day. Now they'll be worrying about my ability to settle the account.'

He pointed his finger, 'Your thought processes are too rigid. You look at me and your brain compartmentalizes what it thinks it sees. Would it interest you to know that last week I attended a performance of *Fidelio* by the Australian Opera Company? Of course it wouldn't, doesn't match up, does it? To you, with all your leisure time and cash, I'm just one more cardboard cutout official getting in the way of things. Well, let me tell you that from my point of view, by degrees you are turning into a one-dimensional villain. Your conversation is so defensive. A person with nothing to hide will discuss things, will open up.'

'To a cop?'

'Why not? The way you are makes me suspect your intentions. Add that to what I already know and …'

'You know I'm here to sell an apartment – how crooked is that?'

The drinks arrived, along with his bruschetta. And then he revealed what was on his mind.

'Your associate, Stan Kriticos.' Just like that, right out of the blue, or left field, or somewhere. The room spun slowly for a moment. It was not a name I had expected to hear. When I failed to respond, 'Are you going to try the "what goes around" philosophy on me again, Mr Holt?'

I gulped the vodka.

'I beg your pardon.' From behind my back the shepherd's pie slipped around my shoulder and met the table with the mashed potato all golden brown across the top. Tomato sauce followed in a wee silver-plate tub. What Karen liked to call 'bubba' food.

Schwartz: 'Working out the solution to a crime is not unlike creating a work of art. You must be flexible of mind. Indeed, if I were to believe any one person's account of a particular event I wouldn't be doing my job. Or if I were to coerce you into telling me what I might want to hear, would that bring me closer to the truth? You understand what I'm trying to say? While I listen to what you tell me, my intuition picks up on what you're not telling me.'

'But I haven't committed a crime,' I said, genuinely puzzled. 'So, what the hell are we talking about here? I'm supposed to believe that you have received some information linking me to an art crime. Where does this information come from? You're not going to tell me. Because there can't be any information, that's why. If there is, it's false. So, how do you expect me to respond to all your talk around the edges of some subject that you're not willing to pinpoint?'

'But your friend, Stan Kriticos. You and him, you see. That's enough to worry the French police. And us.'

'Oh, Jesus Christ!'

'If I was you, Mr Holt, I'd go back to France, throw those balls on the dirt the way they do, petanque isn't it? Bask in the afternoon sun, eat snails, drink Pernod, simply enjoy the good life.'

'Thanks for the advice, but tell me, even if there happened to be a Stan whatever his name is, why mightn't he be in France, too? And anyway, golf is my game.'

Schwartz rubbed his nose and reflected for a moment. I got the impression he thought he had achieved something, although I had no idea what. He said: 'Precisely.'

I knocked back the next vodka the instant it arrived, then picked up my knife and fork. 'What do you mean, "precisely"? I tell you I play golf, not petanque, what's being precise got to do with anything?'

'Now you're trying to put me off my game,' he responded, grinning knowingly, 'Another one of those?'

I nodded. Schwartz ordered me a double vodka. Thinking out loud, trying to resemble a law-abiding citizen, I said, 'The package someone was supposed to be delivering.'

'You've lost me.'

So I told him about being called down to reception to collect a delivery that didn't show up.

'And?'

'For starters it got me out of the room, leaving this girl alone to take a look around.'

'A girl in your room, well I never!'

Oblique bastard.

'That's the sum of my art interest, I do drawings of women.' Although it was clear from this conversation that there were authorities who now realised otherwise. I just had no idea how much they knew. Or cared.

Back in the hotel suite I set up to take a series of macro-focus, high-resolution photographs of the back of the Pont Royale painting I'd bought. That was to be step one in reusing the stretcher in a manner that made it appear not to have been messed about with by anyone over the last eighty years. However, when I switched the camera on its display screen informed me that there wasn't a memory stick inside any more. I sat there, for how long? Just staring at the camera. What, I kept asking myself, did this mean? That there was a fault in the electrics? Or what? Of course, me being only human, my mind didn't want to go to the answer. I took a long while to get it there. When it did I snapped open the door to the memory stick compartment, empty.

Thea and Mandy frigging about with my camera!

Would they have known how to get the memory stick out of there?

What was missing was two centimeters wide, four or five long. A vacuum cleaner would suck it up without blinking a mechanical eye. So, I could have dropped it onto the carpet and then, next thing, whoosh, into the cleaner's apparatus.

That was where I was up to.

But if the models had it then they had a bunch of JPEG images not at all good for the Essington Holt reputation as philanthropic married gentleman and doting father of the prodigious infant, Henry Holt. Even I recognized that I could be in line for some new variety of trouble. Was I going to be asked for money in exchange for a good reputation? That's how we human beings think.

Frustrated, disappointed in myself to be missing all the detail of life, I hung the Pont Royale painting on the wall, in place of the etching of the lotus leaf on a pond, a frog on the lotus leaf, which went under the bed. HV, whoever he or she might have been, wasn't a bad painter, certainly not by the standards of contemporary corporate art. The tones were elegantly stepped across the composition's surface.

Bang, bang, bang, on my door. The phone ringing at the same time. I opened up while letting the phone ring on and two men waving police identities in my face, one with a travel bag in hand, stepped past me into the suite. Something they claimed to be a search warrant was produced.

The phone stopped ringing.

When I said I needed to ring my solicitor they said that was fine, but pointed out all they wanted was the parcel that had arrived for me from France. So, they suggested, we could do this the simple way or, wait for my solicitor and do the same thing, only much slower.

I pointed to where sheets of drawing paper were still having the curl taken out of them, lying flat under the phone books. 'That's what was in the parcel.' They went through the paper, a sheet at a time, checking both sides. 'Don't know why I didn't buy it here. I guess I didn't think I'd find the right kind in Sydney. Magnani Pescia, 300gsm, nice surface to work on.' I could hear myself blurting out this unnecessary information.

The cops looked at each other. 'The package itself, you kept that?' One of them asked, and I indicated where the tube was leaning in a corner of the room.

Expressionless, the one who hadn't asked the question fetched the tube. The two of them compared it with an image they'd brought for identification. They looked inside. 'And this paper in here?'

'Drawings I do.'

'Mind if we take those and the package, you'll get them back?'

'Feel free. Is that all?'

'It's what we were looking for.'

'Regards to Chief Inspector Schwartz.'

No response.

Off they went.

When the phone started to ring again, I let it be.

The following morning, to get away from worrying over of the interest the local police had developed in me, I showered and shaved. Then, as an aftershave, threw half a tumbler of vodka down my throat.

Cleaned my teeth, too.

That felt better. But still pretty flat.

Before I could get further than blowing hot air onto my hair there was a knock at the door. I opened up to find someone called Rebecca who was claiming to be the 10.00 am model. She was standing, tall, muscular, a great deal of colour applied around angry, red-rimmed eyes. Her tangled hair brown with highlights. I asked if she had talked to them at reception before coming on up. She said there was no need, she had the room number. I explained about models turning up at the wrong times and asked if she would mind contacting the agency to sort out the bookings. She looked whacked, I didn't feel right, not a great combination for producing drawings.

Rebecca bridled at the idea of cancelling. She reckoned sorting out the bookings was my problem. She was told to turn up at 10.00 and that's what she had done; if she hadn't been told she wouldn't be here, would she? Which wasn't a bad question.

'Rebecca, Phyllis rings me first, every time.'

She didn't care, she wanted, indeed she expected to be paid, no matter what.

Being out of cash, I walked her to the nearest ATM where I made a withdrawal and handed her a couple of fifty dollar notes. And, taking the easy way out, booked her for another day. She wandered off into the cityscape more or less content.

The agency supplying me with models was called Pretty Girls Inc. It was run by this retired ballet dancer, Phyllis, who seemed eager to share with me a lot of stuff about the arthritis from which she suffered as a result of going to dancing school from when she was four years old. Each time she rang, the same painful history.

I had discovered Pretty Girls Inc by diving into the internet – there must have been something about the way the agency presented itself. The girls with photos on the site weren't too tizzied up, and their smiles weren't over the top either. Neither did they look like a bunch of whores. So I had sent an email and it was on.

Now I called and began explaining to Phyllis about the various mix-ups.

'Who did what, Mr Holt?'

So I went over it, slowly.

'But that's not the arrangement. The mornings at ten o'clock or was it ten-thirty, my mind! For two hours is the understanding that we have, is it not? Their names were, you said?'

'Thea and Mandy, two of them at once. And now Rebecca.'

'I don't have a Thea on the books. Nor indeed a Mandy. There was an Amanda …'

'That could be her.'

'I hardly think so. She left for Thailand four months ago, she sees her future as an exotic dancer over there. Poor thing always hated being called Mandy, I can't tell you how strongly she resisted that contraction.'

'So?'

'Mr Holt, to tell the truth, so far nothing that you have said makes very much sense to me.'

'Couldn't we just stick with Alison, at least I know what she's like?'

'A slight problem, I'm afraid.'

'Sorry?'

'Alison doesn't want to work with you anymore. Too risky, she told me.'

'Risky posing for me! Has she told you about the other work she does? Sex acts for bike gangs, and I'm too risky. I don't believe I'm hearing this.'

'Not that side of the work, it seems that someone was asking her questions about you.'

Pause. 'Phyllis, what kind of someone?'

'She didn't want to say. All she told me was that as she came out of your hotel someone cornered her and asked a lot of questions.'

'A man, a woman?'

'She has left the agency on account of this. Nice girl, I was rather fond of Alison myself.'

'Well, I am sorry to hear that.'

My phone back in its cradle, I took to wondering who this someone might be. Then I was considering why anybody would bother to scare off a model. Unless of course that someone was another model desperate for the gig. And Mandy and Thea could well be thought to have a real incentive to muscle in on the gig, if from the outset they had intended to grab a bunch of photographic images with which to blackmail me.

But if they weren't with the agency, how did they twig to the idea that I was interested in drawing women? Was I gaining a reputation in certain circles? Another question, how would they know I'd have a digital camera? How could they be familiar enough with that camera to know how to extract its memory stick? Realistically, if they were serious wouldn't they have smuggled in their own camera? After all, some were not much bigger than a credit card.

No, nothing was making too much sense for me. Not that much ever did.

Essington, I said to myself, a drink is what you need if you are to come up with answers to this bunch of questions. And so I poured myself a vodka, threw it down my throat and, bingo!

They could have had a camera, but when I produced mine, why use it?

A second drink.

I snapped my fingers! Taking the memory stick let me know for sure they had the images. It was as effective as sending me a bundle of prints. And safer for them: no evidence of criminality.

A swig from the bottle!

But how did they find out I drew from the model?

Because they had been watching me, had noticed Alison, had the presence of mind to ask her the question.

Light bulb came on inside my head! Was this the sort of scam Thea and Mandy would dream up all on their own?

Answer: Probably not. Because how do they know about me in the first place?

That was when I twigged to the idea I was being watched by someone other than Schwartz, other than Mandy or Thea.

My head was spinning with the booze. My life act becoming scrappy at a rate to the power of itself. Worse, people were starting to get away with things. And how was I reacting to the situation? By falling in love with a fantasy Giovanna Cecchini.

I bought myself a maximum capacity memory stick, returned to the hotel suite, spread the morning newspaper across the top of the desk and set to taking the shots of the back of the Pont Royale canvas in which the police had failed to develop an interest – must have assumed it was hotel property. I checked them for quality on the laptop and then converted them out of JPEG into the image-editing program's format. They had turned out fine. Next thing I was removing the rusted tacks from the back of the painting's stretcher. I used a pair of nail clippers to get a grip just below the head of each tack, wrapping paper around it first so that I didn't break through the rust to bare metal and leave evidence that someone had been tampering with the whole assemblage. Removing the tacks with appropriate care took quite a while: some of them proved stubborn and required a lot of manipulation before they let go, like a wisdom tooth.

As they were removed, each tack was placed in its corresponding position on a plan drawing I'd made of the back of the painting. It was of course imperative that the same number of tacks went back into the stretcher as had come out, and that each went into the correct hole.

Thirsty work.

Late afternoon I tried her number. Ring ring goes the telephone down the other end. It was picked up. I asked, 'Giovanna?'

'Who else?' She sounded just so weary of me?

'Why didn't you tell me?'

'Tell you? What would it be this time, Essington?'

'Schwartz asking you questions about me.'

'Frankly it didn't seem important.'

'Want to have dinner?' I rushed it a little.

'Really, no. Why must you always be so …'

'It's genetic. How'd you enjoy moonlighting then, thirty five dollars an hour, come over to my hotel suite, take all your clothes off, I'll do a drawing for you that neither of us will ever forget.'

'Fractionally more interesting, but still no. Anyway, I understand that you already have lots of willing models.'

'And Schwartz has the drawings. Shown them to you yet?'

'No.'

'Oh, and please don't tell Karen I put that proposition.'

'Who'd ever believe it?'

'You might be surprised.'

'Is that so?'

I was too drunk to pick up on the nuances of the exchange – if there had been any. In some way I couldn't quite grasp, it seemed interesting that she knew I had lots of willing models.

More and more, thinking about Giovanna I'd imagine I was drawing while she was half in, half out of her serious career attire. Yes, my imagination would be proceeding along that path when, all of a sudden, it would veer off in the direction of the good Chief Inspector Schwartz. Did he represent danger? Can a duck swim? And yet … I don't know but that danger proved to be a kind of a come-on.

Chapter 6

I passed Grace the camera and showed her the option of holding it or using time delay with it sitting on the furniture. She went for time delay and set to methodically clicking images of herself, holding a gigantic rose she'd brought to the job. The rose here, there and everywhere.

When I got her to put some clothes back on she insisted on holding on to that rose, as if it represented something. But she removed her spectacles with equal determination. While I was drawing she had a way of looking at me. I took it for an unusual level of interest in what I was doing. Later it hit me that I was probably just one more blur at the edges of her life.

Grace wanted to be a curator in an art museum. So she was doing a fine-art major. I told her about a theory that clothes represent different selves that we draw onto our bodies.

'Or you can use body paint.'

Was that her joke or what? It was kind of funny.

I showed her a drawing of herself and for no apparent reason she told me her father disapproved of sex for fun.

'It can be fun,' Grace grinned blindly.

'Do you think more fun than being a curator?'

'Different kinds of fun.'

Once she said, 'Unelephants'. Just like that. Another moment, 'I love pendentives.' It was hard to know what she was seeing through those glasses. She preferred posing undressed. Indeed I got the impression that before turning up she had worked on a sequence of naked poses, but had lost the confidence to adopt them. I imagined her cataloguing positions in her mind. Then suddenly, unexpectedly, she was into Egyptian-esque, stilted, side-elevation posturing.

Knock, knock, knock.

Grace belted into the bathroom, slammed the door.

It was the cops who'd taken the drawings. Wouldn't you know it, not even the courtesy of ringing through from reception.

'Returning these.' They were flat, wrapped in brown paper like a huge pornographic novel to read on the train. For reasons of their own, they'd kept the tube they'd taken them away in.

I didn't say a word, simply received the offering, shut the door.

'Just a delivery,' I called.

Grace emerged from hiding.

Possibly she had seen a Nijinsky-choreography production of *The Afternoon of a Faun.* Or something like it. Nice as she looked, there was too much art already in what she was doing, and so not much I could add.

Grace with this long black hair hanging down her back.

Her mouth only just closed on her teeth. Most of the time she appeared surprised and confused. But happy enough.

Sitting in the clothes she'd arrived in, flipping over the pages of a coffee table book the hotel left around for the bored, she couldn't have appeared more charming.

Reverting to our earlier conversation, I asked, 'When, in particular can sex be fun?'

'That's none of your business.'

'True, but the way you said it made me think you were on the point of elaborating.'

'It was a joke. I might be thinking of sex with yourself.'

'Like being your own curator?'

'But who cares?'

'I was wondering if you'd like a drink? Or we could go out, have some lunch.'

'I don't think so.'

'Fine.'

Silence, charcoal scratching on paper.

'Can I change my mind?'

'Of course. Which would you like?'

'Be fun to get taken out to lunch somewhere smart.'

'But no complications, okay?'

'I promise,' she said.

'So do I.'

And there weren't.

By then I was starting to feel pushed on the drawing front because of too many models and a diminishing inclination to explore the subject on my part. I had been at it non-stop, had alienated Alison whom I'd liked a lot, even more than I'd realised at the time, and been screwed senseless by Mandy and Thea and had this feeling of being steamrolled by Rebecca turning up at the wrong time. And Grace ... well she ordered up big at lunch.

My own moral conduct left room for improvement.

10.00 am a few days later the big, strong and angry-eyed Rebecca was tap, tap, tapping at my door.

I decided to work small, and fast, holding a stick of HB graphite and just letting the tip travel across the paper in the manner of a water diviner's rod, searching for the gravitational pull of form. I suppose I was remembering drawings by Rodin, or even the 1950s sketches of the great German artist-cum-bullshit-artist, Joseph Beuys. Well, form this Rebecca had. I wouldn't have been surprised if she had form in the police's understanding of the word as well. She had come striding into the suite dressed to the nines in a '40s style polka dot frock, white high-heeled shoes with platform soles, the tangled hair piled carelessly on top.

Before I could say duck soup she had kicked off the shoes, was out of the frock and standing before me naked except for the pseudo tortoiseshell clip holding the hair up. A remarkably evenly tanned woman.

'Well?' she asked, or challenged.

I was into the second drawing when she inquired if I liked her tits.

'Very nice' I responded, 'Yes, very nice tits.'

'Cost ten thousand dollars.'

'Worth double that.'

She kept getting herself into girlie poses with a lot of slightly unusual gynecological information tossed in for good measure. So I moved in close, increasing the scale of image to paper so what I drew pushed out the frame of whatever part of her I was concentrating on.

After an hour or so, assuming she was losing interest, I thought to ask if she'd ever had trouble with clients.

'Clients? You're talking about punters – like you?'

'I guess so.'

'Never … well once or twice you can see that there's some-

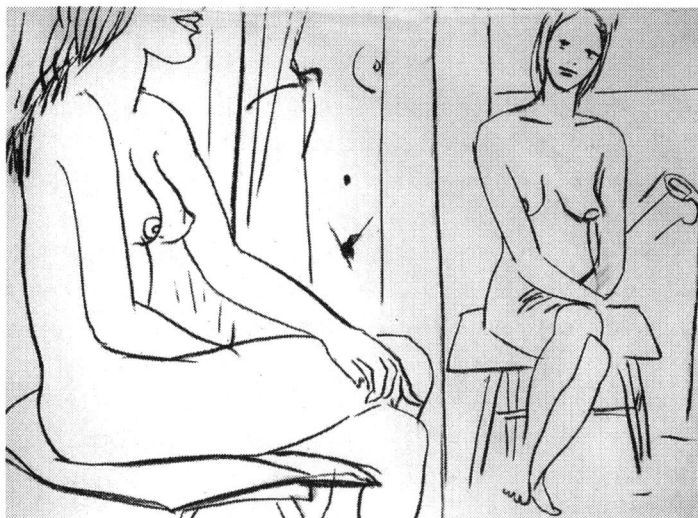

thing more to this than just taking photos.'

'Photos, that's what you'd normally do?'

'You're only looking at last year's Miss Nude 500cc, double page spread in *Two Wheels*.'

'Which involves?' It must have been at about that stage it occurred to me that Rebecca had been born a male of the species.

The Pont Royale canvas came away from the stretcher without causing me grief – backing up my assumption that the canvas and stretcher had been purchased by the artist from an art supply shop way back when, and in La Belle France. Small size canvasses had been manufactured in their thousands from the time in the 19th century when enterprising capitalists commenced marketing paint in tubes and the educated classes took up Sunday painting as a leisure activity. Geniuses and amateurs bought the same materials. Vincent Van Gogh would write to his brother, 'My dear Theo, I have sent off two cases of canvases these days, D 58 and 59 (that's the size), by goods train, and it will be at least a week or so before you get them. There are lots of daubs among them, which you will have to destroy, but I have sent them, such as they are, so that you will be able to keep what seems passable to you.' I love those Van Gogh letters, he's so matter-of-fact. If my canvas had been stretched onto the stretcher by the artist and then it had been sized, as it should have been, with rabbit skin glue before having a white gesso ground painted over the top, there would have been a better than even chance that some glue would have penetrated the canvas fibres and stuck to the wood behind. Not a disaster, but a problem, principally because an expert poking about in the back of the picture like an expert ought to do would notice that the canvas I was going to tack into place had never been accidentally adhered to the stretcher timber. Causing alarm bells to ring. Well, maybe.

Because the canvas on which I'd painted my Derain nude was as old as the stretcher I'd bought with the Pont Royale on it, the linen fibre had become fractionally brittle. So I had to be extra careful stretching it. And it had to take shape around the edges of the stretcher and set into that shape as though it had been there for most of a hundred years. To do this it was necessary to dampen the canvas down and then raise its temperature a little. Since it was a small picture I could do this by holding it over the hotel suite's electric jug while it boiled, at the same time turning the room temperature up as high as it would go. Working naked.

The next thing was to deposit some of the ancient dust I had carried with me from the south of France into the grain and folds of the canvas, particularly at the corners. All of which took a great deal of time. That was fine by me. I needed something engrossing with which to occupy myself.

With the sports channel ticking over on the TV and room service coming close to finishing my sentences for me when I ordered more booze, the canvas stretching project was coming along fine. There was a festival of one in the suite when I finally slotted the Derain into the genuine, water-gilded frame that had come to me around the Pont Royale image. It was the real thing. I was even proud of myself. Great little nude, with the blue-tinted greys reading so cool against the tones of umber, Indian red and Vandyke brown. Signature still to be revealed with the prudent application of solvents. While it wasn't visible, the work wasn't liable to be regarded as a forgery.

In the morning I was out of that hotel and moving about the city streets. Then sitting shoulder to shoulder with the let's-do-breakfast set. The hotel suite must have been getting to me, because it was nasty, and because too many people were focusing on where I was holed up. At the breakfast joint I got into the pleasures of anonymity. Starting with bacon and eggs with a tomato and sausages and hash browns, the lot. Plus a short black coffee to get the human heart working. To follow I ordered French toast with maple syrup, and strawberries and kiwi fruit on the side for the vitamins.

I was so happy.

I had my digital camera sitting on top of the stainless steel serviette holder, zoom set to wide angle, resolution maximum so I could crop without losing quality. I was taking snaps every so often by checking what was in the display at the back of the camera, reaching forward and hitting the button. Usually these were shots of a passer-by who caught my eye for one reason or another. A little bit of art-making.

Just sitting there, digesting, clicking off the photographs, it didn't occur to me that I was close to where Giovanna had her office. Yet it couldn't have been a total accident that I had taken myself off in that direction for my big breakfast treat, could it?

Back at the hotel, my delivery had arrived from Brownscombe Art Supplies. I opened it up and got off on the surface, weight and edge quality of the paper I had bought. More than $4,000 worth of stuff. The best. Hand-made. Averaging close to ten dollars a sheet. Pure self indulgence. More than I was likely to use over the next five years, should I live so long.

Not enough to occupy myself with, I ordered a bottle of French rosé, poured a glass and coupled the camera to the laptop, transferring its contents across. One by one I clicked the thumbnails up to full screen. Boring. Just people in the street, that was all. One, a nice looking girl wearing a summery frock decorated with red roses, talking on her mobile. In another shot the shutter delay had the main subject moving out of the frame while a courier on his bike was coming in from the other side, a crowded bus in the background with one of the passengers, a youth with a blank expression, looking straight out at the camera. In another a couple were kissing, nothing too passionate, just a see-you-later peck on the cheek.

And then a shot filled with one of those chaos-theory type emptinesses that glide through cities unnoticed like an embolism. Just space and the buildings on the far side of the street. And two people right over there.

Two women. To get a better look at them I did a digital zoom into the mega pixels and brought the two of them up full screen.

It had to be Giovanna, her body tilted slightly forward, a fairly aggressive stance; dark blue outfit, white blouse – her uniform. She was gesticulating with her near hand, waving it in Alison's face.

One more zoom in. But was it Alison? Another zoom and the pixels were turning to building blocks. I reduced the image size again. No, maybe it wasn't Alison after all. Hair a little too long, perhaps.

Then it was Alison again, because almost nobody has hair that red.

The Zeiss lens provided the definition. I only started to lose edge quality when I had the two of them cut off at the waist.

Yes, it was a confrontation, had to be.

So what was I supposed to make of that?

Either that or I was seeing what I wanted to see. Or didn't want to see.

Or something.

I dialled Johnstone & Lang and left a message with whoever answered the phone for Mr Julian Anderson to call me back. Must have been the same character who'd been at the desk when I visited the office with Alison. Intent on losing as many customers as possible.

Five minutes later my phone rang. It was Julian Anderson returning my call. Civilities. I told him I'd made up my mind to sell the Derain and asked if maybe I could bring it around in the next few days. Of course I sought and received assurances as to the insurance situation once the painting was in their hands, but he seemed more interested in nattering away about how Derain kept on fathering children by the models he used and how, in the end, his wife had had enough. Julian asked, 'Are you familiar with that portrait of Derain by Balthus?'

'In the striped dressing gown with the semi-naked girl in the background.'

'I expect you have noticed the manner in which he has the tip of a finger slipped in between the buttons of his shirt.'

'Now you mention it.' Thinking, Cut to the chase, Julian, what has Alison told you?

'As well, Essington, the way the cord of his dressing gown is knotted? Representative, I should have thought, of a gentleman's genitalia.'

'Gentleman's or anybody's, even mine I guess. Aren't there canvasses stacked, facing the wall, at the back of the composition?'

'Indeed there are … give me a ring when you are going to bring the painting, be nice to have another lunch … without my niece, this time.'

'Be a pleasure. Oh, by the way, you wouldn't have a phone number for her, would you? I've lost it and it's important I get in touch.' He didn't respond. 'I've got a job for her.'

'I suppose in that case …' He looked the number up, read it out.

I couldn't detect any change in his attitude to me, which probably indicated that no anti-Essington stories had been fed to him by Alison. So I was thinking that it mightn't have been Alison with Giovanna in my photograph.

Checking the photograph again, enlarging it on the screen, it was hard for me to be absolutely positive about the identity of either woman, although I remained convinced that the one with the black hair was Giovanna.

Another glass of rosé.

The other *was* Alison.

The next day, Alison called. I hired a car and we went driving, looking for somewhere to stop so Alison could eat. She had said she was hungry for oysters. We were near the sea where the oysters are, so our chances had to be good.

She said she didn't feel so guilty now about the fact that we'd 'done those things'.

'"Done those things", what are you talking about?'

'You know, Essington … the sex games.'

'You fuck girls on stage watched by hundreds of bikies, now you're talking about "those things"!' I laughed. 'I just don't get you.'

'It's different with you, Essington. You know, it feels different, that's all.' She was staring out the car window as she said that. Sort of looking at everything and nothing. Her fingers clasping, unclasping, intertwining, generally working away.

I said, 'So, how do I know you don't do this with Giovanna, too. Playing both sides for what it is worth.'

The hands turned to fists. 'I resent that.'

'I'm sorry. But think about it, under the circumstances it's not such a silly question.'

How was I going to know for sure? The instant I asked myself that question a little voice piped up inside my head wanting to know if we ever know anything for sure. But then she told me.

According to Alison, Giovanna had been waiting for her in the hotel lobby, approached her and wanted her to put a miniature tape recorder in her bag next time she was modelling. That was all. My own solicitor! When Alison asked why, she was told she didn't need to know. So she declined. Or that was what I was supposed to believe.

And, yes, Giovanna had offered quite a lot of money.

'She didn't need to offer that much, did she?'

'Wanted photographs, too.'

'Kinky. Alison, do you think this means she fancies me?'

'Definitely not.'

In Alison's version of events, when she got home after the Giovanna encounter, she decided that it would be best to cut and run. But first she had to have that meeting with Giovanna, which I had photographed, accidentally.

'I still don't get it, Alison, why meet again? You told me you just wanted to vanish. Next thing you are meeting Giovanna on the street. And if I hadn't had the photograph to show, you wouldn't have told me a thing, would you?'

'Because I felt like it. I met her because I felt like it, all right?'

'I don't believe that.'

'Would you believe this then? I wanted to tell her to leave you alone, that she had no right ... Oh, fuck this, stop the car, let me out.'

On and off all afternoon. We argued. We ate oysters. Drank wine. We argued. We fucked, we argued some more.

I asked, 'Did you fuck her like you fucked ... was it Pixie?'

'None of your business.'

Heading along the six-lane highway, my head empty of everything except guilt and suspicion, and sexual satisfaction, and even more guilt. No doubt by then exhausted, Alison was pretending to sleep. When my brain permitted the exercise, I was trying to develop an accurate picture of Karen, my wife, bring her to life in my imagination, but I'd get half-way and like a small cloud in an otherwise blue sky her fragile image would start breaking up at the edges. I just couldn't reconstruct her as the Karen I reckoned I knew. Then, I'd become frustrated, angry, and set to telling myself what I'd do to the Buddhist, avant-garde artist when I got back home. Greek heroes returning from Troy weren't going to have a thing on me.

Because, that's where we were up to in our marriage. I

didn't want to confront the problem, to face a truth that just might turn out to be true. But there definitely was this fucking Buddhist art-priest or something, and his name was Richard, and he was getting in the way. He did installations in glass cases. Just little bits of this and that he'd found on streets where he walked in his dopey-looking saffron robes; he'd arrange them in the glass cases: for instance all green objects in one glass case, all yellow in another. I mean, he looked such an act in those robes, plus with his shaved head. His art was so very much yesterday.

My opinion is that Caucasians called Crusader names like Richard never really look any good as Buddhist monks.

It hadn't taken me long to learn to hate Richard.

Which only made things worse.

What I hated most was when he pretended to be fond of Henry. It was unnatural.

And, Karen, he was pulsing hot for her, no two ways about it. Some Buddhist shit getting wood for my wife! Was he going to put her in a glass case, too, show her at some fucking art biennale, together with a whole lot more flesh-pink objects he'd happened to collect?

Wouldn't put it past him, Richard.

The worst thing I ever heard from him – and that's saying something – was this Buddhist idea that if you tran-scended desire you'd get what you wanted. Like, I don't desire that man's wife, look around and she's in your bed. How good is that?

Next thing, its owner still playing sleeping beauty, Alison's hand strayed over to my side and was stroking my upper leg, some fingers kind of wandering off on their own to check the field of action.

It was nice and it was wrong. And it was right.

We were doing a little over eighty kilometers an hour.

The good thing was that it stopped me thinking about Richard and Karen and Henry and everybody else back home –

113

Paula, the nanny, the dog, Desdemona.

Instead I was thinking about Giovanna.

Chapter 7

I came awake to the ringing of the phone.

I'd been dreaming of an old man standing on the edge of a wheat paddock, gazing at the horizon. At sunset. I was approaching him from behind when, unexpectedly, he turned around. He was me. But me in drag, with my hair dirty and all hanging down, my makeup smeared, my face sort of smudged? Or it was as it might appear on an artist's unfinished canvas, a mottled ovoid waiting for the eyes, nose and mouth to be painted in complete with highlights and dashes of some darker tone.

From the other end of the telephone connection came the voice of Inspector Schwartz.

'Why don't you just leave me alone?'

'Oh, Mr Holt, I wish I could do that.'

He said he was calling to inform me that he believed the Stan Kriticos we had talked about earlier was now in Sydney. Did I know that?

'How would I know stuff like that? Or is there something you're trying to communicate to me and I'm too slow to get?'

'If it's not important, forget I told you.' He hung up.

Just hung up like that.

The bastard was playing games.

Jesus, don't you just hate it when people play games with you?

But before I could weigh up the actual significance of this fresh snippet of information there was a knock at the door.

A bottle of wine in a bucket of ice, chilled glass as well.

I said, thank you very much but the one I'd ordered had been delivered some time ago. The room service man appeared confused. I was confused too. When things like a bottle of wine being delivered twice happen you shouldn't make too much of it. This is an imperfect world we live in. Still I got to pondering the meaning of the double delivery because I was drunk, and also because I felt as though I'd stepped through a mirror into wherever Alice finished up.

Alice – Alison!

Next thing a rabbit should have come hopping along – a dormouse, a duchess or even something really weird. I poured another glass of wine and started checking through my drawings. I was evaluating them three or four times a day. I told myself I was searching for one work that stood out, something of which I could be truly proud, that would blow them away in a hundred years or so. But really I was fixing on the Thea and Mandy images, and wondering.

Wondering as well why the bottle of wine had been delivered. Letting little things like that hang about inside my head for too long.

I rang room service to ask about the wine and was told it was a mistake, that they were sorry, and please would I accept it with the compliments of the management.

Some time in the next hour or so I went out. I guess I went into the first bar I found, ordered a drink or two and then, just possibly into another bar. Same routine. I shared my views on life with strangers, attracted attention, might even have been refused service. I don't seem to remember.

I assume I fell over at least once.

Later I took to wondering how many of my fellow human beings passed me by until someone stopped to investigate the fallen man.

Then I was regaining consciousness while waiting for the

next stage of whatever was happening to me in the casualty section of Sydney Hospital. Nurses and doctors and porters coming and going. Daily life's victims trundling past on trolleys. People talking in subdued tones. The smell of antiseptic. The anticipation of death. I wasn't in my clothes, no handkerchief, no wallet, no shoes, no nothing.

Talk about the halt and the lame! 'Holt,' I'd say to people, 'My name is Holt.'

The man in the bed next to me was in a straight jacket. Curtains were drawn around the bed on my other side. I was told I was under observation, my blood pressure was up to buggery, my heart wasn't beating as regularly as it should have been. A doctor would talk to me later in the afternoon.

My sense of time passing was like watching glaciers flow. To fill all that time I started to think about how what was going down in Sydney with this Inspector Schwartz had to connect to stuff that had happened on the other side of the world, before I had departed the Côte d'Azur for Sydney.

Yes, it had to have begun on one of those lost but pleasurable days I had devoted to taking care of Henry.

Nanny in residence or not, in our household it was the rule that I looked after Henry half the time. Karen said it would be good for me to do so. Particularly, she said, with me about to go away, my share of child care duties should be ratcheted up to become a more or less full time occupation.

Karen: 'For children, these early memories of being with a father, they count for so much.'

As if I were heading off to climb Everest or fight in somebody's front line!

'How about Paula? What do we pay her for?'

'She wanted time off anyhow. To go back to the States, see her mother.'

'Paula has a mother?'

'Essington!'

She was always pretending to be a believer in that father-son bonding thing, Karen. Which was weird. The Buddha, for instance, my memory of him was that he didn't give a stuff about the family. He just liked to sit by a river going oom or whatever sound it was that he made, and let the kids look after themselves. He was that spiritual.

But possibly not as spiritual as Richard, who hung about the household the way a vulture will stick close by a dying animal. The Buddhist named Richard with his pink skin, blond hair if he'd had any hair, undershot jaw which is not a great look anyway and very bad for mastication. I'd persuaded him to let me point my camera at him, take a snap. There were times I'd click that image up on my laptop, and then try and work bad magic on it. Do-it-yourself voodoo, simple little tricks like pointing the finger and incanting, 'Die, arsehole.'

As far as bonding with my son was concerned, from my side it didn't seem necessary to make a big event of it. I felt close to him anyway. What I liked to do most with Henry was crawl about on the floor, the pair of us playing games like puppies from the same litter – while elsewhere in the house the women plotted their next business move. Desdemona the Second, she liked to play the games too. So much mindless buffoonery worried Dawn even more than it did Karen, Dawn who had never been easy about sharing space with a Great Dane. Although she denied the accusation, I could sense that Dawn wasn't a dog kind of person.

The avant-garde Buddhist, he'd just get this half-smile on his face, raise an eyebrow and fasten his gaze on Karen. Being so spiritual, he wasn't very much into life. And not much into dogs either.

Karen said Richard was a 'people person'.

I said I preferred seagulls to people.

She said, 'You would.'

Taking care of Henry Holt, and getting the hell out of the house – the incense made me sneeze – one day I had parked the car down at the Villefranche-sur-Mer wharf, directly behind the chapel decorated by one of the legendary figures of the 20th century French art world, Jean Cocteau. Mainly a poet, since his death Cocteau's fairly vacuous if once highly fashionable drawings have become a favorite of low-skill forgers, because he's so easy to do. All along the Mediterranean there are chichi apartments and villas with one or two Cocteaus hanging amongst Jean Miro and Marc Chagall lithographs, more of them fake than real.

Because they were easy to do, I'd thought that maybe my son would be entertained by looking at the wall decorations. That's how little I know of the three-year-old mind.

Instantly we were inside and gazing at the art, a switch threw itself in Henry's head. He opened his eyes as wide as they would go, flushed deep pink, blew out his cheeks, bit down on his bottom lip, sat on the floor's terracotta tiles, held absolutely still for a very long moment, then let loose an ear-splitting wail.

'I don't think he goes for this stuff,' I explained to the aged custodian in my very Australian and poorly conjugated French. With faded eyes he half smiled in uncomprehending response, then looked away as if to avoid mutual embarrassment. Locals reckoned that the custodian, a young fisherman back then, had been one of Cocteau's catamites. I went along with that. I liked to believe that for however brief a moment he'd been the weirdo aesthete's muse, and that the sinecure of guarding the chapel was a reward for dreams satisfied by a great deal of whatever they were into. That's the sort of thing that happened in Cocteau's films and stories.

We were out of there.

Into the bright sunshiny day. Just me, the boy, and I couldn't help but notice a black Citroën Maserati parked over the other side of the road. You focus on a car like that if you happen to be into collectables. It was rare, a model with a history and, like the Concorde, a product of General de Gaulle's push to have French industry lead in design and innovation. Manufactured in the early 1970s, after the General had departed the political scene and as a result of Citroën buying out Maserati. Only twelve thousand were built, each packed with innovation.

The doors opened and out popped a couple of social undesirables intent on drawing attention to themselves by leaning against the vehicle's side; black tee shirts, black jackets, black trousers. I got the sense of eyes behind dark glasses watching every move I was making. One, talking into a mobile phone, was about thirty, really bad skin, Groucho Marx moustache.

'Ignore them,' said a voice inside my head. Not often I receive sensible messages from up there, and with Henry in my care I took extra note of that one. There was a light breeze coming off the Mediterranean. I took to settling a now silent but still rather grumpy Henry back in his pusher. I had one of his hands clasped in mine when I was greeted from the car that pulled up beside us. I knew from the voice it had to be Stan Kriticos. Stan the hard man. A unique trans-Pacific accent: Americanised vowels, Australian grammar. At one stage he had been one of my favourite people. That had been when we'd had business to do, a lot of money changing hands.

Comfortably settled beside him in the brand new, yellow, two-door, turbo-charged Mercedes was a girl less than half his age wearing a brilliantly dumb-arsed expression and sunglasses on top of her head of luxuriant, gently curling, red-blonde hair.

'Moonlighting as a wet nurse, Essington, nice. Or are you a daddy now? If so, why hasn't someone told me about this?' Even giving voice to jokey thoughts as prosaic as that, Stan managed to express a certain animosity towards the world in general and some kind of direct threat to me. He was a very let-me-sell-you-something, go-fuck-yourself-sucker type of person, our Stan.

'You never asked around, did you Stan? Or, more probably a person like you has been mixing with the wrong crowd. With some bunch of flash airheads. Like attracting like, you know how it works in society. Flipping coins against the wall with those sad bastards holding up the Citroën.'

Me being pleasant, see, socially enabling, as ever.

Under the bland scrutiny of his new girlfriend, Stan wasn't going to lose it. Hell no, he was presenting himself as Mr Cool. Flashing a look at his companion as if to check the effect he was having, he said, 'Fatherhood, I wouldn't have thought it possible for the original wild man. But seeing you with the kid there, you know, it suits you.'

Next he put on that you-poor-sucker grin people pick up from the facial expression manual we call Hollywood.

'Seems to suit you, too, Stan.' I winked at Ms Fairy-Floss. She puffed out her cheeks pretty much the way Henry had done not so long before in the Jean Cocteau chapel. Only instead of screaming her lungs out she released a pout full of stale air through gloss-painted rose bud lips. Vacant eyes with – did I imagine the dilated pupils? Next thing she was winking back at me, as if signalling that we were the ones with the inside running, she and I.

And that Stan was out there somewhere doing nothing but losing. Interesting.

Don't you hate standing outside a car, holding on to a pusher, having to talk in through the space of a three-quarter wound-down window? It's a strain on the vertebrae, bad for posture in all sorts of other ways as well, and takes away what human dignity you thought you might possess.

'Essington Holt, meet Holly.'

'And this is Henry Holt.' They couldn't see him very well in his pusher. But I could; he was paying particular attention to the swaggering pigeons pecking the cobble stones in search of invisible scraps; he was telling them great truths.

'Henry, brilliant, like King Henry the ...' The accent, Holly had to be from London, England.

'Eighth?' I suggested.

Stan, suddenly all serious. 'Essington, I've been wanting to talk to you about something. A bit of a problem I've got, really. You be home tonight?'

Of course I wasn't to know then that he wanted me to buy back the entire Kriticos art collection.

'Believe so, or any time, you've got my number.' Stan gave the throttle a neat little vroom-vroom. 'Nice to meet you, Holly. Look forward to hearing from you, Stan.'

All of which was a lie.

Last image I had was of Stan's profile as he squeezed the steering wheel in one gloved hand and, staring straight ahead with the determination of a test pilot, shifted the shiny heap into drive.

Then the black Citroën with its smoke-glass windows and load of trash piled back inside, pulled out from the curb and followed in his wake. Whenever you got Stan you got as a bonus his heavy-looking pals, saying nothing and standing off a little from the social action. Say if I'd turn up at his latest apartment to discuss the acquisition of a painting, there'd always be a couple of men in the next room watching some bike race or soccer match on television. If I glanced in their direction one or other of them would just happen to be taking his eyes off me.

Back when we were doing business together, it had seemed to me that Stan was in fact Mr Constantly-Worried. So I thought of him as Con. Like Con-Stan (*How did Constantinople get the works?/That's nobody's business but the Turks*).

I'd decided the reason he'd developed his particular attitude to life was that he couldn't find it in himself to deal straight with anyone. Deep psychological problems. As well, that was what I had heard from other people who'd tried to do business with him. While putting together medium-size property deals all along the coast, Stan had stomped on a lot of toes, some of them attached to feet belonging to more substantial operators than he would ever be – or so I had thought at the time. But there seemed an endless supply of suckers with buckets of cash and hopes of getting even more who were moving into a French Riviera dream from everywhere around the globe.

Stan and I had met when he decided to make a big art purchase. For him, as with most of my clients, to buy art was one more way of declaring to the world that he'd arrived. I'm talking here about Stan of the blue shave, the full, sensual lips, the five-hundred-word-vocabulary – he was a kind of handsome knockabout feller with a lot of attitude, but riddled with doubt at the same time – a shrink might say 'a complex character'.

Back when we had been friends, I'd bump into him on the Villefranche waterfront and he'd be telling me what the Parramatta Eels had done to the Sharks the previous Saturday – oh yes, you have to believe it, a real man of the world.

So, suddenly if Stan Kriticos wanted to talk, should I be worried?

Faster than light the answer had to come back, Yes, very worried.

Any customer wanting to talk some years after the last deal was closed ought to set alarm bells ringing in the head of a person in my line of work.

Of course I had managed not to see the real Stan when he first brought up the idea of me hunting up a painting for his wall. Someone, I can no longer remember who it was exactly, had told him I was the man for the task. First up I procured him an elegant if unchallenging Raoul Dufy oil painting. Stan's first art purchase ever, except for a fake icon of which he was fantastically proud. US$350,000 the Dufy cost him. Title: *Still life beside the sea*. Nice enough looking picture, sophisticated touch with the colour relationships.

Being up-front, Stan told me that he'd be going to want to borrow against the work of art at some time so his banker was likely to want something tangible, something written in real words on a real piece of paper that would guarantee the painting's value.

So I put together a bunch of stuff. The provenance, with one copy adhered to the protective backing behind the canvas, along with an older (silverfish eaten) piece of documentation already pasted there. Typed on a carbon ribbon typewriter, it read: From the collection of Charles Debucourt, (direct descendant of the eighteenth century draughtsman and engraver of the same name). Estate of Madame Charles Debucourt, now deceased. Oil on canvas, signed 'Raoul Dufy' lower right. 33.4 x 46.5 cm. Painted between 1925 and 1928. Literature, Gallery Leslie catalogue, Paris, 1978, (illustrated; with wrong dimensions). Exhibited Belgium, August 1943, catalogue number no. 39.

As well, I'd typed a brief artist's life into my computer and printed it out for him on a laser printer. Stan was getting a lot of service back-up for his measly US$350,000. I'd even bought him an English language paperback on Dufy so he'd have some idea of the importance of what he was getting.

Myself, I admired Dufy's paintings. If that hadn't been the case, Stan wouldn't have finished up with the picture. Dufy's greatest attribute was his ability not to display ambition. In painting after painting he is seen to under-perform where, say, Picasso would never miss a chance to let you know what an over-the-top guy he is with the paint brush – not to mention with his dick.

To the French art world of his day, and particularly to those who made up the numbers of the Fauves, Dufy was an outsider even though he shared their ideas about colour. His first successful show was held in 1922 when he was already forty-five years old. Afterwards he became a regular visitor to Vence up behind the Côte d'Azur, where he produced large numbers of watercolour studies that later, in the studio, were turned into oil paintings. In these he treated the picture space in a flat manner with the painting's motifs reduced to simple zones of color, on top of which he indicated them in a kind of painterly handwriting – bottles, nudes, fruit, trees.

In Stan's Dufy, the subject is a water pitcher beside two squash on a table, his own palette and brushes, then the sea beyond. The work relates to Picasso's seaside still-lifes painted in the early twenties. However, Picasso's are more structured – he never completely threw off cubism. Dufy's objects are informally placed; he's interested in what he liked to call 'couleur-lumière', where picture space is all about the interaction of color.

Despite initial enthusiasm, peaking with a cocktail party to introduce the Dufy to his acquaintances, after a few weeks it became apparent that Stan thought I'd underestimated his potential as an art lover. Somebody must have said something that cut him to the quick because suddenly he wanted to spend much more than US$350,000, and on some 'really important' work of art. 'You hear what I'm telling you, Essington?' And he wanted me to take back the Dufy.

Treating me like I delivered the groceries.

I said, 'Stan, that blue sea in the background, that's Golfe-Juan … see? It's where you've developed all these wonderful properties. What you've got in the Dufy is a significant work by an important artist, but what's more it's connected with your own life.'

But he kept badgering me for a work with more social clout. Eventually, having argued him into keeping the Dufy, I promised to go in search of a work that would knock everybody's socks off. Something that showed off both the artist and the collector.

That was the first time I'd dared venture into Henri Matisse territory. Three months later Stan Kriticos acquired a work by the master titled *Sleeping Nude Woman*; a charcoal drawing about 50 x 70cm.

He blanched when he saw it.

Wanted to know if I was playing games with him or what? The thing wasn't a painting, it was just this simple drawing that a kid could do. He had asked me for a masterpiece, hadn't I understood that? What did I turn up with but a nude girl who wasn't even a turn-on, didn't look as if she could sell her butt in an old people's home!

'Look at those tits! Come on, Essington, could you get wood over her, tell me?'

I can hear him saying those exact words, even now.

The drawing was beautiful, or I wouldn't have been pushing it. In my own humble opinion I'd have to declare it a masterpiece. It was supposed to be from around 1924. Stan started to take it seriously when I pointed out the price. The US$750,000 that I quoted was around US$150,000 under the last auction price for a similar drawing. As with Vincent Van Gogh after death, Matisse prices had been managed by his own astute family, principally by his son, Pierre, who ended up a big time art dealer in New York. They just kept on rising.

Once Stan got to see the paperwork I'd collected to go with the drawing, he became a bit more enthusiastic. I explained to him that for Matisse, drawing became an end in itself. Early on it was subordinate to his painting, considered to be neither more nor less than a means of solving compositional problems. But by the second half of his career, drawing had become central, it acted as a catalyst for changes in his way of doing things. Stan's nude was drawn with what I considered the sensitivity of a real colorist working without colour. Matisse always aimed for what he termed luminous space – similar to Dufy's 'couleur-lumière' I guess – with tonal and colour accents allowing for some play

of light and shade across the paper. Matisse said somewhere, can't remember where, 'In spite of the absence of shadows or half-tones usually expressed by hatching, I don't renounce the play of values or modulation. I modulate with variations in the weight of the line, and above all with the areas it delimits on the white paper. I modify the different parts of the white paper without touching them, rather through their relationships.' I'd copied that into a notebook without the detail of when and where it had been said.

Being a salesman, Stan went for my Matisse quotes. He liked them so much that over the period when we were seeing quite a bit of each other I developed the habit of dreaming up fresh ones for him. For his part he'd quote them back to me as if they were a natural part of his cultural repertoire, wisdoms that maybe I ought to take on board.

The Kriticos art collection expanded over time, with Stan spending a hell of a lot more money than I would have thought possible to extract from his property deals. This should have worried me, but I have always been a bit hazy about financial matters. Anyway, I was having too much fun. With a great deal of help from me he came to possess a substantial Degas, a pastel tracing on translucent paper stuck down on board, reverse side up, with some over-drawing in orange and green. It was still sporting the pin holes Degas would have put there when fixing the sheet into place to replicate an earlier work. The subject was a woman washing herself in a metal hipbath. It wasn't in top condition. Indeed, quite a bit of the pastel pigment had been rubbed off in the top left hand corner.

I was proud of that touch, and a couple of Degas experts were seen to get off on it as well.

Also, Stan acquired a big Sonia Delaunay abstract composition of split concentric circles painted in bold primary colours, white and black. The canvas had rotted away along its bottom edge, as will happen from time to time, and so had been adhered to a newer canvas and restretched onto the original stretcher. I was really pleased with that restoration job on my own painting. The Delaunay was my first pure abstract. As well, to remind him of Australia, there was a Sidney Nolan image of Ned Kelly, in Ripolin, a brand of French household enamel popularized as an anti-traditional paint by Picasso and adopted by Nolan because he thought it chic. Stan also got his hands on two more Matisse drawings. He was starting to notice that having works by Matisse in what had become the master's home territory won him more brownie points than anything else.

Then there was a pause for a full year before he announced that he was ready to enter the market again. I remember the day he told me what he wanted next. He'd asked me to meet him for lunch around the coast at Menton. Why Menton? Christ only knows. Menton's where you go into some smart joint along the waterfront named something like L'Escargot and the maitre d' whacks you over the head with his London glottal stop.

Stan was going to be waiting at Le Poisson d'Or right on 12.30. I turned up at one o'clock because my car, a veteran, wouldn't start, so I had to wait for Karen to get back from her weekly tennis game so I could use her Volvo wagon. Anti-car cult, Karen drove Volvos reckoning they were safe, solid and didn't accelerate too fast. So I didn't break any speed records on my way round to Menton.

Tapping the face of his watch, Stan asked, 'Where you been?' As if he was in competition with the maitre d' to see who could show the least class.

I would have put my money on Stan.

Easing into the role of hireling, which he liked me to play, I explained about the car. And he said, 'You could have rung. I don't believe some of you people.' As if he belonged to another species.

'What's on your mind?' I pulled my sleeve back, had a look at the face of my watch, just for the fun of it, you know. Of course it wasn't a 24 ct gold big brand model like Stan's, but it told the time all the same and there was a chance the gesture communicated the idea that he could back off or I was out of there.

'What will it be, Essington?' grasping by the neck the bottle of Christ-knows-what already on the go in the ice bucket.

'It's all the same to me.'

The waiter was called, poured, departed.

'Exactly what are we celebrating here today, Stan?"

He put down his glass, locked his fingers in a bunch and held them just underneath his chin. As solemnly as if he were telling me he'd been diagnosed with terminal cancer.

He said he wanted to catch a really big fish.

At first I didn't cotton on that he was talking about a work of art.

So, kind of joking, I said, 'You need some heavy tackle.' You know, a funny sex reference. Stan enjoyed rutting humour and I indulged him. Stan was my cash cow. But he let that pass and went directly to the heart of the matter. 'I have in mind a masterpiece, a big Matisse. They like the Matisse drawings you got for me, they go down well with the people. What I am visualising, Essington, is a big value item, a real oil painting, you know, the focal point in any room. The only thing is I want it yesterday.'

I set to searching the menu shoved under my nose, hoping to find a course the chef couldn't stuff up. But there was nothing extra safe there so I ordered the boudin noir with apples, reckoning that at least a sausage is protected from the chef by its skin.

Stan went for the sea bream.

I said, 'What you have in mind might be out of our range.'

'From last week, nothing is out of my price range.'

'That's nice to hear.' I smeared a large grin across my face. 'I won't ask how or why, but, well done anyway, Stan.'

'I'm not joking, here.' Half-standing, leaning across the table, talking right into my face. 'You don't want to agent this, I'll find someone who does. I'm sorry, I was only thinking about loyalty. You have done me those good deals in the past, therefore I stick with you, Essington, but ...'

Suddenly, I was trying to seem overwhelmed by his confidence in me. 'It's not easy to find a major painting by Matisse any more. You know, I know, any market is determined by supply and demand. Off the top of my head we would start by looking at around the four million dollar mark, and these are US dollar figures I'm quoting you, Stan. This kind of thing isn't likely to come up at auction every month of the year. I'm going to have to hunt it out, maybe even offer an inducement to sell, something well over the auction estimate.'

After we'd eaten, Stan was keen for me to have a look at his latest set of wheels, which turned out to be a 1990 silver Lagonda with four doors. Nasty angular piece of shit with a boring V8 motor, which he lifted the bonnet to display.

I kicked the tyres and asked if there was enough room in the back for making the legendary two backed beast in the drive-in pictures, and he said they don't have drive-ins any more, arsehole. And I said that showed how long it had been for me.

Stan held out the keys and jiggled them before my eyes. 'Take it for a drive, see how it feels.'

'Meanwhile you will what?'

'Forget about that, Essington, I'm coming too. I'll be interested to see how you handle the corners in a real automobile.'

For me, playing Stan's games was part of the gig. He decided against Italy for the joy ride, instead he reckoned it would be nice if we headed up to Sainte-Agnes in the mountains directly behind the coast.

Narrow road, sharp corners.

I pushed the Lagonda, which was a heavy car anyway, but

had a pleasant balance to the suspension. It didn't over-steer. Then I pushed it a bit harder just to give Stan a thrill. Outside Sainte-Agnes I was screaming through a series of sharp bends when I had to come close to hanging a couple of wheels over the side to avoid a majestic 1950s Mercedes heading in the opposite direction. Nasty, those mountain roads, twisty, designed for donkey carts, not cars. Two more bends and I slid to a stop at a scenic lay-by.

'It goes.'

A grey shade of white, Stan was in mild shock.

Silence.

Next Stan was tapping out a cigarette, pushing in the lighter. The lighter popped out. The cigarette got lit.

I was thinking that I didn't associate Stan with smoking cigarettes. But he was carrying them.

After a couple of draws he said, 'These painting deals, Essington, don't you ever try to screw me on them.'

'Screw you! What the hell are you saying? Either you trust me or you don't. But either way how am I going to be screwing you on them?'

'Don't do it is what I'm saying.'

'I give you copies of the documentation, the purchase price, everything. We are agreed on the commission, a big discount by the way; if you don't believe me shop around.'

'I know that, I checked.'

'Of course you would, anybody would. What's more we've agreed that from now on anything over two million US is only five percent to me.'

Stan, 'Of course, sure, it's agreed. I'm just warning you, that's all. There is no way forward if you fuck with me, because I'll kill you, okay?'

That was when I should have walked away. And yet, to have done so could have led him to reexamine the deals we'd already done, and I certainly didn't want him to do that.

Instead I asked him, 'What do you do with all these cars I

see you in? Do you deal in them, what?'

'You look after the art, Essington, my business is my business.'

Stan took over the driving for the rest of our excursion.

So it had to be a Matisse oil, nothing less would do.

How was I to know that the word Matisse would one day come to bring me out in goose bumps? Let's face it, I really didn't do anything wrong, not under the circumstances. Impatient as he was by nature, there wasn't any other way that he was going to get the painting. If Stan wanted something he had to get it; satisfaction transformed him, briefly, from a brooding, threatening beast to your standard over-the-top nice guy who couldn't do enough for a pal.

The belief he had regarding the Matisse acquisition was that one way or another I had magicked him an important painting from the master's 1947 to 1948 period. It was titled *Femme Couchée* and measured about 55 x 45 cm. First reaction from Stan was, 'It's so small, Essington. I wanted a really big painting, knock your eyes out.'

'Major means big, but only in quality terms. You were talking about quality, Stan, not square metres. A painting isn't wall to wall carpet.'

It took a while to hose the 'big' thing down. Until I did he was growling like a pig-dog in at the kill and doing this act he did of leaning at you and making grasping and twisting actions with his hands, as if wringing the necks of little birds.

I walked him through catalogues from major collections so he could see for himself that most Matisse paintings were in fact small. I went beyond that by forcing him to concentrate on the real size of Vermeer's *The Lacemaker*, even going to the trouble to bubble-jet print it for him on a sheet of A4 paper, blue-tacking it to his wall. Me asking, 'Can you imagine the impact if you had the real thing hanging up here?' He didn't get the point straight away, because I guess he wasn't sure who Vermeer was.

Femme Couchée was a challenging Matisse with quite a lot of black painted over red and only the barest indications of an interior with curtains achieved by scratching back through the black. The woman's figure was crudely drawn and painted scarlet. Out a window there was an abbreviated garden landscape that might just as well have been a painting hanging on the wall. The image took eight attempts before I got the right level of relaxation into the brush strokes and those calculatedly casual lines scraped into the black with the wrong end of a fat bristle brush. The canvas was of the correct vintage and the whole thing had been put through an elaborate aging process involving smoking, prolonged exposure to an ultraviolet light and begriming with the use of well-aged dust collected with a vacuum cleaner from the bowels of the Saint-Jean-Cap-Ferrat house. Once he got over the size factor, Stan really went for the painting. And he took to correcting me more than ever on quotes and the characteristics of Matisse's output. He was the instant expert, thanks to the educational Matisse video I'd supplied.

For Stan, from that moment on the collection was to be built around this jewel.

To go with the painting he smartened up his own life act, creating a fresh persona with even a touch of ennui as a topping. He did up more shirt buttons, depriving us of the view of chest hair and the solid gold cross on the solid gold chain. He gave up leaning in on people, and if he caught himself doing that screwing action with his hands he'd stop.

He acquired yet another smart car, this one a two-year-old Bristol shooting brake, the body of which was supposed to have been built to order for an oil sheikh. I didn't get to put that one through its paces.

Stan Kriticos had himself featured on the front page of *Nice Matin* where he was described as a 'local identity', only in French. They used a photo of him standing beside a mint condition 1936 Cord coupé with running boards and bright metal exhaust manifolds emerging from the side of the multi-finned engine compartment. On local television it was reported that he was intending to establish a museum and leave his art collection in its entirety to the municipality. That one gesture, no matter how hollow, transformed our Stan from being just one more developer of nasty postmodern blotches cluttering the few scrubland, sea sloping faces left along the Côte d'Azur.

He'd arrived. All for a mere US$3,500,000. Cheap.

Preparing top apartments to sell, he was now in a position to hang the walls with one or two of the minor masterpieces he had been accumulating, and make one hell of a life-style impression. A bit later on I heard that a particularly exclusive English language Côte d'Azur walking tour stopped off at Stan's to get a taste of typical French Riviera high culture.

All the money Stan paid me went into a bank account in Switzerland, something I neglected to mention to Karen. There it sat accumulating interest and doing the compound thing. Not that I was concentrating on the arithmetic but it would have to have been growing by something substantial a year.

We did a lot more art deals, some of them smallish stuff but others were major works, real in-your-face masterpieces any hot-blooded American collector would kill for. A still life of pears and cherries by Derain, a Jawlensky of a woman in a red hat, two primitivist pre-1910 Kirchners, a group of six Maillol drawings. The Kandinsky was still there of course, other stuff too, some small watercolours and a bunch of understated Bonnard brush drawings in pink, purported to be studies for illustrations to Verlaine's last poems, *Parallelement*, one of the exquisite books the Paris art dealer Ambroise Vollard published round the turn of the century.

Then, quite suddenly, Stan's enthusiasm for art vanished. I was told that he went over to race horses. I was told as well that he spent his time flying between Nice and Longchamp to watch his nags running and chat up the business hoi polloi gathered there in their Saturday best, or to visit training establishments and studs up in Normandy. It was proudly reported in *Nice Matin* that he scored a second place in the Prix de l'Arc de Triomphe.

And I thought, 'Go, Stan, you good thing.'

That day, after bumping into Stan for the first time in ages, and him threatening to call me on the phone that evening, little Henry Holt and I played for a while in the sand of the Villefranche beach before settling into the Bar Plage that is set against the wall keeping the railway line from falling onto the water. There I changed his nappy and ordered some ice cream and banana for him while I had a cup of coffee with a glass of water on the side. It was a pleasant place to sit and gaze out over the anchorage. There was a big Greek-registered tourist ship swinging at anchor with launches shuffling between it and the customs and migration check directly in front of the Jean Cocteau chapel.

Usually, whenever I sit at the Bar Plage I think about Africa over the far edge of the sea. But Africa wasn't anywhere in my head on that particular day, instead I was pondering the great mystery of being Stan Kriticos. And thinking how much I didn't enjoy the idea of his phone call to come that night.

Sitting at my side, watching the sea and its birds, a residue of beach sand between his sticky fingers and toes, Henry was turning into Mr Sleepy-Head. There hadn't been a lot of banana eaten, but a great deal of ice cream was smeared across his cheeks, so I stirred him up a little and we got into feeding games, filling the spoon then drifting it into his gaze while making buzzing noises or imitating the fut-fut-fut of a helicopter's rotor. Then slipping the spoon between semi-parted and undecided lips. It made him laugh, playing that.

Henry was sleeping in the room with us. That wasn't unusual. The same with the dog, she shared our room when it suited her, but not, since Henry's arrival, the bed. With Karen suffering bouts of nausea on account of her being pregnant again, and with Desda succumbing every now and then to those doggy bad dreams that lead to whimpering and the occasional growl, a fart, or her deciding to scratch simply for scratching's sake, or attempting to regain possession of a section of the oversize bed, or because of some involuntary sequence of word-type sounds coming out of Henry, or Henry deciding he'd prefer to be awake, it was amazing if I slept at all.

And that night I certainly wasn't sleeping. No way.

Was Richard the monk sleeping three doors down the corridor? Or was he going ooom while playing with his namesake and fantasizing sex acts with my wife?

'You want to talk to me about something, Ess?'

'Not really, Raran.' Karen had turned into Raran the instant Henry took his first stab at pronouncing her name. His vocabulary had grown since then but he was still some way off saying deeply meaningful things. But then so are we all.

I certainly wasn't going to tell Karen about bumping into Stan outside the Jean Cocteau chapel. Once Henry was born, she had lost what patience she ever had with the fake art side of my life, believing that it brought trouble with it the way rats carry plague, mosquitoes malaria. And of all the people with whom I did business, legitimate or otherwise, Stan Kriticos had, right from the start, been the one Karen disliked the most. She hated everything about him, and that even before the rumour began to circulate.

Rumours, the Riviera thrives on them, on the French side of the border at least. That's because it's a dumping ground for this world's falling stars. On the streets of Nice people point out total strangers and tell you all about some appalling crime they committed in the not so recent past. The reason is that there are a lot of monied people crowded together along the coast, and it's hard to get rich without breaking a rule here and there and even the occasional neck. So it wasn't unexpected when one day, and out of nowhere, the story began to spread that our Stan had killed an ex-partner in the Kriticos property business because of a disagreement over profit sharing. An unreasonable number of stab wounds is what the rumour insisted on. Plus the possibility that the victim had been tortured. The body was left for all the world to find and see, sitting on a park bench high up in the grounds of Le Chateau, overlooking the Bassin Lympia in East Nice. As accounts circulated, they garnered the embellishment of a stray rottweiler gnawing on the dead man's left leg, directly above the sock line. And then jokes about dogs' distaste for wool-nylon-mix socks.

The victim, who turned out to be Moroccan was, according to the press, an ex-partner of Stan, or if you listened to street talk this was just one more Niçoise gang war thing. Did it make any difference?

Not to me it didn't. The fact is, the corpse on the park bench had been my friend, name of Moulay. From Morocco, yes. Lived half the time in Casablanca. On the French side of the Mediterranean he ran the Bar d'Azur, a hang-out of mine where softly sung Brazilian lyrics spun magic. I never remembered if I'd met Yassir through Moulay, or if it had been the other way round. Whichever, I'd known him. And I'd believed he had been involved with interracial street politics all across the south from Marseilles to the Italian border. His bar was on the ground floor of a Stan Kriticos development down by the water. A lot of people might have wanted him dead. Stan among them, quite possibly. But there are so many stories that circulate in life – tell me about it.

So, when in the middle of the night Karen had asked, out of nowhere, if I had something on my mind that I needed to talk about, there was no way I was going to bring up the

Kriticos name. I responded, 'Nothing I can think of. Unless it's because it seems I'm doomed to go away, with you pregnant and Henry needing his walks and stuff ...'

'There's a lot of time before the baby, Ess, I don't want you worrying about that. And there's Dawn to help look after me while you are gone.'

'Henry?'

'He's why we have a nanny, isn't he?'

'Is he why we've already got Richard?'

'You don't understand about Richard. Essington, life has a spiritual side as well as the physical. That's what Buddhism teaches us, well one of the many things.'

She turned over, facing away from me.

Quiet. The only sound being our unsynchronised breathing.

'You're not going to go to sleep tonight, are you Ess?'

'Maybe I'll walk around for a bit, give you a break.'

'Perhaps you should.'

At that moment the telephone rang and I scooped it up before Henry was disturbed.

'Mr Holt?'

Couldn't identify the voice.

'You any idea what the time is?' I asked.

Click.

I went straight downstairs to the studio. Desdemona followed. I put on some Keith Jarrett piano renditions of great old tunes. Straight off, 'Blame it on my youth'.

Tell me about it

I slumped into an armchair, poured an extra large shot of room temperature vodka, gulped, pondered the meaning of life and the loss of it – really deep stuff, okay?

The phone rang, somebody inside the house answered it. Then I woke with Dawn standing just inside the door of my studio, fresh as a daisy, and chilly as the peak of Mont Blanc, cropped bleached hair spiked with gel.

'Sorry to intrude on the bear's cave, but it's breakfast time, Essington. And something might be required for your pal, Desdemona, a garden walk for instance. Think poo poos. Wouldn't that be a nice idea for you to develop on, and sooo thoughtful?'

I grunted, blinked, swallowed. 'What time is it?'

'Going on eight, sweetie.'

'Karen out of bed?'

'Couldn't say.'

'That prick, Richard?'

'Praying, I expect.'

'That he can get into Karen's pants.'

'You are so gross, you know that? Oh, and, you just had a call. A Stan somebody who said he was sorry about last night.' She smiled her just-for-Essington smile. 'Is it a secret between you two?'

'You said Stan?'

'So, what did happen last night? You can tell Dawn.'

'Who'll tell the world. First, it's none of your business. Second, nothing happened, I was here, remember, in the bosom of my family. This Stan, he say anything more than that?'

'Just that if he doesn't hear back he'll meet you at the Matisse Museum, mid-morning. Will that be all, oh great king?'

'Mid-morning would be?'

'I'd imagine elevenish, wouldn't you?'

Dawn and I, our little anti-courtship routine.

'Tell you what, Dawn, you ought to meet Stan's current lay of the day. The name's Holly, think of all your Christmases coming at once. Pretty little thing.'

'Darling, I can't wait. But then breakfast can't wait either, and I have a hunch breakfast's a surer bet.'

Dawn and Karen have been in partnership for ten years or so.

They design and print silks for the high fashion market. They started out small and got bigger, then big. In fact it had got to where my inherited riches were becoming less central to everybody's lives. Maybe it was the earning-capacity competition from their silk business that had me wanting to fiddle around again with art forgery, I don't know, but I was beginning to feel like one of those bees or spiders or whatever who have slept with the queen, passed their use-by date, and are due to be eaten.

A sales-addicted business hardhead, Dawn's heart had its soft side nevertheless; she kept falling hopelessly into and out of love or lust or something. As she got a little older, the girls who stole her heart away became younger, and even more beautiful – or was that just the way things looked to me? Quite a few of her partners had been met at one end or the other of the catwalk at Paris fashion parades. Each time she was out of love, Dawn came to stay with us to recover from passion's headlong charge and its bruising aftermath. She was in the house a lot. Next to Karen, Dawn was the wittiest and most creative person I knew.

In truth I had long been in awe of both of them.

Along with Villa du Phare, I had inherited a Bentley Sloper from the aunt I hardly knew (that was Dawn's phrase, Essington's Aunt he hardly knew). The car was what in France you'd call an *item de collection*. There's a big down side to driving an eye-catching car. Off you go and a whole lot of people you don't want to know think to themselves 'there goes that Essington Holt, arsehole, believing his shit doesn't stink.' Or they might think, 'Funny thing, isn't that Essington's car parked outside Mademoiselle Charmont's house, and it's three o'clock in the morning' kind of thing.

On the other hand, the car, like the house, was a memorial of a sort to this relative who looked after me with such generosity from the other side of the grave. The least I could do was continue to drive it around the district. There had been a number of occasions when I'd address a remark to the old biddy as if she were seated there beside me, in her Bentley, as we zoomed along the Corniche with the Mediterranean on one side and villas or flat-faced apartment blocks on the other.

Having time to kill before my meeting with Stan, I parked in Nice, in the shade, one street back from the Promenade des Anglais, just behind Rue de la Buffa. My bank was a block away and there were some arrangements I needed to put in place to cover my trip to Australia. As well I had it in mind to sashay a fraction further to the east of the city in search of something nice to buy Karen. I had thought that, for the woman who has pretty much everything, the way to go was culture, a bunch of CDs perhaps. But there was a Buddha figure from northern Laos that I'd spotted in a gallery dealing in Oriental art. I wanted to take another look at that. But then it had also occurred to me to give her the little painting I'd just spent time aging in my studio – an Andre Derain nude, not the post-Fauves period nude I intended taking with me to Australia but an earlier, really bright, broadly painted picture, pushing the Fauves palette as far as it could go. I was rather proud of the work and as a present it appealed to my sense of humour to have Karen hang it on the wall believing it to be the real thing from her reformed forger. How Buddhist was that?

I had time to kill and thoughts to entertain.

Having unfolded Henry's pusher and seated him in it, I turned back to the open car door to wind the window down a couple of centimetres so that Desdemona could breathe freely while awaiting our return. My mind was nowhere in particular. But the dog's mind! Suddenly she was roaring and barrelling past me, knocking me over in the rush before locking her jaws on the upper arm of a man who'd popped out of nowhere to grab the handles of Henry's pusher. Henry and the pusher rolled forward a couple of metres and came to a stop against the front fender of a parked delivery van. The man, on his knees by then, my dog all over him but still keeping hold of the arm. Man, really in his teens.

First up I was looking to Henry. Who was fine. In fact he was just staring straight ahead, the complex of his thoughts altogether elsewhere. Of course the good citizens walking on our side of the street were crossing over to avoid what might turn out to be an unsavory event.

'Desda, enough!'

She knew the command, 'Enough'. I used it for just about everything.

She let go. Recovering, instantly this guy was kind of half sitting, half kneeling on the pavement, balanced and rising. With a hand sliding in under the lapel of his black suit jacket. Maybe Desdemona registered the movement before I did, because she was onto him again, thrusting across his body, taking that other arm just above the wrist. Next thing he was flat on his back.

And I was up to speed, taking over from the dog, rolling him onto his face, checking through his pockets, retrieving a nasty little lady's .22 pistol with mother of pearl insets on the butt. Only when I rammed the short barrel into his left ear did he give up. And he locked up. Didn't move a fucking muscle. Like he'd been deep-frozen. Still nobody was interfering though there had to be the chance of a call made to the police, because scenes like the one in which I'd scored a major part are bad for the city's tourist and retail trade.

From the other inside pocket of the baby-snatcher's jacket I retrieved a wallet, a hypodermic syringe in its wrapper and a packet of smokes.

Working the gun in his ear, 'What are you on about?'

Not a word. Still not moving a muscle. But looking down I saw he'd pissed himself.

Isn't it a disgusting thing when a young man pisses himself in the street? I'd need a proper medical excuse to forgive that.

But no way could I forgive someone who has just tried to kidnap my son.

On the other hand I didn't have a lot of time. And I did not want to spend the rest of that day involved in a police investigation. Nor did I need a story like this to get back to Karen and Dawn, for whom straight off it would be a case of me putting Henry in danger. I could hear the words, see the way they'd look at me. And then that Richard the Buddhist would be gliding by, him too, with just the hint of a smile playing on his thin, purple-tinged lips.

'Piss off, cunt,' was all it took.

He was off, looking over his shoulder, heading due west for the red-light side of town. Not big, not too tough either. But a man who had been carrying a gun.

Desdemona was looking at me and then at the distance into which the man had fled, then back at me. Like she couldn't believe it. Her eyes were telling me that they handled problems of this kind altogether differently in the animal world.

Mostly I'd like to inhabit that animal world.

If I did, that character would have been a meal, and some time ago Richard the Buddhist would have his balls cut out with a blunt knife.

Putting aside the idea of Karen's present and of doing stuff at the bank, I lifted Henry back out of the pusher, tied him into place in his car seat, got Desdemona in there too – quite pleased with her morning's work she was, expecting a reward, most probably reckoning on an ice cream at the very least.

The Musée Matisse in the Villa des Arenes-de-Cimiez commemorates the master who made his life up there from the late 1930s pretty much until he died in 1954. It is over the road from what's left of a Roman arena and overlooks the city of Nice and the very blue water of the bay beyond. Wandering through the rooms of the house, admiring the fairly thin selection of his work on display there, I have often been reminded that a critic once wrote of Matisse's studies of the female nude, 'the female animal in all her shame and horror', and I have wondered how it can be that one person might so totally fail to comprehend the art of another.

There have been times when I've looked at Matisse's images – and believe me I've had cause to study them closely – and thought how vacuous it all seems. But then there have been times when I've looked at the whole of life and come to the same conclusion.

Walking the museum's rooms up there at Cimiez, checking my watch from time to time, staring at what was hanging on the walls, at stuff like his *Nude in an Armchair with a Green Plant*, *Nymph in the Forest*, a portrait of his wife, Amelie, painted in 1905, it seemed impossible not to be impressed by this master of pictorial ease. There were a lot of seemingly less significant drawings and designs hanging about, too, mostly of flowers and fruits, plus ground-breaking sketches for the Matisse Chapel at Vence. Me, whenever I visited the museum I tended to end up standing, dumb with admiration, before the 1950s paper cut outs, *Créole Dancer* and *Blue Nude* number whatever.

But not while waiting for Stan Kriticos to turn up. My mind wasn't really on art, so I couldn't get a proper grip on its magic. What I found myself doing was glancing this way and that to catch an imagined figure threatening me from a doorway, even checking through the windows for the Mercedes' bright yellow duco. I guess I was trapped in a triangle made up of fear, loathing and the desire to know what was going on.

My mind kept replaying the encounter I'd had on the street not so long before. I was regretting letting the street scrag in the black suit go. To do that, how stupid was I? And yet, at the time with Henry and Desdemona ... I recognized that to even consider bringing my infant son to this meeting with Stan had been stupid. Yet I'd had to, or what was I to have told Karen. For reassurance I put a hand in my pocket, fingered the .22 pistol I'd just acquired, pulled it out, discretely checked it over. I was nervous enough to make sure it was ready to fire.

Then I put it back in my pocket.

Brought it out again, checked it over. Going crazy in a small way.

The Musée Matisse tends to be empty of visitors in the mornings, the skeleton staff running the place don't exactly hang about, either. Most of the time I was alone, with Henry standing by my side in the art-filled rooms. Thinking about Stan Kriticos.

Dangerous stuff, but I stayed. Indeed, the two of us hung about there for most of an hour, during which time Henry dropped off to sleep in my arms, awoke, went back to sleep again. He was getting pretty heavy when, turning my attention away from a view of the car parking area and back to the largest *Blue Nude* paper cutout, I caught sight of a girl who looked a lot like Holly might be expected to look when not sitting with Stan in a nasty two-door yellow Mercedes with electrically heated seats, satellite tracking, the lot.

Stan had sent a messenger!

I assumed she recognised me. She would, wouldn't she? There wasn't anybody else hanging about waiting to be met.

'No Stan?' I blurted out, revealing to myself and to this new arrival how wound up I had become about the assignation.

'I beg your pardon?'

She was right across the far side of the room, standing in a doorway, sunlight flaring behind her. 'No Stan?' I asked again.

She retreated. And I was walking quickly after her, asking her, too loudly, would she wait a minute, please?

Only, finally when she turned and faced me did I realize I had the wrong girl. This one, wide eyed, fearful, I might have thought, was staring at the infant held in my arms. Collecting herself, next thing she was demanding that I leave her alone.

Which was when I realised I had the .22 pistol out of my

pocket, in my right hand; it must have been pressed against Henry's flank.

Out of there, Essington.

Driving down from Cimiez, direction home, cutting across town, navigating Place Garibaldi, I couldn't believe it but I spotted Karen and Richard in the crowd of mostly tourists hanging about fish restaurants, ice cream vendors, boulangeries, and coffee bars. They were two people at a small square table set on the pavement, sitting close together, a water bottle and two glasses in front of them. I sensed a kind of intimacy between them and felt incredibly sad. Then, despite the gun in my pocket, I drove straight on by.

My heart was pounding in my chest as though the regulator had lost control. Was I going to explode? That's how I was as the Bentley rolled back in through the gates of Villa du Phare. Only once out of the car, the dog out too, and me unbuckling Henry from his safety seat, did I notice there was an envelope on the driver's seat. I'd been sitting on it all the way home. Inside a note: 'Not just a pretty face, Essington. That girl you met yesterday, Holly, she is an art expert. Tells me the Kandinsky isn't any good. How are we going to fix this up, Essington? Think about it. Hope your kid is okay.'

Printed with a laser printer on standard paper. No Stan Kriticos signature, nothing. Just three lines of Times Roman printed on the crappy sheet of too-white paper.

Chapter 8

In Sydney, Australia, I woke in the same hospital bed. My neighbour in the straight jacket was still my neighbour. The next bed along was empty. Bobby was sitting on a chair at my side. First up I didn't recognize him.

There was a chart at the end of my bed. Nice graph, nasty graph, I couldn't work it out. Maybe it wasn't a graph at all. Out through the window I could see two paperbark trees and a stretch of green-painted steel picket fence.

'What are you doing here?'

'I brought you here.'

'Why?'

'I'm on the payroll, remember?'

Then he told me about happening to be around when I collapsed in the street.

'You just happened to be there? You and me diluted by– how many people are there in Sydney? You were watching me, weren't you? Who asked you to do that?'

'I reckon you did.'

'I said I'd let you know when …'

'Mate, in my book falling over in the street is like letting someone know.'

I can't remember where the conversation went from there. I have an idea I slipped back into sleep.

And woke with Bobby still beside me, in the chair.

'Don't you have something better to do?'

'Like what?'

'Like getting me something to drink.'

'There's water.'

'I meant something to drink.'

He just shook his head. 'Oh mate,' he said, 'you really do have problems.'

'Then get me out of here, for Christ's sake, do it.'

First things first. So it was out of the hospital and straight away I got out of that hotel suite, too, and moved into the apartment. I didn't do it to save money, but it did save money. Lots of it. On the other hand it created an unexpected cooking situation; it hadn't occurred to me that there wasn't room service in apartment blocks.

The interior was pretty much the way Mister D had left it. Which meant buying bits of cheap modernist furniture and some essential electrical goods like a coffee machine and a sandwich maker. His arm a little delicate still from the break, Bobby was coming and going, doing most of the work. As part of employment deal mark two, he was allocated bedroom number three; back to where he'd been when Mister D was the man. Bedroom number two was to be my studio, so I asked him to fix a padlock to its door.

'Why would you need a padlock? You already have a lock on the front door, and at street level too. Fix one to that door and it is defaced. I'm going to have to drill holes, screw screws into it and into the door jamb as well if you want to make it secure with a bolt.'

'You're telling me about defacing the joint! Look around at what your last employer did. Anyway, if the work offends you, get a locksmith, I don't care. I need it locked up, okay?'

Bobby shrugged his shoulders.

'Have you been seeing anybody hanging about?'

'There's people all over the place.'

'But hanging about? You know what I mean.'

'You collapse in the street, you're just getting out of hospital, mate ...' He was looking at me meaningfully while tapping the side of his head with his forefinger, pointing to the existence of the human brain. 'Paranoia wouldn't be the word by any chance?'

That was when I showed him a couple of images I had in my laptop. I showed him one I'd got of Schwartz in profile, sitting in the Bounty Bar. His head was askew in the frame because I'd taken it wide angle with the camera at waist height when approaching the table where he had been waiting for me. And there were his hands, fingers interlocked forming a chapel. As well I clicked up the zoom blow-up of Alison talking to Giovanna in the street. There they were, the two women, side by side.

He wasn't sure.

I clicked up one more mug shot. It was a photo of Stan Kriticos taken out off one of his property development promotion brochures. Suit and tie, hair fluffed up by some stylist, Stan was wearing the smile of a mass murderer on holidays in the tropics.

'Someone looking very much like that was in the lobby of the hotel, the day before yesterday I think it must have been. Could have been a bit younger. Didn't get a good look but … Who is he, anyway?'

'Bobby, all you need to know is he's real trouble,' I said, my heart sinking.

'Mate, what kind of trouble would that be you're talking about?'

'I wish I knew.' Then I clicked up an image of Desdemona and told him, 'My dog.'

I asked him to arrange the lease on a car as well.

'I've got a car.'

'Whatever, there's a parking spot under the building. Goes with the apartment, might as well use that.'

'I'm in there already.'

'What sort of car?'

'Motor up one end, spare wheel at the other. You know, a Holden.'

There were a few weeks to pass before the appointments that had been lined up for me with specialists who were supposed to work out what had gone wrong inside, and/or if, as the doctors had suspected at the hospital, I was just one more case of middle-aged male depression with a substance abuse chaser. Assuming that the doctors could have been pretty much on the money, I took myself off to a tropical island in North Queensland for three weeks. The place featured an inbuilt health resort with masseurs, dietitians, personal trainers, you name it. My idea was to get healthy, swim a mile a day, fish, snorkel, splash around in one of the resort's many play pools, wink at female fellow guests, female staff, possibly give the occasional one permission to shag my brains out. Most of all I wanted to be at a place where the cast of people crowding in on my imagination were not.

I didn't catch any fish. Didn't get laid either. But I developed some real muscle tone, lowered my blood pressure, and got a tan. On the last morning I looked at myself in the mirror and what I saw there almost smiled back at me.

Grand prix racing, Christ knows where, on the TV. For comfort there was a half drunk bottle of wine in its ice bucket at my side, and a bottle of vodka in the freezer in case of unexpected drops in my sugar levels.

There had been a resolution made. During my brief stay in hospital I got the feeling that to make a decision, whatever it might happen to be, was a good thing to do. Clear goals should help me connect with the world. But what to do now I had moved house and purchased myself a live-in friend in the form of Bobby?

What I had to do was quit frigging around and get my art deal happening, Schwartz or no Schwartz. That way, I convinced myself, I would regain some confidence.

But, oh dear, the maze we call the human brain! No sooner

had I decided to get the art thing happening than Giovanna came into my mind. And then, of course, next came Alison. Before I knew what was going on I was thinking about Thea and Mandy, or had it been Leah and Mandy? and the threat their possession of that memory stick represented to my marriage.

On the other hand there was the Karen and Richard problem.

I'd perform this little play in my imagination. Richard walking through the crowded Place Garibaldi, and me encountering him there as if by pure chance. He'd greet me with a Buddhist smile, a nod of the head, humility. I'd do the same back. We'd stand locked in spiritual greeting then I'd reach forward, cup a loving hand behind his neck, pull his head closer and break his nose with a neat head butt. Tourists all about us, popping photographs, cheering, screaming, 'Go Essington, get the bastard!'

I fetched the vodka out of the freezer.

Other times I'd pull out that .22 and pop a bullet into the middle of his sanctimonious gaze.

Question, from nowhere in particular: Why had Sparrow wanted to get in touch with me so badly? He knew I was no longer happy with him.

Another: What about Stan's insane demand that I buy back the paintings. Could that be real? Was he really in Sydney?

I poured a double shot of vodka then connected with the internet to check for emails that might have accumulated. There was indeed a bunch of them, mostly stuff from businesses I had no recollection of every having dealings with. One, a catalogue update from Johnstone & Lang Art Auctions, okay. And one with attachments from Kriticos Inc.

It turned out that Stan had sent me as attachments a compressed JPEG image of every one of the paintings and drawings he had decided I should buy back. Plus the email itself, a curt reminder that I had promised to do the deal.

So soon, he was telling me I had promised!

What deal was that, exactly?

All I could remember was telling him no way would I do that.

I poured some vodka down my throat and was opening the images one by one.

Next I poured myself a refreshing glass of dry white wine.

Then another vodka.

I was shocked at the quality of these works of art represented by the JPEG images he'd sent. For a brief and disappointing moment I thought they were indeed images of the pictures I'd sold him, and that I'd been kidding myself about how good my own work was. Such low-grade imitations, every one. Definitely not my handiwork. I asked myself, how could Holly have had problems with the Kandinsky, in particular, amongst this lot? These were the kind of paintings, 'in-the-style-of' was the polite way of expressing it, which you could have painted for you in South East Asia. There they had factories full of disappointed artists producing them in the great European tradition of oil on canvas. Send a good quality photo image of a Cézanne Mont Sainte-Victoire landscape over there and for not a lot of money you got back a genuine oil painting.

The hospital experience and just about everything else happening around me had reduced my confidence to where I believed I might have done them. Though to have imagined that was crazy. My art is the refinement of forgery, not its debasement. The JPEG images Stan had sent were so clearly fakes, lacking historical understanding and any sense of the art-ists' real concerns.

A true work of art has confronted a series of problems and found unique solutions to them. It surprises, it tests itself over and over again, exploits the individual language of brush marks, subtle or blatant colour shifts, the interplay of negative and positive space. Real works of art surprise the viewer, not just once but again and again, over the years. That's what it's all about, art.

Without having the slightest feeling for creative processes, Stan had got these pictures made, most probably in Vietnam or the Philippines. I felt sure that an examination of each one's painted surface would leave an even worse impression than that which I had received from the decompressed images I'd been clicking up on my screen.

Sitting there checking the images I recognized the possibility that Stan had lost faith in the paintings I'd sold him, maybe because of what Holly had said about the Kandinsky he'd once tossed contemptuously against the wall. Had other people expressed doubts to him about the authenticity of pieces in the collection? It was possible.

And impossible for me to know for sure. Holly could have doubted the Kandinsky for the wrong reasons, and then shot off her mouth, the way people her age may be inclined to do.

Whatever, Stan was pushing me, that was for sure, keeping me rattled, causing me to fear what he might try next. Coercing me to agree to buy back the paintings, he was planning to keep his side of the deal by delivering cheap copies. Leaving him with the original collection, and his money back. That was his property developer's way of doing business in a life-game the object of which was to be the richest man left standing.

And Inspector Schwartz?

I had a half-empty glass in front of me. And a wine bottle. A vodka bottle as well, three-quarters empty. Directly behind that still life, the laptop's screen was shining silver around the low-grade copy of my Matisse painting, *Femme Couchée*. The tableau seemed to me to be some kind of representation of reality. I pushed the wineglass up against the laptop's keyboard. The two bottles were standing in front of it, one more empty than the other. The scene blurred as my eyes went to focus on some point behind the screen, beyond the wall behind, outside the room.

Thinking about Schwartz. None of it made sense.

There was a moment when I must have wondered if I had it the wrong way round, and Schwartz was after Stan, using me to catch him. He's mentioned Stan's name to me, to check the effect, going so far as calling him my 'associate'! Later he'd told me Stan was in Sydney, again checking how I'd react.

Sitting there, the misunderstood Matisse shining out of the screen at me, wineglass hemmed in by the two bottles, nowhere to move, I could believe police all around the world might be after Stan and exchanging information on him with one another. Because he was the same vicious character everywhere he roamed.

Then I lost the thread.

After the next drawing session, escorting a model called Janet out of the building and into the street, the first thing I spotted was Inspector Schwartz pretending to read a paper while sitting in an unmarked sedan.

I wasn't going to play dumb and sneak past him?

No way.

After only a moment's hesitation, I split from Janet, who seemed happy enough with the hundred dollar bonus for services over and above straight modelling. I wandered over to the car, 'Mind if I join you, Inspector?'

Give him credit, he didn't pretend surprise. He said, 'Whatever you did to that girl, Mr Holt, you certainly made her happy.'

Looking straight at him, 'Which girl are we talking about here?'

'I wasn't thinking of the solicitor. Though it's interesting, isn't it, calling them that, solicitors. When, or rather if you come to think about it.'

'Oh I think of stuff like that all the time. But which solicitor did you have in mind?'

There I was, same situation I'd been in with Stan down near the quay at Villefranche-sur-Mer. I was leaning over talking in through a car window.

'The one you use as your shield, Ms Cecchini. But why would you ask that, tell me, do there happen to be others?'

'There could be.' I straightened up, looked at the sky. Light cloud, a flock of little birds way up there, so high. At his window again, 'Schwartz, is it strictly within the law for you to be stalking me like this? Have we stepped into some totalitarian mind space without anybody telling anybody it's happened?'

'Stalking! I am a busy man with better things to do, Mr Holt. And right now I'm in line for an early tea break. Would you care to join me?'

After a moment's hesitation I said, 'Why not, you creepy bastard.'

He smiled. I smiled.

There was a chichi café round the corner from my front door, stainless steel tables, buttery friands, flourless cakes, home baked muffins. When I'd been in before to ask if they'd send meals up to the apartment they hadn't bothered to answer the question. Treated me like I was one of the homeless. Schwartz ordered peppermint tea. They didn't have alcohol so I asked for a glass of water. For the next fifteen minutes – it felt more like an hour – we talked small talk, the two of us, mostly about how screwed up the world is. He wasn't concerning himself with the big picture. Rather, he got into attacking new software the police department had installed, and the associated training sessions he'd been obliged to attend. And then, in painstaking detail he explained the ways in which the software didn't work and why it should be scrapped, and how much the whole exercise had cost and what the fraud squad could have done with that much money.

Somewhere in all that I must have switched off.

Eventually he noticed. Most likely he'd rehearsed the whole spiel anyway. Because next thing, totally out of the blue he was asking me about Gerald Sparrow, and exactly where he fitted in.

'Fit into what, Inspector?'

'Your plans here in Australia. Kriticos and Sparrow, there's a connection there. Anything you could tell us would be, ah, appreciated.'

A connection? 'Would it surprise you to learn that I know nothing, and there are no plans, other than selling an apartment?'

'As always I am pleased to hear it from your lips. Your interest in art is on hold, then?'

'My interest in art, what are you trying to say? I do my drawings, you'd know that because you've made knowing what I do your business.'

'I was hoping you'd expand on the art theme for me, just a little. Of course I'm fascinated. The arts, they are food for the soul.'

'We know I am into art. It's what I do. You saw the drawings, remember? By the way, every one of those drawings your sad little helpers took away with them, they came back smudged. If you are going to take an interest in the art world you better learn how to handle the stuff. But me, Essington Holt, I'm a rank amateur, you understand? You know, I know, that all manner of nasty little financial tricks are played with art. Casinos, art galleries, these are ways of laundering money, causing suitcases of cash to vanish into thin air. Pay attention to that, why don't you. But me, I draw as a hobby. And my purpose for being here in Australia is a hundred percent tied up with selling an apartment. Boring but true. Or I'd be doing my drawings back home, wouldn't I?'

'Why would you come all this way to sell an apartment. It's never made sense to me.'

'Nor to me either. My wife told me to do it.'

A smile playing round the corners of his mouth, 'Surely, given the excellent relationship you appear to enjoy with your solicitor … I would have thought you could sell the real estate by phone, you know, or fax, even by email, we are in the age of electronic communication.'

'There was a stuff-up and somebody needed to set things right.'

'Which, as we know you went ahead and did, in your own unique fashion. There are professionals you hire to get unwanted tenants out of apartments. Ms Cecchini would know who to approach, surely. Or if not her, then your other solicitor, Gerald Sparrow.'

'Why are we having this conversation?'

He held his arms spread wide and wiggled his fingers as if to illustrate the point. But what point? 'I am not getting a proper feeling for what is at the heart of these matters.'

'Which matters?'

Bringing his hands together till the palms met at nose level. 'The people you associate with …'

His dark Schwartz eyes watching me all the time.

'Put your questions to Giovanna Cecchini?'

'I already have. She insists you are here to sell the apartment.'

'Who were you really watching out for, parked down there on the street? It's not me, is it. You are checking who I have visiting? Chief Inspectors don't do this. You're supposed to be sitting at a desk, giving orders to underlings.'

'Brink of retirement, I'm afraid. Not a lot expected of me.'

'Sad.'

'You don't mean it, and it isn't. I see your friend Bobby Chisholm coming and going. So, you're giving orders to underlings, that's clear enough.'

'His name's Chisholm? Don't know why but I never

thought of him having a family name.'

He sipped his tea, I drank my water. The silence grew until I was conscious of soft music playing in the café. A trained soprano ruining good Scottish ballads.

'Your friend Mr Sparrow seems to have disappeared. Do you know if he's in France?'

'He called me.'

'Long distance?'

'I don't know. Why France?' I asked, shocked.

'The Kriticos link. Will you tell me about it now?'

When I got up to go, Schwartz observed, as if for no reason at all, 'Matisse had domestic problems, too. In the south of France. Of course in your line of business you'd know all about it.'

'Forget you ever said that, Schwartz.'

'Threatening me?'

What a creepy bastard.

With the Matisse observation trilling in my ears I strutted off in search of … well, of psychological calm, I guess. And a real drink.

Sure, Matisse did have a domestic crises, her name was Lydia Delectorskaya. She turned up at his studio at the age of twenty-two, the master was about sixty at the time. At the start she was an assistant. She helped with nursing Amelie, Madame Matisse, before progressing to modelling and functioning as a kind of live-in secretary. Henri always called her Madame Lydia. Amelie regarded her as the princess of bitches and finally demanded that she quit the household, which was when Henri put his foot down, 'Madame Lydia stays,' he said. Amelie went out the door, or so the story goes, and moved on to play the part of heroine while an operative in the French Resistance.

That was history.

Me, my life was now, and there was no way I was going to

let the Giovanna thing break up my happy home. What sort of sad decision was that, anyway, since Giovanna wouldn't let me near her? Worse, if Alison was to be believed, Giovanna was playing games of her own – and very possibly hers were dangerous games.

Could Stan Kriticos have been in touch with her as well?

And now Sparrow was missing in action. Oh dear.

Chapter 9

You live in a big city, you are trapped. In the midst of all that action and noise and glitter there's really nothing to do. It's all right if you are working through the day and substance-abusing and shagging yourself stupid through the night, but for the unemployed like me the daylight hours can really drag. I had my drawings, sure, but usually after a couple of hours my concentration gave out.

I headed for the street where I could switch off from being me for a while, melt into the throng, get human. That's me there wandering along Macquarie Street, hands clasped behind my back, maybe I'm whistling, or am I just in search of an innocent occupation, for once, something with which to occupy my mind that doesn't have guilt tagging along behind it.

I reckoned I could have done with Henry in his pusher trundling in front of me. With Henry about I felt more like your natural man.

Some say the fact that travelling men want to shag women they meet along the way is to do with nature, with the desire of the species to survive by broadening the genetic pool. Crusaders raped their way through the Balkans for Jesus, didn't they? At the same time, other people reckon it would be better for those same travelling men to take a cold shower, read Gideon's bible and watch Attenborough nature programs on television. Generally, travelling, my thoughts and inclinations are pushed this way, then pulled that. It's kind of like moral perpetual motion, me oscillating, be good – be wicked.

Did I wish I were circumnavigating the globe single-handed in a rowboat?

In a bar some people stipulate the brand of vodka they'll drink, being hip connoisseurs, I suppose. A person like me who takes vodka for its medicinal properties, I don't care which magazines advertise what I drink. I want a high proof percentage, that's all. To calm me down.

It can take a lot of vodka to calm me down.

Mid-afternoon I was sitting on a bench and gazing across the road at the gates to the botanical gardens. Pigeons were hanging about my feet, no doubt in the hope that, on a late lunch break, I might pull out a Tupperware box stuffed with crumbly sandwiches and lamingtons shedding their grated coconut, lovingly put together by the little woman back home. It was nice there on the bench. Behind me, patients were visiting their specialists to get the bad news. In front cars were streaming past, tourist buses heading for the Opera House, couriers on their bicycles, the knights of the business district.

My mobile rang. Bobby. 'Essington, what's the weather like up there?'

'I'm down here, Bobby. What's new?'

'These people you showed me pictures of, two of them just came out of that café round the corner, the one with the cakes you wouldn't want to eat.'

'Which two?'

'Cakes or people?'

'I'm not up to repartee … by the way, you never told me your name is Chisholm.'

'Repartee, is that some kind of a cake?'

'Enough. Who did you see come out?'

'Firstly it was the cop, Schwartz. I'd swear we locked eyes for a moment. Then that other guy, the one with the hairdo and the shirt and tie. You told me he was Greek.'

'They were together?'

'Pretending they didn't know each other. The cop came out first, walked away without looking back. Either that or it was a coincidence them being there at the same time, in a city of three million people.'

I grew cold, then hot, and then I said, 'The fact is you don't know for sure. People on the street don't look like their photographs, because their faces are in motion. Could it be you're telling me what you think I need to hear, Bobby? But why would I want to know those two were hanging out together?'

'You showed me their pictures and I just …'

'Maybe you're suggestible. You sure it was Schwartz?'

'Certain.'

'And Stan Kriticos?'

'Hard to say, really. Could be just a Greek-looking guy.'

'Same age?'

'Might have been younger.'

'So it could have been anybody coming out of the café with Schwartz?'

'Now you put it that way, well yes.'

For two weeks I couldn't get in touch with Karen. I'd ring and be talking to the answering machine. Or I'd try the other number and get Yassir. English wasn't Yassir's strong suit – although I got the impression he understood it better than he spoke it – and his French was a little worse than mine, from what I could work out.

At last Karen answered and told me that she'd been out of contact while on a trip up to Grenoble with Dawn.

'You carry a phone around with you, can't you answer it?'

'Actually, you're not going to like this, but we were at a Buddhist retreat.'

'You're not long off having the baby.'

'It's months yet.'

'What did you do with Henry while you two were up there going ooom or whatever tantric noise it's supposed to be that you lot make?'

'You are so antagonistic! Ever since I met you I've felt that there was something not quite right. Now I know it's this anger you have, Essington. There's a bomb inside you and it's waiting to go off.'

'I was asking about Henry.'

'Of course he came with us, and he adored it. You might not have thought this through properly, but even Buddhists have children. The difference is that unlike some people they enjoy spending their time with them.'

'I bet they like making babies, too.'

'Essington, you are so …'

'You think that for me Buddhists are just men in saffron togas, begging alms while concentrating on appearing to be absolutely calm. But when they're travelling the world they put up in five star hotels?' Silence. 'Karen, was it just the three of you, or did Richard tag along as well?'

'Where on earth does this anger come from? You seem to have an anti-me philosophy worked out, it's word perfect. Perhaps you should think more deeply about these things.'

'About …?'

'Buddhism, for instance, Essington, it could be just what you need. I've told you that before.'

'Karen, as far as children are concerned, I like being with Henry, understand? If I'd been offered the option I'd be with him now. Me being here was your idea.'

Once we'd got past bitching at each other, I asked Karen if Dawn had met up with the English girl I'd recommended,

Holly. The one who had been hanging about with Stan Kriticos. Karen didn't know. But she did add that she'd heard a story
circulating within the Australian expatriate community down
along the coast that a lot of people were after Kriticos's blood.
It was rumoured a big scheme of his had come unstuck and the
banks were chasing him for a considerably more than he was
worth. 'I never liked him, Essington. I know you were thinking
of doing some sort of art deal with him, but I never liked him.
You knew that, didn't you? Right now it looks like it was lucky
you pulled out. Even if a fraction late.'

'What do you mean a fraction late?'

'Your name has come up in connection with his. They're
talking about an Australian mafia. People are talking about Stan,
and some of that expat crowd living it up in Monaco, as well.'

'People are saying that about me?'

'There's no point breaking the law just for the thrill of it, is
there Essington? You get caught and ...'

'Australian mafia! I hear what you're telling me, too clearly.
Still, there's no need for us to go over that getting caught stuff
again. I told you how many times, that part of my career, it's
been closed down.'

'It should never have opened. And why was it? Because
you were looking in the wrong places for life's meaning. You
thought thrills equalled meaning. Essington, the truth is quite
the opposite ...'

'You said creditors are after Stan, has he gone missing or
what?'

'I wouldn't expect he's being missed. Only by those idiots
he owes money to. You recall the rumours connecting him with
that dead man they found in the park around Le Chateau, sitting on a park bench? Hadn't a dog been eating the man's leg? A
business associate. Well, Essington, you're his business associate
too, that's what they're saying in the papers.'

'They mentioned me?'

'Well, not directly, no.'

'You are holding back. Karen, what are you working up to telling me?'

'Give me time, Essington. It's just that it has been such a shock.'

'What has?'

'That the story has surfaced again. There was another, a double page article on Kriticos in *Nice Matin*. I guess you'd call it an exposé. Sensationalist. Drugs as well. Exporting cars with drugs hidden inside them. They were as good as asking why is this man living in our midst?'

'Reasonable question.'

'There hasn't been a connection made. But they've found another body.'

'Connected to Stan?'

'The paper insists on a connection, yes. A bizarre story. The body was imported. Somebody sent it by air to Marseilles, sealed in one of those big plastic chemical containers. Sent from Australia. That's why it's such a news story. Because it came from Australia.'

What could I say? My hand was trembling and a void had begun to form in my stomach. I couldn't tell her that Bobby had just seen Stan in Australia, talking to a cop who happened to be tailing me.

Karen asked: 'Essington?'

Maybe, really, the worst thing for me at that instant was the kind of distance Karen seemed to be putting between us. There was a tone she had adopted: uncaring, hard, arm's length. The old Karen would have at least displayed some real anger.

Was it true, I'd been sent to Sydney to get me out of her life?

'Why are you calling me Essington all the time, as though we've become strangers? You call me Ess, remember?'

'Have I been doing that? Sorry.'

But she didn't sound sorry, or worried about it. It was me who was worried. It wasn't as if I was talking with a woman who loved me.

'Anything else you would like to share with me, Karen?'

It was her turn to fall silent. I should have cut the call at that point, but I held on. Eventually she said. 'I promised I'd say something.'

'Promised who?'

'I'm, well, sort of involved with a person from the retreat.'

'Of course you would be, that's why you go there.'

'He's an artist, Essington, a real artist. From Bremen, he does assemblages.' She mentioned a name I vaguely knew.

'So much for Richard, then.'

'Essington.'

'I can see why the Taliban blew up all those fucking Buddhas. Thank you very much, Karen … for nothing at all.'

I'm not sure what I did immediately after putting the phone down, but some time later I was on all fours under the shower, rocking backwards and forwards like a chained elephant. I got myself out of the bathroom, towelled dry, and started speed-walking round the room, naked, picking things up, putting them down, talking nonstop, about me I guess. Along the way I tried to expunge from personal recall the bits about Karen's romance, then set to working obsessively through the rest of what had been said. Over and over. It was hard to tell what was the most dispiriting, the possibility of the banks putting Stan's art collection on the market – because that's what they do if you go belly-up – or a body turning up in a chemicals container, from Australia, and the press linking it to Stan.

Also, unforgivable, I'd forgotten to ask about Desdemona! That dog, nobody much for company other than the enigmatic gardener. It worried me, Desdemona and Yassir seemed to be forming an alliance of the taken-for-granted classes.

As far as the art collection was concerned, what would happen would be that the obvious forgeries he had offered to sell back to me would be what went to the banks. No doubt the law would check them over as well. Mister Banker would get them valued and some arty guy, most probably in London, would point out that they weren't worth anything. Stan would explain that they came from me and no matter what happened from then on, my name would be linked to the idea of forgery. Any painting out there in the world with my name showing up in its provenance would come under scrutiny. And it didn't take much imagination to work out what would happen next. It didn't matter that I'd had nothing to do with those pictures, the mud would stick.

All of which constituted an argument for me buying the paintings back. But not those cheap imitations Stan had sent images of, what I needed to buy back were the paintings I'd supplied him with in the first place. I could manage that, and sell them off one by one. Yet something inside told me not to do it. Call it pride? Might have been pride. More like stupidity.

A big problem, reputation-wise, was clearly the fact of me ever having being tied in with Stan Kriticos.

Going for the ice cubes, it hit me how strange life is, what with Karen turning into the kind of girl who goes for artists. They needed to be into Buddhism as well, sure, but art was the common denominator. Starting with me. She'd been working her way up from a lowly forger whose sensibility was stuck in what they used to call 'modern' art, via Richard the avant-gardist who placed found shards of glass, colour coordinated, into glass display cases, on to this hot-shot from Bremen who did installations with, I had been led to understand, video.

A clean reputation is important in my line of business. That was where I was really screwing up. Or being screwed. Once they think you are a crook, they won't believe what you have to say about a work of art, because art is supposed to be so spiritual.

The body in the chemicals container? Being dead would be an even worse blow to my business and not in the slightest bit spiritual, no, not at all.

One more fuse went in my brain. There had to be a lot of circuits down by then. Very possibly too many. But as it happened I still had a few to go.

I was watching the broadcast of a tennis match from Indian Wells, tippling at the same time, occasionally walking round the apartment, checking out the drawings I had strewn all over the place, from that morning's session, of a model named Sally who seemed to be more frightened than anything else. I'd said to her, 'I'm not going to hurt you, for Christ's sake!' She said, 'There are a lot of ways a person can get hurt.' So, I'd elected for silence through the rest of the session. Silence and Johnny Hartman singing over the top of John Coltrane. Funny thing was, the drawings turned out really good. And, the ultimate compliment, Sally had wanted to take one home with her.

Bobby had put the bolt and padlock on the door of the second bedroom. The two of us had set the room up as a studio with ultra violet lights, work benches, an easel. It wasn't particularly spacious, but it was fine for what I wanted to do. But before I could really get going I had to conclude a pact of some sort with Bobby. Already it was worked out that he'd be out of there whenever a model was booked. That suited him fine. He wasn't interested in my drawings, or in me doing them. I guess he reckoned it was just a sex thing I had going. As far as life was concerned, Bobby wasn't easy to surprise. Except when it came to my drinking, maybe.

About three in the afternoon Bobby knocked at the door, came in.

He'd kind of come into a room, Bobby, and nothing would

change in his face. He'd just look at you the way a raptor might. Uninvolved but alert. Always alert, Bobby.

It hit me then, I suppose for the first time, that I was seeing a subtly transformed character. If you knew what to look for you still might suspect that he'd done time, though I'd noticed he didn't loop an arm protectively around his plate any more when eating at a table. He'd changed his get-up as well. Still the alligator skin cowboy boots, yes, but now he was in a loose-fitting microfibre suit with dropped shoulders, black tee shirt under. Three days growth. Could have been a hard man, could have been a fashion designer fresh home from the pin-and-tuck end of the catwalk. Funny what regular blobs of money will do for a man.

Bobby avoided looking at the drawings, of course.

I asked if he'd eaten and he said he was fine.

'Maybe you'd like to sit down then.'

So he sat down.

We were like that, awkward with each other. Neither of us knew what we were supposed to be doing next. I guessed that was why he snooped around behind me, to feel employed. Either that or he was lying, and Schwartz or Giovanna or Stan or Christ-knows-who had been asking him questions about what I was up to.

'Bobby, I don't like to pry, you know.' Slumped in a chair, staring at me, massaging the elbow area of the arm that had been in the sling. He didn't say a thing. 'But, as soon as I came across you being called Chisholm I realized that you have a history.'

'Reckoned I was found in a basket floating amongst the bulrushes? Get real, Essington, what are you trying to say?

'Well, tell me something about yourself?'

Which he did. Yes, he'd spent three years in jail and was still on parole.

'You are reporting?'

'Regular as clockwork. Mate, you do time in jail either you

can't wait to get back inside there or you are like, no, never.'

'And before that?'

'I was a clerk in the public service.'

'You were a what?'

'Essington, you are so like everybody else. Did you know that? You have these attitudes that are really fucked. I tell you that I worked in the public service and you go, "You did what?" As if I told you I had walked on the moon. Except that isn't what you are meaning, is it? Same in prison, they go, "Here's Bobby the public servant, who wants him for a bum boy?"'

'Hold it, is it possible you are getting a little carried away here?'

'Mate, actually I wouldn't say so.'

'Then I'm sorry.' He appeared surprised to hear me say that. 'What kind of department were you in?'

'Public health, I did run-of-the-mill stuff, working on estimates, outcomes, you know, it's a language.'

'And?'

'Manslaughter, a car accident … I was drunk.'

'So, you're not like, a criminal?'

'That's the whole point, Essington, I am a criminal.'

I don't know why but I said, 'So am I.' And out of nowhere other than an excess of booze – so what was new there – I told him all about Stan and Schwartz and the painting deals I'd done since way back when. Before I'd finished we were standing in the bedroom that was now a studio and gazing down upon the Derain nude looking snug and very genuine in its water-gilded frame. Signature revealed. But I didn't actually spell it out about forging the works of art.

Ready for delivery to Julian Anderson. In fact it's delivery becoming a fraction overdue. Which was often the case with me. Hard not to get attached to the products of my craft.

It was getting to where I had to argue myself into leaving the apartment. While Bobby was in and out like a jack in the box.

I asked him, 'What do you do out there on the street?'

'I get away from you, because it's so depressing watching you drink, and I observe the world.'

'What are you seeing out there?'

'It's what I'm not seeing that's so interesting.'

Mysterious.

A few days later we were sitting watching a quarter-finals game at Indian Wells, Bobby was drinking diet Coke, I was working my way down a bottle of chablis. He was telling me about how he'd been employed by a promotions company looking after a couple of star tennis players from Russia. When I asked what that involved, without being the slightest bit interested in his reply, he got into explaining to me how people get fixated on sports stars. 'Sexual fantasies, or they want to kill them. Driven by this thing inside them. It's a bit like that with people in prison, Essington. The moment they lock you up, your head is emptied of anything you might have been hoping for. Mate, because of being that way you are like a wounded dog in a pack. They all turn on you, the guards, just about everyone. In the end you have to work out how you are going to get through this time, and doing that starts to teach what you are capable of.'

'I don't see the connection, the people stalking sports stars, prisoners behaving badly. No, I don't get it.'

'I had six years, minimum, right?' From there he went on to tell me about how he'd been in the army, but that hadn't been any kind of preparation for incarceration. 'Put a bunch of battle-trained guys from the army against prisoners who've done some time, you know, guys who are about the same age, the same fitness, the army wouldn't stand a chance.'

On television a tie-breaker had run up to thirteen-twelve. Both players as extended as you could get. Of course, I didn't ask Bobby what happened to the three-year sentence he'd told me earlier he had been given for manslaughter. Nor about his public service career. There didn't seem to be much point, did there?

Bobby was making up his life story as he went along – for my benefit.

Some people will do that to you.

Gerald Sparrow, for instance, before I cut off all contact with him, it had got to where I couldn't believe a word he said.

We sat in silence watching the ball go backwards and forwards across the television screen. Then Bobby said, 'Oh, but mate, somebody dumps you in a prison cell, how you feel then, you wouldn't want to know about it. When you lose it you're like, unstoppable, mate.' A rare smile, 'You're not a civilized person any more.'

Another time he had launched into a story about his aborted rugby league career.

I had a fantasy factory in my employ.

'You haven't spotted Schwartz or Stan again?'

'Nope.'

'Wonder what that means? Maybe the police department found something socially useful for Schwartz to do.'

'But I saw that girl, Essington.'

'Who?'

'Alison, I think it was, going into Giovanna's building. Tell me, how do you get to know all these people if you don't even live here?'

'Bobby, I don't, they get to know me … and too well, or so it seems. But you said you saw Alison visiting Giovanna, when exactly?'

I did a lot of thinking. Some vague planning, too. And I went walking because one of the specialists I'd seen told me to. She claimed that a tendency to withdraw from society could get hold of a person and not let go. I had to fight it, I had to go out there on a daily basis, eyeball my fellow citizens.

There I was, a mental wreck with muscle tone and a suntan, walking down Martin Place, heading for the city's hub. Coming to one of those men's clothing shops that dare you to pay for what they've got on display, I entered and emerged half an hour later decked out in a light-weight Italian suit, straight off the rack because I'm a standard size kind of a person.

Next I found a place to eat and settled at a table snug against the window and ordered a bottle of sauvignon blanc to go with duck and fennel risotto. Facing the street, I sat and watched the girls go by.

I was bringing a loaded fork to my mouth when I couldn't believe my luck, there was Inspector Schwartz standing across the road. Amazing. Like he just happened to be there. He was talking on a mobile.

A bus propped, blocking my line of sight, rolled forward a couple of metres, propped again. Then it drove away. No Schwartz over there.

Medicos and hospitals notwithstanding, I had to be staying at least half crazy, didn't I? Everywhere I looked the same cast of people kept popping up and if I gazed back inside myself as often as not I would be imagining performing some sex thing with Giovanna.

When, right out loud, I instructed myself 'go back to go', a waiter hurried over asking if everything was all right.

'Just talking to myself.'

He said, 'Oh, I do that all the time, it saves having to buy drinks for acquaintances.'

'My father said it's the first sign of madness.'

'Very old fashioned.'

He left me to feed myself, sip wine and muse.

A phone was ringing somewhere in the restaurant. Next thing the waiter is coming towards me, holding a cordless out from his ear. 'Mr Holt?' he asked.

'Who wants to know?'

'It's a call, for you.'

'Yes?' I asked the telephone.

'Stan Kriticos.'

'I was just talking about you.'

'I wouldn't advise you to be talking about me to anybody, particularly not since you are eating on your own.'

'What can I do for you, Stan?'

'You can do the arithmetic. I'm asking you for the last time, add up what I paid you for those fucking paintings, deduct ten percent, get a bank cheque to me.'

'I thought you understood, I'm not going to do this.'

'I say do it. That's the choice, Essington. And don't forget there's that kid of yours, what was his name, Henry?'

'Don't think about it, Stan …'

'All you've got to do is pay the money. It was a guarantee you gave me.'

'I told you before, Stan, I guaranteed you the quality of the work.'

'And we all know about that, don't we? So, do it.' Raising his voice.

I was looking around in the restaurant, out in the street. Where the hell was Stan? Which continent? 'Where are you?' I asked.

'Tell your wife, Karen isn't it? Tell her what I want and what I'll do if I don't get it. Her opinion counts. Mothers, you know how they are, Essington. Tell her that if I don't get the money I get your boy. Then I'll be asking her nicely just like I'm asking you now. And so it goes.'

He disconnected.

I went to ice inside.

Schwartz came striding in through the door and straight to my table.

'This is a surprise.'

'A really nice one,' I replied. 'Where's Stan?'

Life is a see-saw, while you are going up nothing is more certain than that you are going to head right back down again. Me, I always hoped to be riding once more the kind of upswing that had led me to the inheritance of millions, not for the money itself, but for the feeling of being blessed that comes with it. Yet in my heart I knew that crap like a fresh suit of clothes was about as good as things were likely to get for me from then on. By degrees my brain, my liver, my skin, my just about everything would wither and die.

What's worse, my risotto had gone cold before I could finish it.

I had finished the wine, but of course. Even ordered another bottle, while Schwartz pushed down the plunger on his green tea.

'You're the police, so say if I was being threatened, would that concern you?'

'Actually, in your case, I don't think so.'

All the pieces on the chess board had been moved, or was it the goal posts? The truth is I don't play chess, I don't play football any more either. I get too wound up when things start to go against me in real life to be capable of handling parlour games. So I bid Schwartz farewell, paid and got the hell out of there.

'What are you trying to prove, Pops?'

I looked sideways and up. Fresh-faced character, in his mid-twenties, wearing one of those bottom lips and jaws they get through orthodontic intervention. White cut-away collar, striped shirt. Nothing in his eyes, except the excitement of reckoning he was somebody on the way up. It must have been him shouldering me along the bar. And I had been holding position, protecting a little line of vodkas.

I picked up vodka number three, tipped it down my throat.

The fact is there was a bit of a crush at the bar. It was that time of day, after six, they'd let the loonies out of the high rise offices after hours pretending they had the foggiest idea of what was going on in the global markets.

'Did you hear me talking to you?'

There are some people it is hard to believe.

Because next thing he was addressing some third party, but in a voice loud enough for me to hear over the bar's general din. He was saying something particularly disparaging about me.

In that bar I wasn't receiving the respect a distinguished international art forger deserves.

So I slid off the stool backwards, shoving my butt out to push whoever was behind me back a little further. So many people there we were nose to nose. I said, 'Course I heard you talking to me.' Reached my hand into a gap being filled at the bar, picked up the last of the vodkas, threw it into his face at the same time as I grabbed his balls and twisted.

Gasping, he dropped out of my line of sight.

'Don't you just hate it …' I had started to say something along those lines to a dumb shit with the noose of his tie loosened, who happened to be looking straight at me from too close, when somebody walloped me on the side of the head. Must have been a pal of the character with the crushed balls. Hard to comprehend what those types see in one another. Indignant, I brought my forehead down onto this fresh assailant's nose, spun around, elbows out, to make some space for myself, but already a third party had got an arm around my neck, attacking from behind. So I hit reverse into the crowd, still with this arsehole riding on my back.

And so it goes.

The mêlée developed a life of its own during which I extricated myself, somehow, made it to the street and into a cab before eager cops had alighted from the Paddy wagon just pulled up outside.

And home I went.

When I came in through the apartment door, this wall of sound hit me. A whole bunch of violins and whatever hitting their straps. Bobby was on his feet. Happy expression. Close to ecstatic. Then seeming to resent the intrusion.

He said, 'Essington, look at you.'

'The noise, Bobby! Think of the neighbours.'

'It's called romantic music. And we don't have neighbours. On this floor it's just us. Everything else is unoccupied. Remember?'

'In my book romantic would be something like *Harvest Moon*. Anyhow, I don't care about this, just get it out of here.'

He walked to the machine, turned the volume down a whisper. I slumped into a cheapo armchair, rested there maybe twenty seconds, got up again, went to the freezer, pulled out the bottle of vodka.

I was taking a second swig, so cold my lips were sticking to the glass, when Bobby confronted me. Standing straight, hands on his hips. He seemed to be launching into some kind of a speech. I could sense he'd been workshopping it in his mind. Like a wronged wife. Or a parole officer. Or both.

'We have to talk.'

'Be easier if you turned that noise off.'

'That noise is Rachmaninov. It's called the radio.'

'People like you don't listen to shit like that. You want Willie Nelson.'

The orchestra calmed down and some slow piano playing came in over the top.

'People like me! What do you mean by that?'

I took another suck at the bottle, still so cold it was making my hand ache.

'Forget it. I don't mean anything.'

'Of course you do. Mate, I've been in jail so I'm doomed to listen to country music, isn't that what you're saying? And you're half right. Except, in there they have an education program, for what it's worth. I started with guitar, then that teacher quit and we got this other one who did music appreciation. The high spot of the week. What had I been missing?'

'Damaged ear drums.'

'Essington, it's changing all the time, the volume, the rhythm, even the key.'

'Doesn't make an iota of difference to me, Bobby.'

'I am beginning to think nothing does. You are a lost cause. I mean, mate, how did you get in the state you are in right now? You've been in a brawl. You're wearing a cut above the eyebrow.'

Another swig. 'Bullshit.'

'Don't believe me, go and look at yourself.' I went silent. I suppose sullen, too.

'Music might be what you need. All this art you go for, and you're an ammunition dump waiting to explode.'

Extended silence. Him looking at me. Like he was trying to remember some next point he'd intended to make. Something about music learnt in jail.

The slow piano kept on going, with some soft violin behind. Not too bad. But I wasn't going to get to like it.

Returning to the prepared script, Bobby said, 'You've got more trouble connecting to you than you can wave a stick at. But do you think it through? No way. You get pissed. You stuff up. People out there in the street, what are you saying to them? What do you tell Schwartz while you are falling to pieces in front of him? It's anybody's guess.'

The orchestra was gathering strength, becoming really objectionable. And the pianist was fighting back, full bore.

Bobby: 'I don't want to know what's going on inside your head. But mate, I'm employed by you, I've got responsibilities.

So, cut down on the drinking and get a life or you are on your own.'

'How I want to be, on my own, right.'

'Exactly wrong. You're the kind that can't stand being alone. So you drink. You don't get it, do you? Good music is a be-on-your-own type of thing.'

'Choirs?'

'Listening to music. You do it in your head, by yourself. Alone. The way you're supposed to do life.'

Chapter 10

I had thinking to do. A great deal of it. Some done already, at close to the speed of light. I had acquired a first class air ticket to Nice via Paris. Four hours later I was on the plane, having tried Dawn's mobile at the airport and, amazingly, managed to catch her on the other end. Of course I'd tried Karen first and got a message that her mobile service was no longer connected. How Buddhist might that be? I gave Dawn the flight number and estimated time of arrival. Yes, she was in residence at Villa du Phare so, again yes, she could pick me up. Of course Henry was fine. As a matter of fact he was there with her, well, he was with Yassir in the garden but she could see him as we spoke. Yes, Desdemona was fine too. Desdemona was also with Yassir.

She had sounded like a different, would I dare imagine a new Dawn? No banter. Plus, strangely, I got the feeling she was going to be glad to see me.

Riding to gay Paris I eschewed alcohol, popped sleeping tablets, lay back hoping that I didn't talk too much in my sleep. I'm not sure the evangelistic executive from Minneapolis-St Paul in the next seat would appreciate me sex-talking a Giovanna of my dreams through the flight's sleep stage.

At Charles de Gaulle airport I watched my species in all its wondrous variety until called, right on schedule, for the flight to Nice.

Me, I was daddy coming home. It was just that daddy wasn't expecting mummy to be waiting with a batch of scones in the oven.

A prescience which turned out to be right on the money.

No mummy. Just Dawn and a friend.

'You didn't bring Henry along?'

'Essington, some consideration please, if the flight happens to be late what are we going to do to entertain him in an airport.'

Her friend said, 'Airports are so boring.'

Of course I was disappointed. But I was very tired too. I suppose I was suffering the after-effects of the sleeping tablets.

'So, who's looking after him?'

'Paula.'

'Of course. How could I forget?'

'Paula's fine. Karen adores her, trusts her implicitly, won't hear a word against her.'

'A fraction grim, wouldn't you say?'

'Henry adores her, too. I have a hunch it's mutual. She's more than competent.'

'Whatever you say, let's just go.'

Since I had only one piece of hand luggage and my laptop, we were out of there and into Dawn's Audi before it registered on me that Dawn's friend had said, 'Nice to see you again,' when we were introduced.

I'd responded, 'Nice to see you, too,' but without a clue who this was with the lime green hair that looked like a thatch of those threads they weave to make lycra. We were coming around the sea front with its palm trees, past the red-onion dome of the Negresco Hotel, when this friend reached back from her position in the passenger's seat, touched me on the knee, 'Holly,' she introduced herself.

Dawn laughed. 'For once in your life, Essington, you were right.'

'I was right?'

'About Holly.'

'Oh, yes, of course.' I didn't have a clue what she was talking about. My mind not functioning properly after the flight.

When we got home, Henry was working beside Yassir, in fact Henry seemed to be working harder than Yassir. Desdemona was doing everything she could to get involved as well. Henry's wheelbarrow was heaped with twigs and leaves, Yassir's was empty. There was a stern-looking, unadorned middle-aged woman sitting under an umbrella a little way off, watching what was going on.

'Remember, Essington, be nice to Paula,' Dawn said. But I was already breaking into a trot, on my way to Henry. Who chose to ignore me. Some kind of punishment, I guess, for abandoning him. All the same he looked to be doing pretty well on it. By contrast, Desdemona didn't possess the guile that comes naturally to us, even in our infant stage; as soon as it registered on her that I was me, she came bounding.

Eventually, a creature of habit, I settled down at the iron-frame, glass-top table on the second storey balcony. From there I was able to contemplate the mystique of the Mediterranean. A little later Dawn and Holly joined me. Henry stayed below in the garden where he would have been slowing Yassir down, if that were possible. I could see Paula there too, under her umbrella. She was talking to somebody on a mobile phone. Who isn't, for Christ's sake?

I thought, Paula!

I asked Dawn, 'Where did we get her from, do you remember?'

'Essington?'

'Which agency?'

'I don't recall. So long ago now, anyway. Karen arranged it all, or was it you, Essington? What I do know is she was in the United States Army.'

'Rings a bell. Major career shift. And Karen, she's going to be away, how long?'

'Vague about that.' Dawn looked to Holly, as if seeking guidance.

Too late I realized that I didn't need the conversation drifting in a Karen direction. I had come home to protect Henry, nothing more. Once sure he was safe I was returning to Sydney to do what I had to do. If I could work out the moves.

'I never knew much about her.'

'About Karen? For heaven's sake, Essington! How long have you been like this?'

'Paula, I meant.'

'Then ask her.'

We were drinking rosé. Didn't the sea look blue? Wasn't the grass green? Weren't the shadows a tone or two lighter on the Med coast than in Australia? Look into them and, it was true, you could see those complementary colours lurking, that luminosity Bonnard got off on all his life, and which was the trigger I guessed for the wild colour play of Derain and his fellow wild beasts. And wasn't that human nature – a bunch of young men find something new and critics are coming out with 'Incoherents', 'Invertebrates' and then, seeing a small bronze in a gallery with some of these paintings, exclaiming, 'Donatello parmi les Fauves!'

Henry and Yassir were sitting side by side on the lawn, Desdemona was standing a little way off, watching. Paula was checking us all out, the dog included, glancing up from time to time at me on my perch on the balcony. Then she was dialling on her mobile, was talking again to someone.

Dawn was telling me about how the fabric business was progressing. Seemed there were sales all over, suddenly everybody wanted silk, woven or printed. The challenge was turning out the designs and anticipating right now the colours people would go for a year in the future.

I butted in. 'I get it now, but of course.'

Dawn, 'Get what?'

'Holly, you were with Stan Kriticos, in his car.'

'And you were walking Henry.'

Dawn was smiling.

Uneasy, I was counting the ways Stan was reaching into my life.

Then looking back in Paula's direction. But she had gone. So had Henry. Desdemona too. I was off the balcony and running down stairs, first to the front door. Nothing there. I called, 'Henry!'

From somewhere towards the back of the house Desdemona let out a half bark. That was about as loud as she ever got. One cool dog. I whipped through two reception rooms, into the corridor leading to the kitchen, and the main rear entrance. Sure enough there they were, Henry sitting on the terrazzo floor sucking fruit juice from a plastic bottle, Paula mashing a banana.

She looked at me, grey eyes, no expression. She'd looked worn out the first day I clapped eyes on her. Hardly even any interest. I said, 'Hello Paula, I'm back.'

'I already figured that out.'

Dog, child, Paula, me, mashed banana. I asked, 'What agency did you come here through, Paula?'

'Instant Angels. But they've closed down now.'

'I'm concerned about Henry's safety.'

'Why is this? Have you done something to put him in harm's way?'

She stared blankly. And the mobile went off in the pocket

of her linen jacket. It rang 'Yankee Doodle'. Little gold cross on a thin chain round her neck. Thick grey hair with a fringe and bangs.

'What did you do before that?'

'Before what, exactly, Mr Holt?'

'Registering with Instant Angels.'

'You already know that. I was in the United States Army.'

'I never really believed that. What rank.'

'You won't believe this either then. I made Captain.'

'So …?'

'It happens I love children, if that's all right with you. Biggest regret, not having a child of my own.'

'We make choices, Paula.'

'Or the Lord makes them for us. Tell me about it, Mr Holt.'

Well, I might have gone gaga in Sydney. But back home for a few hours and my view of life was turning out to be the same. I was suspecting the worst of everybody. Paranoid. Working on it. Worse, I didn't care that I was doing it.

For instance, whenever I glanced at Holly something about her presence at Villa du Phare worried me. I couldn't help it, it just did.

Was that unreasonable? Hadn't I met her with Stan Kriticos?

A little later on, working at my laptop plugged into a telephone connection, Instant Angels didn't respond to a Google search. I couldn't find it in the phone book, either. Which proved what? That Paula had told the truth, it was defunct? Back in the kitchen, when I asked Paula more about herself, Dawn asked me again why I was being like this all of a sudden? 'This house, Henry, everything, it's going like clockwork. Thanks to Paula.'

Passive, expressionless, Paula stood by a marble bench-top over the far side of the room, a window behind her, the cerulean shutters open; she let what would be said be said. The kind of person life washed over.

'Well, now daddy's home maybe Paula's not needed any more.'

'Essington!' Dawn exclaimed. Then, 'Excuse me a minute,' to Holly and she steered me out the door and into the pool area. Plastic ducks floating on the synthetic-looking water, plastic lounges on the sandstone paving. A big yellow rubber ball.

'Essington, how many days did you say you intend to be here? Was it three, at the most? That's what you said, isn't it? So, who do you think is going to look after Henry if Paula goes?'

'I don't like the idea of her, Dawn.'

'What exactly is it that's worrying you?'

'Earlier I was watching her watch Henry while talking on her mobile. I can't say why but she made me feel uneasy.'

'Male intuition! Okay, if you want a reason to feel uneasy I'll give you one.'

'I don't, actually. I've got too many as it is.'

'Then one more won't hurt you. A body turned up in some kind of heavy duty plastic container.'

'I know about that already, Karen told me.'

'But she couldn't have told you who the body is. That only hit the news since Karen headed north.'

'Is this a guessing game?'

'It was Gerald Sparrow.'

I walked around to the far side of the pool, picked up the rubber ball and kicked it high, right over the top of a row of variegated oleanders.

Watching me, Dawn stayed where she was.

I shouted, 'How could anybody around here know that?'

Walking towards me now, 'Identifying the victim seems to have been too easy, from what I saw on the television at any rate. We know the box doesn't lie, does it, Essington? It seems that someone popped a wallet in with the corpse, complete with credit cards, business cards, a driver's license, everything you'd need to establish identity. And your name in there as well. Amongst the documentation.'

Straight away I thought of Stan Kriticos. Moulay up there in the park. Sparrow delivered to where I live, dead.

Stunned. I felt angry at the same time. It's okay to get so you can't stand someone you've known most of your life. But to think of them dead, and, worse, stuffed into a plastic container, that brings back a whole lot of misgivings. My failings, Sparrow's failings, the two of us trapped in the moral squalor of this life. Yes, too many memories, okay?

As well, too much responsibility for what was happening. Henry in danger. Sparrow. Karen out there somewhere, in the world. Beyond my reach.

'Dawn, I have to tell you this, he tried to get in touch with me just recently. It couldn't have been much more than a month ago.'

'And?'

'Well, if he's turned up here dead, already ...' I was looking at her eyes, intently, hoping to find a sign of something there – good faith, bad faith. 'And Stan Kriticos, he called too, at the time I couldn't work out how he got my number. By the way, you didn't give it to him, did you?' Still watching her for signs.

'You know I wouldn't do a thing like that.'

'Sparrow, he had attempted to call me via Giovanna. How could he possibly have known to go by that route?'

'Giovanna's rung here every other day since you went away. She's talked to me, she's talked to Karen. Maybe Kriticos got your number from her.'

'Must have.'

'But how would he know she existed?'

Throughout the conversation we had been standing, facing one another – combatants.

'The newspapers, they said the container was from Australia?'

'Essington, I don't know. Though, they did say the body was in a dreadful state, decomposed. I assume that the container had been sealed. Or somebody would have ...'

'You are talking about it as if it were an experiment of some kind. Shooting a fox terrier into space, for Christ's sake! That corpse could be you, it could be me, or anybody. Think about it. It was a human being sealed in there. Worse, it was the person I've known just about the longest of anyone.' A terrible thought – had he been dead when they put him in?

Dawn turned away from me. There was a flock of long-necked birds overhead, heading south, to Africa. All the time I'd lived on the Mediterranean I'd never travelled beyond where the sea ended and into Africa. It was this unknown place that I could still believe in.

'I start to wonder if it was Sparrow attempting to get in touch with me in Sydney. Could have been Stan playing games, couldn't it?'

She asked, 'Whoever it was relaying messages through Giovanna ... Well, there's something else I ought to tell you, Essington, about Giovanna.'

'Yes?'

'She isn't what she seems.'

'Meaning?'

'She's ... how should I say, well putting it bluntly, I've always considered her to be more than a little schizoid. At school, where she was the top of our year in just about everything, she didn't connect with people properly. All her relationships were fantasies inside her head. Look, I know I'm not expressing this properly, but what I'm saying, it's the truth. You could never rely on Giovanna. She's totally amoral. I have a feeling as well that she hated Karen. Envied her. Of course she never showed it, but there were so many small signs ever since we were teenagers.'

'You and Karen, both of you told me to use her.'

'That was Karen, Essington. My mistake might have been not getting worked up enough to object. Anyway, why should I have objected? What of importance could you be doing in Sydney other than selling an apartment? I mean, of that kind of importance which calls for a solicitor. For the apartment, surely Giovanna was as good a choice as anyone.'

'Except that she'd give my contact details out to the world.'

'Her brother was the same. Dino we all called him. Don't know his real name.'

'Maybe it was Dino.'

'Probably. He looked more Greek than Italian. But so handsome. My first boyfriend. First obsession actually.'

'Nobody ever mentioned Dino.'

'Possibly, Essington, because there isn't any reason.'

'Your first boyfriend, it has to mean something.'

'He'd bring this Italian food in his lunch box, his mother made it for him. He'd share it with me, sometimes. Depended how he was feeling. A really moody character. First boyfriend, yes, but that was the funny thing, he wasn't interested in sex. At the time I wondered what was wrong with me. He just wanted to talk, to hang out.'

'Same as Holly, here.'

'I'll ignore that. But Dino, I suppose he was like Giovanna … in not connecting properly. As well, he was forever dreaming up these money-making schemes.'

'Write a book, Dawn, call it *Why I Swapped Teams*. Blame it on Dino.'

'Essington, what do you mean by "blame it", for heaven's sake?'

The sun was thinking very seriously of going down. Must have been close to six o'clock. Equinox. We stood there, side by side now. This was a new relationship we'd established. I got this weird feeling that Dawn was someone I could trust. Holly came out of the house, bearing a brightly painted ceramic bowl of olives. She was asking 'Drinkies?'

I said, involuntarily I suspect, 'Come to think of it, Giovanna couldn't have given my number to Sparrow because he tried to contact me through her.'

Holly: 'I beg your pardon?'

'Nothing.' I picked an olive out of the bowl.

Bringing the conversation to a conclusion, Dawn said, 'Karen and I never agreed about Giovanna's reliability.' Then she smiled at Holly, 'A dry discussion, this.'

As I was heading inside to keep an eye on Henry and his minder, it occurred to me that the last time I'd seen Holly her hair had been red-blonde, not green.

It was strange, but Paula's unsmiling presence, her alert if arid personality, seemed to be just right for Henry. He had really taken to her. When she asked him to do something he did it, and willingly. For instance, 'Time for the bath, Henry,' she announced. And straight off he was heading up the stairs, gleefully crying out, 'Bath, bath.' Paula giving him quite a start then following, athletically, two steps at a time.

I trailed after the pair of them, excluded by their domestic routine. I'd toss in the occasional daddy-ish snippet in a desperate attempt to bond again with my own flesh and blood.

Had I been away so long? I didn't really think so. But for Henry, I seemed to have become a creature of a lost past, irrelevant as far as the present was concerned.

After the bath she was on the nursery floor, drawing with coloured felt-tip pens, smearing glue on a sheet of paper, sprinkling glitter on the glue from little bottles and keeping up a childish exchange with him all the time.

Night with a quarter moon. It got to be very quiet out there on Saint-Jean-Cap-Ferrat once we, the residents, were back in our mansions or water-views apartments. Just the sound that the sea makes. Occasionally a night bird. Villa du Phare's steel grill gates were secure. Yassir was in his one-up-one-down house by the main gate, I could see that as always his lights were on. (He told me once that he never slept for more than a few minutes at a time. People who say that are usually kidding themselves, but I suspected Yassir was telling the truth.) He helped me feel secure. I believed that the religious and social alienation of his group of nationals in the area rendered him trustworthy as far as my family and its affairs were concerned. Villa du Phare was his sanctuary, had been for quite some time, and he didn't have any anger to spare for us.

Once Henry was in bed and had indicated a preference for going through a picture book with Paula rather than with me, I took to a bottle of wine and to thinking about Gerald Sparrow.

Oh dear, death, it is such a powerful drug. Maybe that's why certain of us get hooked on it. A decomposed corpse in a plastic container or not, my name in his wallet, Sparrow was back with me. We were children together. It wasn't till I was sitting there in the gloom that I realized how important his life had been to me. And yet, there I was, without an intention in the world of putting my hand up, telling the authorities that I was back, that I had known this man. I was constructing stories in my head to cover the fact of him carrying my name around. My problem being that if the local law connected me to Sparrow's death, it would be months before I could get out of the country.

And right then I wanted to return to Sydney and become pro-active. At least, that was what I planned to do after I had secured Henry's safety.

However I was going to achieve that.

Paula didn't join us for dinner. Dawn told me that while Henry slept she liked to keep to herself, mostly watching television in the room she was occupying next to Henry's nursery.

'You really are on the wrong track with this newfound distrust of Paula, Essington.'

'I haven't said a word.'

'Your animosity is palpable.'

Holly had prepared a marinara pasta, with a haricot and walnut salad on the side. I occupied myself selecting, opening and serving the wine. Dawn was at the head of the table, playing patriarch.

I'd already done the 'I remember where I met you before' thing with Holly. By then twice. Which didn't appear to phase her. Then, wiping my plate with a chunk of bread I asked how she could have teamed up with scum as obvious as Stan.

Looking straight at me, 'I didn't team up with him, certainly not in any sense that you might be implying.'

Dawn: 'Look at her, Essington, you're so insensitive to how other people are. I would have thought it obvious that she's my kind of woman.'

'I'm insensitive! She was sitting there in his car, the classic rich prick's trophy chick for all the world to see. There were Stan's enforcers at the ready across the road. Leaning against that car. You remember them, Holly?'

'She was working for him.'

'You recall, don't you, Dawn, I said I'd met this girl who'd be perfect for you.'

'You got that right. But we don't have to go over this territory again and again. Or do we?'

'Except back then she had pink hair.'

'And you were with Henry. Actually, Essington, Dawn and I have talked about how lucky that was so many times, the coincidence. Now, would you like some more pasta? It'll be lukewarm but the sauce is still piping hot.'

Holly picked up my plate, took it to the kitchen.

'Working for Stan, in what capacity?'

'She answered an advertisement in a London paper for a short term position, as a curator with a corporate art collection. As it turned out it was Stan Kriticos' collection.'

Holly brought back my plate, replenished, then asked Dawn if she'd eaten enough. I got to my feet, did the honours with a fresh bottle of chablis from my cellar. Dawn asked me, disingenuously I might have thought, 'Didn't you have quite a bit to do with Stan's art collecting?'

'A long time ago, but he really did it on his own.' I was thinking of the images of improbable fakes Stan had emailed me. 'Looked fine to me, but then I'm not an expert.'

'Take it from me, Essington, Holly is.'

Holly streamed on, 'Of course I was excited by the opportunity the job represented. But as for Stan himself, and his people! To tell the truth I was shocked by the situation I found myself in. Trapped, really.'

I decided to give it a go. 'About that time I got the information that in your precious opinion the Kandinsky wasn't the real McCoy. Did you happen to tell him that?'

'In the end she wasn't offered the job, anyway.'

I asked, 'But you put in some time on the collection, it wasn't just a job interview?'

'Oh yes, I was in the house for the full week.'

'And you let him know you suspected the Kandinsky was a fake. At what stage in all this did you meet me down there outside the Cocteau chapel.'

'Second or third day it would have been, Essington. He was enjoying driving me about the place, taking me out to lunch. I had the feeling that he was showing me off.'

Dawn reached across and placed her hand on Holly's forearm.

One of those silences settled over the three of us. I thought, 'time to leave, Essington.' I was on my feet when Dawn asked, 'It's none of my business, but did Giovanna get you into her bed?'

Getting Holly off the hook with that.

Holly shaking with stifled laughter.

Dawn joined in the fun, openly.

'Would she do that, with a best friend's husband?'

'I wouldn't describe Giovanna as a best friend to Karen.'

'So you said. Whatever, the answer is no, and that's the truth.' The laughter subsided. 'And the rest of the paintings, what was your opinion of them?'

'A particularly interesting collection, I would have said. I couldn't find any of the pictures in the books I searched.'

'You searched?'

'Although a few were pretty similar to some of the more obscure works I've seen.'

'Artist's paint the same composition again and again. Even if it looks spontaneous. They'll do it a different size, maybe. Three or four paintings in an afternoon, ringing small changes. Not even cleaning the palette, so the same set of colours. Van Gogh, several versions of the same picture … his *Portrait of Doctor Gachet*, painted in June, 1890, one in the d'Orsay, the other sold at auction in 1990, and his *Two Children*, also June, 1890, one in the d'Orsay, the other a private collection. Or, turning you into an instant expert, didn't they teach you that kind of stuff?'

Dawn: 'Essington, I thought you weren't an expert!'

'It's just that there are all these know-nothing experts, Dawn. I've had them up to here with art. Okay, Holly, she didn't know at the time, but if you put some idea in the head of Stan Kriticos, doesn't matter how small, how innocuous, sooner or later it's going to come back at you. Tell me about it.'

They looked confused. Silence descended.

Whenever there had been a conversational lapse during the meal, I'd think about Sparrow, dead and decomposing. Then I'd think about Stan and how crazy he was.

It had got to where there were moments I'd chill with fear, just thinking about him. My stomach would want to collapse in on itself. I'd freeze and sweat, both at the same time.

Then more booze to top up sugar levels. Very important, sugar levels.

Or return to the image of Paula sitting under the umbrella with her mobile phone. I had this picture in my head of her talking into it, listening more intently than was usual, then talking again. It hadn't seemed the kind of relaxed conversation you have with friends and family, unless something very important happened to be going down. She'd been doing business of some kind. She had a right to do that. Yet still she made me uneasy. Everybody did.

I'd be thinking about Paula conducting those conversations. Then I'd start working out how you get into the stored numbers in somebody's mobile phone. There wasn't any point in stealing it, because I didn't know the code to get the thing going.

Heading upstairs to what had long ago come to be regarded by all as my sitting room – the beast's lair – I spotted Paula standing outside Henry's door. Facing away from me, the mobile pressed to her ear. She wasn't so far from where I was propped but obviously hadn't heard me coming up.

I didn't make a decision. I just did it. I covered the distance between us like a cat pouncing, bumped heavily against her and in the same movement, as she was falling sideways, snatched the phone from her hand.

Okay, a crazy thing to do.

Still, I did it.

After all, I was supposed to be just one more crazy male with no Buddhist mind reconstruction to render him reliable.

So true.

Paula was scrambling to her feet, screaming abuse, clawing to get the phone back. To hold her off I grabbed a handful of hair then pushed her face hard against the wall. My other hand brought the phone to my ear.

There was a French voice asking, 'Miss Bartles?'

When I asked, 'Who is this?' he hung up. I'd swear it had been a he speaking.

Paula was a tall woman, and fit with it despite appearing to be so tired. Bags under her eyes. What she didn't have in her favour was a suntan and the benefit of a month working out in the gym of a North Queensland health resort. She wasn't protecting her own flesh and blood either. They reckon that provides the extra strength. Whatever, she put up with me frogmarching her along the corridor, into my sitting room and setting her in the chair at my desk. I still had hold of her mobile phone. For leverage I opened the desk's middle right hand drawer, reached to the back and pulled out the .22 pistol I'd taken from the man who'd tried grabbing Henry in Nice a couple of months earlier.

Paula almost let loose a gasp when she saw the gun. But didn't. I wouldn't have thought displaying shock or fear was in her character, yet, just for a second, she came close to losing it. More, she appeared surprised. I was talking at her most of this time. Telling her why I was worried. Explaining that I needed to know for certain what was going on in my own house, that I wasn't going to let up till I knew Henry was a hundred percent safe. Then, standing at the door, the only way out of there, I opened up the numbers she'd stored in the mobile phone. There weren't a lot, only five in fact. Not a big social life.

Because there was no way I could hold the gun and the phone, plus a ball-point to write down the numbers and keep an eye on my captive at the same time, I had to ask her to write the numbers as I called them out, and write down her mobile's code as well.

Funny thing was, well, it's true I didn't get it at the time, but looking back it surprised me that she appeared to be so submissive. Surprised me, then seemed to indicate that she mightn't have been totally happy with whatever double act she'd felt obliged to play in the recent drama of our lives.

We'd just finished transcribing the fifth number when her phone started to ring. Not 'ring' really, it played 'Yankee Doodle'.

Softly, 'Who's this going to be now, Paula?'

'I really couldn't say.'

I folded the list of numbers, slipped them in my back pocket. We watched in questioning silence till 'Yankee Doodle' stopped.

At first I offered her money to tell me what was going on with her; that had come to be one of the principal Essington Holt responses to the world's troubles.

And Paula responded, 'No'. Acted offended. 'You pay me already, Mr Holt. Beyond that point I'm not for sale.'

'To me?'

'To a single soul.' Long pause, the two of us. 'You don't understand, do you Mr Holt?'

'You've told Kriticos, or at least his people, that I'm back.'

She nodded agreement, but seemed indignant rather than shamed.

'Told who, exactly, Paula?'

'Gilles, his name is Gilles.'

'A local? What was his response to that useful snippet of information?'

'He asked if I knew your plans. Wanted me to describe you, so there couldn't be a mistake, you know. Then said he'd have to make an overseas call, I remember that clearly. As if he didn't do that very often. Said he'd call me back tonight.'

'Which he did? You were talking to him when I grabbed you?'

'I'd rung him.'

'Why?'

'The only interest I have in any of this is to protect little Henry.'

'I'm so fucking stupid? Would I believe that? Jesus Christ!'

'Please, you blaspheme.'

I didn't know I was doing it but I guess I had the .22 pointing straight at her. Between the eyes. The world-weary, fading hazel eyes.

She held a crooked arm across her face as if to protect herself.

I lowered the gun. 'We should go into Henry's room, you and me, have this conversation with him watching you.'

Said she didn't want to disturb him.

'You are happy for these bastards to kidnap him.'

Lowered her head, closed her eyes, actually brought the palms of her hands together and raised them as if in prayer.

There was the little gold cross dangling on its fine, bright-gold chain around her neck.

She opened her eyes. 'Mr Holt, there's been nobody here. Not a soul I could trust. You people, you are so tied up with yourselves. All of you. Where have you been? You've been in Australia! Meanwhile, day after day, night after night, I have made decisions in the best interests of the boy. I don't know why but out of the blue a caller informed me that Henry had almost been kidnapped in the streets of Nice already. I asked myself, how could that be? These people who called, I asked them that too. They said he'd been with you at the time. Said it had been almost too easy. Precisely the words they used, too easy, and that they were merely giving you a warning on that occasion.'

Now, beating herself on the chest with the flat of her

right hand, a slow, steady rhythm. 'Knowing that, what would you expect me to do?'

Was this Paula being straight with me?

I said. 'That happened on the street, yes.'

'Precisely what did happen, Mr Holt?'

'This character made to grab Henry off the pavement as we were getting out of the car. Some time back.'

'You didn't judge it important enough to tell anybody about this? The police for instance?'

'Desdemona got hold of the guy.'

'It took the dog to save him, in the company of his own father! And they weren't trying. What kind of a man are you? What kind of parents does Henry have? Think about it. He doesn't know any of you. He knows me. In need of protection, it is me he comes to. Even you must have noticed that.'

Swinging the .22 onto her again, 'This was the gun the guy used.'

'Oh,' she said. 'Small bore,' and blinked at that.

Which was when I caught myself inhaling big chunks of air. On automatic once again. Needing the oxygen. She'd hit me right on the spot. Okay, my mind was jumping around in denial of what she had just said. But my body was saying 'Mea culpa.' Screaming it out.

Not knowing what to do, Paula Bartels had been playing for time. She couldn't talk to Yassir about the threats because she had no idea what he might do, or of where he stood. The first call had come the day Karen left for her Buddhist retreat or whatever. Clearly Paula regarded Dawn and Holly as a pair of airheads.

She hadn't been able to contact the law because there were no direct threats. Just the calls. They'd told her not to attempt taking him out of the region. They were watching.

I asked, 'Why didn't they just come and get him.'

Disbelief at my stupidity spread across her face. 'I would have killed them.'

'They couldn't know that.'

'I knew that.'

'But why do you think, Paula? Really?'

'They told me it was in connection with a business deal. Wanted me to contact you so the thing could be settled and Henry would be safe.'

'And?'

'I didn't believe that, no way. I thought about it and it didn't ring true. I've had a lot of training, Mr Holt. I've been taught how to respond under pressure. How to think not for myself, for the welfare of a bunch of people.'

'Give it up, Paula, trying to throw this back onto me all the time. For Christ's sake!'

'There you go again, blaspheming. You don't have to believe what I'm telling you. What you choose to believe is of no concern to me. But your son, Henry, knowing he may be in danger, my only concern is to protect him. Whereas you, Mr Holt, do you mind my saying that you seem a little mad. Unstable. And so uninterested in that child's welfare.'

Her story was she was playing along with these guys till a solution occurred to her. She believed that my return might represent that solution. If they got me then they would leave Henry alone.

Her logic.

Maybe hard to fault from Henry's point of view.

Of course she was quite mad. But then we all were by then.

I dialled Yassir from my desk phone. He picked up straight away, the man who never sleeps. I told him to bring the dog up to the house, pop her inside the main door, then lock it. Lock all the rest of the external doors as well. But first to call up a few of his friends because, I explained, there could be trouble at Villa du Phare. Explaining what we might expect, I suggested not securing the main gates because I wanted these people to come in and get caught. I needed to talk to them. Then I made sure he had my current mobile number so we could stay in touch on the hoof.

You just love people like Yassir. He didn't ask why, how many people might be breaking in or anything. He acted like this was routine. And I had confidence that in half an hour there'd be three or four hardened, bitter men occupying the moon shadows beneath my trees.

Paula had proved to me that the mobile's pin number she gave me worked. So I passed the gadget back to her, told her to ring Gilles and tell him I'd got drunk and passed out.

'Whatever you do, Paula, just have him think that everything is going as he might have planned. Encourage him. And don't fuck up.'

She looked at me, concerned now. But not for me.

She did it. She explained she'd had an accident when talking before, that she'd scalded herself and I'd taken the phone from her because I'd been falling down drunk. She babbled on about the problems of trying to do too many things at once while looking after the child. Blah, blah, blah. Fools in the house getting in the way.

Her French, perfect.

I listened as she spun the story.

It had to be fifty percent convincing, at least.

But me! She'd been planning to give me to those bastards! Just when I could have been softening towards her in a very small way, a fuse burnt out in my head. Suddenly I was like: damned Paula! Tired but fit, corrupt Paula! That Paula with whom my Henry had established such a bond. And I was screaming at her. 'You bloody …'

Waving the gun.

She was on the verge of weeping.

SHE HAD STARTED TO WEEP! COULDN'T BELIEVE IT!

Straight off, I'm like, shoot the bitch. I could feel it inside me. A surge. I was getting that wound up. Because there is nothing worse than waiting for an event that can only turn nasty. Your adrenalin begins to pump. Like, after a bad event I will tend to go dead calm for a bit. But not while waiting for something to happen, knowing it's going to happen. No way.

Then I heard panting behind me, followed by a low growl. Maybe sensing who was on whose side, Desdemona had sat herself down right next to me and was staring at Paula as if she'd never seen her before. The growl at the back of her throat like the distant beginning of rolling thunder. Paula's gaze switching between me and the dog. Relaxing a little, I let it register whose side Desdemona was on in this life. That I did have a friend. Your own child might shift his loyalties, but your dog, never – ancient Buddhist saying.

I opened the nursery door, let Desdemona in there, watched as she wandered over to the bed. She sniffed, looked back at me, then folded herself into sphinx-like repose on the pale blue carpet beside a yellow and red plastic tricycle.

There wasn't anything further for me to say to Paula. I had the names of the people whose numbers were stored in her mobile. There was a mother in Seattle. There was the Villa du Phare number, of course, and some friend she reckoned she had. At the top of the list there was this guy, Gilles. Plus a second number for Gilles or whoever to leave a message with in an emergency.

I'd asked, 'What would be an emergency in this case, Paula? Are we talking about me having a heart attack? I don't think I'm going to believe that.' I'd steered her along the main top storey corridor and down the back stairs because I didn't want to meet up with Dawn or Holly – I had no intention of talking this over in a reasonable fashion with a pair of love birds. The intention I did have was to get down to my studio. It was in the basement, mostly underground, opening out on one side to a sunken courtyard with a pond full of fancy-looking goldfish that my aunt reckoned were put there a couple of owners back, not long after the Second World War.

In the basement I unlocked the door connecting the studio with the house and guided Paula in. Only then, having to push her through the door, did it occur to me that she had received some message from my unstated 'Shoot the bitch' thought. Still, I didn't have time to waste on her intuitions. I flicked on the light, headed straight for the storage wall down the end of the long, art-cluttered room, opened a drawer at floor level and, the petite .22 in one hand, reached behind a stack of antique drawing paper and pulled out a .32 automatic. Checked the clip, full. Dropped the .22 into a pocket.

Paula should have been close to wetting herself by the time I steered her back up the stairs, but no. She was contained, right back in control of herself.

If I couldn't realise why she was like that, maybe it was because by then I wasn't seeing anything not connected with the immediate present. And the present had to be all about protecting Henry, but my way.

Outside the nursery door I said, 'Anything happens to the boy, you will be killed.'

She gazed upon me with contempt.

She even chanced a smile.

'You hear me,' I went on, 'even if something happened and you got out of here alive I'd find you and kill you. If I can't find you I'll find your mother in Seattle. Do you understand what I'm telling you?'

'Mr Holt …'

Blocking her out. 'You hear me, I'm doing you a favour, I'm offering you a chance nobody in their right mind would offer.

Pure Christian charity, okay?' I suppose I was swinging that .32 automatic around quite a bit in front of her face, emphasising my point. Why shouldn't I? I was agitated. I was angry. Angry with myself, with Karen. Jesus, was I angry with Karen? Angry that the pair of us had been fingered by this nanny as uncaring parents.

'Please Mr Holt, listen to what I am trying to tell you. It's Henry I'm interested in. His safety, I love the child.'

I said, 'Miss Bartels, or is there a Mr Bartels in the background that I ought to look up, too?'

'Hear me out before you make yet another terrible mistake.'

'You'd better hear me out. I don't even know why I'm standing here, wasting time. You do a deal with this guy to snatch my child …'

'I have told you that I didn't. You are so wrong … in everything Mr Holt.'

And suddenly it was her turn to be angry. Not that she showed it. She became very still. Her face expressionless, yet deeply troubled. Grey hair standing out all around, framing her sallow face. Her honey-coloured eyes displayed the anger. 'Henry is emotionally deprived. Where have you been, tell me that? The loving father is a joke. I can't even get in touch with the mother. This child had nobody until it had me. The dog cares more about him than you do. I didn't come here to hurt the child but when somebody informs me he's in danger because of a deal you've done …'

She'd said it all five, ten minutes before.

'All I can think of is to protect the child. All you can think of is guns, doing business, brutalisation, revenge. A nursery filled with trappings of love, but there's not even the hint of love's bond in there. This isn't a family you've set up in your grand house, Mr Holt. That's why Henry turns to me, because here is someone who is interested in him, as a person. An eternal soul. Somebody for whom he is more important than they are to themselves. So I'm sorry if …'

In the rest of the house, things were quiet. Dawn and Holly had to be off somewhere, doing what girls in love like to do. I hadn't received any sense of Holly representing a problem. Not yet. For some reason I had elected to believe her story of applying for a job with Stan. Maybe I believed it because I trusted Dawn's judgment. Well, most of the time I trusted it.

I was prowling the corridors, going in and out of rooms, or standing on one or other of the balconies, watching for signs of action below. And the night rolled on. I saw a bunch of men arrive at the gate, talk to Yassir for a bit, then melt into the garden. The .22 was still in my side pocket. I didn't have much confidence in it, no whack. Most of the time the .32 was in my hand.

I'd check on Paula and she'd be hanging about, anxious, protective. Just in case she relaxed, in passing by I'd show her the .32.

I'd just walked past her when I heard 'Yankee Doodle' riding on his pony. I turned. She looked at me, asking the question. I signalled back: Okay, go ahead, answer it.

Coming down from agitation and confusion, I must have nodded off. From somewhere a voice was calling. 'Ess, Ess, hey Essington, wait for me.'

Snap woke. Sparrow had been calling to me. He must have found himself falling behind.

Another time there was a tiger in the roof cavity of the villa, wire mesh stretched tight instead of a plaster ceiling. I had the shotgun in my hand but couldn't remember where I'd left the cartridges, or if they were only bird shot. The tiger totally enraged.

It was after midnight. Still not a peep out of Dawn or

Holly, not that I could hear anyway. Hardly a breath of wind out in the garden either. I thought I could smell the approach of rain. Upstairs, Paula had taken to pacing up and down the corridor. No sign of Yassir or his friends. No cars on the street outside the gates.

How many times had I looked in on Henry contentedly sleeping the night away. Desdemona alert beside his bed.

The phone was ringing in my shirt pocket. In response to my 'What?' Yassir was saying that two men, maybe three, had come in through the front gate. No sign of a car so he reckoned they must have been dropped off some distance away and walked up. That told me there was at least one more Kriticos operative on the outside somewhere. Yassir told me the two he had spotted were moving across the lawn towards the front door. While talking with him I'd been barrelling down the stairs. By the time I was doing the three locks on the front door I heard shouting on the outside, then a window smashing. It had to be a window leading into the reception room beside the lobby where I was standing.

Yassir had said 'maybe three'! How could he not know?

There was more noise from outside.

Holding the gun out in front of me, my finger moving through the trigger's first pressure, I stepped into the doorway leading to the dark reception room. As I flicked the light on the intruder turned to face me. He had one hand covered in blood. Eighteen years old, he might have been, if that, just one more of your street animals out of west Nice. No gun, so he'd have a knife on him. Really panicky, he looked, to be cornered. So I squeezed off a shot, aiming to miss, to frighten. The .32 made a big noise inside the room as the bullet hit the marble floor and, zing, ricocheted to Christ-knows-where.

Within the gun report's echo the sound of another shot. But not in that room.

No time to think about that one. Because the guy was

crouching four or five metres from me, his eyes wide open, round as marbles; he was kind of shifting his weight from side to side, like a caged primate watching a kid approach with a peeled banana. Aiming for his chest, again I had squeezed the trigger through its first pressure, I said, 'Nothing can stop me killing you.' Only in French. My pure Australian French. *Alors!*

Yassir was coming in through the door at my back, and as he came, telling me what was going on. One of his friends was using the butt of a pump action shotgun to break away the jagged glass of the reception room's window before stepping through to join our party. A dazed-looking man of about thirty, with blood pouring from his nose and mouth, was unsympathetically supported by two of Yassir's pals. Meanwhile I continued holding the gun on the piece of street scum with a gash in his hand who'd come in through the reception room window. To steal my child. The two of them we'd caught had to be worried to find themselves at the mercy of energetic followers of Islam who'd already seen too much of this imperfect, Christian society.

Yassir wanted to check outside for the third intruder he might have spotted. He didn't respond to my suggestion that there had been a second gunshot. He was too concerned that Kriticos' men would still be on the streets of Saint-Jean-Cap-Ferrat, outside our gates, preparing to come in. Twice he told me they would have heard the report of the .32 from a kilometre away.

But first I had to check on Henry and Paula. They too would have heard the gunshot, or shots.

Puffing from belting up the stairs I found her, still outside the door, but on the floor, her knees drawn up, arms clasped around them, her face tight with concern. Beyond the door Henry was crying, and Desdemona barking deep, troubled, angry. And then Dawn and Holly came along the corridor like a pair of excited Roman choir boys, swathed in sheets and demanding answers.

For instance, they wanted to know why Paula was being like that? And hadn't they heard a couple of shots? And what the hell was going on?

They'd heard two shots!

All I could think was Paula, was Holly – both of them could still be Stan's people. How to know for sure about anyone, what to do about them?

The .32 still in my hand. With those three women, their eyes fixing attention on the weapon, I shoved it down the back of my jeans.

And why not mistrust Dawn as well, her judgment screwed to buggery by infatuation?

I told them: 'Only chaos going down.' I didn't say it was chaos inside my head, too.

Dawn: 'Essington, what are you trying to do here?'

'It's too important to talk about.'

'But …'

Paula didn't move. Then said in an unnaturally steady voice, 'I believe he's right.'

First off I wasn't too sure if she meant that I was right or that Henry was fine.

Next thing Dawn was kneeling beside Paula, her arms wrapped around her, and I was through the nursery door, grabbing Henry. Awake and a fraction wide-eyed till I picked him up, next thing he was screaming blue murder, banging at my face with small clenched fists. Nevertheless I got to the window just in time to see a car pull up beyond the gates.

My gaze tracking over the lawn, the shadows thrown by trees and shrubs, maybe I noticed something extra down there, one more patch of darkness where it shouldn't have been. Later I found out that what I believed I saw then had in fact been the body of the third of those initial intruders.

Eliminated with one head shot.

What was I sensing in the room? Hanging there in its atmosphere? Surely something like cordite in the air.

Or did I create these details out of the thin air of remembrance?

And hadn't my foot kicked against a long and heavy object? Didn't it slide under Henry's high-sided bed?

Perhaps, right at that moment I should have thought, 'Very like a rifle.' But I didn't. Really, nothing much registered where it might have mattered.

Except that Henry was still screaming.

A man eased out the driver's door of the car and moved stealthily towards the gates.

Maybe Henry saw him, too.

Suddenly quiet. Softly then, anxiously, 'Paula …' And then, 'Raran.'

'That's not Karen, it's a visitor,' I explained while pressing a finger on my mobile's redial button.

'Yes?' That was Yassir.

Paula came from behind and gathered the boy out of my arms as I turned.

'Another one, and we don't need to scare him off, either.' I cut the call, pulled my list of numbers out of my back pocket, unfolded the sheet of paper, punched in a bunch of digits as I was moving out through the nursery door.

And hoping that a mobile ringing in his pocket could put Gilles off his game, if only for an instant. Assuming I was right and that was Gilles down there.

I was heading out the back door.

Travelling fast too, but even so by the time I came around the side of the house two men were wrestling a third to the ground.

Considerable damage had been done to the first two characters who had come through the Villa du Phare gate. Yassir assured me that those two had to be knocked senseless before his friends could head back into the garden to grab interloper number three. I said fine, I understood.

Which I did.

I mean, Jesus, they'd only been after my son!

Number three turned out to be Gilles. I'd seen him before, that first time I'd clapped eyes on Holly, down by the Jean Cocteau chapel, he'd been leaning against the side of the black Citroen Maserati. Up close, the skin across his cheeks looked like a photograph of the surface of the moon. No sunglasses, it was hard to tell what both of his eyes were like, but the one he could still open was delivering me an unforgiving message.

We were downstairs in my basement studio, Gilles and me, bonding in our own way, my mind jumping between there and Paula's emotional collapse, and the rifle under Henry's bed, and the shot that had come directly after I'd fired the .32 in the reception room.

I had decided it was best this way because I urgently needed to find out a few things the rest of the world didn't need to know about. Two of Yassir's friends had helped me bring Gilles there, and with the aid of gaffer tape had fastened him to a ladder-back chair. No way he was going to shift position without having the tape removed.

Elsewhere, Yassir was tidying up, his friends checking that Gilles' fellow workers didn't screw up.

Watching over my captive and contemplating my next move, I dialled Paula's mobile. She answered on the third 'Yankee Doodle'. I asked if there was anything she wanted to tell me before I had my in-depth conversation with Gilles. No, she had nothing to say. I asked how Henry was doing. She explained that the three of them were looking after him, and he was fine.

I asked her to put Holly on.

That open eye of Gilles was watching me. Not nice. Below

the moustache, his mouth was letting loose with nasty growling threats, in his native southern French, together with a small quantity of blood-stained spittle.

I hadn't had a drink since I couldn't remember when. Not that I was feeling the need. Hardly at all. Quite the reverse in fact. I seemed to have gone into my extra calm phase. Like all the levels of this and that, potassium, vitamin B12, single malt whisky, whatever, they were in equilibrium.

'Essington?' Holly not sounding at all uppity, none of Dawn's feminine-masculine shit there. I reckoned that by then even the in-house lesbian love birds would have worked out something of the wee drama that had just played out.

'Don't leave the house for a while, Holly.'

'I wasn't intending to.'

'Just don't. And, the pictures, remember you told me how interesting Stan's art collection was? Particularly interesting, you said.'

'What's that got to do with …?'

I cut her off. 'Is it possible he owned more paintings than you saw? A week of conversation with the guy, drifting around in his smart car, doing lunch … you must have formed quite a picture of the man and what he was involved with, art-wise, any other way. Like is it possible he was storing pictures somewhere else?'

'Only what I saw on the walls of his place, and the crates. I didn't look at what was inside the crates.'

'What crates?'

Still that eye watching me, Gilles, his shoulders working as if trying to free up his hands.

'The paintings he was putting into storage.'

'News to me, Holly. I hope you aren't jerking my leash here. These crated paintings, he never showed them to you?'

'They were already properly packed.'

'How would you know that?' Then, to Gilles, 'You following this, arsehole?' in English. Incomprehension. I got back more of the evil eye. But when, also in English, I asked him where his mother lived because I wanted to fuck her again, he became so agitated he tipped the chair and himself over and in doing so cracked his head against the corner of a workbench.

'Essington?' Holly must have been wondering what was going on.

'Thanks for that about the crates, Holly. There wouldn't be anything else important you haven't told me, would there?'

'How can crates be important?'

The night's disturbance hadn't upset her. I cut the call. Impossible to know which Kriticos art collection she'd seen. What I'd supplied or the junk. Holly, a student of art history, quite probably she wouldn't have had a clue about quality.

Dear oh dear, falling over like that, Gilles had given himself a nasty cut directly above the eye that wouldn't open. Blood flowing into its socket and down the side of his face to be absorbed by the cloth of his snappy, all-black outfit.

'Priests and pimps wear black, has to mean something.'

Gilles acted as if he hadn't heard what I'd just said.

Hundreds of years ago, or more, before anybody was born, there was a television program featuring this lower-middle class British spook in the Cold War. He was a no-nonsense character who collected toy soldiers. On one occasion, interrogating a particularly difficult adversary, he hung him by the wrists and practiced fairway shots at him in a long, under-furnished room.

The scene had possessed a certain *je ne sais crois*, a poetry to it you might say; it had travelled well with me through the years.

My studio at Villa du Phare happened to be the right kind of long room. There was a bag of golf clubs shoved under one of the work benches, souvenir of an attempt to fill time after relinquishing my art forger career. I'd shoved them out of sight. (I could recall too-new golf gear, me carrying the brand-name bag stuffed full with gleaming, top-of-the-range clubs, whacking divots out of the fairways, slicing drives, missing metre putts, getting plastered at the nineteenth – all to entertain one of Karen and Dawn's customers from the US of A.)

It took a lot to set Gilles and his chair upright and to get him in front of a blank expanse of wall. Nothing to say, blood oozing through his lips.

No sound as I selected a number two iron, scrunched up a sheet of A4 laser paper, pushed it around till it was stable on the terracotta tile floor, balanced the ball on top.

He was watching me.

I did a couple of practice swings before squaring up to the ball.

Gilles, he'd worked it out, suddenly every muscle in his body tensed. He turned his head to the side as I swung and connected better than I had ever connected on the course up there in the hills behind Nice. I'd have to say – a lovely shot. Just enough slice on it to miss his head by the length of a tube of paint. The ball rebounded to the wall behind me before touching the floor. Six cans of fixative fell, clattering on the tiles. Gilles let loose an involuntary squawk.

I shifted position so there was less chance of being hit by the rebound; disappointed in myself not to have thought through the physics of the exercise.

Setting up the crumpled A4 sheet of paper and the ball for my next shot, I took to explaining to Gilles that he had choices. Like, we could play this game till the sun came up, if he was still alive by then, or he could consider accepting a certain amount of money from me in exchange for what he knew.

'Gilles, you think Stan Kriticos is some kind of heavy character, right? Tops people he doesn't agree with, leaves them on park benches for dogs to chew. Great if you are a dog. You want to remain loyal in the interests of good health. I understand. That's how scared you are. But let me tell you, because I am so pissed off that my kid's been put in danger, from now on your life is hanging by a thread. Hear what I'm saying? Is my French good enough for you?'

I addressed the ball for a second try.

Then I said, more to myself than to him, 'Problem is, Gilles, how can I neutralise you without killing you?'

This time, leaning back a little too far, I hit over the top of the ball, it went straight to the floor, bounced, hit him close to full force on the shin bone. He let loose with a yelp.

I said, 'Isn't golf a bitch of a game?' In French, of course.

Addressing that little white ball is what golf is all about. It's the highly trainable who become good at it. There are certain activities, contact sports mostly, where it's the animal inside that gets you there, which is definitely not the case with golf.

What this Gilles did for a living involved keeping in touch with the wild beast within. Gilles and his pals took wannabe Moroccan entrepreneurs who'd tested Stan's patience for walks in parks around Nice, where they killed them. His type had no worries about snatching children from their beds, or grabbing them from their pushers on the streets of Nice. There was no way a person like Gilles was going to change. Because he had kept the wild beast alive inside himself but most probably didn't play football.

With golf, a person who effects small corrections to the manner in which he addresses a golf ball might commit fraud in his spare time, or even forge a work of art, but essentially there is something savable inside there, a possibility to be worked on. Someone like me, for instance, I could improve.

But definitely not Gilles.

So I adjusted the way I was standing, checked my grip on the club, thought about how I bent or didn't bend my arms on the back swing then … whop! Almost totally lovely. Just the hint of a slice still. Something remaining for me to work on, to perfect.

The ball collected Gilles in the ribs, had to have broken something in the region because Gilles came alive with pain. So much so, in fact, that I got the feeling he was approaching the point of establishing dialogue.

Yes, indeed, I had got to where I could sense these things. For instance, Gilles' closed eye had sprung half open. And the good one was trying to pop right out of its socket – life of its own.

Once more I was setting the ball up on its paper tee. Taking extra care to do it right. And Gilles was attempting to tell me he'd like to strike a deal.

Addressing the ball, getting the stance, the grip right, I was explaining at the same time that there wasn't any deal you could make with low-life scum who snatch children.

Challenging him to prove me wrong, see.

Something which, as it turned out, he was only too anxious to do.

Of course I couldn't sleep.

What did I finish up worrying about? Such is the human mind, at the end of a night like that I was really distressed to discover that the bullet I'd fired in the front reception room had ricocheted into the chest area of the small Derain nude, Fauves period, I had given Karen on the morning of my departure for Australia. Hit it pretty much where the first golf ball to hit the target had got Gilles.

The Derain, her birthday present in advance.

Yet at the time I hadn't even noticed it hanging there.

Had the painting given her some pleasure? Was she affected by the thought behind it?

Down there, in the room, the light on, damaged painting askew on the wall, through the broken window I could see rain falling.

I had learned that on Stan's instructions, Gilles had delivered the crated paintings to an ancient stone house at Sainte-Agnes, up behind Menton. Stan had trusted him enough to do that. Stan's top man. Clearly, betraying his boss was starting to hurt him more than the golf balls had done.

The house was empty. Crates full of artworks were cluttering its unfurnished, damp and dark interior. With the assistance of two of our enthusiastic guardians they were manhandled into the back of a truck, which Yassir had caused to materialise out of nowhere. The rain falling down hard.

Returned to Villa du Phare, Gilles had to be a deeply troubled man knowing it was because of him that Stan was left holding the collection of South East Asian art copies I was supposed to buy 'back', while I now had possession of what in the context rated as the originals. Stan was in line to lose face, or worse.

Stan's three men at Villa du Phare still represented a problem. When I asked Yassir for his advice, he told me that they were not good men. Gilles in particular, he said, was well known. Miming the cutting of a jugular, he explained that Gilles' trade was causing individuals to vanish.

'Or be found dead?'

'Yes.'

I asked which people might they might have been?

Yassir explained that Niçoise race conflicts connected with control of illegal activities. That it wasn't so much Christians versus Muslims as drugs, or protection money, or pimping for women who had no rights because they didn't have papers. In his view, every iniquity in this world was a consequence of trade.

I told him I didn't bother with that kind of abstract stuff.

When talking to Yassir it was impossible to get even so much as a hint of what was really going on in his mind.

'They were trying to snatch Henry, Yassir.'

He said that he would resolve what to do with Gilles and the other two. Yes, it would be best for me to leave it up to him.

Yassir's friends, whom Dawn and Holly had dubbed 'the bachelors' – Dawn: 'The way they look at a girl, Essington!' – were over the moon when put on the payroll as live-in minders. Yassir handled negotiations. The bachelors grimaced and nodded in my direction. From that moment on, around the place, one or other of them would give me a man-to-man kind of look with as much as to say 'You can count on me.'

I felt I was getting a grip on life at last. Within forty-eight hours of Gilles entering the Villa du Phare garden, I had a plan of action formed. My own Matisse *Femme Couchée* and the Kandinsky *Schloß and Church* were out of their frames, off their stretchers, photographed and rolled, painted side facing out – carry-on-luggage-size parcel less than half a metre long. The problem of stretchers would be solved in Australia. Customs controls there would insist on treating the wood of any stretcher arms to ensure they didn't carry insect pests. Such a process took time, not to mention compromising authenticity with evidence of up-to-date chemical residues.

The rest of the original and recovered Kriticos painting collection was stored where it would prove considerably more difficult to find than locked away in some Sainte-Agnes house.

Images of those inexpert copies of the Kandinsky and Matisse Stan had emailed with the rest were still nestling on the hard disk of my laptop, so I contacted my friend, Alain Taylor, at his photo lab in Nice. I understood that commercial realities had forced him to go over to doing a lot of digital work, so through him I had them laser printed onto canvas textured paper. These I packed with 'art work' and 'handle like eggs' slapped all over the package, and express couriered to Essington Holt at the Sydney apartment. On the better than even chance Schwartz was checking what art work was going into and out of the building.

I called Bobby, told him to expect the package and leave it unopened.

'You're the boss.'

What had he been doing? I pretended interest.

Nothing, he told me.

'Any messages?'

'Unreal, your social life. Who hasn't tried to get in touch? Do you happen to know all these people?'

'Depends who they are.'

'Mate, reading from the list. Alison, does she mean anything? Was he being facetious? Someone called Thea, said you'd know who she is – rang three times, pushy. Pixie from a model agency. That one tempted me.'

'Bobby!'

'Stan Kriticos, he rang twice and left a contact number. He's a hard case, leaning on me the instant I pick up the phone.'

'Have you got that number?'

'Of course.'

'Because maybe we are going to need that. He's the reason I'm calling as a matter of fact.'

'I can't wait to meet him, Essington.'

'Don't be too sure about that.'

'Giovanna Cecchini.'

'You didn't tell any of these people where I am?'

'North Queensland, recuperating.'

'You told them I was recuperating? From what?'

'Overwork. Isn't that why people go to north Queensland? I didn't mention drying out.'

'Drying out! Screw you too. Bobby, this is what I want you to do. But first you have to download two images. You'll need an internet address.'

'And a computer I suppose. I'm not that kind of person. Rachmaninov, remember?'

'Go out and buy one. Pay for it to be hooked up to the net, broadband. By yesterday. All it needs to do is receive messages, and you have to open these two images, called attachments. Have them show you that at the same time.'

'I can work a computer all right. The basics, turn it on type of thing, write a letter.'

'Pity you're not into porn.'

'Where did you get that idea from?'

'Make it part of the deal, they set it up within the hour or you don't buy it.'

'Consider it as done.'

'Then ring through the email address. Straight away, more than urgent. Better still, email it. As well we need a publicist. Because this is the story.'

And I told him the story.

'Mate, better write that all down, email it so I get it word perfect, okay? Then I just have to hit reply, isn't that right?'

'So you can do it? And the publicist, Bobby?'

'Would be under P in the Yellow Pages.'

'I don't think so. Ring Julian Anderson at Johnstone & Lang.' I read out that number and told him it would be repeated in the email. 'He'll understand what to do. Ought to be keen. It's good for him, and good for me.'

'Like a thrashing. You're going to save the world.'

'In one.'

He didn't say a word. I didn't either. Holding on, we let the phone bill grow, little meters going tick-tick-tick.

'Bobby, the truth is I don't remember how much I've told you about Stan Kriticos.'

'A bit.'

'The one person in the world he doesn't want to kill right now is me.'

'You're saying, mate?'

'He's after me for a lot of money. Applying pressure,

threatening people I care about. But he can't kill me because the money he needs is in a bank account. I've got to be there, authorising its withdrawal. What I have to do is stop him hurting these people I care about. You understand what I'm saying?'

'Oh mate, I hope you aren't saying you care about me.'

'Bobby, this is not a joking matter. Of course I don't give a shit about you, but, come to think of it, Stan doesn't know that.'

'I think I follow.'

'Make sure you do.'

Another pause. It was getting awkward, Bobby and me. Neither of us the friendship type.

He must have been thinking 'friend' too, because, 'In the paper, mate, this report, an Australian lawyer's body found in some kind of plastic bin or something in France.'

'I know.'

'They said his name was Gerald Sparrow. Wasn't there some …'

'Used to call him Gerald Fucking Sparrow, Bobby. Yes, he once was a good friend of mine.'

What remained for me before returning to Australia was to get Henry out of there, keep him out of there, too. Place him back in the care of his mother, wherever the hell she was holed up, and explain that it would be wise for her to vanish for a while. On the other hand I was reluctant to initiate the move. Because, of course I wanted him to be where I was, not that there was a chance of carting him off to Australia without consents being signed by Karen. So no chance.

On several occasions Dawn took the trouble to remind me that Australia was where Stan was.

'Is supposed to be at this moment.'

'Essington?'

'He's everywhere, or at least his men are. We just witnessed that. Loyal psychopaths everywhere. I could be heading for Sydney as Stan is very likely coming back here. Who's going to take care of stuff then?'

'These men you've filled the house with. Essington, I really don't believe what's gone on here since you came home.'

'Those men who invaded the place were what, Dawn? On a moonlight garden tour, do you think that explains it? What about Paula, for Christ's sake?'

'Everything was fine with Paula till …'

'Was fine! What's fine about a home invasion?'

'You bullied her. But why, Essington?'

Paula was playing with Henry all the time. The pair of them making me feel like a rhinoceros that had found its way into a house and needed to get the hell out of there. Mostly she avoided me and if confronted went straight into talking the science of nurturing. Totally defiant where the welfare of that child was concerned.

Holly tended towards lying in the sunshine wearing basically a G string. Decorative she was, yes. But she wasn't doing anything for me. Except represent one more concern because of her possible connection to Stan – he was like the sun, everybody else planets spinning, me included.

So the doubt just festered inside my head along with so much else.

The bachelors took a lot of care guarding the pool area when Holly was on her banana lounge.

So we remained for the next couple of days. Dawn attending to Holly's every want. Me watching Desdemona, her hanging around Yassir. The world turning. Sun rising. Sun setting. The level of the Mediterranean rising and falling with the tides. Schools of fish unseen. Dolphins. My alcohol level held pretty much in check.

Villa du Phare an impregnable fortress. Yassir had a couple more of his friends on the job. They walked the garden night and day, pump action shotguns over their shoulders. Just lounging in the garden was like playing mafia boss in a Hollywood movie. Only difference being we had more and thicker moustaches in our little drama. There was one guy with the thickest moustache of all, and a close cropped beard, his name Tareq. Two fingers remaining on his right hand. He spent his time cruising the loop of streets leading to the house. I guess he did it in shifts swapping with some other illegal. I liked those men. They weren't kids, more like individuals of my own age. None of them smiled, ever, they just did this grimace thing.

I was working on the Fauves Derain nude that had taken a hit to the body in the front reception room. There wasn't any real need to restore it, but doing so kept me busy. And Karen would appreciate it when she returned. Particularly if she never knew it had been damaged. Unlikely. I knew she'd find out. Actually, working on it gave me a break from pondering why Karen was keeping out of touch. She'd told me Buddhists liked having children around, hadn't she? I remembered that much about Buddhist's collective spirituality. Now there she was, pregnant and deliberately out of contact, not just with me, in the greater scheme of things maybe I didn't matter, but out of contact with Henry, with her own son.

All the time remembering Paula's judgment of us as parents.

It wasn't like Karen to vanish. She was the practical type. Into life's detail. Getting all that interpersonal stuff so right. Okay, she'd turned Buddhist and fallen for a German artist, but, what the hell? She was still Karen.

It didn't fit that the influence of Richard, or anybody else for that matter – for instance a German avant-gardist – could turn around the way she saw the world.

The rain had been coming on hard, setting records across France. On Saint-Jean-Cap-Ferrat it had the theatrical accompaniment of thunder and lightning when, around midnight, I lifted the phone jangling beside where I'd drifted off slumped in a armchair.

I hadn't finished asking who was speaking before Stan Kriticos told me I still didn't get it.

'What don't I get?'

'That I'm serious. I offered you a fair deal. Why would I do that? Because I'm a businessman, understand what I'm saying. And it's good business to behave in a reasonable way.'

'Killing my friends –'

'Now please –'

'Wait a minute, what exactly are we –'

'I'm fucking speaking, loser. And you're listening. Some men working for me came round to your place to talk sense with you. If that's possible, which I must say I doubt. Where are they now?'

'I'm hanging up.'

'I hear you are back home, so I send these people round because I am running out of patience to close the deal.'

'And steal my son. Goodnight, Stan.'

'I definitely don't advise hanging up on me.'

'Stan.'

'I don't advise that, I said. My people were going to have one final attempt at negotiating, all right? Because I don't like to do things the other way. Are you keeping up with what I'm saying? But now, for you, Essington, it is too late. Too late for you, and too late for your family as well. A promise.'

'Stan …'

'I said I'm doing the talking here.'

'You said "negotiate", mentioned being reasonable …'

'Shut the fuck up!'

'And Gerald Sparrow?'

'You are going to be begging me for ...'
I disengaged just before a lightning strike killed the line.

The bullet wound in the Derain painting didn't seem particularly inappropriate. The artist had been a man very much of this world. After his Fauves period he'd fought at the Somme and at Verdun, two of the major battles of the Western Front. Maybe it was that experience which turned his art around. In stuff I'd read, certain art historians suggested that the war took the fun out of Modernism. Wild and often flippant young men of the pre-war period turned to look again at life and at the old masters. As well, the great dance company, the Ballet Russes, got itself restarted in 1917 and in doing so attracted Picasso, Matisse, Derain and Braque to design for it. Maybe they adapted to the practicalities of costume and set design, and to the fact that they were working for a much larger audience than that made up of weirdo collectors of avant-garde art. All these factors affected Derain, to some extent. But the main thing for him was he became the recognised leader of this 'return to order'. That was the kind of man he had turned out to be – very possibly the result of war experience. He cherished his role of leader in this new conservative movement. It seems that playing wild games with the idea of 'art' and overturning the conventional means used to create it could no longer constitute for him a real life.

Always his work of that post-war period harked back to the evocative poetics of Renaissance painters. Compositions within which you can see what's depicted, but the meaning itself remains elusive – something to play about with in your mind. A lot like life itself, really.

So the forged painting which I was working to restore for Karen's return represented for Derain, and possibly for me as well, that spark which flies, catches, illuminates. If the burn is too hot, you get to tread its ashes for eternity.

It hadn't stopped raining. On the television it showed a huge cloud mass stretching west, all the way to Canada.

My mobile. Yassir telling me there were a couple of gendarmes at the gate who wanted to speak to me.

I looked out, saw the car, Yassir getting wet opening the gates.

The bachelors were the type to know the law had arrived before it arrived. No sign of shotguns. No sign of bachelors, either.

Dawn and Holly upstairs.

Three pigeons pecking about a paved area sheltered from the rain.

The police car rolling up towards the house.

I was preparing stories in my head – to cover just about everything.

It had to be about Sparrow's body. A connection would have been made – a small matter of communication between French and Australian law authorities.

No wonder the bastards appeared to be alert, so grim, climbing out of their car.

One, the driver, was wearing one of those antique-looking hats on his head. The other wore a gabardine overcoat, brown felt hat and a plaid scarf hanging loose.

'Monsieur 'olt.' They'd sent an English speaker.

I said yes and he introduced himself. At the same instant, I swear it, upstairs Henry let out a banshee wail.

'I have some terrible news for you, Monsieur 'olt. I am so sorry ...'

Without saying boo to one other human being in the compound, I was out of there, with the police.

We were heading up the Route Napoleon to where, they deeply regretted to inform me, Karen's Volvo had dropped off the side of the road into the river below.

'She was driving?'

'Her companion.'

Seems they'd been half in, half out of the water for twenty-four hours before being discovered. The trees and scrub the car had dropped through had closed over them, 'like curtains at the end of a play.'

'Like the curtains at the end of what, Monsieur 'olt?'

'I beg your pardon.'

They exchanged a look.

'Nothing, it was nothing, really.'

'Monsieur 'olt?'

'Hello?'

'I beg your pardon?'

'That's my wife who's dead, for Christ's sake! I loved her ... it should have been me.'

'You are saying ... I don't quite understand ...'

We were standing there, looking down. One of the white posts on the side of the road had been snapped off at the ground. Splinters of wood spiking up from its stump. There was a lot of evidence of the car being dragged back up. Parts where the rock had fractured under the pressure of the chains and cables they had used. All that and more. But I wasn't really seeing any of it. Instead, I guess, trying too late to gather her into my arms, to protect her.

'I want to see her.'

'That is a necessity, monsieur. We are heading there now. To Grenoble ...'

It is about there that I have a blank. Just the impression of being assisted to my feet after falling down. Or had I been trying to go over the edge. Or both.

Or whatever.

Rain pissing down.

The foaming, mud-stained river water roaring below.

'There was another vehicle involved.'

I don't know if I was listening. My head was somewhere else, trying to reach Karen before it was too late, even though it was much too late.

It was a dreary ride on along to Grenoble. The nearest hospital. Nearest morgue.

We kept on turning those sharp corners, going into tunnels and out the other side. Light, darkness, light.

Once I said, 'New Jersey.'

'Monsieur 'olt?'

'The light at the end of the tunnel.'

Another time I said, 'Stop the car and I'll shoot myself.'

The windscreen wipers swept backwards and forwards.

'To be with her.'

Nobody said a word.

'How un-Buddhist can you get?'

'How Buddhist for what, Monsieur 'olt?'

I sensed that they became extremely protective of me, those two cops; and in my company, by degrees, increasingly protective of themselves.

The sheet was drawn back. There was her perfect face, not registering me. Her skin grey-white. I put my cheek against hers. To stay there forever.

Gently, gently, they pulled me back from her.

'It is your wife, Monsieur 'olt?'

I couldn't keep from sobbing.

The artist from Bremen, I identified him, too. Well not really, because I'd never seen him before. But I gazed upon him, like they say. Me, full of hate before they pulled back the sheet. His face, mop of blond hair, wispy little beard. The skin colour of the dead. Again. Too soon. Be twenty-five if he was lucky. But hadn't been lucky. Wishing still, somewhere at the dark recesses of my mind, that you could kill the dead.

That was when they told me about the other car. A Citroen Maserati, black, 1974 model. Most unusual, as they observed. It had been found abandoned at the scene. Initially the police had assumed that the accident involved just that one vehicle slamming against the rock-cut, high side of the road.

I must have said, 'Stan Kriticos!' Or something along those lines.

Because that was when they started to ask questions. And, a little bit at a time I got to answer them. As best I could. Not giving much away but explaining about having met Stan a few times and then, recently, having a conversation with him at Villefranche-sur-Mer, him in the yellow Mercedes, a couple of his pals in a black sedan like the one they'd just described.

I'd break down. They'd wait patiently till I recovered composure, then ask more questions.

The Citroen Maserati had been badly damaged. There was blood inside the vehicle as well. So, someone had been injured. They were checking hospitals and doctors to find out who might have received attention in the past couple of days.

The car was registered to a property development company on the Côte d'Azur. A Kriticos company.

They wanted to know what other connection I might have had with Stan?

'I hardly know the guy, ask him yourselves, why don't you?'

Which was when they told me he had left France. To avoid being interviewed in connection with a murder committed quite some time before, apparently. Did I remember the murder? They described Moulay, my Moroccan acquaintance dead on the park bench.

You close your eyes to find Stan Kriticos laughing into your face. Stan Kriticos hurting you every way he can.

Close them again, and there is the presence of Karen but her features losing definition. Already she is far away from you. You call out, but she doesn't hear you.

We were sitting in a small town restaurant up there in the mountains, just off the main road. A woman and her daughter cooking and serving. Basically a truck stop. Wine in carafes, water in jugs, soup of the day which happened to be *soupe a l'oignon*, probably was every other day as well. A choice between trout in butter with capers, a dish belonging up there in the mountains, and *coq au vin* that happens all over France, the *vin* being red wine. I went for the trout. The gendarmes taking care of me, they had chicken.

The one not in uniform waited till he was mopping up the juice of the chicken before asking if an Inspector Schwartz had been in touch with me in Australia?

I said, 'No, in touch with me about what would that be?'

'It would have been in relation to our investigations of Stan Kriticos.'

'Okay, well, yes, he has.' My mind's mechanism turning this information over: tick-tick-tick.

Some red wine poured to top up my glass, some into each of theirs, too. The gendarme in the uniform watered his down. They kept on looking backwards and forwards between each other. Like they'd caught an escaped gorilla and it was a responsibility they felt less than comfortable with.

'Schwartz has been checking out what I am doing in Australia. He believes I'm breaking the law in some way. He's fraud squad.'

'Whatever you say, Monsieur 'olt.'

I lifted the backbone out of the trout, laid it on the side of my plate. Picked up a chunk of fried potato, bit off half of it.

The plain-clothes cop explained that he believed Inspector Schwartz's real interest was Stan Kriticos.

'You communicate on this?'

'On an informal level, but of course. Interpol is developing some interest at the same time.'

Remembering Karen, I dropped out of the conversation. So it died.

I stood up, walked around the restaurant, watched through a window the rain still pissing down and a figure scurrying from the building next door to a white van with a plumber's name in block letters along the side.

Back in my seat. A moment's more clarity. Bells ringing! I believed that I'd got it at last. These police in France had known I'd had contact with Stan Kriticos. And that we were both Australians living on the Côte d'Azur. A bit of a rarity. Therefore for them I was worth thinking about.

I ate half of another chunk of fried potato. Picked up my fork, lifted a thin slab of pink trout flesh off the skin and into my mouth.

They all thought I'd lead them to Stan?

Which explained Schwartz hanging about in Sydney, being a perfect pain in the arse. Making me feel guilty, causing me to act accordingly, distorting the way I looked at the world because I felt so guilty. All the time he'd been watching, waiting for Stan to get in touch.

Another fork of trout. A caper balancing on it as the fork travelled to my mouth.

The law watching.

Tears rolling down my cheeks.

A kind of Jobim Mark 2 played in the Bar d'Azur at wharf level in one of Stan's apartment building developments. Nice enough singing, but the place had never had the ambiance since its founding father, Moulay, had got himself killed. The rain pissed down outside. Hadn't stopped, wasn't going to stop. Neither was I.

And the girl from wherever the fuck it was went walking/ and when she walks all the drunks she passes just cry/Oh yes they just cry.

'Another drink, Monsieur?'

'You reckon I'm a Buddhist or what, garçon?'

I couldn't get hold of my loss, my sorrow either. There wasn't a bottom to it. Or a top. No dimension at all. Couldn't describe back to myself how I felt anymore. I was lost, forever. Karen dead, people around me didn't seem real, emotions couldn't be trusted. All my circuits were blown.

Yassir steered me through most of what followed. He had someone assigned to watch over me down along the quay. I'd screw up or pass out or both and next thing I knew I was being assisted in through my own front door.

It rained for the funeral.

Blank-eyed priest incanting. I had told him yes, of course she had been baptised, confirmed, a firm believer still. Had to, only way he'd do the honours.

He took my word for it.

Had Karen been baptised? Confirmed? How could I know?

I didn't say she was a Buddhist.

So she went into the ground. Half her luck.

Too wet for Buddhists there.

We stood side by side, Dawn, Holly, Paula, with Henry hanging onto her. Lots of other people behind. Henry didn't have a clue what was happening. It must have seemed strange to him that for once everybody else was crying.

Hanging back, Yassir with Desdemona on a leash. At Villa du Phare she'd taken to howling for no reason, sitting at a window watching the rain, every now and then letting loose with a long and plaintive cry.

I decided on taking Henry away with me. Yassir and his friends were going to look after Villa du Phare. Dawn and Holly were off to see the world, hand in hand. The fabric business could look after itself for a month or so, that's what Dawn said.

'Everything has a time, Essington.'

Almost a grin, 'Past tense for me.'

'You'll see.'

That was Nice airport, Dawn and I held onto one another, we wept some more tears.

'Dawn, do you communicate much with Giovanna?'

'That was Karen, Essington.'

'Are you likely to? I need to know.'

'Can't see a reason.'

'Whatever, don't tell her about Karen's death, okay? Do that for me. Not after what you told me about her hidden dislike of Karen. On a need-to-know basis let's just say she doesn't need to know.'

Her eyes full of tears, red-rimmed, mine the same I guess. We held on to each other some more. She whispered, 'I won't say a word, and you look after yourself, Essington, promise me that.'

'Sure, Dawn,' I replied, 'and you too.'

And off they went.

Henry waving at the aeroplane as it taxied through the rain. First stop London.

'Goodbye aeroplane, Dawn, Holly, bye bye … bye bye.'

Not coping well, I made up my mind about Paula with the toss of a coin. Heads she stayed with us. Superstition demanded I use the Australian two-shilling piece my father had given me so long ago. I tossed. There from the small tarnished circle lying at my feet was the unsmiling profile of King George V of England.

So Paula Bartels came to Sydney, Australia.

Paula. Dear oh dear. But Henry, he really did adore her. They played together, so, as people predict, they stayed together.

Chapter 11

Back in Sydney. Big surprise, Giovanna wanted to see me. Her initiative. No, nothing to do with my taking out a lease on the adjoining apartment; that was signed, sealed and ready to deliver, she told me. We could take it over the next day. 'Try not to mess it up.' Her joke. Giovanna coming over all friendly.

The owner, Damien Berry!

'Interesting. Consider the property trashed.'

'That might be unwise.'

Clearly, news of Karen's death hadn't reached Giovanna. Not yet, anyway. Not in any way I could pick. I wasn't going to tell her, either. For my part, right then Giovanna's lips, her hair, her skin, the cloth of those white blouses pulling across her breasts, those things no longer existed.

And yet, now, much, much too late, she wanted to see me! Not in some bar or café, nor at her office, but where she lived. The reversal of form was sufficiently abrupt to bring vividly back to mind Dawn's observation that Giovanna was schizoid. Here I was in mourning, four days back in Sydney, Henry and Paula crowding the apartment, Bobby adapting, and she rings me up, asks me over – for what? My clear impression was that it had nothing to do with business.

Paula. Well, I'd filled Bobby in about Paula. And he had appeared to listen.

Strangely, Bobby had taken Karen's death as hard as anybody. Bobby who had never met her. He had no idea what she looked like.

Could I remember how she looked? Karen who didn't break up into little erotic fragments the way Giovanna had once done. No, I couldn't. Because Karen was all of Karen; she had been this one amazing person who had taken me on board, formed me, transformed me into something approaching the human.

All the time I had been thinking: Beauty and the Beast.

Jean Cocteau made a film once, *La Belle et La Bête*. Used to make me cry watching a video of it. The beast keeps Beauty in his enchanted castle. But has problems communicating his feelings.

Dawn used to ask Karen, 'How's Le Projet coming along?' And they'd laugh. The three of us by the pool, that breeze coming off Africa, Desdemona watching every move any of us dared make. Karen and Dawn laughing. Le Projet simply sitting there, acting the allotted part. Happy as a pig in shit.

'Mr Holt?'

'Yes, Paula?'

'I thought you said something.'

'Did I? I don't think so. Is it time for Henry to wake up?'

Paula appeared concerned for Henry, and for me, wifeless, motherless. It was close to getting on my nerves. Her eyes upon me while with her hand shovelling spoonfuls of mashed vegetables into the boy's mouth.

Or, walking along the waterfront, Henry in his brand-new three-wheel stroller, eternal-life joggers streaming past, huffing and puffing, Paula glancing in my direction to make sure I wasn't falling to pieces.

I was even getting to trust her – because she was getting on my nerves? But not enough. If I wasn't around the pair of them, then Bobby had to be.

Giovanna lived in East Sydney, right on the edge of the city; smart address, within walking distance. So I took a taxi. A neat block of four apartments, the street face ornamented with pseudo pediments and arches painted silly colours. Milky green glass sheets masking unusable balconies. The same glass for the feature entrance, 'Dalton' sandblasted into its surface. Dalton!

Directly opposite was a three storey hotel built in the 19th century. But it too had gone up market with a 'ye olde English' style name plate swinging on little golden chains, 'The White Horse' as if written by a scribe. Underneath, 'boutique hotel', same style of lettering.

Giovanna's top floor, views across The White Horse's roof to Hyde Park.

What's more she had a Burmese cat called De Pussy that appeared to have lost interest in life. (Join the club, De Pussy.) I sensed the cat's dirt tray was past its 'empty' date.

She said hello and the chill wasn't there. She was dressed as for the office. The lights were on full strength. No soft music. There was the telephone on top of a bench-height beech veneer bookcase running the length of a wall, the rest of which was filled with mirror. Looking that way, I saw myself more as an object than as a sentient being.

Giovanna went for sparse modern. I spotted one of those vast Italian designer lounges which can look so much like a bright red Zeppelin at its mooring. The same sort of thing that vanished from my apartment and was indeed in place in the adjoining one we were leasing.

My gaze kept switching between the phone, the mirror and the bright red wannabe dirigible, abstractedly. Whenever I spotted myself I was filled with loathing.

Giovanna indicated where there were bottles of gin, whisky and brandy, told me to help myself, she'd be with me in a minute.

'Vodka?'

'Sorry.'

A very long minute.

My attention was attracted to the only artwork in the

room. Right over the far side from the booze, a group of about twenty framed images, maybe more. At first glance they looked like one more boring contemporary art piece. Collectively the images formed a grid of equal sized rectangles. Delicate, vaguely Oriental art works; washed out colour, sharp-edged but low-contrast delineation. Stepping up close I realized they were more interesting than they seemed. A Chinese Kama Sutra-esque comic book, each scene portrayed as graphically as was possible. The varieties of boy-girl coupling, each arrangement in a room with an open doorway leading to a garden where old men behind flowering shrubs peeped out from time to time as if to catch a piece of the action. A maid was in constant attendance, applying lotions, towelling the lovers down, occasionally joining in. One particularly beautiful image featured the female lover naked except for constricting shoes, her body an arch on the high-perspective bed, the fully clothed maid applying a surprisingly long, lizard-like tongue to her clitoris while the tip of the man's horse-scale penis worked small miracles in her mouth.

In a cage, a cricket, which would have to have been singing.

I'd thrown down two neat gins while taking in the detail of the art – they were all originals as far as I could tell, and would have been worth a substantial amount of money. Giovanna the art connoisseur, news to me! Heading back for a third drink when she came back into the room, wearing a kimono.

It was an Eastern culture thing again. Cousin to the Buddhism which had captured Karen.

And perfect for Giovanna, sure, because she kind of looked Japanese with that glistening black hair. However, right then she appeared to be a little crazy, well, at least about the eyes – gone were the huge spectacles.

And of course I thought, 'Essington, pal, you ought to be thinking, Wow!'

The kimono was such a lovely deep blue silk across which floated a gold embroidered bird with its wings spread wide.

And yet I wasn't thinking Wow! I couldn't do it.

'Music?'

'I don't mind, really.' Filling the glass, emptying it just as fast.

She picked up a remote, hit a button and flat speakers connected to a flat, wall-mounted player loaded with flat CDs behind a flat transparent cover began to pour out the kind of music Bobby had learned about in jail.

'Puccini,' she said. 'Italian,' she went on to explain, as if believing I couldn't know about such a high-culture thing.

Almost right about that.

Giovanna's lips particularly moist, her eyes dilated. Was she on something?

In the front of my mind was Dawn's voice saying, 'You can never rely on Giovanna.'

But another drink and I was any woman's man, I guess. I was all over the place, totally, my emotions running wild. Plus I was sobbing, yes, sucking on my fist and crying like a baby. Because it hit me that everything was too late. There could be no forgiveness, no going back, no day-before-yesterday, ever! Jesus Christ! Giovanna telling me, 'You poor darling, I know how you must feel.' Cool fingers on my chest, her undoing my shirt a button at a time. Fingertips a fraction warmer now, sliding onto the sides of my torso, up and gliding across my armpits before peeling the shirt off.

Me, lying there, letting it happen. Needing it to happen. My breath steadying down, this contact with another human being.

I was on the floor. My arms spread wide. Giovanna licking my armpit, savouring me. Making little growling noises. Fingertips walking up and down my chest, each journey down venturing further.

Unzipping. Taking hold of my dick.

Again she said, 'I know how you feel.' I doubted it.

Feeling me.

It had got to where I didn't feel anything except what was happening right then.

I was the object I'd spotted in her mirror.

Dead inside.

But my dick standing up when it was told to. Throbbing.

Giovanna kissing my eyes, my lips. My nipples. Her fingers lightly stepping up my inside leg, across between my legs down the other inside leg.

'Does that feel better?'

Throwing a leg over me with the spring of a jockey at the picnic races. Taking my dick between thumb and forefinger, guiding me inside. Slipping down onto me. Her eyes, my eyes. Were we reading each other? The heels of her hands flat on my pelvic bones, pressing with them to lift herself up, relaxing to let herself down again. Then rolling off to one side, still connected, taking me with her, the pair of us lying there face to face, my hands groping for her small breasts, my eyes tight shut.

Meanwhile somewhere in my head I was searching after an image of Karen. Weird, that, I remember thinking.

A lot later, some pushing of buttons on the remote, I remember Giovanna explaining that we'd arrived at where Madame Butterfly takes a sword to herself.

And Giovanna was demanding that I semi-strangle her, to supercharge the orgasm.

'There are times when it goes wrong, Giovanna, you know that.' Slurring my words.

'All right then,' she responded, kneeling on the bed like a doll in a digitalised science fiction movie, at that stage squeezed out of shape by a leather corset with wee brass eyelets running all down its length. And she'd put her glasses back on. Around us, her sex toys scattered. 'You're the artist, surprise me some other way.'

I'd emptied the bottle of gin.

In the fog of my mind the thought: 'What sort of an artist does she mean?'

Was she telling me something? Was she saying I was the sort of guy who could only copy other people's work?

Only fake love? Fake sensual engagement too?

She wasn't supposed to know about me counterfeiting anything.

And yet, of course she had to. The whole world knew.

Ask it.

I said, 'Giovanna, why don't we tie ourselves together and jump off the fucking roof?'

'Essington!'

'A love-death type of thing. Chic. Could take off, so to speak.'

'Why not?' As if breathless at the beauty of my idea. But acting. Next thing she was telling me to get the hell out of there.

When I stepped into the street, the sky was tinted pink, shading into a pale turquoise over at the eastern edge and to deep indigo above my head. I could sense the spinning roundness of everything, the sun getting ready to appear over the far edge of the Pacific, just one of a billion dying stars.

For an instant, anything I feared or desired was of no account.

I should have been feeling ratshit in every way, a rag doll on a street empty except for drifting plastic wrappers, crushed drink cans, societies of Indian mynas waking in palms and fig trees, comatose sedans, coupés, four wheel drives, and closed ragtops with electric everything inside.

I stood there knowing I was never going back. That she didn't want me back, either. She'd taken from me what she'd wanted. Or had it been from Karen that she'd taken her portion? Without knowing that Karen was beyond being hurt.

Never again to be hurt by me, by Giovanna, by anybody.

And I'd stepped towards that desire I'd let build inside my head, stepped right up to it, and walked through it out into the ice and ashes of the other side.

Most probably I was just standing there taking it all in when a single gunshot rang out and in the same instant I was tackled from behind, dropped flat on the pavement and in one continuous movement rolled and dragged into the shelter of the line of parked cars on my side of the road. Three more shots, bang, bang, bang, smashing star patterns into the security glass of the doors and side panels of Giovanna's apartment block entrance. The screech of a car burning rubber. Silence.

Except for mynahs squawking in their palm trees.

Somewhere within that burst of action I must have shut my eyes in anticipation of a bullet's impact, and kept them shut so I wouldn't have to watch the world's colours fade from view. Eventually, after God knows how long, I dared take a look around. Of course I knew I'd find Bobby standing over me, his features set in the expression of some left-over person watching grass grow.

He pulled out his mobile, hit a button, waited, then told it the car's make and registration number. 'Your message bank, Essington.'

By then I was sitting on the pavement, my back against the wall of the apartment block. At the same time realising I had been an easy target. Indeed, impossible to miss.

So, this had to be one more crazy go at getting me to play ball.

'I told you I was useless to him dead.'

'What are you talking about?'

'Henry! Bobby, you're supposed to be watching him!'

'They're safe. Do you reckon I don't understand you've set up something you can't control?'

'Where are they?'

Jerked a thumb over his shoulder, in the direction of The White Horse, boutique hotel.

'Bobby, I could murder a drink.'

'One more, my guess is it will murder you.'

'Something or somebody has to, can't go on like this, can I?'

There was a police siren sounding not too far off. Bobby steered me up to The White Horse's door and we slipped inside past a character mopping the entrance. And stayed there till mid-morning, in a suite done up to make Charles Dickens feel at home: patterned wallpaper, dado, picture rail, a couple of British hunting scene prints. Then travelled by taxi back to the apartment building.

Henry appeared to have enjoyed the adventure. Paula Bartels had no comment to make.

For me that was it. I wasn't going anywhere ever again. Life out in the world was just too dangerous. I couldn't trust it, couldn't trust myself in it.

My relationship with Bobby, a total reversal. I was the screwed-up individual discarded by society. He was pulling strings, making the puppets dance, so to speak. He was looking after Henry's interests too. Everybody's daddy, that was Bobby.

As for fiddling about with forged paintings – I couldn't bring myself to think about doing that. Rightly or wrongly, I had put Karen's death down to my insistence on misrepresentation. Misrepresentation of a painting, that was just the starting point. I knew I was guilty of misrepresenting everything else in life as well – feelings, for instance. Was there ever a way out of doing that sort of shit?

If so I couldn't find it.

Next thing I was looking up Buddhism on the internet.

I'd open the laptop, connect, and get to reading the different texts and interpretations. Mountains of the stuff, most mutually contradictory. It didn't matter, I absorbed it anyway, like a sponge soaking up dirty water. I absorb some Buddhism, maybe I'd get a bit of Karen back with it.

Bobby would interrupt. 'Essington, that stuff you asked me to do. The publicity ...'

'I don't want to know.'

As well I had a problem with Henry. As an idea, my son, our child, he was fine. But I couldn't stand being in the same room with him.

I was inhabiting the apartment, our apartment, the one Karen had wanted us to buy.

They were next door, Henry and Paula, with Bobby playing at being daddy. Part of the ever-changing job description.

I'd poke my head in the door. There would be Paula fiddling round with stuff in the kitchen. Or playing a toy glockenspiel while Henry banged on his tin drum, Bobby picking out a tune on a green plastic ukulele decorated with hoola girl transfers.

Either that or there'd be classical music on the radio, changing key all the time, discordantly. Or how many times did I catch a snippet of Paula singing opera type stuff, Puccini nonsense?

I'd enter. Pretty soon they'd stop.

If I stayed in my own play area I could just catch the fun and music as a vibration of the walls.

A letter addressed to me at the apartment: 'How was being shot at? You'd understand they were paid to miss, okay. By the way, Essington, sorry about your wife. Bad luck the guy fucking her had to die too, be nice for me to swap stories with him. We've got to talk, but only when I'm ready. That you'll be ready by then is a promise.'

Laser printed message. A reasonable person would have taken it straight to the police. Maybe I should have done that. But I couldn't bring myself to trust the police to protect Henry, principally because I knew they wouldn't do it. How was I going to convince them it was worth setting up a 24-hour guard? And if they did, would any of their people be capable of standing up to Stan and whoever he'd recruited as his back-up? Answer: no.

Of course I should have gone to the police. But I was not well.

The French cops had told me they were interested in Stan, that they had been sharing information with the law in Australia. So my guess was that Stan was keeping a very low profile in Sydney, anyway. Only signalling his punches to me.

I decided to have another stab at drawing from the model. Great therapy, it had kept Matisse going through the darkest days of the Second World War. My first thought was to contact Alison. But I'd promised myself, definitely no fucking this time. So I reckoned that no Alison was the best way to go because there'd been moments when I was conscious of missing her too much, the way her eyes opened wide at the prospect of scanning a menu, the way she treated me like a human being, too. Maybe she resisted the idea, but she had seemed to like me.

Was I going to let on what I felt about her? Did I even understand it?

I rang Phyllis, set the wheels in motion.

Celeste wore thick, grey-white-grey matt makeup, which gave her the look of a clown, say Giulietta Masina as Gelsomina in *La Strada*. And caused her eyes to shine by contrast, powder blue marbles stuck by a doll maker into two holes beneath a high, fragile brow.

She went at the modelling session like a hardened pro, not

saying too much. When I asked how tall she was she answered, 'Small.'

So I let that subject be. She would have been lucky to make what King George V would have called five foot. Straw-blonde hair half way down her back. Drawing, I got the feeling that her hair was the only thing in the world she found interesting. That and maybe the bright red lipstick shining against her matt makeup.

To smile was clearly inappropriate. She said she was from Goulburn. I guessed about thirty years old. She had arrived dressed like a 1930s coal miner's daughter, maybe from Harlan county, USA. She told me, 'I don't do porn, only art.' The first drawing had her pulling an old fashioned cotton dress up over her head.

From the start alert for trouble, even half-way through the second hour, while doing things to her straw-coloured hair in front of an oval mirror, her eyes never left me.

Unexpectedly, out of the blue of those eyes she asked, 'You know that painting by Claude Monet with this nude lying on a bed, there's a maid holding flowers and there's a black cat, and oh I can't remember what else. It's called *Olympia*?'

Yes, I knew it. I didn't correct Monet with Manet.

'I read this book about the woman who posed, she was called Victoria someone. There was a picture just of her head on the cover. You pick up the book, she is looking straight at you, in this sort of bitter way, with a flower in her hair.'

'Why don't you try a flower in your hair?'

'That's the point I'm trying to make. She was an artist. But nobody was giving her the time of day. She was just this nude model. Monet, he got famous. Nobody talks about Victoria.'

'Victorine Meurent.'

'What?'

'That was her name, Meurent. But you just told me somebody wrote a book about her.'

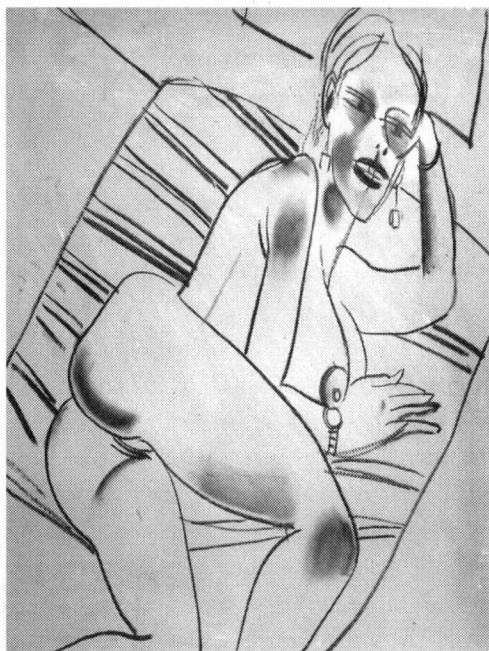

'All these years later. It said that by posing she was satisfying men's desires. But what did she really want, that's the question.'

I said, 'She's got this thin black ribbon tied around her throat, with a pearl hanging from it.'

'Something like that.'

'Anyway, Celeste, no need to worry, nobody's liable to regard me as more important than you are. Think about it, this drawing turns up and someone says, "That's Celeste doing her hair while some poor sad bastard is having to draw her." '

'You don't have to humour me, Mr Holt.'

'You are a hard man to pin down, Essington.'

'Julian, nice to hear from you.' Not that I meant it. I wasn't enjoying talking to anybody.

'The Derain painting?'

'Sorry?'

'From recollection you were intending to offer a Derain through us.'

Since getting back to Sydney I had been experiencing trouble bringing detail into focus. And he was talking then about things discussed before the sky fell in on my world.

'Which one was that, exactly?'

Hesitation. Hopefully, 'We did splendidly with that publicity for you, by the way.'

'So I believe.' I was trying to get a grip on the subject.

'The Matisse you sent the information on. A front page in the national daily, actually, beautiful coverage. Pity we can't get that sort of publicity for our own sales. More of a pity, indeed, that you intend gifting the work to a public collection. We managed to make mention of your Kandinsky as well. But no picture.'

'You know how it is, Julian, give something back.' I was asking myself, Give something back for what? For having a bastard like Schwartz watching every move you make? Trapped in a police state.

Julian rattling on. 'A priceless piece, I had no idea you were collecting at this level, or at such depth.'

'A passion with me, an addiction you might say. Got its grip young, never let go.'

The exchange had lasted long enough for me to reconstruct where it was coming from. 'I'm glad you are there, Julian. And I don't want you to think I've abandoned plans to sell the Derain I mentioned either. Just put it on hold is all.'

'As Mr Chisholm mentioned.'

'Chisholm? You've lost me there.'

'He got in touch with me on your behalf, with the request that I bring the gift to the public's attention.'

'You mean Bobby, yeah?'

'From memory, that was the man, Bobby Chisholm. More interested in music, he said.'

'And not to be crossed. Tell you what, Julian, I'm going to have to get back in touch with you in a week or so. I'm not … like they say I'm not myself right now. A lot of things have been going wrong, personal stuff. They tell me I'm not handling it too well.'

' "They tell you?" Ill health, very sorry to hear it.' About as concerned as if I'd just told him my model train had come off the rails in a papier-mâché tunnel.

'Let's get some action happening around here.'

'I beg your pardon?'

'Let's get some action happening … I was just trying to lighten up a little. But I'll get that Derain to you straight away – a promise.'

Extended break in the conversation.

Julian asked, 'Are you still there?' When I answered in the affirmative he went, 'You don't sound … how should I say?'

'Tell you the truth, I'm a mess right now. Stuff going wrong with my life you certainly don't want to know about.'

Another long silence. Julian keeping the connection open. He didn't want to miss out on any Derain paintings, that was for sure. Or maybe just the prospect of talking about a favourite artist sustained his interest in me. Difficult to say.

He cleared his throat.

'By the way, Alison, would you mind asking her to contact me? Something about her I liked a lot.'

'I'll say you inquired after her.'

'Julian, I'll be in touch, you can count on it.'

Obviously Henry adored Paula. Thinking about it I'd have to say he'd never had a person dote on him the way she did. What's more, she had been perceptive because for me, even for Karen, it was true, Henry had functioned as a kind of ornament. I didn't like admitting that sort of thing to myself but it was true. I'd never understand why Karen took off into the Buddhist wilderness of the mind – first with Richard, then with his German replacement. Name of Werner somebody. *Nice Matin*'s obituary page gave him quite a send-off. One of the local art crowd summing up his career in glowing terms.

I'd shredded that page of the paper; seriously entertained the notion of buying up all his work for a public burning. Really avant-garde that would have been. I was still trying to work out a title for it.

One day I'd gone in next door to sit with them, with Henry I guess. I had a semillon bottle by the neck, the stem of a glass between my fingers. Bobby was heading out into the wild world, the post-WWI Derain nude wrapped in bubble plastic and brown paper tucked under his arm.

My entrance. Henry stopped what he was doing, took a look at me, went back to the enterprise. After a few minutes he got to his feet, walked up to Paula and wrapped his arms around her right leg, in a show of affection for me not to miss. The child exploiting the moment.

The nanny with her eyes on me. As much as to say, 'See.'

Pleased. Yet I noticed how tired she looked, too. More than usual. Worn out.

I filled my glass. The wine warm, but that was all right.

'Paula?'

'Mr Holt?'

'Oh, nothing.'

I set to destroying brain cells.

They got on with life.

Two hours later Bobby returned. He announced, 'It's raining.'

Maybe his presence gave me courage. I had another go. 'Paula?'

She was steaming vegetables. Never stopped, Paula. She cast a look in my direction.

'Stan Kriticos, his people, none of them have tried to get in touch?'

'After what happened to those men, nobody will try and get in touch. Believe me, Mr Holt.'

'For Christ's sake, why don't you call me Essington? You're making me a stranger to the boy.'

She crossed herself when I said 'for Christ's sake.'

' "What happened to those men," what are you trying to say? Nothing happened to anybody.'

She looked up, as if to God. In reality to the ceiling with its recessed halogen lights coupled to a series of dimmer switches. The ceiling was much too low.

Bobby put on some piano music, softly. He said, 'Henry enjoys this, *The Children's Suite.*'

'There's no beat. It's just like water in a lake or something. We want the sound of hard surfaces colliding. Bang, bang, bang. Like that. Something to stamp our feet to.'

Henry was hanging in close to Paula again.

'I didn't do anything to those men.'

Paula said, 'We will all be judged when the time comes.'
That was it.

I stormed out of there.

I was thinking, 'Bobby!' It seemed even Bobby was taking
Paula's side.

Paula! Always believing she was on the side of the good, the
just! I couldn't believe it.

I needed something, more like someone.

Jesus Christ, I guess I just needed someone close to me, to
hang on to.

Chapter 12

There were two phone messages waiting for me. The first
from Phyllis of Pretty Girls Inc. fame, the model agency.
The second from Bobby asking me to ring on his mobile, which
I didn't need to do because he was there with me. Well, not with
me so much as standing where I had been. I was on the move.
Depleted sugar levels had beamed me, as if on automatic, to the
freezer and the vodka bottle waiting there filled with sub-zero
possibility.

'Something soft for you?'

'If you're up to boiling water, Essington, I'll grab myself a
green tea bag when it's ready.'

'Planning on living forever? Schwartz, he drinks green tea.'

'I feel sometimes … oh mate, like my life hasn't even
started.'

I poured a triple vodka, threw it down, then blinked. It was
cold and it was burning. 'Can you get hold of a handgun?'

'In Sydney it would be harder to find a hamburger in a

proper bread roll. For my pal Dranko, a handgun would be a piece of cake, but if you are in urgent need you can always take a lend of mine.'

'You carry a gun?'

'Didn't have it on me that time in the apartment or else I guess you wouldn't be boiling water for me now.' His eyes cut back to dead gaze for ten seconds, more, then he laughed. But not as if anything in the whole world actually struck him as being funny.

'I haven't put the jug on, Bobby.'

'The car that took a shot at you outside your girlfriend's place, I rang its registration number into your message bank.'

'So?'

'Mate, when you checked your messages it didn't occur to you to do something about it? Like write the number down for me and I'd chase it up. I know people who can hack into the system, find out that kind of stuff.'

'I don't like the idea of a message bank.'

'Could be useful, to know for sure whose car that was.'

'Most likely stolen, wouldn't you think?'

'Essington, I wouldn't think a thing, I'd do the sane thing, check the messages.'

'To tell you the truth I played them back then wiped them.'

'You wrote the rego number down, but?'

'Sorry.'

After that exchange he studied me for a whole minute, could have been longer, as if trying to solve the mystery of my existence.

Violin bows scratching away on the radio. More of that classical music.

'So,' I asked, 'what's this shit?'

'Don't know, but it's nice, don't you reckon?'

'There isn't a tune.'

'More like you can't hear it. Why don't you try … listen. See, in fact it's two tunes isn't it? The both at the same time. You have to follow the pair of them, like doing two things at once sort of thing. A bit of a challenge for some of us.'

'You learnt this in the slammer! They ought to go back to having you bastards break rocks, you'd get a feel for rhythm that way. And think of the beautiful buildings they used to make, the bridges, too.'

'Music lessons had their moments at Long Bay. There was this recidivist called Gino. He'd done so much time it wasn't funny. Meant he knew the ropes, pretty much ran things inside. And he was … well, your kind of guitar player, Essington. Willie Nelson standard, at least. So Gino was teaching the guitar teacher a few things. Even doing flamenco and classical. He'd say, "here, let me show you this," and his fingers would be working up and down the strings like ants on a dead rat.' The radio was telling the world what we had just been listening to. 'It got to where even the guitar lessons turned into a kind of music appreciation. The teacher and Gino playing duets, showing each other things, the rest of us, listening. Well, those of us with the wiring still intact were listening.

'The two of them playing, us sitting, most bored to tears I guess, then outside the room, like out of nowhere – this is in the education wing, Essington, peace and enlightenment – there's thumping, and screaming, someone groaning with pain, being beaten up in the passage right outside the window. The teacher drops his guitar, runs to the door and is saying something like, "What do you reckon you're doing?" but Gino is onto him. Pulls him back inside, gently. But firm. Telling him leave it alone. Maybe that was the moment I connected with classical music. Because you should have heard Gino play, it was pure magic. Even John Williams stuff you'd reckon doesn't have a tune.'

No response from me.

A little later on, remembering something, 'Bobby, did you

happen to receive a package, a couple of colour laser prints of paintings I sent?'

'Here?'

'Where else?'

'They didn't turn up, definitely not.'

Eight o'clock that night I was watching a program about upper class degenerates in England when the phone rang.

Schwartz.

For what?

To welcome me back home?

'A pleasant trip, Mr Holt?'

'Perfect.'

'Pleasant weather, I hope?'

'Blue skies, sunshine.'

'On the news there were reports of flooding right across southern France.'

'They make the stories up, Inspector. A man in your position ought to know that by now. What can I do for you?'

'Your friend, Gerald Sparrow?'

'Hasn't been in touch.'

'Small wonder.'

'Sorry?'

'His body turned up in a chemical container, in France of all places. Nice.'

'*Quelle coincidence.* I still don't get why you're calling me.' I had a vacuum where my stomach should have been.

'Another interesting news item, in my humble opinion at any rate, an anonymous collector offering a Matisse to one of the nation's public galleries.'

'To the Louvre, would that be? It happens all the time, very generous, the French.'

'To an Australian gallery, actually. All over the papers a little while back. In the article the donor is quoted saying he wanted to give something back.'

'You know who this anonymous donor happens to be?'

'That's the mystery.'

'Why "he" then, you said "he wanted to give something back."'

'An assumption on my part. A painting very much like one in the Stan Kriticos collection.'

'I wouldn't know anything about that, Inspector. Except I was told the Kriticos collection was worthless crap. Whereas, this painting offered by the donor, if it was featured in the press, you'd expect it to be a work of quality. You know, here in Australia with fellers like you deciding on quality. Unless, of course, like the flooding in France, they made the story up.'

'Only thing is, Mr Holt, from a strictly legalistic point of view it would be breaking the law to import such an artwork without notifying the proper authorities.'

'Tax and excise. Surely, Inspector, not the criminal law.'

'*Touché.*'

'Nobody says "*touché*" any more, Schwartz. More like we say, "shove it up you".'

'You'd have to agree it's an interesting point I raised, nevertheless?'

'You know you're wrong about that, if the paintings are personal possessions. Not all art's for sale. Or more likely what if the paintings have been in Australia since someone bought them way back when? Did you bother to think about that? Those rich Australians of the 1920s, a few of them had to have had taste. My guess is the pictures have been hanging in someone's country mansion, and very sensibly they don't want anyone knowing where.'

My mind was hunting, all the time trying to locate specific Karen moments that could have lodged in my memory.

Too soon, each time I tried I would astonish myself with the realization that I never really knew her. The Karen I'd shared so many years with turned out to be a mirage hovering up there above the horizon of my imagination. Out of reach.

Maybe that was because, as far as thinking in a day-to-day type of way was concerned, I was no longer up to it. No, not at all.

Indeed, Bobby seemed to be doing life on my account. I knew that, was letting it happen. He knew it too. Yet I really didn't know him. Like, Bobby, he couldn't even stick to the one life story; he'd been in jail, that was the one constant in an ever shifting mix of events and injustices.

The most recent account he proffered had him framed by the police. He wouldn't tell me what he'd been framed for. 'You don't need to know, Essington. If I tell you then you're involved, understand what I'm saying? Just because I've done my time doesn't mean it's over. I still have scores to settle, other people might feel the same.'

Well, me, I had scores to settle, too.

In an unexpected moment of lucidity I realised I had to tell Bobby what was really going on with me. Take the risk of doing so. Someone, a pathological liar, why not, who could conjure hand guns off the streets of Sydney, I reckoned they had to be worthy of my trust at a time when I was least able to trust myself. I had three tries at explaining, each on a different occasion. Then came the moment – in the corridor between the doors of the two apartments, at the time of the changing of the guard as I had come to think of the manoeuvre each time I took up a few hours residence with Henry and Paula. The truth was I didn't look forward to going in there. A glimpse of Henry made me think of Karen. And made me realize how little I meant to him. Paula protecting him from me made it worse. Anyway, standing out there in the corridor, the two of us, I told Bobby what my business was about.

No change of expression. 'Your business, you're telling me …'

'At the start, coming here this time, what I had in mind …'

'Are you going to tell me about forging art? Oh, mate.'

'Why would I …?'

'As if I don't know. You are so much inside your head, it's unreal.'

'You knew?'

'You've only got the Chief Inspector on your tail. Fraud squad, right? And all that stuff down there in the locked and bolted bedroom.'

'That's why it's locked.'

'Tell me about it, mate, I put the lock on. Of course I've taken a look at what you have inside there. At the start I was living in the same apartment, right? And there are things I don't do, won't be associated with, you hear what I'm telling you. So, a little investigation all of my own was in order.'

We were pacing up and down the featureless corridor. Right down the end we'd prop at the fixed window giving a view of city lights.

'What that Mister D was into didn't seem to worry you. Kiddy porn as I remember.'

'You think I'm into that stuff?'

'Littering the place, it was. Impossible to miss.'

'No way, mate. Not me. Mind you, though, it wasn't like little girls and boys stuff. Not as far as I could tell. More like, you know, flat chested hookers, waxed like billiard balls, dressed up as high school girls. That was what he was into.'

'And Jesus.'

'That as well, sure.'

Still, Bobby allowed me to explain that the stuff he'd seen in the room was a game I had hoped to play. I was going to sell the Derain onto the Australian market. To keep myself interested in what I do best.

'And now?'

'Now I've got a real purpose. I am going to have to get rid of Stan Kriticos, forever. That or go crazy. He's got me by the balls, I'm thinking about him most of the time. Because he is a threat to Henry, right? Henry's all I've got left of my wife. But Stan, he's never going to leave me alone, I know it. He's a type, a classic psycho. I know what he's like.'

'You sure you know what anything's like right now, Essington?'

'Stan Kriticos, yes. I guess I always did. It's just that I was too caught up flogging him paintings to let it register.'

'The publicity you had me get that Julian Anderson onto. It has something to do with this?'

'It was just an idea I had, catch Stan's attention. He'd have to know it was his painting. Even Stan.'

'What effect is that going to have?'

'Confuse him, I guess. Confuse Schwartz at the same time. They'd see I wasn't making any money on the deal, so where does that leave them?'

'But, mate, so you're poking a stick into a hornets' nest. Doing that can't make this Mr Kriticos any less a problem. Has to be the other way round. He's going to come after you.'

'That's the idea.'

Drawing, there are moments, the very best moments, when you don't know you're steering the stick of charcoal across the paper. You kind of don't even know you are there. The feeling of being absent might last a few seconds, often does, but every so often you don't come back till you've finished the thing. Even then it's not till the next day, maybe, or a week later you recognise you've done something so much better than everything else you ever tried. Could take a year for the penny to drop.

In a kind of way I'd lucked it unconsciously with Stan, too. Unless I was deceiving myself. Without understanding what

I had been attempting to do by parading the Matisse *Femme Couchée* in the Australian media I had to have got Stan's attention. Given his capacity to explode, chances were Stan would forget all about Henry, or any other party for that matter. Instead, with his fuse burning, he'd come directly after me, his mind focused on revenge.

The following morning I was in the studio, with Bobby. Laid out on the bench, the Matisse and the Kandinsky. Just the canvases, waiting for plausible stretchers.

I was explaining stuff to him. 'The process starts with selecting someone the market wants. Otherwise you are wasting time. There are lots of small players out there on the edges of the forging game, bitter little artists mostly, with not a lot of talent and who don't take much pleasure from painting. Not selling too well, probably never will. They produce under-ambitious fakes, many unsigned, "in the style of", so to speak. Pictures that look as though they might or might not be by some dead, middle-reputation painter. Works like that, slipped into the art auction system of a regional centre, can be picked up by dealers who tart them up with a varnish, shove them into water-gilded frames, maybe add a signature and offer them onto the retail market from some smart shop with location. At, say a two or three thousand percent mark up. But, Bobby, that's not art forgery's arsehole, that.'

'Mate, you're saying you've either got it or you haven't.'

'The art in art forgery is at the top end of the market. You take a really big value artist like Vermeer and you are testing yourself as a forger. Like climbing Everest. The greatest forger did just that. Chose Vermeer. He met the challenge.'

'What do they look like?'

'I'll show you.' We went back to the living area, I clicked up a search engine on the laptop, typed 'Vermeer' and after vetting the crap sites found an image of *The Studio*, with the artist at his easel and his blue robed model holding a book and a trombone.

'That's surreal. The way the chandelier stands out from the map, oh, mate.'

'Weird thing is, two hundred years ago nobody was interested in Vermeer. They didn't know who he was, just didn't get it. His paintings were pretty rare – not a lot of paintings so not a lot of reputation. To get a good price, if one came on the market they forged the signature of Pieter de Hooch; a contemporary of Vermeer's they couldn't get enough of in the 19th century.'

'But you copy the lot, signature, everything.'

'I reinvent, is how I like to think of it, Bobby.'

'You design it from scratch!'

'That way nobody's going to surprise you by coming up with the original. Forged Vermeers created a big problem for the art world's experts. In the late 1930s fakes began to turn up, one here, one there, and they sold for a lot of money. Before that there had been convenient misattributions, sure, but these new ones surfacing, they were Vermeers or they were nothing. Curators in museums, the top critics, they believed in the new works. Conservator's chemical analysis seemed to demonstrate that the period and the paint technique were right. Professors of fine art went into raptures over the use of colour, the symbolism, too. Others celebrated the strongly religious subject matter.

'Surprise, surprise, after the Second World War a bunch of American soldiers discovered a painting, *Christ and the woman taken in adultery* it was called, stored in a salt mine with a lot of other artworks. Purchased for a fortune by the German Field Marshal Goering, during the war.

'The sale was traced to an artist, Van Meegeren. Interestingly, having sold the painting to a German, facing trial he had to choose – he could be tried as a collaborator, or admit to painting the Vermeer. He elected going to trial for forgery.'

'You'd do less time?'

'A lot less. If you ask me he should have been hailed as a hero having suckered Goering. But in the art world the players don't like being shown up as a bunch of posers. They'd been praising the Van Meegeren Vermeers for too long, and suddenly had egg all over their faces.'

'Van Meegeren died a year later. In jail. Not much older than I am now.'

'Would have hit it off with Miss Leary.'

'Sorry?'

'Took the art classes at Long Bay.'

'You did music, remember?'

'Took a lot of courses there, doing my time.'

'Vermeer was great at clouds.'

'You are talking like he's your hero.'

'Hadn't thought of it before, but no. Van Meegeren more like it. He made a point that right up to today nobody seems to have grasped.'

'Which is?'

'People who reckon they can pick a fake, doesn't matter what their qualifications, all they can do is pick a bad fake. For me, now, of course, Vermeer's out. Because of Van Meegeren and because the world's has been scoured for anything he touched. The chance of being able to establish the authenticity of a previously unknown Vermeer is nil. The bastards would test the layers of paint every way known, for pigments, for binders not existing at Vermeer's time or not in use in his part of the world at any rate. The gesso ground beneath the pigments, that too, the date and quality of the canvas or maybe the oak panel he painted it on. If you got it right, still no one would believe it. If it was a real Vermeer, they'd knock that back on principle.'

'Miss Leary reckoned the art bit was all in here,' Bobby said, tapping his forehead, 'But from what you're telling me it sounds more to do with your wallet.'

'The market establishes the reputations.'

'Thank you very much.'

I searched 'Matisse' on the laptop, clicked up the image of a model on a bed with a view of Paris out the window. A painting done in 1916 when he was having a hard time financially.

'This man's all right for me because he'd produced a lot of work over a long career and documentation was screwed up by the Second World War and the misrepresentation of just about everything that had occurred which followed directly after. The same situation that worked for Van Meegeren. Forging art for the Nazis was a flourishing industry right across Europe in those days; even modern art, despite the anti-modern-art Nazi party line.'

'If you're not planning to sell it, where's the crime?'

'Depends on your point of view, I expect.'

Then I explained to him about the process of stretching the canvases. The importance of the stretcher itself. And the tacks. Clicking open images of the back of the Pont Royale painting.

'I can see now why you like it, Essington.'

'Sorry?'

'You get into it and you focus. Kind of keeps you sane, I'd reckon.'

'Therapy, never thought of it like that.'

'Maybe you should. It's why they have those courses in jail. Miss Leary, I remember she was teaching us how to do clouds, with watercolour. She reckoned that the stuff happening with the watercolour was the same as happened in the sky, only in reverse. Like a negative process. Follow?'

'Not really.'

'Where the most water is, with the paint in it, is the blue sky, where it's thin, or you leave it dry, that's the clouds. That picture you showed, with the trumpet or whatever, it's an inside painting.'

'Yes, but his skies, lovely.'

Bobby was off to the Blue Boy gallery with the measurements in his pocket and I hoped a clear memory of dates and a mental picture of what the stretchers ought to look like. And to make sure he didn't finish up buying any forgeries. Before he went he asked, 'Why not go yourself? Go out that street door, mate, how hard can that be?'

'Schwartz has already talked to the man at Blue Boy. I turn up there again he's certain to be told.'

'What can he do?'

'With Stan feeding him bullshit, plus his own suspicions. Christ knows what kind of answers Giovanna has supplied him with. The man has to be trouble.'

'Oh mate! That's life, isn't it? For instance, me, there I was minding my own business, going to be married in three months, down payment on a house in Fairfield, big block – you looked out from the verandah over paddocks and bushland. Could have kept a horse in the back garden. Next thing I'm in court facing so many charges you don't want to know.'

'For what Bobby?'

'This importing/exporting thing I'd got conned into getting involved with. I was the fall guy. The rest, local politicians, not a trace of them in any of the documentation.'

'You were importing …?'

'Very much like your line of work, these bronze statues from Cambodia, the Buddha and stuff.'

'Lets get those stretchers. Oh, and Bobby, might as well take the gun, just to play safe.'

'Can't leave it around the place anyway. On account of the kid, mate.'

Chapter 13

A Siamese pair of lady finger bananas to munch while travelling this life's long and winding road. Bananas ingested,
peel next to an empty glass on a coffee table, I pulled out
my mobile, located the stored number for Pretty Girl Inc.,
and pressed the button. I seemed to recall Phyllis had left a
message.

She picked up as promptly as usual and went directly to
complaining about her aches and pains. 'It's my hips, Mr Holt,
the nights are … I can't begin to tell you. But more than the
pain I fear an operation.'

'Mine's inoperable.'

'Your … which is that?'

'Pain, Phyllis. In my soul.'

'Oh, I see.' And she started to laugh.

Then she was telling me about a new girl named Thea who
had joined the agency. It was a Phyllis rule to use only first
names for the models – so rogue clients didn't pester them. She
wanted to know, would I like to book Thea?

'Did she express interest in modelling for me in particular?'

'Not in so many words, but …'

'I'm interested.'

'She did say she'd heard through a friend that my agency
had work with an important artist. Of all the gentlemen, you
are my only real artist, Mr Holt.'

'She said, "important"? That is nice. Unfortunately not
true.'

'Not what I'm told by the girls.'

'On second thought, it might be best if we give models
named Thea a miss. No Mandy's either would be nice.'

That got Phyllis chuckling. Lifted my spirits a little when
she chuckled. 'When I was younger, Mr Holt, a mandy was one

of several terms for a certain illegal substance.'

'Most probably it still is.'

A letter arrived from the south of France, international express post, addressed by hand. In the sender's spot, Yassir had written his name, inelegantly, and his address as Villa du Phare; that made me feel displaced. Inside the envelope was another envelope, posted in Australia and addressed to me in the south of France. Like those Russian dolls, inside that envelope I discovered another, which had been slit open and tucked beside a note from a solicitor explaining that due to the circumstances of the death of Gerald Franklin Swallow there had been a delay in following the instructions of the deceased in forwarding the enclosed letter to me. The writer added that the letter's contents had been made known to an officer of the New South Wales police force, as required by law since those contents might prove to be of assistance in ascertaining the manner of Sparrow's death.

I'd never known about the middle name, Franklin. The names given to the dead can be so affecting, principally I guess on account of the optimism involved in their choosing.

The letter itself had been written by hand in ball-point (not the usual Sparrow-style Mont Blanc fountain pen dripping blue ink) on a sheet of lined paper from the kind of pad students use when taking notes. An extremely un-Sparrow sheet of paper.

My father said to me, I can't remember when, that if you know in your heart of hearts that you can trust a person then you ought to have your head read. While holding Sparrow's letter in my hand it occurred to me, having read it through twice, that my father's piece of wisdom worked just as well the other way round: if you know in your heart of hearts that you can't trust a person then you ought to have your head read.

I suspect Karen would have said that a person ought to seek the middle way.

Was I going to accept the idea that Sparrow was more sorry than he could say? Or that for many years he'd had trouble dealing with those changes in our relative fortunes which had led him to resent me? Resent me, that was something new. He went on to say that after inheriting from my aunt I seemed to have changed. I had become presumptuous and careless of other people's feelings. I had taken him too much for granted; he ceased to be a valued friend and had become instead a functionary.

He explained that he had developed a positive dislike of me, and found himself, against his better instincts, desiring my downfall.

I was thinking of Inspector Schwartz and how many others, picking over the neatly formed words crowding the page. What had they made of his unguarded accusation that I'd sold myself short as an artist by copying the work of others instead of developing a manner of my own?

Was that a reference to forgery, or was he simply referring to the paintings I had produced in my late teens and early twenties, tentative studies in the manner of other artists?

Whatever Sparrow's intention, Schwartz would have relished the possible reference to forgery.

Would Schwartz as well have picked up the hint of some kind of unconsummated homo-erotic relationship on the go between Sparrow and me? That possibility struck and I realized it had to be at least half-way true: we were these two unlikely boys who bonded because of what?

Schwartz wouldn't have been so keen to read the succinct account of his own approaches to Sparrow, or of his use of the law to gain access to correspondence relating to certain business deals I'd done.

And then came the stuff about Stan Kriticos. Sparrow more or less admitted that he'd gone over to Kriticos, spilt his guts to him about what he referred to as 'the nature of your art dealing,

Essington.' He didn't stipulate precisely when he did that. But he did indicate that Kriticos put pressure on him.

There was confirmation for Schwartz. Well, almost.

Close to the bottom of the back of the page, nearly out of space, starting to run two lines of his neat writing within each pair of ruled lines, he explained that he had called a halt to collaboration with Stan Kriticos as a result of information coming his way concerning Stan's 'unconscionable activities, Essington, of the very worst kind, evidence of which I came upon by sheer accident'.

He wrote, 'I can imagine you smiling when you read that now I fear for my life. You who once told me I was physically insecure – do you remember saying that? Well, Essington, I am in deadly earnest when I write that I am equally concerned now for your safety.

'Because in the end it has to be you that he is after, Essington.'

In tiny letters along the bottom of that page he wished me well for the future.

All those years with the art thing, telling me nothing – hear no evil, see no evil – the bastard had been working out what I did!

The whole thing so sad. And so very Gerald Fucking Sparrow.

By the sound of it, working out where Stan's money came from. In that agreeing with Karen, after death. The pair of them at loggerheads while alive.

I picked up the knife and fork and began making my way, surgically, through a grilled flounder, while sampling the potato wedges in one side dish, and the Greek salad in the other. As it happened I was still under the weather from the excesses of my afternoon, and the food-laden fork was shaking a little and shedding each time I brought it to my mouth.

I must have experienced a slippage of time, because next thing the booze was gone, the food gone too and the television was cruising with the sound off, showing some bullshit film.

Bobby had come and gone back next door, that's what it meant.

And I was losing it one more time – on each occasion in a bigger way. Falling apart completely, a total wreck, sometimes naked and weeping, or gasping for air and for sanity or for both at once; occasionally wrapped in sheets and wandering up to the window, pressing my hands and nose against the glass, staring at that bridge the way a goldfish or a guppy stares unknowing at the world beyond the fish tank.

You live smart in Sydney, you'll finish up staring at the bridge. And at night the doomed birds circling above it.

Or I was in the bathroom, all the taps running, steam building. Or at the freezer and screaming at its tundra interior because the vodka had run out.

Some time later, probably another blackout.

'You have a member of the fraud squad on your tail day and night and you want me to believe there isn't an issue concerning you that's causing him to act this way? Or do you think I'm incapable of putting two and two together? The apartment isn't the principal reason for your being here. So, don't you think it would be wise to fill me in? Your legal representative.'

The cordless phone in one hand. The little finger of the other mining lint in my navel.

'Are you hearing me, Essington?'

'Of course I am hearing you. I understand your problem, too. Unfortunately I anticipate that you won't believe whatever answer I give. Of course you should know about any legal problems I might have while I'm here. The fact is I still don't understand what interests Schwartz so much.'

'He mentioned a letter from Gerald Sparrow.'

'Why don't you ask him, then?'
'Essington, we both know he's dead.'
'I'm not hearing you, Giovanna.'

Celeste. Still fiddling with her hair, but relatively relaxed.

She went out of her way to tell me I was a real artist, like Monet.

'Manet.'

'You're the expert.'

'That's called pronating, isn't it?'

'What?'

'Your feet turning.'

Celeste: 'Pigeon toed. Pronating is when you kind of roll over, inwards.'

'Must look it up.'

'Look it up, that's a guy thing.'

'You think so?'

'Last time you checked if Greenland is a different shape on different maps.'

'I did?'

'Essington, you know you did.'

'Or is that half way to ... which position is it in ballet?'

'What are you talking about?'

I stood up, placed my feet just so. '*Le position premier* ... or is it *la position*?'

'You lost me.'

'When I was young, it didn't matter how thick you were, if you could talk French you were in.'

'In where?'

'With the culture crowd.'

'We did Japanese, a lot of use that is.'

I was working my way through the ballet positions. 'Finish up with *plie*, like this.'

'More a clown than an artist.'

'Same thing.'

She had brought along a cape she explained was part of her medieval costume. It was much too big for her.

'Medieval, for what?'

'I'm into the medieval.'

'I got that, but what do you do exactly?'

'You know, jousting tournaments, computer games, banquets, we have these nights that are the best thing, drinking honey mead and stuff.'

'I love honey mead.'

'You could have warned me, I'd have brought a bottle.'

'Next time.'

'Maybe I'll bring two, the other for that poor sad character living on the street outside your block.'

'Was he begging when you arrived?'

'Was he what?'

Chapter 14

I hadn't set foot outside the building, for how long? I'd stopped counting. But I patrolled its corridors, stairs and lifts; the car park, the roof. I'd developed a thing about the security system the governing body had installed soon after my trouble with Mister D. There were supposed to be state-of-the-art video surveillance cameras to cover just about every angle. Frightening. Yet I couldn't locate the TV monitors the surveillance system fed, and nobody was going to tell me where they were.

Revealing more of the caring side to his nature, Bobby reckoned I should consult a psychiatrist and work out what had gone wrong inside my head. I was against that. Anyway, seeing someone about losing the ability to go outside would involve leaving the building. That I definitely did not intend to do.

I did, however, elect for indoor physical exercise. Twice a day I worked out in the gym on the sub-ground floor – one level above the car parking slots – where I got off on pulling against springs and pushing up weights, walking the conveyor belt, not to forget beating the shit out of a punching bag that looked as if it had never before taken a blow in anger.

Other times I'd ride the lift to one level below the penthouse and swim fifty laps of the heated, twenty-five metre pool.

Destroyed mind, healthy body. I was sustaining my tan and vitamin D levels by lounging naked on the narrow balcony. If there'd been any other sun lover on that level we could have compared the condition of our primary and secondary sexual characteristics. But no. Paula kept the doors to that balcony locked, claiming that the thought of Henry out there frightened her. And there certainly wasn't any sign of people further along, in either direction. Not even a pot plant.

Meanwhile Bobby was doing reality on my behalf. For instance he magicked a little double-action 9mm Walther with a spare clip and a box of ammunition. He reckoned it would be a great idea if we took a spin out into the country for some shooting practice.

'Sick in the head, remember. Not going Sunday driving. Anyway I know about shooting handguns.' One bullet, which hit the Derain nude, the sum of my target practice in ten years.

Whatever he'd done, whichever crime they'd put him away for, something about forgery was getting its hooks into Bobby. He'd come in from next door, stepping out of all that fuzzy violin music he reckoned turned him on, and pretty soon he'd be keen to go to where I was doing my art thing. My own drawings did nothing for him. But he was getting some feel for old and brittle canvas, the way paint is mixed and applied, for yellowing and patterns of cracking, and for varnishes. The whole thing.

'Don't tell me, pure alcohol.' He'd picked up a laboratory

style bottle with a glass stopper, three-quarters full with clear liquid. 'Don't answer that. Be empty, wouldn't it?'

'I'd add orange juice first. Give me a break.'

'Mate, doesn't sound like you.'

'Bobby, I told you before, didn't I? That's distilled water. Working on these paintings you have to use it for everything.'

'Because?'

'Think about it. The chemicals they put in town water today leave a residue. Test the painting and you're liable to discover a substance that wasn't known about until thirty years ago.'

'Be the same with rain water, then.'

'Exactly.'

'You could still drink it, be good for you.'

'Except no minerals, either.'

Funny thing was I liked doing this with Bobby. Showing him what I knew. Was that because I was one more aging ego-maniac crowding out the world? Or was it some kind of passing on knowledge thing? I couldn't say.

Next I was showing him a model I had of one of Derain's fingertips. I only had a couple of these, the other was a Kirchner thumb. Kirchner, the German expressionist.

He couldn't believe it. Picking up the jeweller's lupe from the bench top. Turning the fingertip under it. 'This is his fingerprint?'

'High-tech casting putty, Bobby. Very fine surface quality. You find finger imprints on paintings all the time, particularly with Impressionists, and the Moderns of course. They worked a lot with their fingers. The same back to the Renaissance, once oil painting was developed. Oil is slow drying, so an artist can push it around by using a brush, obviously. Or a knife, a block of wood or just hands and fingers – often the ball of the thumb to smooth out some blending.'

'And the pattern of the finger print is left there?'

'Takes a lot of looking to find it. But turn the idea around, Bobby. What if there's a print in the paint that isn't the artist's? That's going to raise suspicion. A forger leaves his prints in the paint, then there's the evidence he doesn't need to provide. Make sense?'

Bobby just shaking his head. Then pulling out one of the paintings from the Blue Boy Galleries. Checking the surface for fingerprints.

'They've got too much varnish on them, Bobby. Well, all except ... try that one with the girls in hats, the flowers up above. The technique looks about right. Smeary, see. Looks like it was painted quickly, and thick. If you don't find fingerprints you might find a cat hair, or some dog's, all sorts of stuff stuck to the paint. Plus the parallel grooves the bristle brushes make.'

He reckoned he was finding hair up in the white-pink tones of the flowers.

Me observing someone finding things in a work of art.

Nice feeling.

I looked at the distilled water in the bottle. Realised it was time for a drink.

'Oh, mate ...' Bobby was muttering, 'Fantastic, a whole world, this.'

After midnight. Nina Simone singing 'Summer wine'. Drunk, alone, sliding the glass doors onto the balcony wide open, I taped a paper towel roll to the railing. A paper towel roll is close to the size of a man's head. I refilled my vodka glass, switched over to FM radio, found dance music, turned the volume up. A citizen's nightmare is some crazy guy high in his head, high too above the world, a glass of booze in one hand and a Walther in the other. I was fifteen paces from the target. On the other side of the wall Paula and all would have been wondering what the boss was up to now. Most probably I was swaying like the mast of a moored yacht. Beyond the balcony, the night and all that

CBD stuff I didn't give a shit about, most of it empty.

I put the vodka glass down, turned the amplifier on full, raised the gun and fired – just like that. The report was followed by a ping and the high whine of a ricochet; did I invent the ricochet? Don't think so. The shot hit the top of the iron railing and sailed into the night.

I turned the sound down, emptied my glass, inhaled acrid cordite hanging in the room.

I'd always assumed Karen would outlive me. She was a lot younger, what's more I was a man and had bad habits. Not that I thought about outliving much. That I loved her had seemed enough – I wasn't going to find out how much I'd miss her till some time after she died. At some level I must always have understood that emotions work on time delay. So, after the initial shock of her death, apart from falling to pieces altogether, for the second time in as many months, the fact that she wasn't going to touch me again didn't actually register. One reason for that might have been this inability to remember what she looked like. I didn't have photographs. There were photographs, hundreds of them, but all back in France, stuck in different drawers around the house. Karen somewhere, smiling. Karen in London with Dawn at the launch of a range of fabrics for summer or whatever. Karen talking to River Phoenix on the waterfront at Villefranche-sur-Mer, Dawn paying a lot of attention to his companion. Karen pregnant, on a banana lounge, Desdemona at her side, panting. Karen and the baby.

Yes, they'd all be there. But without their aid I couldn't actually recall what she looked like. I couldn't get her to come alive in my imagination. I couldn't look at her memory, into some souvenir of her eyes and say, 'Karen, I am so sorry, so terribly sorry.' I had a more complete recollection of each painting and drawing in the Kriticos collection than I had of my dead wife.

So I stood in the room sniffing cordite, gun in one hand, an empty glass in the other hand, knowing I'd failed Karen yet again.

I sat on the floor, cross-legged. Stayed that way a long time, a ghost of music leaking through the speakers, from time to time an announcer cutting in, more mindless music, the announcer, more music.

The gun in my hand.

The barrel of the gun in my mouth.

Then out of my mouth.

Sweating.

My eyes shut, inside my head searching for the image of Karen.

The barrel of the gun pressed against the side of my head, just above my ear.

My eyes wide open.

Then Bobby knocked twice and came striding in through the door saying, 'What the hell do you think …!'

But he knew. Of course he knew.

'Essington, you can't do that, you're my meal ticket. Oh mate, you top yourself and I'm finished.'

I lay flat on my back on the floor, the ceiling up there – too low I would have thought, those nasty little recessed lights connected to their nasty little dimmer switches, and I laughed. 'I kill myself,' I splutter, 'you're finished!' Laughing so much I could hardly get the words out. 'You're finished … Jesus, what about me?'

'Wouldn't worry you, mate, you'd be dead.'

Laughter crossing into hysteria territory.

Cool as you like he picked up the gun where it lay beside me on the floor, smelt the barrel, removed the clip, emptied the chamber as well. Meticulous. And acting like a man who knew a lot about guns.

'A drink, Bobby?'

'That's exactly what you don't need right now, Essington. In the state you're in if I let you have a drink I reckon I'd be breaking the law.'

'Breaking the law!' Very likely I laughed so hard at that I wet myself. I'll never know if I did, and he'll never tell me.

Headache. Headache tablets doing battle with it. Heartache – no heartache tablets. Yet there was that feeling again. Didn't I know that guy over there abandoning the conversation he was pretending to be having? I was watching them both through the front door of my apartment block. I'd go down there from time to time, checking things out, and to see if I could actually bring myself to open the glass security entrance door. There'd been times when I'd stood there for an hour, attempting to find the resolve to push the button, open the door, step out into the street. People would enter while I was trying to overcome the fear, but I'd just prop there, acting the cool dude while looking like nothing so much as the in-house intellectual defective. Residents who already knew me by sight would mutter stuff like 'Nice Day' and off they'd go into the wild, threatening world of the street, or up to their nests. Coming, going.

Not a lot of residents, to tell the truth. Had to be a lot of empty apartments up there. Damien never mentioned that when we were buying.

Nor Sparrow.

But I wasn't in a mood to hold grudges where Sparrow was concerned.

I'd pretend to myself I was collecting my mail. In reality Bobby collected the mail. Still, the excuse would have me down there trying to reach the outside world – three times in a day, ten times? Watching passers-by. All the time thinking to myself that different individuals looked like someone I once knew; or that the person over there sitting in a car, wasn't that the man who'd … but then I'd forget what the connection might have been.

Was that Giovanna hailing a taxi?

There was that bum living on the street who seemed to come by with the regularity of a cut-out target mounted on a continuous travelling belt in some shooting gallery. I knew him from somewhere, didn't I? If I could have opened that door I would have rushed out calling …

And he would have asked …

But I couldn't do it.

Three times I'd spotted Stan Kriticos exiting through the open door of the coffee bar across the road. On each occasion he looked straight at where I was standing in the lobby, then averted his gaze, slow, a movie camera sliding up the face of the building.

Each version of Stan Kriticos was markedly different from the previous one.

Had I forgotten what he looked like as well?

Karen, then Kriticos.

On more than one occasion I took the lift to the car park below the gym, down there in the bowels of the earth where the water, gas and drain pipes ran free. Wandering among what slumbering automobiles were in residence, all of a sudden I'd drop into a crouch and, doubled over, sprint between the cars, often as not with the 9mm Walther shoved down the back of my pants. Then prop, take a look around like a fugitive in a TV cop show, run for the next cover.

Gun held in both hands, cop style.

Taking cover behind Bobby's Holden with its bright blue passenger side door not matching the grey duco of the rest of it.

I guess I thought I was checking the place out.

Maybe I was doing just that.

I don't know.

I wasn't me any more.

I really did not know what was going on in my mind at that time.

I was emotionally exhausted. Fit, tanned, and gaga.

Back up to the apartment for a shower, in the door, the sweat pouring off me. Paula and Henry in there. Like there was this moment, me staring at them, the pair of them staring straight back, as if we'd never met before. Strangers. The moment lasting forever.

'Showing Henry where his daddy lives.'

'He bloody well knows where I live, Paula.'

'I've asked you before, about the rough language.'

'I pay for everything. Everything, do you hear what I'm saying, and you want to pick faults with my vocabulary!'

'That's another thing, Mr Holt, your moods. You might not realise it but there are times – the walls in these apartments are so thin – we hear you roaring in here. And banging. It's as if we are renting next to bedlam, if you don't mind.'

It had been Bobby's idea that Paula have a key to both apartments. He'd argued that the situation was safer that way.

Bobby taking over.

I wasn't sure I liked the idea of Paula nosing about in there.

That third bedroom was stuffed full of paintings that had turned up from the Blue Boy Gallery. When I asked Bobby if he preferred any one to the rest he responded by raising his eyebrows.

'What would your Miss Leary have said?'

'Who are you talking about?'

'Woman who ran the art classes.'

'Which art classes? Essington, I can't follow you on this one.'

The truth was, all the paintings were dreadful. Yet once upon a time people had liked them enough to buy. Stuff like those varnished, deep green and brown landscapes with their generalised European feel had been doing the rounds of dealers and auction rooms since forever. Always a seller and a buyer.

I'd forgotten to do it earlier, so I asked him about the reception the Derain got at the auction house.

'Fine.'

'What do you mean, fine?'

'Like you said, I gave it to Julian Anderson. Took the paper and the bubble plastic off like he was unwrapping an emu egg, he held it out at arm's length, smiled, I suppose you might call it. Then he wanted to know the reserve.'

'Jesus, I forgot to tell you that. And now you've forgotten to ask me.'

'It wasn't so long ago he got it. You can ring, or are you telling me you can't punch numbers on a phone any more?' Bobby had been walking from room to room as we were talking. As if assessing the apartment itself, checking it for further indications of my mind's deterioration.

He found something in the cooking department.

'Oh mate, I don't believe it. Nobody keeps a gun on the drain board. Think about it, Essington. I'm responsible, you understand what I'm saying? I get you that gun, and you leave it around the place like it's a packet of biscuits.'

'I only just put it down.'

'If that gun was legal, licensed and all, mate, you'd have to have sworn on the bible to keep it under lock and key. You leave it there, say Henry comes in …'

'Henry never comes in here.'

'Just say he did, is what I'm suggesting.'

'And I'm telling you he doesn't like it in here.'

'Please don't leave the gun lying around, Essington. And if you wouldn't mind ringing that Julian Anderson, because I told him you would.'

'Treating me like a child.'

'You don't like it, I'm out of here.'

Bobby was holding the 9mm Walther out in front of him. Shooting stance. Aiming at the TV where, with the sound off, somebody was telling the rest of us about something important.

'We have a break-in here, pick up the gun, where does that leave you?' His face expressionless. 'Before my life turned to shit I used to play a bit of league. Essington, that's what I really wanted to do, I reckoned I was cut out for it, be a football star. All right, I hear you ask, who doesn't? I was good, though. Yet I didn't make the grade. The truth is I never really thought the right way, I wasn't positive enough. Still, I learnt a few things while not getting there. Essington, you ever play?'

'I lacked the talent.'

'One thing always sticks in my mind. The coach said that a genius player knows where to run. Knows it in his head and gets there. A dud hangs about where the ball last landed.'

'Meaning?'

'We're going to need to know about what's out in front of us, mate, not what's in the past. All those paintings I picked out for you, at life's big moments they only represent a waste of space. Okay?'

Sitting, silent, we watched TV with the sound off for half an hour.

Then, 'Mate, you don't know a lot about me. You can copy a painting, and you can brawl, I wouldn't dispute that, but in life you've had it too easy to learn much.'

'I've had it easy!'

'You never went to jail.'

Left to my own devices I checked the new paintings' measurements. I'd do something like that and my mind would start working properly. Or I'd sit around remembering stuff and go nuts. There were two paintings in particular. Both early 20th century. Their frames were more authentic in terms of fashion; not properly modernist, but they'd pass since the

French used to go for out of date frames anyway. One was fishing boats with the tide out, a couple of sea birds in the sky. The other showed women in wide-brim hats sitting under a flowering creeper of some kind.

It took a while to get them off the stretchers and my Kandinsky and Matisse on. Then I popped them back into the frames. In each case the match between image and frame wasn't too unlikely.

But then reality began moving back out of my reach.

Bobby came in with buttered toast and a hot chocolate – for me!

Next he wanted to use the bathroom.

He returned shaking his head, 'I don't know if you want to hear this.'

'Hear what, Bobby?'

'That guy you told me you see watching from the coffee bar over the road. He's not in your head, he's real. What's more I spotted him visiting your pretty-girl lawyer, too.'

'At her apartment?'

'The office, where she works. That photo of him you showed me, it's not a great likeness, but it's the same guy, that's for sure.'

'You are talking about …?'

'The Greek, Kriticos.'

'There are a lot of offices in Giovanna's building.'

'Don't I know it? But he was visiting her. I checked. I asked this receptionist they seem to share on that floor.'

'Asked if it was Stan Kriticos?'

'No way, if someone just went in, would I have to wait? She said if I didn't have an appointment there was no way …'

'So they know you were interested?'

Bobby got to his feet, wandered over to the window as if to admire the view and stopped there, 'If you reckon I'm that thick, what are you paying me a wage for?'

Taking another look at the two canvases I'd stretched, I don't know why, but I got this idea of something extra to do. Most probably it was just me wanting to get back that illusion of being an effective human being.

Or it was a further step into craziness. I don't know. But I decided to stretch the original paintings back over the top. Mostly, I suppose it amused me to do that. I was smiling all the time I was working. The Matisse over the women in the big hats, the Kandinsky over the fishing boats.

It took a bit of doing. In fact I couldn't get them absolutely flat because the canvas wasn't pulling properly at the edges despite strips of computer printing paper I'd laid there as a buffer between the two surfaces. Still, I figured I was the only person in the country liable to notice the problem. Only me because the real experts weren't going to grant those two banal paintings the time of day.

A little later, a fair bit drunker, it hit me, not for the first time, that I do with paintings what I do with life. The sort of person-ality given to faking everything. The paintings – I'd layered one lot of shallow sensations over another, just piled bullshit onto bullshit. It was as if every move I took was a step away from understanding.

From understanding anything.

That crazy character sleeping out the front of the apart-ment block, him and me, with our lack of connection we had to be mirror images of one another.

An email from Giovanna. Terse. She asked me to open the attachment, look at it, think about it. She would send another email in one hour.

The attachment was an image file. Me fucking these two girls. Thea and Mandy. Nice clear shot.

I just sat in front of the laptop. When I came back to my

senses I remember thinking how still and how absolutely quite everything around me was, soundless as death.

I tapped in a reply, 'Pretty picture.'

Her response, when it came. 'The owner wants to meet you.'

I walked to the wall separating me from Henry and Paula. Bobby would be in there too. I pressed my ear against the plaster rendering and could pick up the sound of Henry crying. Then Bobby's voice, telling him something. Then Henry settling down a little.

I drank a glass of iced water, spread my women-in-states-of-undress drawings all over the floor, the bed, everywhere. Collectively they had to mean something, well, you'd reckon, wouldn't you? But what?

Chapter 15

I'd been sitting with Henry and Paula. In dispute. Paula wanted to get out of there, said they needed air. She reckoned being locked up would have a bad effect on Henry's development. She said he was starting to ask about his mother.

'That took a while coming.'

'It's been there all the time, but I've kept him so busy he hasn't been able to get a proper grip on what's gone wrong in his life.'

'And now?'

'You aren't listening to what I'm telling you, Mr Holt.'

'I heard. Believe it or not, I almost understand. But one minute you were telling me we neglected Henry, Karen and me. Now he's missing her. Don't you think I miss Karen? I think about her all the time.'

When I returned to my apartment Bobby told me that seconds before someone had buzzed from the street entrance, but when he picked up there hadn't been anybody there.

He asked me, 'That wasn't you buzzing, Essington?'

'From the street, definitely not. Did you say anything into the door phone?'

'Nothing, pretty much I just grunted.'

'Not so many residents but there are a lot of apartments. I guess people push the wrong button from time to time.'

'You'd think.'

'Yet strange it's never happened before.' My mind was hunting for where I'd last put the gun. I sat down.

Still on his feet, Bobby watching me. 'He's threatened your kid, right? I mean do you sit around and wait for the thing to unravel?'

'You're telling me I've got to kill someone?'

'Mate, it's very possible you don't have a choice,' he said very slowly.

Checking in the bedroom, I found the gun, it had been under my pillow. No memory of putting it there.

I walked to the glass doors giving onto the balcony. Blue sky, a few puffy white clouds, tops of palm trees and Port Jackson figs, yachts and all that bullshit. In the 180 degree view not a hint of trouble.

I followed this one yacht tacking up a reach of the harbour, butterfly decoration on its sail.

'Bobby.'

'Mate?'

'Anybody watching will know your car, right?'

'Just a Holden.'

'With a bright blue door on the passenger side. It stands out. So hire a commercial van of some sort. Have them bring it into the carpark. Okay? Make it a white van. And next time that buzzer buzzes, get Henry and that Paula woman out of here, understand. Straight down in the lift, don't take a thing, just go. You understand me?'

Two days later the buzzer sounded and I picked up the hand-piece connecting to the block's front door.

'Essington, buzz me up, we have to talk.'

I hung up the hand piece.

The thought: would Schwartz be around there somewhere, watching Stan failing to make an entrance? And if so …

Bobby must have heard the buzzer because he was standing at the door, observing me. I was getting used to him doing that.

'Get them out of here, Bobby.' He vanished.

This time it was the phone that rang.

From before I picked up Stan was saying. '… Essington, I've got a deal, fair to both parties.'

And I was thinking, 'Jesus Christ!'

'I'm a businessman, a realist …'

I was saying, 'I don't have a trade to make.'

'Let me come up there so we can talk it over, face to face.'

'Stan …'

'Essington, a final offer, hear what I'm saying?'

'You're at the street door?'

'Was, I'm in the car now, double parked. I thought you'd be watching me from your balcony. Or do you have vertigo?'

'On your own?'

'Are you?'

'Give me five minutes.'

Would Schwartz have someone checking movement in and out of my place when it mattered? Then I remembered the gun, where did I put the gun?

Silence.

Just me standing there without the gun. I was surprised to catch my reflection, hunched and panicky, in the sliding glass doors giving onto the balcony.

Junk coursing through my head as I belted around the apartment, looking for where I'd put the gun.

And dripping sweat.

I opened the freezer. Would I put a gun in the freezer? No way. I took the top off the vodka, poured a shot down my throat, taking care to keep my lips from touching the glass. Straight to the drawers in my clothes cupboard, I emptied the lot.

No gun.

More vodka.

The buzzer sounded. I pushed the button to open the street door.

More sweat.

They reckon there's a moment when a trapped animal knows it's doomed. The eyes glaze over, breath is coming fast, it sweats buckets.

Body temperature falling, I was trembling a little. Pathetically, the handle of a carving knife was tight in the grip of my hand when a different buzz announced that the visitor had arrived at my door. Wrong visitors, though.

I opened up to find Thea and Mandy standing there, and frightened. Their eyes were looking every which way to avoid contact with mine, then going to the carving knife.

Mandy opened her mouth to say something but no words came out.

Behind them was a man I'd never clapped eyes on, herding them in through my door. Looked kind of film-actor Italian, but I'd never seen him before. A blue shave.

They were inside, the three of them, awkward and crowding the space there. No Stan. Weird.

I had been retreating before their advance. The carving knife still in my hand. Thea watching the carving knife till …

'I've been chopping something up.'

'Cooking something up, Essington? I'm Dino Cecchini, yeah. I'm sure this won't take long.' He swung the door most of the way shut behind him and was reaching into a side pocket, pulling out an A5 manila envelope. 'Some photographs I was hoping you'd be interested in buying.' The knife didn't phase him.

'Dino,' I repeated lamely. 'So you're Giovanna's brother. That's it, right? Somebody told me about you.'

'Mind if I sit down?' That was Mandy. And she sat down.

But before I could indicate yes or no the buzzer sounded again at the apartment door.

'And this will be?' Dino asked.

No answer. Just the three of them caught off balance by this fresh arrival.

'I didn't let them through the street door, so it's probably the police.' I lied. 'What would your guess be, Dino?'

Mandy stood and made as if to leave. Only to be blocked by Stan Kriticos coming through the open door. A couple of the kinds of pals he collects were following along behind him. Never happy to be alone, Stan.

'A party!'

'Till you turned up.'

'You guys, you mind if I take your host outside for a minute, we need to talk. Isn't that the truth, Essington? We got some business to clear up.'

Mandy, 'We ought to be going now, anyway.'

One of Stan's pals walked over to Dino, whacked him in the solar plexus with the heel of a hand. Dino sat down right next to Mandy. Thea perched on a dining chair on the other side of the room. She was starting to cry.

'And you, bitch, shut the fuck up.'

The obedience those three displayed must have come from the fact that Stan had pulled out this nasty-looking gun. Shiny chrome plating. Very short barrel. A revolver. Not that he was pointing it at any of them.

He was pointing it at my face. Standing a metre away, I could see just a little way down the wide muzzle.

I have this idea that I was thinking that I didn't really care.

'Lets talk outside,' Stan said, and led the way to the sliding glass doors. He was so full of purpose. Masterly almost. He kind of knew already that there would be a balcony there, understood that it was the place to talk. It being a small area, narrow, and a long way above the ground.

I must have been getting the idea. Getting his idea. Because part of me was already experiencing going over the railing. I was spreading wide my arms and legs the way sky divers do and flying out over the harbour, the yachts, ferries, the palms and Port Jackson fig trees, the shining white crests on a trillion waves; sharing my thoughts with passing birds as on and out I went gliding over the blue Pacific Ocean.

Stan slid the door open. 'After you, scumbag.'

I stepped onto the balcony.

He slid the door shut behind him.

'Pity about the girls, Essington. But they'll have to go too. Material witnesses.'

'Not if I give you the paintings they won't, Stan.'

'Too late, after all the damage done. Those men you had killed … doing that was a mark of disrespect to me. I can't let something like that happen. Can I do that, Essington? Of course not. There has to be a payback.'

'What are you talking about, had killed?'

'My people who came to your Villa du Phare to do the same deal I'm doing now.'

'I had nothing to do with what happened to any of them.'

It was tight out there on the balcony. There was the banana lounge. There was me and there was Stan still holding the gun out in front of him.

'You better put that knife down, Essington, while we talk this over.'

I tossed the knife onto the banana lounge. It bounced, went through the railing, and fell.

All this in full Technicolor and sharp focus was being picked up by my receptors. 'I don't get, Stan, what is there to talk about? You're going to kill me anyway.' I could feel this trembling starting up somewhere right at the core of my being. Not fear, not excitement either. It was a lot more fundamental than that.

'Henry, Essington. We are negotiating about the boy.'

'Negotiating what, for Christ's sake?' The trembling, more like vibration within an inorganic body, it was spreading out from some epicentre. Me looking into the barrel of the gun. My gaze lifting from there to Stan's nasty dark eyes, then back to the gun. Stan's finger on the trigger. I could spot that he was sort of up and getting off on anticipation of the violence to come.

I asked, 'Did you know I can fly?'

A question like that put him off his game for an instant. But only for an instant.

'You protect the boy by just writing a few things down, Essington. Where all those fucking fake paintings you got for me are right now. The one that was in the papers, that too and the rest.'

'It was a Matisse in the papers, Stan.'

'Don't get too clever, you don't have the time. Plus I want you to sign this authority for me to withdraw money from your bank account. It's like a legal document, Essington. Think of it as giving me power of attorney. Do it right and I leave the boy alone.'

'You think I remember shit like account numbers and stuff?'

'Be really great for Henry's future if you could.'

'Where are these papers?'

Still gliding, I had entered a thermal current and was circling slowly, rising as I did so, higher and higher. Looking back towards Sydney, and down, I could see far, far away these two figures talking on a balcony. A banana lounge on the same balcony. Was there something else I should have been picking up as well?

Stan was patting his jacket with the flat of his free hand. His gesture letting me know that's where the papers were.

Dino inside with a manila envelope. Stan with papers in his pocket.

Dino who was going to leave the apartment in a bag.

Dino whose great little blackmail scam had turned out to be not so great really.

'Show me the papers then, Stan. My father told me, never sign a contract till you read the small print.'

Hard to tell if I was actually saying that. Because I was still in the thermal current, circling, watching.

I got a fresh feeling about something that I couldn't quite get a grip on. Right at that point in the conversation I felt this other presence. Like, for instance, there was Stan and me and suddenly this third party. But I didn't actually look to see because I knew it was inside my head. And I didn't seem able to take my eyes off that gun. The brutish emptiness of its short barrel. The emptiness in Stan's eyes, too.

Emptiness behind the eyes.

A revelation! That must have been the actual moment, yes. It hit me that Karen was right, there had to be a spiritual side to this life. Or everybody in the world was going to finish up being variations of Stan Fucking Kriticos.

There was the wheel of life. And sitting beside a river going ooom, over and over again. And there was needing nothing. And there was the transcendental moment, too.

I knew there wasn't any point in looking to see, because this presence was a spiritual thing that I was sensing.

Like it was Karen willing me to protect Henry, our son.

I heard his voice as if from a long way off. 'Your fault, arsehole. I had to have your wife killed, your friend, Sparrow … didn't you understand I was trying to get through to you. But no, too stupid …'

I felt myself lunging forward, outstretched arms, hands grasping for his throat.

A loud bang as he shot me. Then, had there been a fractional delay? Another bang and Stan pitched forward, taking me with him as he fell.

A searing pain in the general area of my chest.

People like my aunt get rich because they can't think of anything to do with life. They just don't get it, do they? No idea at all. When they think 'life', they think 'acquire things'. They're not into letting the material world slip through their fingers.

Kind of like small children in that, really.

I'd picked up this little bit of a car body, painted metallic burgundy, just a box-like piece of metal with some plastic of the same colour attached to one of its sides. I was on a mountain road, on one edge a sheer drop to the river, a hand-hewn rock face on the other. I was stopping traffic; the drivers winding down their windows, asking me 'why?' with their eyes. I'd ask, 'Is this a piece of your car?' The drivers would shake their heads, wind up the window, drive on.

It was raining. Of course it had to be raining. Those hairpin bends that never end. Autumn leaves on the roadway's shining blacktop.

Thea and Mandy were washing me. 'I'm just going to roll you on your side now, Mr Holt. Here we go, that's it … what a good boy.' Then, Mandy to Thea or Thea to Mandy, was it? 'God, he's a weight!'

A balcony railing. Way over there, Africa. A hot wind coming off it. Drums beating out complex rhythms. Placing one delicate white foot in front of the other a geisha is walking along the railing. A great golden bird embroidered on her kimono.

'How are we today, Mr Holt ...? Here, let me take a look. Dear oh dear, so much damage.'

In hospital they never called me Essington.

I was telling the doctor about how life itself is damage. You can live it in a Tupperware box, or swim right out into the ocean where the sharks will get you. Damage either way. I was telling him about this character who swam way out because he'd fallen in love with a shark. 'Doctor, tell me, have you ever fucked a shark?'

'Nurse what is he trying to tell me?'

'Just the noises he makes, Doctor. He's in a great deal of pain, too.'

'Let me see that chart again ... oh yes.'

'Doctor?'

In the next minute, or day or year, he gave me an injection.

'Bobby.'

Bobby leaning over me.

'Bobby.'

'Don't try to talk.'

Looking around the room, it wasn't too bad. Like that's another justification for greed, so you get rich enough to die in a room all by yourself.

And there were flowers. Two vases of flowers. All the different colours. There were the red colours and the blues – it's amazing how many blues there are in nature. Same with the colour yellow.

'Alison, she sent you the flowers.'

'I would have thought Schwartz.'

'You're not making a lot of sense, mate. Better just rest, okay?'

Close my eyes and I saw Alison being a Modigliani, her rich-red hair, her eyes. 'Sensitive little thing like me,' she seemed to be saying. Southern twang on the 'thing'.

I realised I had liked her a lot.

News item: Colour photo in the morning paper showing a collection of second-rate paintings in gold frames: the paintings I'd bought from the Blue Boy Gallery. 'Police make progress in investigation of the shooting of mystery art collector, Essington Holt.'

Bobby held that out for me to see. It made him smile – and that's something. Mostly only Henry could make Bobby smile.

Another time he was telling me that Paula hadn't gone down in the lift with them. It had been just Henry and Bobby. Paula had told them to leave, that she had to rush to the bathroom, she was going to vomit.

'Oh mate, what could I do? Henry too, he was torn, you know how it is.'

I attempted to say that I didn't know how it was.

Truth is I reckoned I had said something.

'You just lie there, Essington, don't tire yourself. I'll talk. The nurse says that's all right.'

'I like to talk.'

'What's that? Just rest now. What was I telling – don't answer that, it's like a …'

I could sense him searching for the word, 'rhetorical'. Would have been a creative writing class in jail, you'd reckon, wouldn't you? And if there was, Bobby would have been there, expressing himself all over the page.

'What could I do. I went down in the lift with Henry. We drove off in the hired van. Went to the Botanic Gardens because

I reckoned I'd be able to see the apartments from there. I mean, what kind of good was it to see the apartments?'

'And your gun, Bobby?'

'Easy now Essington. Yeah, so she stayed there. Was there the whole time. Says she heard the shots and knew not to open the bathroom door, not to anyone. Even the police, she wouldn't let them in there either. Called me on my mobile, said she reckoned it was safe to bring Henry back. How could she know if she was locked in the bathroom? I wasn't sure what to do. But in the end what could I do? Had to go back there some time or it would look just too weird. So, mate, I'm up there. And you've been taken away. Stan Kriticos as well. He's dead. One shot and he's history. But you, taking a hit in the chest at that range, even just at the side, the medicos were having trouble keeping you going.'

I didn't want to know. 'Why bother to save me?' I was thinking.

'Seems our friend Inspector Schwartz was hanging about the joint anyway. On the spot. Straight in there. These two models were still there. Sitting in the room holding on to one another. Apparently three guys were grabbed going out on foot through the car park. Two of them Stan's people, and this other one. Stuck down there – security door into the parking area wouldn't open for them and Schwartz or somebody had the lifts stopped.'

'Ah, Mr Chisholm, we should let Mr Holt get some sleep now.'

'Whatever you say, nurse.'

'There's this problem with the gun. Nobody can find the gun.'

'Your gun, Bobby?'

'You said?'

'Which gun?'

'Sorry, mate. The one that killed Stan Kriticos. I don't have

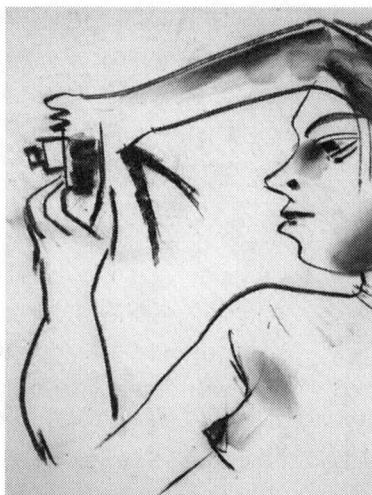

a gun, I want you to remember that, okay. Never did. Nor you for that matter. There were no guns.'

I would have been nodding my head, or trying to do so: I had received the message.

'They know the shot came from the balcony. Only person who could have been there was Paula. Except she was locked up in the bathroom, vomit everywhere. Very bad way. And definitely no gun.

'On the ground, everywhere, the police have searched. Crime scene tape marking off the area. But no gun. No shooter either. It's a proper mystery, I'm telling you. Mate, what I reckoned to the police, it has to have been one of his own people shot Stan, the guys who went up there with him. Would have been waiting for the opportunity. Suddenly there it was, the chance to top him.'

I drifted out of it about then.

The same day, or the next, they rushed me back into the operating theatre. I couldn't figure out why, except that something had gone seriously wrong. After that no visitors. Just drowsiness. Drifting on nothingness.

Once I believed that I was leading Karen by the hand. We were wading in an artificial lake, all around our legs were eels and carp and water plants.

Different flowers.

When I asked who sent them, Bobby told me Alison again.

I said, 'Different colours.'

'I guess they are.'

'You're hearing me better.'

'You're talking better.'

'Isn't it strange, Bobby, you get to my age and the only friends you've got are people you pay.'

'Some people have real friends.'

'You?'

'Came out of the slammer, nobody wanted to know.'

'Now you've got me.'

'And you've got Alison.'

'I'm probably her first near-death acquaintance. Bobby, Henry?'

'He's outside with Paula. She's had to hand in her passport.'

'What's that for?'

'Nobody else could have got onto the adjoining balcony to fire the shot.'

'Bullshit, Bobby, because you left the door open when you took Henry away from there. Or don't you remember doing that? Paula locked in the bathroom, throwing up, the door left open. How many people would there be wanting an arsehole like Stan dead? Why not one of those guys trying to get out of the building? That one, Dino, for Christ's sake!'

'Excuse me, Mr Chisholm, do you mind waiting outside for a few minutes?'

That was the nurse. She fiddled around with me, took my temperature, wrote down the levels of the drips. 'Time to get some rest, Mr Holt.'

'My son, outside … I'd like to see him.'

'For a minute and then you must sleep.'

I was coming in low over the CBD. My spread arms had sprouted white feathers. My vermilion-ringed eyes gazed in wonder. I landed on the balcony railing because I understood there was something there for me. Bird lovers all in the high-rises.

Preening myself.

A geisha in a kimono with my image on it, embroidered in golden thread. She was reclining on the banana lounge.

Looking straight down from my perch, the street bum who slept in the garden outside the apartment block; he was watching me, giving me the thumbs up, grinning from ear to ear.

'Bobby.'

He leaned in because my voice still wasn't carrying too well.

'Bobby, the gun's gone forever. She dropped it off the balcony. They won't find it. I bet they didn't turn up a carving knife either.'

'A carving knife? How do you know this, Essington?'

'Non tax deductible donation to charity. And I bet, you check down there where the planting is in front of the apartments, there won't be that crazy character living there any more.'

'Why, Essington.'

'Because he's got the gun, and the carving knife. All he needs now is a microwave and he qualifies as properly domesticated.'

'You're pulling through.'

'Tell me about it. But Bobby, listen to what I'm saying. Believe it. You told me already that they put crime tape around the area. That would be at ground level, too? And they haven't found the gun! So someone's removed it. That madman living down there, if he heard something hit the ground, he'd be onto it like a flash.'

My life is testimony that I'm not a particularly fast thinker. Dawn and Karen used to make jokes about me taking the longest route to solve simple arithmetical problems. With percentages I'd calculate what a tenth of a hundred was and then halve it or divide it by three or whatever was required and then multiply by the number of tens that were in the initial figure and so on. Whatever answer I'd come out with Dawn would say, 'Nearly' and Karen would say, 'Not too bad this time, Ess'.

It was a ritual with us. That and a whole lot more. A million small life things. But no more. The arithmetic had been humiliating but, Jesus, I'd enjoyed it. Why? Because I love my wife, that's why. And I love the whole family thing, and the dog, Desdemona. All that is gone now.

Chapter 16

Finally they let me out. I replaced Giovanna with a Mr Ng who had put his plate up outside the building two along from my apartment block. Nothing surprised Mr Ng. He'd been on one of the last flights out of Saigon. At least that's what he told me. Now he was working on keeping the police from interfering with Paula Bartels' child minding duties.

We were getting along a lot better, Paula and I. We'd never be friends, I knew that. Even though I paid her wages. But there were times I'd be sitting at the table taking some part in the feeding of Henry and there would be one of those pauses that happen in life. Nothing said, no movement. A lull. And I'd look at her and see she was watching me. Each wondering what the other might be thinking.

Then, if that moment went for too long, I'd say something like, 'Do you think Desdemona would recognize who it was if I sent a DVD of us for Yassir to play?'

And Paula would say something like, 'A very cruel man, Yassir.'

'Not true, it's just that he has suffered so much.'

'Suffered what, exactly?'

'Who can say?'

News item: Well, to tell the truth, Julian Anderson rang it through to Bobby. The post-WWI Derain nude I'd put in their hands made A$75,000. Private buyer. Same collector who'd purchased the Derain still life they'd told me about earlier.

$75,000 more or less covered my medical expenses. So that was all right. But I wasn't. I was into physiotherapy in a big way. Working on shoulder and back movement on my left side. At the same time coming to terms with pain spasms. They'd come out of nowhere and get me considering the medicinal benefits of vodka.

But the prescribed recovery regime involved no vodka at all, just a lot of tablets, pink ones, the blue, the green, some of which weren't so bad the way they could hit the old human mind out of the stadium.

'In Brief' news item: Gun control activists demand action after one of Sydney's growing community of the homeless was arrested for having fired seven shots from a handgun into the face of a hair shampoo girl reproduced larger than life on the side of a Watsons Bay bus. Nobody was injured.

There were days when I could have murdered a drink. Really could have.

Mr Ng didn't like to say too much about anything. I got the feeling that he had lost faith in the world long ago – maybe even before Saigon fell. He gave the impression of being one of those people who breathe out in the evening, satisfied just to be alive.

I gathered he'd filed some kind of complaint against Chief Inspector Schwartz. At the same time, he announced that the offer of the Matisse *Femme Couchée* to a public collection had been withdrawn because of difficulties caused by the Australian legal system. From my point of view, not a bad outcome. I had all the pictures. I still had Stan Kriticos' money, too, which I found nice even while hunting after spirituality.

Mr Ng didn't have any luck with attempts to contact Giovanna Cecchini. Seems she'd gone where Cecchinis hide when things turn sour. And was unlikely to join the bun-fight involved in popping her brother into jail.

Thea and Mandy? Mr Ng reckoned they'd score some kind of suspended sentence and go on to distribute more small moments of pleasure around the community.

I really liked Ng's style.

A sub-tropical low pressure system slid down the coast bringing with it high winds and torrential rain. Rivers on the New South Wales north coast flooded. On television they ran news coverage of residents of towns up there rowing aluminum boats down the main street, sand-bagging levee banks, moving treasured items up into the rafters. Reporters hovering in helicopters grabbed shots of isolated houses built on the flood plains, their residents standing on the roof, clinging to the television antenna, waving, grinning, happy to be alive. Horses, cattle, sheep stranded on high ground. Those not so lucky drowned and washed up against fence lines.

In Sydney, trees standing since European settlement were bowled over by freak winds. Electricity lines came down, sparks flew, drains blocked, roads flooded. Cars aquaplaned on highways, they rolled, they piled up when visibility came close to zero. A tanker brim-full with some toxic chemical capsized and spilled its load into a drainage canal south of the city, causing authorities to evacuate thousands of people till the poison dissipated.

A weekend's football games were abandoned, round four of the season. Total disaster.

Me, hour after hour I'd been standing at the glass doors looking out beyond the banana lounge and the railing, through sheets of rain, at a world turned grey, gone fuzzy at the edges. Muted beauty all over.

Then back to the television and more digitised images of an infrastructure not coping.

Me thinking that I didn't need to be up there. That a proper person would be down in the world not stuck in a box high above it. I should be losing control of a car on some sweeping corner five centimeters deep with water, flipping it, skidding to my death with wheels spinning silently, significantly, in the air.

Or up there on the Macleay or Clarence rivers, one more link in a human chain, passing sand bags to hold back the flood.

I couldn't do it.

But I was drinking cranberry juice.

The phone rang quite a bit. Legal stuff mostly. That meant the extremely reserved, indeed taciturn Mr Ng telling me no more than I needed to know.

Julian Anderson from Johnstone & Lang, he rang too. I was getting the feeling that he liked talking to me. It was a pleasant feeling. Was he a friend in the making? Would that mean I'd have two friends? Slow down Essington, did Bobby really qualify while on the payroll?

I was listening to Cassandra Wilson's remake of an old one, 'Harvest moon'. Hippy romantic bullshit really getting to me, sipping on cranberry juice. Watching even more rain come down even heavier.

Ring, ring, goes the phone.

I picked up, recited my number.

'Essington?'

I knew that voice. I knew it, definitely.

'Alison?'

And she said, 'I was thinking it could be nice to have a meal or something.'

My eyes watering, don't know why, I suggested, 'How about both, a meal and then something.'

'If you like, we could always give it a try.'